Double Deal

Also by Jenny Pitman

ON THE EDGE

Jenny Pitman

Double Deal

MACMILLAN

First published 2002 by Macmillan
an imprint of Pan Macmillan Ltd
Pan Macmillan, 20 New Wharf Road, London N1 9RR
Basingstoke and Oxford
Associated companies throughout the world
www.panmacmillan.com

ISBN 0 333 90808 2 HB
ISBN 1 405 00560 2 TPB

3 5 7 9 8 6 4

A CIP catalogue record for this book is available from
the British Library.

Typeset by SetSystems Ltd, Saffron Walden, Essex
Printed and bound in Great Britain by
Mackays of Chatham plc, Chatham, Kent

TO MY FATHER AND MOTHER

Double Deal

1

It was half-past five in the morning. Jan Hardy glanced in the rear-view mirror of her Land Rover. Briefly, she was dazzled by the sun rising behind her, until the road turned sharply into a deep, tree-lined gorge as it snaked its way towards the Irish ferry port at Holyhead.

She smiled nervously at her reflection – clear green eyes in an even, round face, beneath a dishevelled mop of blonde hair. *Could be worse for a thirty-two year old mother of two in the habit of working sixteen hours a day*, she thought.

Of course she looked tired. She could have packed half a pound of sugar in the bags under her eyes; she'd already been on the road for two hours, but soon her excitement and the pink-blue dawn, magically lighting the tops of the Welsh mountains, would cure that. Maybe she'd be able to grab an hour's sleep during the ferry crossing. But it wasn't only excitement that was making her tremble and tying her guts in knots. If she was honest, it was downright fear.

Fear of the unknown; fear of failing her children; fear of letting down those people who were committed to supporting her.

I just don't know if I can hack it, she silently questioned herself.

Jan glanced at her father, Reg, slumped in the passenger seat of the old Land Rover and for a few disloyal moments she wished it was Eddie Sullivan beside her, laughing and making life seem one big joke, as he always did. She wondered if she wished it because there was no chance of him being there, not while he was lying low in the back of beyond in western Queensland.

But she smiled with affection at Reg's furrowed features beneath cropped tufts of shiny white hair. His russet cheeks twitched and his lips quivered with the gentle rhythms of deep sleep. He had insisted on coming with her and on paying his own way. Although during seventy-seven quiet years he had never travelled further from his native Cotswolds than Wales, he couldn't let her go on her first trip to an Irish sale all on her own. It was as if he thought she was still the twelve-year-old he used to cart around the local gymkhanas with her pony in the sheep trailer and she couldn't do without him, especially since John had left her a widow so young.

Jan knew she could easily have handled the trip on her own, even though she, like Reg, had never crossed the Irish Sea, but she also knew that when she got to the sales she would be very grateful for his knowledge and advice. Reg Pritchard was as good a judge of livestock as anyone she knew.

Price and pedigree weren't factors as far as Reg was concerned. Since his birth in 1925, he'd lived on only two farms in the Cotswold hills and had grown up with the working horses his father had always used. As a boy he'd been intrigued by the stallion men, who came round each season to offer their horses' services to the farms' mares. He'd listened carefully to his father's judgement of each animal and had learned where to look for strengths and weaknesses. He had kept horses on his farm long after his neighbours had replaced them with tractors, and he had needed very little pushing to buy Jan a pony when she reached the age at which ponies were the most important thing in her life.

A big Irish stock lorry bore down on them, filling the narrow gap between the river and the rocky side of the gorge. Jan turned her attention back to the road, then thought about what lay ahead of her. She had no idea what to expect in Dublin or, for that matter, at the horse sales being held over the next two days at Fairyhouse. Although she had never been before, she was sure that all the well-known English National Hunt trainers would be there, probably nudging one another and looking down their noses at her – a penniless new trainer daring to take them on at the most prestigious sale of young jumping horses in Ireland.

Since she had been granted her public licence by the Jockey Club two months before, she'd been shy of making direct contact with her new rivals. She had sent out half a dozen runners already and broken her duck with just one winner, but now all the horses were out at grass for the summer and she didn't plan on taking any more to the races until the back end of September, when, she sincerely hoped, the ground would be much easier.

It had been Colonel Gilbert's suggestion that Jan should go to the big summer sale of three- and four-year-olds, when she had mentioned that two other owners had asked her to buy them horses. He had said at once that, if there was a bargain to be had, with her eye she would be likely to see it sooner than most. She had hoped that he would come to Ireland with her, but he'd said he didn't need any more horses at present, although he wished her luck.

It was strange, she thought, that the colonel should be one of her strongest supporters. He was her father's landlord, and a polite but rather distant figure when she was a child. Despite that, when she had moved from Wales after John died to set up an establishment on the steep western edge of the Cotswold Hills, the colonel had been one of the first to send her a horse, albeit an old pointer well past its prime. He'd been so pleased with the way she'd taken care of Sorcerer's Boy that he had encouraged her to apply for a professional licence and then had urged her not to give up when the Jockey Club turned down her original application. Now he had sent her Wolf's Rock, a far superior horse, and he had also encouraged several other owners to do the same, despite the fact that his daughter, Virginia, was also training horses on one of his own farms.

Jan's budget was modest compared to most buyers at the Derby Sale – so-called because it was held on the Thursday and Friday before the Irish Derby. She could have found horses in England, but once the colonel had put the idea in her head she'd found herself dreaming that she might discover a potential star among the four hundred or so youngsters on offer. Besides, sooner or later, she was going to have to become au fait with the Irish bloodstock world, and in her book sooner was always better than later.

As her battered vehicle lurched its way through the serpentine valleys, she couldn't help feeling vulnerable, despite her father's company. To keep the cost of the trip to a minimum, she'd made up her mind that she would drive to Holyhead, cross the Irish sea on the ferry and stay in the cheapest guest house she could find. She was sure she would have felt more confident if she hadn't being doing it all on the cheap, but she had no choice and, anyway, she could hardly expect her staff to abide by her frugal practices in the yard if she went off and slept under fluffy duvets at £100 a night or more.

But as the sun climbed Jan's apprehension began to be replaced by a growing buzz of excitement. Whatever happened, she thought, jutting out her chin, she wasn't going to be intimidated by any egotistical trainers.

🐎

On a shimmering blue sea, the big twin-hulled ferry nosed into Dun Laoghaire harbour as passengers made their way down to the car decks or gathered up their belongings to carry them off.

'Dad! Dad!' Jan hissed in her father's ear. 'I'm sorry, but you've got to wake up.'

Reg Pritchard, half-lying on a curved upholstered bench, blinked his eyes, bleary with tiredness and what looked like a touch of flu. He had found it hard to wake up when they'd driven onto the ferry three hours earlier and Jan had to support him up three flights of iron stairs to the passenger deck. She had hoped that a good sleep during the crossing would revive him, but now he looked worse than ever.

Jan sighed, mainly because she knew Reg would be angry with himself if he thought he was being a hindrance. But her anxiety was increased by the suspicion that her Land Rover was about to pack up. She knew the engine tone so well that she was sensitive to any tiny variation, and she was sure she had detected a jerky spluttering as she had driven the car into Holyhead an hour before the ship sailed.

'Come on, Dad,' she said gently. 'You can have a really good kip as soon as we've found somewhere to stay.'

Reg eyed her reproachfully. 'You should have booked somewhere.'

'Maybe I should, but I'm sure we'll find something. Now you'd better shift yourself, or they'll be heading back for Holyhead before you're off this ferry.'

On the car deck Reg heaved himself into the passenger seat of the Land Rover and flopped weakly against the door.

Jan's lips tightened, but she said nothing as she inserted the key into the ignition and turned it on. An ominous clatter of random clicks was followed by silence. Feeling her guts tighten, she tried again. This time there was only a single click as the red ignition light faded. She clenched the steering wheel, leaned forward and closed her eyes.

Oh shit! she thought. *This is all I bloody need.*

She'd been counting on getting to the sales as early as possible for the preview day, to give herself time to inspect as many horses as she could before the bidding started the next morning. She glanced at her watch. It was just before ten and with a knackered vehicle and her father not looking much better, she knew by the time she'd dealt with both of them, and got Reg settled into a guest house somewhere, most of the day would be gone.

'What's the trouble, love?' Reg croaked, with one eye open.

'Damn thing won't start. I thought there was something wrong with it before we reached Holyhead. It must be the electrics; it may not be much, but we'll have to get it off the ferry before we try to get it repaired.'

'Do you want me to have a look?'

'No, Dad. You don't look too well yourself. Just stay there.'

Ten minutes later, with Jan at the wheel and Reg still leaning against the passenger door, the Land Rover was towed down the ramp by one of the Stena Line service vans.

Jan was told that she could leave it in the compound while she arranged for a breakdown truck to come from a garage in town and deal with it. With a promise that she'd be back as soon as she could, she extracted Reg and their two holdalls from the vehicle and headed for the taxi rank outside the ferry terminal.

Jan had been wondering how she would find the Irish in their own country, and whether they would live up to the voluble image of them she already had from those she'd met in British racing. Her preconceptions were quickly proved wrong by their taxi driver – a dark-eyed, sombre man, who seemed reluctant to get into any kind of conversation with her.

Nevertheless, Jan thought, he looked trustworthy.

'Would it be worth looking for a B and B out near Fairyhouse?' she asked him, trying not to think about the cost of a taxi ride out to the sales ground.

'I wouldn't know. The nearest village is Ratoath; but with the sales on . . .' He shrugged.

'Then could you take me and my dad to a B and B somewhere in Dublin, which is handy for the buses?'

The taxi driver nodded and drove them in silence across the humming city, before pulling up outside a small, gloomy guest house on a back street a few hundred yards north of the River Liffey.

'It looks clean enough, I suppose,' Jan said. 'What's it like?'

'They won't overcharge you,' the driver said. 'And your father looks like he could do with a rest,' he added, nodding at Reg.

'OK, that's fine,' Jan said. This was no time to be picky. 'Could you give us a hand with the bags?'

A heavy stream of traffic slowly surged both ways along Dublin's O'Connell Street. Jan looked on with distaste; the noise and the fumes were as bad as London.

She'd put Reg to bed in a quiet room at the back of the guest house, with strict instructions not to move until he felt up to it.

'You'll be no use to me at the sales if you're not on the ball,' she'd told him with affectionate bossiness. 'But here's forty Irish punts for a taxi in case you feel like coming out this afternoon.'

'How will I find you?' Reg asked nervously. 'It must be a big place.'

'When you get there, find somewhere to sit in the main reception area, and I'll check it every so often. But for now just get some sleep.'

She'd spent half an hour showering and changing in her own cramped bedroom and somehow, despite the journey and the hassles, she had blossomed again. Her skin looked fresh and her blonde hair gleamed in the sunlight. She was wearing jeans with a light cotton jacket, and had a bag slung over her shoulder and a thick sale catalogue tucked under her arm. She stood on the edge of the pavement, waiting to cross on her way to the bus station. She was about to step out onto the busy road when an old white minibus juddered to a halt right in front of her, and the side door slid open.

A small red face appeared from the gloomy interior. 'Is it Fairyhouse you're going to?' A pair of pale turquoise eyes glanced meaningfully at her catalogue.

Jan nodded with a shy smile. 'Yes. I was told to catch a bus over there.'

The owner of the face, a short wiry man at least seventy years old, emerged from the vehicle and stepped out onto the pavement beside her. 'There's no bus stops anywhere near Fairyhouse. But you needn't worry; we're going to the sales and we've just enough room for a little one. Hop in!'

Jan shrugged her shoulders and stepped up apprehensively. Inside were a dozen more men, all of a similar age, apart from the driver.

The little man who had invited her to join them waved an arm at him. 'That's Liam, my son, at the wheel,' he said. 'And I'm Micky Byrne.' He turned to the three men perched on the back seat. 'Come on, now! Make room for the lady.' He ushered Jan down the aisle and she managed to squeeze between two men in flat caps and linen jackets.

The door slid shut with a bang and the minibus pulled out into the traffic. As far as Jan could tell during the journey from Dublin, all her fellow passengers had been connected with steeple-chasing – mostly as jockeys and a very long time ago, she guessed. They began to bombard her with questions, advice and anecdotes about their own experiences and other historic racing scandals, which they punctuated regularly with gales of laughter.

One of them, sitting beside Jan and much quieter than the rest, wanted to talk to her about point-to-pointing in England. 'I had a few rides myself between the flags in Wales back in the fifties,' he said, as if he were a well-seasoned adventurer. 'I've always kept my eye on it since.' When he found out her name, he commanded the attention of his fellow passengers with an expansive gesture. 'D'you realize, this woman is a serious trainer? Seventeen winners she had last season – a couple under rules, and a hell of a good run in the Foxhunters' at Liverpool – you remember – Russian Eagle, wasn't it?'

He looked at her closely, nodding his head in admiration; for a moment, she shivered and was chilled by the memory: Russian Eagle powering over the final fence in the big amateur chase at Aintree with the race at his mercy, before a loose horse had cannoned into him and Eddie Sullivan, forcing them across the track. The impact caused Eddie's saddle to slip right round under the horse's belly, but with his usual luck Eddie had fallen clear.

Now Jan could feel tiny beads of perspiration trickle down her back as she remembered peering through binoculars from the top of the stand at the motionless figure on the ground, praying that he would be able to move again.

He had moved, of course, Eddie had a knack for cheating disaster. But everyone agreed they would have won and comfort-ably beaten Supreme General, A.D. O'Hagan's heavily backed hot-pot.

It had been a devastating blow, but it had been that result which had produced a knight in shining armour just when Jan needed one.

'I'll never forget it as long as I live,' she said with a wry smile.

The other men were looking at her more intently, now that they had a tag with which to identify her. Evidently they all remembered the race, run just three months before. Very probably, Jan thought, they'd all won money on their countryman's hot favourite, but she couldn't hold that against them. Now every one of them was pressing invitations on her, either for a drink in one of Fairyhouse's many bars or to come home one evening and meet their family, or, in the case of Micky Byrne – who told her he had once ridden for Fred Darling – to marry him.

Jan arrived at Fairyhouse hot and rumpled, but as she clambered ignominiously from the minibus, she thought that it was the first time she had come across so much uninhibited, open-handed friendliness. She felt a little ashamed that her English reserve still made her wary of it, though she couldn't deny that the Irishmen had made her laugh and feel more at ease. But they soon scattered like leaves in a gale to the stables, bars and tea rooms that filled the site, leaving her to fend for herself.

She stood beneath a pale blue sky on an expanse of thick grass and gazed around her at the unfamiliar scene. The sales complex was alive with people and more good-looking horses than she'd ever seen gathered in one place. This was potentially a big pay day for hundreds of breeders and dealers from all over Ireland, and few of them would consign a horse to the sale without it looking its very best.

Among the deceptively casual crowd, Jan saw several faces she recognized from English race courses – trainers, owners, agents and the other middlemen that racing seemed to produce. Few of them gave her a second glance. She shrugged and reminded herself that they also had work to do.

Leaning against the rails of a parade ring in front of the octagonal sales hall, she focused her attention on the glossy horses as they were walked around, or were trotted up or held still by their grooms for prospective buyers to inspect them and check their all-important limbs. Her eyes flickered from horse to catalogue as she tried to assess each animal's potential from the pedigree listed on its entry page and the visible qualities of the horse in front of her. She wished her father was alongside her to give his opinion and prayed that he would turn up before too long.

In the meantime, Jan realized she was going to have to organize herself and be more methodical; there simply wasn't enough time to view the physique of every horse in the sale. Back at home in Gloucestershire she had already made a preliminary search through the catalogue for the horses whose breeding appealed to her most. Now she needed to plan her way through the series of industrial-sized barns where all the horses were stabled. She also needed to sit down after the ten hours it had taken her to reach the sales. And she badly wanted a cup of tea and a sandwich.

She walked from the warm, bustling atmosphere of the paddocks into one of the tea bars beside the sale ring itself, where she settled at a table with her lunch in front of her. But as soon as she opened the catalogue her eyelids began to sag. She was still blinking hard in an effort to keep them open when she sensed another body settle on the bench beside her.

'Hello.' A man's voice, soft and Irish. 'Are y'all right?'

Jan braced herself. Feeling too tired to deal with any more banter, she slowly turned to face a pair of the brightest blue eyes she had ever seen.

'Yes, thanks,' she returned guardedly.

'I thought you were about to drown yourself in your tea.' The man, who was in his forties, nodded at her cup. 'Were you out on the town last night?'

'No, I was not,' Jan answered crisply. 'I got up at three o'clock this morning in Gloucestershire, drove to Holyhead and came over on the *Swift*. Then my Land Rover conked out and had to

be towed off the ferry and my Dad, who's seventy-five, looked
like he was at death's door. We had to take a taxi into the middle
of Dublin and book into a guest house. I left Dad there and got a
lift out with a gang of pensioner jockeys in an old minibus. And,
I admit,' she allowed her tone to soften, 'I was finding it rather
hard to concentrate.'

'Well, I'm sorry to have woken you, but now I have I'll
introduce myself. I'm Sean McDonagh.'

Jan looked at the man's nut-brown, symmetrical features and
grey-black crop of wavy hair. She smiled and shook the hand he
held out. 'Jan Hardy.'

He nodded in a way that told Jan her name didn't mean
anything to him.

'I'm a trainer; I've been granted a full licence,' she added, still
savouring the words.

Sean McDonagh put his head to one side. 'But you've not had
it long, eh?'

'No,' Jan admitted with a smile. 'I only had it for the last few
weeks of the season with half a dozen horses. But I'm trying to
get a few more with a bit more quality for the next.'

'So, you've come across with an order book?'

'Not much of one,' Jan answered wryly. 'I've got a couple to
buy for some existing owners if they're not too expensive, and
someone suggested I come here.'

'Never been before, then?'

Jan looked at the man. There was nothing obviously predatory
in his manner. She felt that, without being patronizing, he was
rather like a schoolmaster giving lessons to an eager pupil.

'No,' she said, determined not to lose sight of the fact that
some people might consider an inexperienced buyer like herself
a soft target.

'Well, I don't want to be disparaging about my countrymen,
or my colleagues in the bloodstock business, but I should warn
you that not all of them . . .', his eyes swept the roomful of people
eating, drinking and engaged in seemingly interminable, sotto
voce conversations, '. . . are entirely trustworthy.'

Still wary of his frankness, Jan couldn't help laughing. 'You don't say?'

Sean smiled. 'Good. You're not a total debutante, then. Tell me, what sort of yard do you have in England?'

'Not much of one,' Jan said. 'It was a twenty-acre smallholding when I got it, mostly on a slope. I put in sixteen boxes last year and I'm hoping to put up another dozen this summer.'

'Will you fill them all?'

Jan made a face. 'I bloody hope so.'

Sean looked at her shrewdly. 'Do you have any backing – if you don't mind my asking?'

'I do mind, although it's pretty common knowledge.' Jan shrugged. 'I didn't have the money the Jockey Club wanted for the guarantees, and someone put it up for me. He's supposed to be sending me six horses, too, though they haven't actually arrived yet.'

'And who is that?' Sean McDonagh asked.

'A.D. O'Hagan,' Jan said and waited for the reaction. O'Hagan was one of the biggest owners of National Hunt horses on both sides of the Irish Sea.

'Is that so?' The Irishman's eyes widened. They seemed to express surprise, awe, caution and concern all at the same time. 'So, you're the pretty little blonde I heard about.' He tilted his head to one side. 'You look a bit more than that to me.'

'Thanks,' Jan said with a hint of sarcasm.

'No,' he smiled. 'It's a compliment, I promise. Whatever they said, I knew A.D. wouldn't back a woman – or any trainer for that matter – who wasn't up to the job. He'll be sending you good horses, that's for sure; he never hangs onto the rubbish. Now, Jan Hardy, I've a lot of horses to look at before the selling starts tomorrow, but here's my card. If you ever feel you need any advice or a second opinion, I'd be very happy to oblige.' He handed her a card and stood up. 'I hope I'll see you again.' His eyes twinkled briefly before he turned and disappeared into the crowd.

Jan stared after him for a moment. She had been poised throughout the conversation to deal with any advances he might make; but none had come. At the least she had been expecting him to try and sell her a horse. She also felt a little indignant that her connection with A.D. O'Hagan had clearly altered his attitude towards her. O'Hagan might be her backer, but he didn't own her and she wasn't going to allow her relationship with him to dictate who she dealt with or talked to. Not for the first time she experienced a twinge of doubt about the man who had effectively underwritten her new career.

Although Sean McDonagh might just have been seeking to land another punter, it would have been very helpful to have someone to talk to besides O'Hagan and his cohorts – at least until her father arrived. She looked at the card McDonagh had given her. It described him as a bloodstock agent who also specialized in breaking young horses and preparing them for sale from a farm in County Wexford. Jan tried to imagine the farm and then wondered, for some reason, if there was a Mrs Mc-Donagh and a house full of little McDonaghs. Impatiently she pushed the thought from her head, took a gulp of lukewarm tea and turned her attention back to the catalogue.

She shortlisted the ten horses that she most wanted to see and identified the barns where she would find them. First, she checked at reception, to find that there was still no sign of Reg and, once again, she wished desperately he was with her to guide and con-firm her judgement. She knew that he would always spot a flaw; they'd often joked that he could see a pimple on a horse's backside from fifty yards. It made no difference to him whether people thought an animal was worth five pounds or five million, he knew if it was sound and ready to go to work. But then it was her job to decide if it had that special quality that would raise it above the norm and make it a frequent winner. She would be the one responsible for training any horse she bought at this sale, and she had definite ideas of her own about the type she liked to train – strong but athletic, with plenty of bone and well-rounded quarters.

Each barn in the sales complex housed about forty horses in big airy stables. Most of those being sold over the next two days had already arrived, so the maximum number of potential purchasers could get a chance to look at them. Jan's nostrils were filled with the familiar smells of soggy straw and horse dung as the horses' minders pushed cartloads of muck to the heaps at the back of the barns. The complex was bustling with prospective buyers and breeders and grooms from the studs, who were doing everything they could to make their stock look as handsome as possible.

The vendors clipped ropes onto the polished leather head-collars of their animals and led them out to stand in the barn, or to trot up the ash-covered walkways between the buildings for small clusters of potential buyers, who tried to hide any hint of a reaction unless it was outright rejection. Even then, Jan thought, they could be bluffing; in this land of horse dealers and card players she realized a good poker face would be a vital attribute.

Jan found the first two horses she had marked in the catalogue. She had only to glance at them in their stables to see they weren't robust enough. With so many horses on offer, she thought it was a waste of time to look at any that obviously failed to match up to her high standard. The next horse appeared to have the bone and well-developed back end she liked, but Jan was immediately turned off by the whiff of medication wafting from its box.

The fourth horse she had earmarked, however, seemed more promising. He was a four-year-old big brown gelding described as 'broken and ridden away'. He was by an unfashionable sire and although there weren't many names of winning horses in bold type among the extended pedigree in his entry, his dam had already produced a winner. No one else seemed interested in him and Jan noted that he was the only one consigned from a small stud in the south-west of Ireland.

A short, raven-haired girl with nervous, droopy eyes in a spoon-shaped face was perched on a bail of straw beside the stable door. She looked up when Jan stopped to glance inside and quickly got to her feet; she hovered uncertainly, not wanting to make a fool of herself by offering to bring the horse out if it wasn't wanted.

Jan smiled at her. 'Could I have a look at him?'

'Oh yes,' the girl said, excitedly picking up a head-collar rope. She slid open the stable door on its runners and a moment later led out her charge with defiant pride, daring anyone to find fault with him.

'Could you just walk him for me, please?' Jan asked.

The girl led the horse up the middle of the barn, between groups of people standing around the other stables. Jan watched his long stride and rounded quarters as the horse walked away from her, and the broad chest with front legs set well apart as he walked back again.

'Would you mind trotting him for me, outside?' she asked.

'No, of course not!' the girl said eagerly in her soft Kerry accent and turned the animal back to lead him out of the big opening at the end of the barn.

Jan followed, as nonchalantly as she could, and wondered if anyone else was noticing her, laughing at her for inspecting an animal which, on paper, had little to recommend him. At the same time she was beginning to feel a distinct tingle that everything she had seen in the horse so far looked right and closely matched her idea of what made a good steeplechaser, until she suddenly became aware that she was smiling. She straightened her mouth and clamped her jaw, damned if she was going to give anyone else the benefit of her views, even if no one had a clue who she was.

She watched as the horse was trotted up a couple of times and, when she'd seen enough, she shook her head. 'That'll do. Thanks.' She walked away as if that was the last time she would think about the gelding. While she was aware that no one was probably taking any notice of her, she was worried that even the slightest sign of approval from her might bolster another buyer's confidence. She couldn't allow herself to feel sorry for the groom, who had almost burst into tears at her indifference.

After all, she thought, *I'll be putting my hand up for the animal tomorrow and that's what counts.*

By the time Jan had seen ten horses, she had decided that she would bid as far as her meagre funds allowed for the fourth and the eighth lots she had looked at. Now she planned to sit down with her catalogue again and earmark another twenty or so to look at. First she checked to see if Reg had arrived. Once again she was disappointed, but as she made her way back to the tea room she had used earlier, she was aware that someone was a few paces behind her. Jan had noticed a well-turned-out woman in the background while she'd been examining the last two or three horses, but, until they arrived at the door of the tea room together she hadn't felt that she was being watched.

The woman looked directly at Jan. She had warm, brown eyes with dark chocolate hair. She smiled and followed her to the queue at the counter, where they each picked up a tray. Jan looked at her more closely.

She was about her own age, perhaps slightly younger, in her late twenties. She was lavishly dressed – rather over the top for these sales, where everyone seemed to make a point of dressing down. Her short dark hair had been freshly cut and she wore a neat, dark suede jacket and tailored brown trousers, in contrast with the jeans which most of the women her age were wearing. Jan judged that she had spent some time in front of the mirror that morning, but felt she had an honest face.

'Seen anything you like, then?' the woman asked suddenly.

Jan detected a hint of English West Country in her voice. 'A few,' she answered cagily, wondering if the woman had been watching her after all.

'I noticed you having a good look at a couple. Oh, I'm sorry,' the woman went on quickly, as if abruptly conscious of a social gaffe. 'I know who you are, but you don't know me, do you? I'm Angie Sharp.' She held out a tanned, well-manicured hand.

Jan shook it. 'Jan Hardy.'

'Yes, I know. I've seen you at the races and I saw that article about you in *Horse & Hound*. My mum and dad have a few horses, but I like going to the races more than they do. They're getting on a bit and find it easier just to watch on TV these days.'

'I know how they feel,' Jan said, though for her watching horses run in the flesh was a hundred times more exciting.

'Are you here on your own?' Angie asked.

'At the moment I am. I couldn't afford to bring a load of hangers on like some of these big shots.' Jan nodded in the direction of a well-known Lambourn trainer who had just walked in, trailing a large entourage. 'My Dad's supposed to be meeting me here, but he hasn't turned up yet.'

'Oh. Well, I'm on my own too. Would you mind if I join you while you have your tea?'

Jan wanted to look at her catalogue, but, on the other hand, she was feeling a little lonely after her long tour of inspection through the barns and Angie Sharp seemed like someone she could get on with. 'No, not at all,' she said.

They shared a tray and carried tea and cakes to a spare table.

Angie took a gulp. 'Coo, that's better,' she said. 'It's bloody exhausting wandering round those barns all day and in the dust.'

Jan agreed with a laugh. 'It's murdering my feet, and I thought I was fit, riding out two or three times a day and chasing my kids all over the place.'

'You've got kids have you?'

'Yes,' Jan said. 'Two. Megan's nearly seven and Matty's coming up to two.'

'Does your husband look after them while you're away?'

'No. My husband died eighteen months ago.'

'Oh, I'm sorry.'

'That's OK. You weren't to know. I'm still not used to it myself, but I'm getting there.'

'So, what *do* you do with the kids?'

'I'm quite lucky really. There's a couple of girls that work in the yard who're very happy to do a bit of nannying. They'll look after the kids while I'm at the races. And, anyway, my parents live near by. Mum's always happy to have them and Megan sometimes comes with me now. She didn't use to like horses, but she loves them now she's got her own Welsh pony called Smarty and she's getting on really well with him.'

Angie nodded in admiration. 'God, you're lucky! It must be so exciting when your kids start showing interest.'

'Have you got any?'

Angie made a face. 'No. I haven't found a man I could put up with for that long.'

Jan thought it wouldn't be wise to probe further in that direction. 'So, what brings you over here then?' she asked.

'Mum and Dad asked me to look at a couple of horses for them, but they never like to spend money so I doubt I'll buy anything – unless the trade's real crap,' she added with a laugh.

'At least if you come with that attitude, you can only take home a bargain.'

'Or nothing at all, which is what usually happens.' Angie grinned ruefully. 'But I like coming to the sales. It's a great gas.'

'Have you been to this one before?'

'Oh, yes. It's the best for good-quality young jumpers.'

'What have you got at the moment?' Jan asked, hoping she would recognize some names.

Angie reeled off half a dozen, faintly familiar as runners.

'Some of them are all right. We had a few winners last season, but I think the trainer's pretty useless. Mum and Dad won't hear of changing, though. They sort of helped get him going three or four years ago.'

'Who's that?' Jan couldn't stop herself asking.

'Martin Hunter.'

Jan felt a quick pang of sympathy. She'd met Martin Hunter, and rather liked him, when he'd been a good amateur jockey ten years before, but she'd heard that his training yard hadn't really taken off and now there were rumours that he was gambling, losing heavily and struggling to stay in business. Angie Sharp's parents must be amongst his biggest owners, Jan thought, and tried to dispel a quick surge of excitement at the thought that they owned several racehorses and sounded as if they were soon going to need a change of trainer.

'Oh,' she tried to say flatly.

'Yes, I know,' Angie answered, apparently reading her thoughts, 'but Mum and Dad'll never take their horses away from him. How many will you have for next season?'

Jan told her a little about her yard and the plans she had for a house there, which she hoped would begin to rise from its foundations during the remaining summer months.

When they had finished their tea, Angie smiled apologetically. 'I'm sorry, Jan. I expect you've got a lot of work to do and I've stopped you getting on with it. It's been great talking to you.'

Jan agreed. She did have more work to do, but meeting Angie had been like coming across an oasis in a desert of unfamiliarity and had done a lot to restore her self-confidence. Besides, the idea of having a companion to back her up – her own small entourage – appealed to Jan. 'I was going to look at some more horses. Do you want to come with me?'

'Gosh,' Angie said, impressed. 'I'd love to!'

'Right then.' Jan opened her catalogue at the next earmarked page, happy to abandon any reticence she might have felt when Angie had first talked to her. 'Let's have a look at what else is on offer, though you won't find me sniffing around any of the star lots.'

When eventually Jan announced that she had seen as many horses as she could take in for the time being, Angie told her that she'd come across from England in her Range Rover and offered to drive her back to wherever she was staying.

'That's really kind,' Jan said, 'but I've arranged to go with the old boys who brought me here this morning. I've seen a few of them around during the day and I promised to have a drink with them.'

'I know how it is; you don't want to break your word.' Angie nodded in understanding.

'I was hoping my dad would have got out here today, but unfortunately he felt pretty lousy this morning. He came over on the ferry with me and I don't think he got much sleep last night, so I've left him having a lie down at our guest house in town.'

'Oh, are you staying in Dublin?' Angie asked with surprise.

'Yes. I haven't been here before so I didn't know the ropes.'

'It costs quite a lot to get in and out by taxi and there are no buses. I tell you what, you could both move out to where I'm staying. It's a private B and B on the other side of Ratoath. I know they've got a couple of spare rooms from a cancellation.'

Jan wanted to put her guard up. She didn't like to feel obligated; but then, with Reg feeling so awful, the nearer they were staying to the sales the better.

With these thoughts going through her head, she nodded. 'Thanks, that would be a big help. We'll go there tomorrow.'

Angie's eyes shone with delight that she was obviously going to see more of her new friend. 'Great! I'll pick you both up in the morning and run you out there before the sales start, if you like.'

Guiltily Jan thought of Reg and the cost of taxis. 'Thanks a lot,' she said. 'I'd really appreciate it.'

❧

When Angie had gone, Jan felt that on balance she had put in a good day's work. The sales complex was beginning to feel more familiar, as were a lot of the faces, which she'd seen several times as she'd worked her way round the barns. People were beginning to nod in recognition the third or fourth time their paths crossed. Although she had spent quite a lot of time talking to Angie Sharp, she had managed to identify five horses which she thought might not attract too strong bids and which she would be happy to take home to Edge Farm.

Jan decided to walk around the stables on her own one last time that evening, to check on a few more horses that she would look at more closely the next morning before the auctioneers started selling. When she returned to the main bar at the back of the sale ring, she found Micky Byrne acting as master of ceremonies among a circle of laughing friends.

'Hello, Jan Hardy!' he called as soon as his sharp little eyes had spotted her. Jan shrank back as she noticed a few people nearby glance at her, craning their necks to see why she was being welcomed so enthusiastically by the group of gnarled old jockeys. 'Where have you been all day? Jimmy—'. Micky Byrne turned to a quiet man on the bench beside him. 'Would you get a drink for Mrs Jan Hardy from Gloucestershire,' he boomed.

Her companions questioned her eagerly, anxious to know how she had got on. Had she seen anything good enough to take back to her yard? She smiled, but was careful not to give any indication of what she thought about the horses she'd seen that day.

'That's right,' one of them laughed, tapping the side of his long red nose with a wiry finger. 'Don't let on. If you've an eye for a horse, you keep it to yourself.'

'Well, now, she'd be safe enough telling us, wouldn't she? Nobody with any brains ever listened to what a jockey thought of a horse.'

'Speak for yourself!' the other crowed back as a glass of whiskey was thrust into Jan's hand.

'I'm not sure I want this,' she said.

'For God's sake, drink it, will you?' Micky chided. 'It'll get rid of the tension that's been knotting you up all day!'

Jan acknowledged the truth of what he said with a smile and felt the fierce spirit slide over her tonsils. Somehow she managed to avoid having another drink, although they didn't leave the bar for another hour, when they all crowded outside to clamber back into their minibus.

On the way back into Dublin, as they passed the now closed race course at Phoenix Park on the outskirts of the city, the little men described how they had pushed and jostled each other's horses around the tight bends of the narrow track, and how, subsequently, the quality of the racing there had deteriorated so much that no one came to watch it any more.

Back in town, Jan turned down an invitation to join them for more drinks in their favourite bar off O'Connell Street, so they dropped her outside the small guest house where she and Reg had booked in that morning.

The owner welcomed her back and asked her how she had got on at Fairyhouse. It seemed that everyone in Ireland had an interest in the sales, and had a brother, cousin or friend selling a horse.

'I had a great day, thanks,' Jan said. 'I saw a lot of horses I'd like to buy, which I probably can't afford, and I met a lot of nice people and most of them have been really helpful.'

'They would be,' the owner agreed ambiguously, but Jan was too tired to look for clarification.

'Have you seen anything of my dad?' she asked.

'I have, he said he was feeling much better. As a matter of fact, he's just taking a turn around the block. He said he wanted to go and have a look at the Liffey.' The man shrugged. 'He may be a little disappointed; it doesn't look a lot. Ah,' he went on as the door opened behind Jan, 'he's here right now.'

Jan turned and was relieved to see that Reg was looking his usual bright-eyed, red-cheeked self.

'Hello, Jan,' he said. 'You back already? I thought you had five hundred horses to look at.'

'It's not possible to look at them all; but I rechecked about a hundred. I couldn't face any more. There's half a dozen I want you to take a look at for me tomorrow, since there doesn't seem too much wrong with you now.'

'I'm fine. I just needed a real good sleep.'

'Thank God for that,' Jan laughed. 'The last thing I need is an invalid on my hands.' She turned back to the proprietor, who was still standing in the hall with them. 'I'm afraid we'll be moving out tomorrow. A friend has booked us into her B and B near the sales.'

The owner nodded. 'That would be better, for sure.'

'In the meantime, is there anywhere nearby where we can have a quick meal and a cup of tea, while I tell Dad what I've been up to?'

After an enjoyable hour discussing all the horses that had caught her eye, Jan left Reg lingering over a pint of Guinness while she took herself back to the guest house and went up to run a bath. She lay in the water for a good, long soak, thinking of the people she'd met and the horses she'd seen during the day, and she prayed that she had enough money to buy at least one of them. She climbed out of the bath completely relaxed and, nineteen hours after she'd woken up in Gloucestershire that morning, she clambered into bed and fell asleep within seconds.

2

When Jan came downstairs the next morning she found Reg finishing an enormous Irish breakfast. He was wearing his best tweed jacket, with a V-neck sweater, a checked shirt and his Sunday tie. She was sure he would be wearing a vest, too, even though it was midsummer.

'Dad, you'll boil in that lot.' She shook her head in despair, knowing he wouldn't take any of it off.

'I ain't going to risk catching a cold, or your mother'll go mad; she didn't want me to come in the first place.'

'All right.' Jan sighed. 'But we'll have to get our skates on; Angie Sharp'll be here any minute. She's going to drive us out to her B and B in Ratoath. We'll quickly dump our bags there and go on to the sales. We've got a lot to get through, the first horse I'm interested in should be in the ring at about half-past eleven. Now I'd better find out what's happened to our Land Rover.'

The indulgent owner of the guest house lent Jan a cordless phone, and when she had finished her breakfast she tracked down the garage which had collected the vehicle and replaced the solanoid. She groaned at the cost, but didn't want to upset Reg by telling him how much it was.

As she put down the phone, Jan saw a gleaming black Range Rover pull up outside the breakfast-room window. 'That must be Angie. Are you all packed?'

'Course I am.' Reg said. 'Who is this woman you've befriended?'

Jan knew he would be suspicious about someone she had only

just met. Reg had known most of his friends for at least sixty years and didn't like to call people by their Christian names until he'd known them for a couple of years, at least.

'She's a really nice person. We met in the tearoom and got on like a house on fire. Her parents own quite a few horses in Martin Hunter's yard.'

Reg was a keen follower of form. 'Oh dear,' he muttered, then he brightened. 'Perhaps they'll be looking for a change?'

'I've already thought of that.' Jan chuckled. 'But Angie says they've been with him since he started and they won't move them.'

'Seems a bit of a waste. Is this her?' Reg sounded reluctantly impressed. He was looking towards the door.

Jan turned and saw Angie looking as glamorous as she had the previous day.

'Hello, Ange,' she said. 'I'm sorry you had to get up so early to come and get us.'

'That's all right. I'm always awake by seven and I knew you didn't want to miss any early lots.' She smiled at Reg. 'This handsome man must be your dad.'

'Reg Pritchard: Angie Sharp,' Jan said in introduction. 'I told Angie you're my secret weapon at the sales, Dad, so you'd better be on your toes.'

Jan found the atmosphere at Fairyhouse palpably more tense than the day before. Yesterday people had been looking; today the real business started.

Angie disappeared as soon as they arrived, promising to see them around lunchtime. Jan tried to get her plans in order. She had whittled her list of potential purchases down to the six which she particularly wanted Reg to see. Reg was already looking around in wonder at the number of high-quality jumping-bred horses on offer, but she was confident that however many animals he saw he would always be able to pick out those that weren't up to the job. The two of them set off to give Jan's choices a final inspection, starting with the lots that would come up for sale soonest.

The vendor of the first animal she wanted Reg to see was a sharp-looking little man from County Down. He was leaning against the wall beside the stable door, but pushed himself upright when he recognized Jan from the previous day. His eyes gleamed in anticipation when she stopped outside his box.

'Could we have a look?' she asked.

'Sure you can.' The man glanced at Reg, as if he were trying to assess Reg's status in the decision-making process. 'Good morning,' he said politely, in case Reg held the purse strings. He slid back the door of the stable to lead out the freshly groomed horse and walked him up through the crowds already milling around in the barn.

The animal was very much in the mould of Jan's ideal, broad-chested, big-quartered – a preference inherited from her father and grandfather. She and Reg followed the horse.

'Don't let on what you think in front of him,' Jan said in a whisper, nodding towards the vendor.

'And don't you teach your grandmother to suck eggs,' Reg muttered back.

'Sorry, Dad.' Jan grinned. She sometimes forgot how sensitive her father could be, especially when he was away from his home territory.

They caught up with the horse and asked its handler to take it outside, where he could give it a trot up the ash track for them. They stood side by side, slightly crouched to get the best possible view of the horse's action. Being careful not to show what they thought, they asked him to do it again.

'OK, thanks,' Jan said with a curt nod, before walking briskly towards the next barn.

They walked round a corner and stopped. Jan pulled the pen from the holder dangling around her neck and opened the catalogue at the page of the animal they'd just seen.

'What do you think of him?'

Reg raised a pair of appreciative eyebrows. 'Not bad. Good

slope to his shoulders, moving dead straight, nice and even. He looks clean enough. Nothing wrong with his legs. I should think he'll make a fair bit of money.'

Jan knew that his reference to the horse being clean had nothing to do with its shining coat. 'He looks nothing in there.' She nodded at her catalogue.

'That's as may be, but when you've been breeding stock as long as I have, if you want to buy an animal to do a job, pedigree ain't everything.'

'Of the ones I like he's the first to go through the ring, so we'll have to see if he's anywhere near our price range.'

Reg nodded with a grin. 'Right, what's next?' he asked sniffing the air like a hound on the scent.

Jan didn't tell her father that the second horse was the one she liked most. She'd studied the gelding carefully the evening before and concluded that, with her budget, he might well be the most desirable lot for her.

She pointed out the stable to Reg, and let him go forward and do the talking.

A lad brought out the horse, and Jan tried not to let her interest show when he looked as good as she remembered.

'Just stand him still for a moment,' Reg said. He gazed intently at the horse for a few seconds. 'What's that on his knee?' he asked the horse's handler, a small man of twenty or so in well-worn jodhpurs.

'He'd a bit of a knock loading.'

'That's a shame,' Jan said, although she knew it was almost certainly nothing to worry about.

'That'll do, thanks,' Reg said abruptly, and turned to walk away.

Jan almost had to run to catch up with him. 'Didn't you even want to see him move?' she asked.

'Nope.'

'But that knock on his knee was nothing. I spotted it yesterday.'

'Couldn't you see what else was wrong with him?'

Jan liked the horse, but she didn't want to admit that she might have missed something. 'Erm, no. I didn't see anything else.'

Reg stopped and looked at her. 'It can be dangerous to be too sure of yourself,' he warned. 'That knock wasn't his only problem. So you better go back and have another bloody look!'

'All right, Dad,' Jan conceded. 'I admit I saw nothing else. What did you see?'

'It had a bog spavin on its off hind. You get a swelling like that on the hock of a young horse and it'll never stand any serious work. Let me tell you, young lady, there are problems you can live with and problems you can live without, and that's one of them. There's no need to go buying trouble; you'll get it soon enough.'

Jan sighed. She knew there was nothing to be gained by going back to check for herself. If her father said the horse had spavins, then it most certainly did and that was that.

She led him through the next barn to the horse being tended by the spoon-faced Kerry girl. The girl recognized Jan at once and smiled shyly. Jan didn't smile back.

'There it is, Dad,' she said, as if she didn't care what he thought of the horse.

Reg nodded at the girl. 'Can we have a look at him, then?'

The girl opened the stable door and led out her charge.

This time, Reg watched him walk and trot before letting him back in the box. He didn't say anything to Jan until they were well out of earshot of the groom.

'Nothing wrong with him,' he said approvingly.

'He's not very well bred,' Jan remarked.

'I've told you before, that doesn't necessarily mean anything.'

'It means he might be pretty cheap,' Jan corrected.

Reg smiled. 'I'm used to buying stock for a job, not for the hopes and dreams they might give a man.' He shook his head and tapped the page of the catalogue. 'This proves nothing. The proof of the pudding's in the eating.'

'I know you're right, Dad, but the vendors *are* selling dreams, not reality. There'll be people paying over a hundred thousand pounds for untried geldings here when they know the chance of ever earning back that kind of money is minuscule.'

'That's a side of your game I'll never understand.'

'Never mind, Dad. I didn't bring you here for that – just to tell me which animals will stand their work, and that's well worth a few pints of Guinness.'

Reg was really enjoying himself, but after they'd spent two hours walking what felt like several miles around the barns, Jan knew he was ready to for a rest, and the first lot they were interested in was due through the ring soon.

'Where do you want to sit?' Jan asked him as they walked into the octagonal building, which contained an almost complete circle of steeply racked seating, walled with dark timber panelling.

'Let's sit opposite the auctioneer,' Reg said, 'so we can see who he's talking to and what's going on in the entrance.'

They found a couple of spaces in the top row, which gave them a clear view of the rostrum where the sales were conducted. The auctioneer was trying desperately to drag out some bids for a moderate-looking animal which was ambling listlessly around the ring.

The horse Jan wanted to take home was due in next, and she quickly spotted the sharp-featured man from County Down who was selling it. He was standing by the roped-off opening where the horses entered the arena, and was systematically sweeping his eyes around the spectators for likely bidders. When he spotted Jan and Reg his eye stopped momentarily, before moving on without showing any reaction.

Jan suddenly felt anxious at the thought of bidding here for the first time. Auctions both scared and excited her, whether she was buying or selling; there was such scope for drama, deceit, weakness and greed, and above all the chance of sucess.

The auctioneer, a smooth-voiced young Englishman who had come over from Newmarket to share the workload with his Irish colleagues, gave up on the horse in the ring. 'Not sold,' he said with a hint of admonition to his audience, and the horse was replaced by Jan's first prospect.

Of the ten animals she and Reg had inspected, this one had really excited her. She couldn't explain what it was that made him stand out more than the others, but for her there was a presence about him, in the way he held his head and seemed to listen when she spoke, which made her feel he was a horse that would want to work and please her.

Then she leaned in towards Reg. 'I've got up to eight for him,' she said.

'Are you sure?' To Reg eight thousand pounds seemed an awful lot of money for someone to be spending on a hobby.

'That's what Ray Bellamy's given me, and I'm sure he'd like the horse.'

The man on the rostrum shot his cuffs and audibly cleared his throat, as if to punctuate the change of animal in the ring below. 'Right. Lot number sixty-three . . .' He reeled off the horse's particulars, stressing its lack of a single flaw, and glossing over the absence of any heavy bold type in the catalogue entry, which would have denoted its blood connection to proven winners. 'A very handsome individual,' he went on approvingly as the animal continued to walk round. The vendor leaned on the wooden wall and gazed at his horse.

Jan studied it longingly too, clutching her catalogue tightly to her chest.

'Now, who'll start me for this nice trainer's horse? Who'll put him in at ten thousand?' His eyes and those of the red-uniformed women on either side of him swept the amphitheatre, the rails around the back, and the clusters of people in the doorways. 'All right, give me eight . . . Two thousand I'm bid.'

Jan with her right arm tucked in close to her father's shoulder, twitched it in readiness.

'Hold on, girl. Don't give 'em too much ammunition; make 'em sweat a bit.'

Jan forced her arm to stay where it was and tried to see who

was bidding – someone to her left whom she couldn't identify. Another bidder, apparently down by the entrance, raised
the price to three thousand, after which there was a lull in the
proceedings. Lot 63 continued to stride around the ring, glancing
at the crowd from time to time as if he couldn't care less about
the lack of interest in him, until the bidder on Jan's left, with a
little encouragement from his companion, went to four thousand. The man on the rostrum, with neatly parted, short blond
hair, looked at the entrance and raised an eyebrow. 'Come on,
now. This is very little money for an animal of this quality.'

Jan spotted the bidder when he shook his head.

'Come on, now. Who'll give me five?'

Jan gulped, still gazing at the horse; she felt she already knew
him; she could see him back in the yard at Edge Farm with his
fine head and intelligent eyes looking over his stable door. She
waited another twenty seconds, which felt like an eternity, before
she shifted her weight on the seat so that she could extract her
arm from under Reg's shoulder and raise her hand.

The auctioneer's hawk eyes spotted her at once. 'Thank you,
madam. Five thousand. Five two. Five four. Five six. Five eight.
Six thousand,' he rattled on smugly, his head darting from side
to side like a tennis umpire's.

Jan glanced at the electronic display board that showed the
lot number and the price it was currently selling at, in both Irish
Punts and English guineas.

She dropped her gaze down until she saw the man who had
brought the animal here to be sold, still staring at it without
expression.

'Six thousand I'm bid. Not enough to buy a horse like this,
I'm afraid.'

Jan raised her hand again.

'Six two, thank you,' he nodded. 'Ah, a new bidder.' Another
rapid volley of bids took the price to eight thousand. 'At eight
thousand guineas I'm bid. Eight; all right, eight five.' He glanced
at Jan.

Nine thousand Irish guineas would be approximately eight

thousand sterling. That was her limit, however much she liked the horse. This would have to be her last bid. She started to raise her hand.

'Steady, girl!' Reg muttered. 'I thought you were stopping at eight thousand.'

'Nine thousand in Irish money,' Jan said, and raised her hand once more, and for the last time.

'Nine thousand, then,' said the auctioneer with a little more animation. 'But he's worth more than that. Who'll give me ten?'

Jan found it hard to breathe. She was determined to stick to her budget and not allow herself to get carried away.

'Come on, who'll give me ten for this big, strong horse?' He and his spotters swept the sea of faces in front of them once more. He glanced down at the entrance, where the vendor was now looking back at him. 'All right,' he said. 'I'll take a half. Nine and a half thousand I'm bid. Who'll give me ten?' Now he was staring at Jan, daring her to go on.

Jan's arm was once more wedged against Reg's. She stared back and slowly shook her head. She didn't miss the quick glance of annoyance that clouded the auctioneer's face. 'You'll be sorry to lose him now. Come on then,' he resumed his mantra. 'Nine thousand five hundred I'm bid; who'll give me ten?'

Jan shook her head again.

The auctioneer looked around the room with a faint look of disdain, and abruptly gave up. 'Not sold.'

Reg leaned in to Jan. 'He was running you,' he whispered angrily. 'I reckon the horse had a reserve of ten, that's why he had to take a half bid off the wall.'

Jan was still shaking. She had never felt so nervous and wound up, and then so completely let down. Now that she'd lost the horse, she realized just how desperately she'd wanted it.

'I should have stayed in there, then, shouldn't I?'

'They might have run you even higher.'

'But who was running me? That little Northern Irish bloke who was selling it hardly moved his head.'

'You can bet he had a couple of mates around the ring to keep it going.'

Jan took a deep breath and sighed hopelessly. 'I've got a hell of a lot to learn about this game,' she admitted.

'S'long as you know that, there's a good chance you will learn.' Reg nodded approvingly. 'You'll get there, don't you worry. Bloody hell, pet, you've never even been in this country before. It's got to be bloody strange, ain't it. Anyway, there'll be others. There's that nice Good Thyne we saw at the end. He'll be well worth going for.'

Jan nodded. Reg was talking about an animal similar to the one they had just lost, perhaps on paper a little better bred. 'There's nothing else we've looked at coming through now until after lunch. Let's have a quick cup of tea.'

The cafe was much fuller than it had been the day before now that the sale was in full swing. The auctioneer's patter, which was relayed over closed-circuit television in all the bars and by loudspeakers outside the building, was backed up by the electronic display of the lot numbers and prices.

Jan found a table with space for them and went to get two cups of tea and a snack for Reg.

While she was waiting in the queue, she heard her name being spoken by a voice she immediately recognized.

She turned and found Sean McDonagh standing beside her with a tray.

'What are you getting?' he asked.

'Just a sandwich and a cup of tea.'

'And who's that you're with?'

'That's my dad. He's come over to guide me. He wasn't feeling too well yesterday, though.'

Sean nodded. 'OK, you go and sit down. I'll get your tea and bring it over.'

Jan wanted to say no, but she didn't have a good enough

reason and, besides, her feet were in agony. 'Thanks,' she said, careful not to show too much gratitude.

'Who's that?' Reg asked when she rejoined him.

'That's the man I was telling you about. I don't trust him an inch.'

'Why's that?' Reg asked.

'I don't know; just a gut feeling. I think maybe because he seems too good to be true.'

Reg laughed. 'He's certainly a good-looking chap.'

Sean was making his way towards them. Just as he arrived some people beside Jan got up, leaving a space.

'D'you mind if I join you?' Sean asked.

'No,' Reg said. 'Sit yourself down. Thanks for getting our tea.'

Sean held out a hand. 'I'm Sean McDonagh.'

'Reg Pritchard.' Reg nodded comfortably.

'So how have you been getting on?'

Jan told him about the horse they had been outbid for.

Sean nodded. 'I saw the horse. I didn't notice you were bidding, though. You could have had it for ten.'

'That's what Dad said.'

'I could probably get him for you, if you like. I don't think there was much of a rush for him outside the ring.'

'I'm not sure if I still do, after they've tried to run me.'

'Listen, do you want horses in your yard or a few puddles of hurt pride?'

'Of course I've come to buy horses, but there are others.'

'Which are you looking at?'

Jan didn't want to tell him, but Reg joined in. 'There's a nice Good Thyne. Lot 190, late this afternoon.'

Sean looked doubtful as he opened his catalogue. 'You should be able to afford him. He won't make a lot of money; there's a little problem with that horse.'

'What sort of problem?'

'They've already tried him and he doesn't like the job; I heard he's temperamental and nappy when he gets on the gallop and won't co-operate.'

'But it says he's unbroken.'

'That's not the Holy Bible you're reading there, you know. It's only a catalogue and not every word in it is bound to be true.'

'So you're saying we shouldn't bid for him?' Reg asked.

'I am; I think it's unlikely he'll be an easy horse to train.'

'We liked the look of him, though, didn't we, Dad?'

'Yes, but if Sean here thinks he's not up to it . . .'

Jan looked sceptical. 'We'll see.'

Sean glanced at her. She thought he was going to make more of it, but evidently decided not to. 'It's up to you,' he said, shrugging his shoulders.

As he spoke, Jan saw the familiar face of another Irishman she knew make his way across the room towards her. Eamon Fallon had been a client at Edge Farm before she'd got her professional licence.

'Hello, Eamon,' Jan called out. 'I thought I saw you in the distance yesterday.'

Fallon nodded. The ring dangling from his left ear glinted in the sunlight shafting through the tall windows. 'His nibs didn't know you were coming, but he would like you to join him for lunch since you're here.'

Jan knew he was referring to A.D. O'Hagan. 'Why couldn't he have asked me before?' Jan protested. 'I've already arranged to have lunch with someone else.'

'A.D. is what you might call a spontaneous individual and he thinks everyone else is the same. He gets very disappointed if they're not.'

'I see,' said Jan, sensing that A.D.'s influence over her life was already making itself present. 'I suppose I'd better come, then. Where is it?'

'In the restaurant. He has a large table there always. Come about two.'

'OK,' Jan sighed. 'I'll see you then.'

Eamon grinned and winked. 'Be seein' you, Reg.' He melted away into the crowd.

Sean's eyes followed him for a moment. He turned to Jan.
'Do you know Eamon well?'

'Yes. He had a point-to-pointer with me last season – a good
horse called Dingle Bay.'

'I heard he had a spot of money trouble. So he's doing a bit
of work for A.D., is he?'

'I think they've known one another quite a long time.
Eamon's in charge of the breeding operation now.'

'A.D. makes a big thing of always being surrounded by the
lads he used to hunt rats with as a kid.'

'I suppose that's better than dropping all your old friends like
a lot of self-made millionaires.'

Sean smiled. 'That's true enough. Anyway, I'd better be going,
but best of luck, Jan. I hope I'll see you around later.'

He stood up, shook hands with Reg and walked out of the
room.

Reg watched him go. 'Nice, genuine bloke,' he remarked.

'Gosh, Dad, do you think so? I'm not sure I'd trust him
further than I could throw him.'

'I think he's all right. And I think we should leave that horse
alone.'

'What? And ignore our own judgement?'

'Well, we can't tell the horse's temperament just by looking
at him. If Sean's heard he doesn't like the job, where's the point
in pretending?'

'But, Dad, I thought you had stronger views than that.'

'Maybe, but I'm not so stubborn that I don't know how to
change them.'

Jan knew perfectly well what he meant, but she also knew
she didn't feel comfortable accepting Sean's advice. 'I'll think
about it,' she said lamely, wondering if perhaps she should
swallow her pride. Her attention was distracted at that moment
by the arrival of Angie, who was weaving her way towards
them through the swelling crowd, waving her catalogue, her gold
bracelets jangling.

'Hi!' she said breathlessly when she reached their table. 'Hello, Reg. How are you bearing up?'

'Fine thanks,' Reg grunted.

'What shall we do about lunch?' she asked.

Jan made a face. 'I'm afraid one of my owners has asked me to join him and I don't think I can refuse. But why don't you have something to eat with Dad? You can exchange notes on what we saw this morning.' Jan glanced at Reg, who was shuffling uncomfortably.

'Of course I will,' Angie gushed. 'I'd love to.'

Jan left them, smiling at her father's apprehension, but confident of Angie Sharp's tact in handling any resistance he might put up. For herself, she wasn't at all sure that she was going to enjoy lunch in the restaurant, which was the smartest place to eat in the sales complex, surrounded by the sycophantic gofers she guessed would make up most of A.D.'s entourage.

But when she saw him, A.D. O'Hagan seemed relaxed amongst his friends, some of whom might almost have been equals. 'Jan Hardy!' he boomed when he saw her. 'How glad I am that you've decided to join us. Why didn't you tell me you'd be here?'

'I'm only here to buy a couple for clients – nothing too expensive, mind.'

'Well, if you see something else you like and don't have a client for, let me know. I'd be happy to follow your judgement. After all, it was me who didn't think much of that horse you bought at Doncaster and it would certainly have beaten mine at Aintree if it hadn't been rugby tackled by that loose animal, so naturally I take your opinion very seriously.'

Jan wondered for a moment if he really meant what he'd just said, but there was no reason why he shouldn't. It sounded clearly like an order for another horse and she should have been excited about it, but for some reason, however charming and plausible he seemed, all her instincts were telling her not to let this man end up dominating her yard or her life.

She was also acutely conscious that the six horses he'd already promised her were not due to arrive at Edge Farm until the end of July or early August. A.D. liked his horses to summer at Aigmont, a big estate he owned near Dublin with a magnificent stone mansion, built by an eighteenth-century English earl on the western slopes of the Wicklow mountains.

Jan felt that she wouldn't fully earn his respect until she'd shown him what she could do with his own animals.

'I'll certainly tell you if I see something I think might suit you,' she offered, although she'd already made up her mind that she wouldn't risk sticking her neck out too far this early in their association. Besides, she thought, it wouldn't do their relationship any harm if she managed to buy a good horse here for one of her other clients.

Suddenly, Jan felt that acquiring that elusive equine star was more important to her than ever.

'You do that.' A.D. nodded, without any sign that he'd sensed her reluctance. 'Now, what will you have to drink?'

He ordered the tonic she asked for and introduced her to the gathering of a dozen or so men, some of whose names she already knew, either from their connection with racing or their prominence in Irish business. Others made no pretence at being more than working countrymen, long-standing friends of A.D.'s whose generosity they were happy to enjoy without a trace of embarrassment, in a way that wouldn't have happened in England.

Jan watched him during lunch, while the men on either side of her were otherwise occupied. She couldn't help being impressed by the way he seemed to know what was going on in every corner of the room and to have a well-informed view about anything that was being discussed.

She guessed he was in his late fifties, but he looked younger and curiously, she thought, a little like Sean McDonagh, though undoubtedly more forceful and more enigmatic. She had only met the Irish tycoon half a dozen times. He had visited her yard at Edge Farm with a small entourage on two occasions, when they had talked at length about her plans. As she had told Sean

McDonagh, it was O'Hagan who had put up the thirty-five-thousand-pound bond the Jockey Club asked of new trainers to ensure that staff, vets, farriers and suppliers would be paid out if things went wrong. While the arrangements for this were being put in place, A.D. had kept his promise and had done everything he'd said he would do: he had sent in his accountants to look at Jan's set-up and to advise on management systems; he had assured her that if she ever needed more financial support, she only had to ask. He had also taken her and her staff out for a meal at the pub in her local village, where he had behaved with impeccable manners, finding out about her own family. But she knew that she had come nowhere close to knowing him yet.

For a few minutes towards the end of lunch no one spoke to Jan. Glad of a rest from the constant need to be on her guard, she was still pondering A.D.'s elusive personality when his unmistakable, mellifluous voice cut across her thoughts.

'Now then, Jan. I haven't decided for sure which horses you'll be getting, but I'll definitely be sending you a nice five-year-old called Tom's Touch. He's not run yet, but he showed a hell of a lot of promise on the gallops last summer and it looked as if he favoured the top of the ground. I'd say he's an early season horse and you should be able to run him within a few weeks after he's arrived with you.' A.D. dropped his chin and looked at Jan from beneath shiny black brows. 'And, with any luck, he should get you off to a flying start.'

Everyone else round the table had stopped talking. Jan guessed they were making a mental note to back A.D.'s prediction. He had, in effect, offered her a public challenge – with the implied belief that she would rise to it.

Clever bastard, she thought, *he knows exactly which buttons to press!*

'I'm looking forward to seeing the horse,' she said brightly, rising to her feet. 'But you'll have to excuse me.' She nodded at the CCTV screen in the corner of the room. 'I've got a few other horses to bid for.'

A.D. accepted her departure with a smile. 'Of course you have,' he said. 'Thank you for joining us.'

As Jan walked from the dining room, the tension created by lunching with A.D. seemed to have heightened her awareness of her surroundings, and as she made her way towards the door she felt as if every eye in the room was on her.

Outside the building a stiff breeze had sprung up, dissipating some of the sun's heat. Jan stood for a moment and took a few deep breaths before carrying on down the path to the sale ring. In a crowded bar she found her father well ensconced at a table, with a pint of Guinness in front of him and smiling happily at Angie.

'How have you two been getting on?' she asked, delighted that her father appeared to have come round to her own view of Angie.

'Great!' Angie said, grinning.

Reg nodded.

'He knows so much. It's fantastic. I can see why you brought him along.'

'She didn't bring me.' Reg grunted indignantly. 'I insisted. She's never been here before and I didn't want her getting into trouble.'

'That's true,' Jan said, 'but I'm making sure he earns his keep.'

'You want to get yourself into gear, pet. Lot 173's coming up soon; that's the big brown horse by that stallion I never heard of.'

Jan nodded. 'I know, Dad. That's why I'm here. I'm afraid I had to leave A.D.'s lunch before anyone else.'

'What was that like?' Angie asked in the secretive tones of one who enjoyed her gossip.

'I don't know. I was so bloody nervous I hardly tasted a thing.'

'No, I meant what's he like?'

'Full of charm, of course, but he doesn't miss a trick. He'll

certainly want to keep me on my toes – not that he'll need to,'
Jan added. 'Anyway, he says he's still not sure which horses he's
sending me, but there's definitely one coming that'll be half fit
already, so hopefully I can run it in September – "somethin' to
get me off to a flyin' start".' Jan mimicked A.D.'s voice with a
grin.

'But isn't it great he's taking you so seriously?' Angie said.

'Yes, I suppose it is: anyway, let's go and put in a bid for this
Kerry horse.'

Angie and Reg followed Jan through to the saleroom, where
they went up the stairs and managed to find a space close to
where Jan had tried to bid for Lot 63 in the morning.

They watched Lot 172 being sold, a star lot by the most
fashionable stallion in the catalogue. The horse was exactly the
sort Jan would have loved to buy if it had been remotely within
her budget, but the bidding had already passed seventy thousand
when they came in, and as the bids gathered momentum the
crowd grew silent. Jan could hear her own breathing. She glanced
at her father and saw his look of bewilderment as the price
reached a hundred and twenty thousand.

An almost tangible pressure had built up under the gaze of
the Irish auctioneer's intense blue eyes as they swept into every
nook and cranny of the hall for signs of a fresh bid. Quietly, not
needing to galvanize the audience as his colleague had with
earlier lots, he recited the current bid, glancing from side to side,
from bidder to bidder, raising the pitch of his voice a quarter
tone with each increment, until there was only one buyer left in
the race.

He turned to address the under-bidder. 'Are you going to tell
me you've come all this way just to lose him?'

With a rueful smile, the under-bidder revealed himself with a
shake of his head. A moment later, the gavel hit the top of the
lectern and the animal was sold for a hundred and sixty thousand
guineas to a burst of applause from the watching crowd.

There was an instant release of tension amid a hubbub of

murmured excitement since everyone in the room felt they had been part of the drama. Even Reg was smiling, in spite of his cynical views about the wisdom of such a transaction.

People were still talking loudly about the spectacular price the handsome horse had achieved, and prognosticating its future, while it was led from the ring as the spoon-faced Kerry girl led in her big brown gelding, almost unnoticed.

Jan felt herself stiffen as Reg's hand squeezed her forearm. 'This is it, girl,' he said. 'Let's hope he doesn't fetch so much as the last one.'

Jan looked at her father and squinted her eyes.

The auctioneer, quickly adjusting his demeanour from the high point of the last lot, was reading out the horse's particulars in a measured, businesslike way, which gave no hint that the animal in the ring now was in any way inferior to its predecessor.

'And his dam, Balkan Ballerina, has already produced a good winner with her first crop. Now, who'll start me at twenty thousand for this big, strong horse?'

'Twenty thousand?' Jan gasped to herself.

Reg felt her alarm. 'Don't worry, love. He's just winding it up.'

The Irishman on the rostrum gazed sternly around the room. 'Now we're here to do business and we all know that an individual like this deserves a strong opening bid. Who'll give me fifteen? All right, five?'

'I can't see no bidder,' Reg murmured resentfully.

Jan waited to see if there was any real competition. The auctioneer was showing a hint of impatience. 'Come on, now. There should be a show of hands for him at this price.'

Tentatively, hardly able to believe her luck that no one else had reacted, Jan raised her hand.

One of the spotters saw her bid at once and drew it to the attention of the auctioneer, who nodded at her with the ghost of a smile. She wondered if he'd noticed her as she'd traipsed around the barns for the last two days.

'Thank you, madam. Six thousand I'm bid for this lovely big

gelding – he could make a real fine chaser; maybe we'll see him winning a National one day. Come on now, bid on if you want him. Six two; six four; six six; six eight; seven thousand. Thank you sir. Seven thousand I'm bid. Seven thousand. Now come on gentlemen, we've a long way to go.'

'God, I hope not,' Jan murmured between tightly clamped teeth.

'Easy, girl,' she heard Reg whisper beside her. 'Don't go too fast.'

With a great effort of will, Jan restrained herself from lifting her hand for a few moments longer, then slowly, without showing too much commitment, she raised it once more.

This time the auctioneer was waiting for her. Again in increments of two hundred guineas, he took the bidding up to eight thousand. Once there, he went on cheekily, 'Eight thousand I'm bid. Who'll give me nine?'

The crowd had thinned since the sale of the last lot, and those who remained had more important things on their mind than the big, unfashionably bred animal currently on offer. There was a persistent buzz of unconnected conversation in the air as the man on the rostrum tried to raise interest in the horse.

Jan gazed at him, willing him to stop, to accept that he'd had all the bids he was going to get.

'For God's sake,' she murmured. 'Sell him to me!'

As if he'd heard, the man seemed suddenly to give up. 'All right, eight thousand I've got. Does anyone have any more for him?' He raised his wooden gavel and waved it back and forth over the top of his lectern.

'Please!' Jan pleaded silently. 'Just knock him down!'

A second later, her prayer was answered.

'Going once – for the second time – I can't dwell.' There was a sharp rap of wood on wood. 'Sold, to the lady in blue.' He indicated Jan with the handle of his mallet. 'Can I have your name, please?'

Jan flushed bright red as the realization that she'd bought her first horse at the most prestigious sale of National Hunt horses in Ireland hit her. She raised herself a little from her seat and opened her mouth. At first only a quiet croak emerged. This time she knew every eye in the room would be on her. Clearing her throat, she tried again. 'Jan Hardy.'

'Thank you, Mrs Hardy. I hope you have a lot of luck with him.'

And that was it.

Limp from the emotional drama of bidding, Jan stared at the mournful features of the girl leading her new horse from the ring and, after the morning's setback, tried to get her head around the extraordinary sensation of seeing the vague fantasy of training one of the many animals she'd inspected over the last two days turn into reality.

'Well done, Jan!' Angie was saying. 'I'm sure that was a really good buy.'

Jan nodded absently and turned to her father. 'What do you think, Dad?'

'I told you this morning he was worth going for, and compared to the horse that sold before it, I'd say you had a hell of a bargain.'

Jan didn't feel like explaining again that it was the bold type which attracted the high prices, and anyway, she felt inclined to agree with her father. The horse did look like a bargain, and she was delighted she'd bought an animal that she was sure Toby Waller would like for a couple of thousand less than the budget he had set her.

'Let's hope you're right.' She grinned at her father. 'Come on, let's go and have another look at him. Our next lot's not due to go through for at least an hour.'

With a spring in her step, now that she was a bona fide buyer, Jan led her entourage of two out of the sale ring and through the reception area.

'Well done, Mrs Hardy.'

She turned and saw the weasel features of the man who had been selling Lot 63. 'Thanks,' she said, without offering him a hint of a smile.

'I'm sorry you didn't get mine,' the man said.

'Well, there's not much point coming to a sale with a budget if you don't stick to it. I expect you've sold him by now, anyway.'

'As a matter of fact, I haven't.'

'Oh well, that's the way it goes,' Jan said lightly and turned to follow Reg and Angie, who had gone on ahead.

'Sean McDonagh said you might still be interested, and I see you've a few wealthy friends.'

Jan stopped and looked at him. 'I haven't been asked to buy horses for Mr O'Hagan, if that's who you're referring to. And I also reckon I was being run when I was bidding for your horse this morning.'

'OK, OK,' the Ulsterman said quickly, seeing the conversation going from bad to worse. 'Are you interested in the horse or not?'

Jan shrugged a shoulder. 'What do you want for him?'

'Ten K.'

'Forget it,' Jan said, growing stronger now the initiative was with her. She spun round and carried on towards the door, to be called back once more.

'Hang on, now.' There was a satisfying shrillness in the man's voice. 'You obviously liked the horse, so tell me what you'd give for him?'

Jan turned back and faced him. 'Seven and a half.'

The man winced. 'Irish or English?'

'We're in Ireland aren't we?'

'Sorry, no can do.'

'So you'll have to take him home then, won't you?'

This time Jan spun round in a way that offered no comeback. She heard him mutter a few obscenities and was still grinning when she found Angie and Reg outside, eager to hear what had happened.

'Let's get around the corner and I'll tell you,' she said quietly. 'I tell you what – I think I'm starting to get the hang of this place!'

3

The day after the sales had ended at Fairyhouse, Jan drove her Land Rover through the village of Stanfield in Gloucestershire. She turned onto a newly surfaced tarmac drive, which led up the steep incline to Edge Farm. Until a month before the track had been little more than a pair of rutted gullies which the winter rain had gushed down; now the girls and lads who worked in the yard called it the 'motorway'.

The stable yard was built on a plot of ground which had been levelled from the steep hillside several hundred years ago. A large barn beneath a stand of Scots pines was the only original building on the site, and where the old farmhouse had once stood, the footings of a new but traditional Cotswold stone house were beginning to sprout, as if they had grown organically through the thin soil covering the soft rock of the hill. Fifty yards further up the slope perched the caravan which had been Jan's and her children's home for a little more than a year; there, against everyone's predictions, they had survived the winter.

Jan pulled up on the tidy parking area that had been laid the year before. She turned off the engine, wound down her window and sucked in a deep gulp of the familiar air. She gazed across the broad valley of the Severn, lit by the late afternoon sun. She longed to see Megan and Matthew, but they would be safe and happy in the caravan with their grandmother for a little while longer.

As soon as she stepped down from the Land Rover she was mobbed by her dogs; a terrier, a lurcher and an arthritic sheepdog. She fussed over them for a few moments, but was keen to check her paying guests – eight horses in a long, thin paddock that stretched almost to the top of the hill. She could see a couple of them now, grazing lazily in the afternoon sun. At least there was still some grass, she thought. And she was glad her father had urged her to spread the turf with a liberal measure of calcified seaweed earlier in the spring. 'It don't matter how much you put on; it costs hardly anything,' he'd argued, 'and it'll do your 'osses good.'

Roz Stoddard, twenty years old, big-boned, strong and devoted to the horses, emerged from the end block of stables, saw the Land Rover and started walking towards it. She waved and a welcoming grin spread across her russet cheeks.

Jan smiled back. 'Hi,' she called. 'How's everything?'

'Fine,' the girl replied, 'No problems at all, apart from Eagle trying to barge his way through the fence into the mares' paddock.'

'Did you stop him in time?'

'Sure.'

'Have you checked them every day?'

Roz laughed. 'Of course I have. But I suppose you won't believe me until you've done it yourself.'

Jan nodded. 'I'm afraid so.'

She was always relieved that the girls understood her diligence. The lads weren't so easy; they took it personally if she wanted to see for herself that things had been done correctly. Roz was beside her now, walking towards the gate into the big field.

'So, how did you get on?' she asked.

'Not bad; I bought three. One for Frank Jellard, which is a bit of a punt – he rang me at the sales and asked me to bid for it. A nice horse for Toby Waller and one for Mr Bellamy.'

'The bloke with the pub in Bath?'

'It's more than a pub; it's supposed to be one of the best restaurants in town.'

'No wonder he's so huge,' Roz observed, forthright as always.

'He'll like the horse I've bought for him. He's a big strong lad, a bit like Russian Eagle.'

'How much did he cost?'

'I bid up to nine thousand guineas – Irish – and then the bidding stopped at nine and a half. Dad was sure they ran him up to try and get me to the reserve of ten. Anyway, I wouldn't have bid that – not that he wasn't worth it, but I didn't want to overspend on my first buying trip there.'

'How did you get him, then?'

'The chap selling him came up to me in the afternoon; someone had told him I was still interested and he must have seen me having lunch with A.D., so I suppose he thought I had big money. He said I could have the horse for ten. So I told him I didn't think there'd been another bidder and I wasn't amused at being run up just because I was a new kid on the block. I said I'd give him seven and half, Irish; he cussed a bit and I walked off.' Jan grinned at the memory. 'He found me again later, though, about six o'clock, and said he'd take it.' Jan nodded with satisfaction. 'So I underspent for Mr Bellamy, which'll make him happy and prove to him I'm not about to rip him off.'

'I can't wait to see the horse. What were the others you got?'

As they reached the gate to the paddock, Roz pulled back the long bolt to open it and let them in. Closer to, Jan saw that the grass was a lot shorter than it had been a few days before. She made a mental note to supplement the horses' diet with concentrates and to split the geldings into two groups to start grazing the lower fields, leaving the fatter ones on the shorter grass.

'There's one that's really nice. Nothing great on paper, but just the sort I like. He came from a small stud down in Kerry. The girl minding him had come up to the sales on her own. She was a quiet little soul, but was so excited when the horse sold. Not that he went for much – another eight grand touch. So Toby'll be well pleased. And I bought one more on spec, possibly for Frank Jellard; it's a bit smaller than the others but tough-looking.'

'So Mr Jellard hasn't seen it?'

'No, but I hope to God he likes it; as I haven't had any money from him yet.'

'And that was it?'

'There were a couple more I bid for, but they went for forty and fifty grand a piece – a bit out of my league, you might say!'

'For the time being,' Roz added.

'Let's hope so. I reckon A.D. would have bought one of them if I'd asked him, but I didn't want to commit him to that kind of money when I haven't had his other horses yet. I need to show him what I can do with them first. Mind you, there were other horses I really liked which were cheap enough. But Dad spotted one of them had spavins, and another one I was warned off – I think.'

'How do you mean?'

'I'm not sure, to be honest. The horse looked great – Dad and I both agreed. But I'd met this Irishman, Sean McDonagh, who told us the people selling him had tried the horse already and found he was nappy on the gallops and not interested in the job, so they put him through the sales as "unbroken". Can you believe it?'

'What did you think?'

Jan grimaced. 'I just didn't feel I could trust this bloke; I still don't, but anyway I left it. I thought I'd feel such a fool if I got the horse and he did turn out to be a wrong 'un. He sold for practically no money to someone I'd seen talking to a big trainer from Somerset – so I don't know. It must be very easy to start a rumour about a horse to keep the price down.'

Roz laughed. 'Well, we'll just have to wait and see if it does any good, then you'll know whether this Sean's straight or not. But why didn't you trust him?'

'That's what Dad asked. I don't know – I can't put my finger on it. I think it was because he was too good to be true – too sort of considerate and friendly. It didn't feel quite right. But Dad liked him.'

'And your dad's a good judge.'

'Of horses; not people.'

🐎

Once Jan had made her way round all the horses in her care, checking them for any cuts or blemishes they might have picked up and inspecting their legs and feet, she was satisfied that all was well. She thanked Roz and made her way to the caravan, ready to concentrate on the two children she hadn't seen for nearly four days – the longest she'd ever been away from them, which felt even longer when so much had happened in Ireland.

As she walked up towards her long, green, mobile home, she thought about the new house, which was taking shape on a site halfway between the yard and the caravan. The house had been a long time growing because she was determined to borrow not a penny more than she had to during her first few years as an independent, licensed trainer. Most of the building material – timbers, stone, slates – had been found and gathered up by Eddie Sullivan the previous year. He'd owned Russian Eagle then and had often come to ride the horse or to visit her. Since then Gerry, her builder, had worked on the house, for little reward, whenever he had any spare time.

🐎

As Jan reached the steps up to the caravan, Mary Pritchard opened the door. She was wearing a blue fluffy cardigan under a floral cotton pinafore, just like the one she'd worn when Jan had been a child.

Jan sometimes thought her mother's life was stuck in a time warp in the early 1950s. Grateful for her support, she started to smile affectionately, but something in her mother's face froze her.

'Mum? What is it?' After all the warm feelings of expectation, Jan felt a sudden, violent panic. 'Is everything all right?'

'Oh, Jan! I didn't know you was back. Matty's not well,' Mary said with a quiver of guilt in her voice. 'He's really sick.'

Jan stepped up into the caravan, almost pushing past her mother. 'What on earth's wrong with him?' she asked, trying to stop herself from panicking.

'I'm not sure, but he's been grizzling all day and now he's got a temperature of a hundred and four.'

Jan's alarm grew as she heard strangled, uncontrollable sobs coming from the far end of their cramped home. With her heart thumping, she hurried through to the partitioned area where the children slept. Megan looked up wide-eyed from where she was leaning over her younger brother. 'Oh Mum, Matty's really upset; he just won't stop crying, whatever I do.'

'Hello, darling,' Jan tried to say lightly as she too leaned over the little boy's bed. 'Poor Matty. He does sound unhappy.'

Matthew stopped his whimpering just long enough to acknowledge his mother's presence. Jan pulled back the sheet covering him. His pyjama top was rucked up, as if he'd been trying to pull it off to get cool. With a horrified gasp, Jan saw that his bare, chubby torso was discoloured with a blotchy rash. She looked hard at his face. There were signs of it there too, on his forehead and lower down.

'Oh my God! Mum,' she called, 'have you seen this rash?'

Mary was already behind her, leaning over her shoulder. 'Oh, Lord,' she croaked. 'No, it wasn't there half an hour ago; it must have come since I changed him.'

'Do you know what it is?'

'Looks like the measles.'

'Meg,' Jan asked, 'has anyone at school had the measles?'

'No,' Megan answered solemnly, responding to the sense of crisis in the air.

'I'm going to call the doctor – right now.'

'I phoned the surgery,' Mary said. 'But being as it's a Saturday, there's no doctors in. They said to call back if there was an emergency.'

'This *is* an emergency for God's sake!' Jan's voice quivered with fear for her son's safety and with a touch of guilt that she hadn't known her mother would have phoned automatically. 'Maybe we should get an ambulance.'

'I know measles can be dangerous . . .' Mary said shakily, a little in awe of her daughter's passion.

'It may not be measles. It could be . . .' Jan found she couldn't even say the word, as if it might turn the thought into reality, '. . . something much worse.'

Meningitis!

The word echoed round in her head. There had been several recent outbreaks in the county.

She stood up, brushed past her startled mother and went through to the living room to use the phone.

Almost without seeing the buttons, she punched the surgery's number.

'Hello, Health Centre,' an officious woman's voice answered.

'This is Jan Hardy, Edge Farm, Stanfield. My little boy's got a high fever and a definite rash. I need someone to see him, right now.'

There was a moment's pause. 'Mrs Hardy, did someone else phone earlier?'

'Yes, my mother was looking after my children while I was away.'

'Right, I thought so. Well, as I told her, unfortunately, our duty doctor is out on call and I can't contact him just at the moment. What is your son's temperature?'

'A hundred and four.'

'And the rash, where is it?'

'His face, his body,' Jan told her impatiently.

'Well, as you say, there's a chance that these could be the symptoms of something serious. So I think it would be best if you took him to the A and E at Cheltenham Hospital right away. Can you do that?'

Jan wondered for a second what the woman would have suggested if she said no.

'Yes. I'll go right now.'

'All right, and I'll inform the doctor so he's aware of the situation.'

That'd be useful, Jan thought sarcastically, then chided herself. It wasn't the woman's fault. 'Thanks,' she said more warmly. She put the phone down and turned to Mary who had followed her. 'We've got to take him to hospital in Cheltenham.'

'You take him,' Mary corrected. 'I'll stay here with Meg.' She paused. 'That is, if you want me to . . .'

'Oh Mum, please. Course I do, but Dad'll want you home. I dropped him there about an hour ago and said I'd be bringing you right back.'

'Don't worry, I'll phone and tell him what's happened. He'd expect me to stay and help.'

🐎

Four hours later Jan emerged from Cheltenham General Hospital, feeling totally drained but clear-headed. As she walked briskly back to her Land Rover, the late sun was shafting across the pristine playing fields of the boys' college opposite and through the big leaves of the plane trees that lined the road. She took a few deep breaths and thanked God.

A young, conscientious paediatrician in the children's ward had reassured her that, despite Matthew's raging fever and alarming rash, the early results suggested he didn't have meningitis. Nevertheless, in view of the recent outbreaks locally, the hospital didn't want to take any chances and they'd decided to test him with a lumbar puncture. The consultant wanted to keep him in overnight while his temperature came down and they waited for the test results, although his opinion that Matty was suffering from measles and not meningitis was strengthened by Jan's guilty admission that her son had not yet had the MMR vaccination.

Jan had sat with Matty until he was asleep. Having made up her mind to come back first thing in the morning, she felt that she'd now done all she could. But the experience of leaving her children only to arrive home and find one of them with a possibly life-threatening disease had shaken her badly. Now she was fighting against all the feelings of guilt that had assailed her ever since she'd moved back to Gloucestershire following John's death. She'd decided that the only way she could support herself and her children was to use her knowledge of horses and this had meant she was often away at the races for a whole day at a time, or for the bloodstock sales in Doncaster or Newmarket, when she had to be away for longer. She guessed that all working mothers, whether they were employed in a factory, in an office or even on television, suffered form this same sense of guilt.

'How is he?' Mary asked, with tears in her eyes, as soon as Jan was through the door.

Jan sighed, reluctant to say too definitely what her mother wanted to hear. 'They're keeping him in for some more tests, but they're ninety-nine per cent sure he hasn't got meningitis. He was out for the count when I left, and will be for most of the night, they said. I'm going back first thing in the morning. I'm hoping to bring him home, but I'll drop Meg and Smarty off on the way so I can spend the day with him if necessary. Is that OK?'

Reg appeared behind Mary. 'Thank God he's all right,' he said. 'Of course Megan can stay.'

'Hello, Dad.' Jan hadn't even noticed his old Daihatsu outside. 'What are you doing here? I thought you'd be knackered after that journey.'

'Soon as your mum phoned and said what's happened, I came over. I wish you'd phoned us from the hospital.'

'Oh, I'm sorry,' Jan said, suddenly conscious of her thoughtlessness. 'Of course I should have – I was just trying to take it all in myself. I didn't think. Anyway, he's OK – they're pretty sure he's got measles.'

For the next twenty minutes Jan tried to recall every word the doctors had said and repeat them to Mary and Reg until her mother was prepared to believe that her precious grandson would live and would suffer no ill-effects.

Reg sat quietly, listening and nodding, knowing his wife far too well to belittle her concerns. When Mary was finally reassured, he got to his feet. 'Come on now, love. We must get off home. Megan's already fast asleep.' He nodded at the little girl curled up on a bench at the end of the caravan. 'And Jan's had a hell of a long day.'

'Thanks for coming,' Jan said. 'Mum, thanks a lot for having the kids all that time and, whatever you do, don't go blaming yourself. It's not your fault; it's not anyone's fault.'

'No, love; but if you need any more help, you just let me know.'

Jan watched them leave and Reg's old car creep slowly down the steep drive. She looked down at Megan, still sleeping soundly, and decided to leave her a little longer. Suddenly she felt very alone and badly wanted someone to talk to. She wished Annabel hadn't gone away.

She made herself a cup of tea, then sat down on one of the benches at the table which was fixed to the wall and picked up the phone. She was wondering who she could talk to when it rang out, startling her.

'Hello?' she said, stifling her tears.

'Jan, it's Gerry. I just wanted to know if you were back from Ireland.'

Jan tried to hide her disappointment. She didn't feel she could cope with Gerry right now. 'I got back this afternoon,' she said, 'but then I had to take Matty into hospital and I was there for hours.'

'Oh no! Is he all right?'

'I thought he might possibly have something very serious, but it looks as if he's going to be fine. Everything's under control and he'll be home tomorrow, all being well.'

'Just s'long as he's going to be OK.'

'Thanks, Gerry. Anyway, what did you want?'

'I wondered if you'd be in tomorrow?'

'I'll be going over to the hospital for most of the day, I expect.'

'Then, maybe, I know it's late, but could I come up now and tell you what I was looking to do on the house tomorrow?'

Jan looked at the clock on the wall. It was half-past ten and she wanted to go to bed. 'All right,' she sighed. 'But I don't want to be too late.'

When Gerry arrived, Jan asked herself, not for the first time, why she found him so awkward. He was absurdly shy, but extremely kind and thoughtful, as well as generous. He was very fit from the work he did and not bad looking, either. But Jan found that his unquestioning devotion sometimes made her feel embarrassed, though there was nothing threatening or demanding in his manner and she didn't want to hurt him by turning down his generosity.

He came into the caravan, making it seem smaller with his big, fidgeting presence until Jan asked him to sit at the table.

'Would you like a drink?' she offered.

'Yes, please.' His face flushed under his thatch of fair hair. 'A lager, if you've got one. Don't worry about a glass.'

Jan took a bottle from the fridge. She handed it to him with an opener and topped up her own tea.

'So,' he asked, 'what was it like in Ireland?'

Jan told Gerry about the horses she'd bought as he listened intently, but when he asked her about the people she'd met, she didn't mention Sean McDonagh.

'They don't hold back in Ireland,' she said. 'The first morning I was picked up by a gang of retired jockeys going out to the sales to meet up with their old mates. They were really friendly; in fact, most of the Irish folk were very helpful. Then I met this great girl, Angie Sharp, who's about my own age, maybe a bit younger.'

'Is she Irish too?'

'No.' Jan laughed. 'She's English, really smart, great company. She wasn't there to buy herself, so she came round with me for a while on the first day. Actually, it may turn out to be quite useful because her parents have got several horses in training – guess who with?'

'God, I don't know. I hate guessing games.'

'Martin Hunter.'

'How many have they got with him then?'

'About half a dozen.'

'That'd be half his yard.'

'Not quite, but he's not doing at all well.'

'Any chance we'll get them?'

Jan didn't miss the 'we' and shook her head. 'I doubt it. If it was up to Angie, there'd be no problem. But apparently her parents helped Martin set up and they're committed to staying with him.'

'But they can't go on shelling out to someone who's forgotten what it's like to have a fit horse, let alone a winner.'

'Anyway, you'll soon meet Angie, I should think. I've asked her to come up here and visit as soon as she's got the chance.'

'Where does she live then?' Gerry asked, though Jan could tell he wasn't particularly interested.

'Somerset, I think; anyway, near Bath. Her parents have got a hotel in Bristol, and various other businesses – obviously making a lot of money.'

Gerry nodded at her with a soulful look in his grey-brown eyes, and Jan sensed he was already jealous of Angie, as he was of Annabel for the closeness of Jan's relationship with her.

'Anyway, Gerry. You came up here to talk about the house, you said.'

'Oh, yes. Sorry. You must be tired after driving back from Ireland and then having all that worry in the hospital.'

'Yes I am. So we had better get on with it.' Jan tried not to sound too impatient.

'It's just that I don't start my next job till Thursday so I can crack on here for a few days, if that's OK by you, but I need a load of sand and cement before I can get on with the block work.'

Jan struggled as she always did between the need to have a proper house for her children, and the tiny budget she was operating on at present, with no full training fees coming in and the wages still to be paid.

She nodded her head. 'OK, you may as well while you've got the chance, but I can't afford any big bills for materials just at the moment.'

'That's fine, Jan; we won't be needing to buy anything much for a few months yet; I've got most of what I need to be going on with and, like I said, you don't have to pay my bill until you've got the money to spare.'

'But I don't like owing you all the time.'

'Jan, you've got enough on your plate. You know I want to do it for you.'

'Thanks, Gerry, you've been really kind,' she sighed. 'Anyway, you get on with it and get the stuff. I don't know if you'll see me here at all tomorrow, though, if Matty's awake and needs me.'

'That's fine, Jan.' Gerry drained the last of the beer from the bottle and put it down on the table with a thump, before sliding out from the bench and standing up. As he opened the door, he looked back at her.

'May see you tomorrow, then? Take care of yourself.'

She could see he wanted to lean down and give her a casual kiss on the cheek the way people like Eddie always did. Instead, he reddened a little, took a deep breath, turned and let himself out into the starlit summer night.

🐎

Gerry's visit did little to distract Jan from her worries about Matthew, and she lay awake for a few hours praying that he was comfortable and asleep, and that he wouldn't be a victim of the one per cent element of doubt in the consultant's diagnosis.

In any event, she wasn't completely surprised that Matthew

had succumbed to the measles; she'd often felt he wasn't as strong and healthy as Megan had been at the same age. He'd always been less active as a baby and a toddler, but perhaps more thoughtful to compensate.

Megan, with Jan's own pert features and John's lean physique, was already showing signs of becoming a stunning girl, brimming over with confidence at school and on her pony. It just showed – Jan thought – even bringing up a child in a caravan on a windswept hillside, you could still point her in the right direction. But she didn't discount all the support she'd had in this area from her parents and the girls who worked in the yard – Roz and, in particular, Annabel.

Jan found herself thinking about Annabel and how much she missed her.

At the end of May, when they had sent out their last runner for the season, Annabel announced, quite unexpectedly, that she was going away for ten weeks to stay with friends in Italy and France. Of course she had known it would be hard for Jan to pay her wages over the summer, and she would probably have gone on helping out for nothing, as she had the previous year when they were setting up the point-to-point yard. But she also knew that Jan found this kind of charity embarrassing – maybe that was why she'd decided to take herself off.

It wouldn't do her any harm, Jan thought. Annabel was a beautiful, serene girl of twenty-four who had come to work with Jan when she'd still lived in Wales and, despite their obvious differences, they had become very close friends.

Annabel's father, Major Halstead, was a wealthy man; he had inherited from his aunt a large estate in the Welsh Marches and enjoyed living there like an old-fashioned squire. But he had always treated his daughter with complete indifference, leaving her insecure and too naive to cope with all the men who pursued her. Jan was sure she had run away from university back to the country to avoid them.

But whatever problems had blighted that side of her life, Annabel was the most loyal friend Jan had ever had. She didn't work for Jan because she needed the money – in fact, her wages barely covered the cost of the cottage she rented in Stanfield – but because she loved the horses and the yard, which they had worked so hard to create from a cluster of abandoned farm buildings which no one else had seemed to want.

When Eddie Sullivan had sent his horse to Jan the previous year, she had been worried when she discovered that he and Annabel had once had a relationship that had obviously gone wrong. But Annabel handled the situation sensibly enough, and she must have forgiven Eddie for whatever he'd done because on her own initiative she had bought Russian Eagle simply so that Eddie could ride him in the Aintree Foxhunters' in April – a race which, even though they hadn't won it, turned out to be an early watershed in the history of Edge Farm.

Amidst uneasy, muddled thoughts about Annabel, Eddie, and about Matty, hospitals and A.D. O'Hagan, Jan finally fell asleep.

A.D. was the first person to enter her thoughts when she woke the next morning. The phone beside her bed was ringing. She picked it up and heard his greeting before she had even looked at the clock.

'Good morning, Jan.' His deep, musical voice seemed to project his powerful charisma down the line.

'Morning, A.D.' Jan tried not to sound too croaky.

'I've woken you,' the Irishman chuckled. 'I don't blame you; it's a hell of a drive back from Anglesey.'

'And I'm afraid I spent all yesterday evening at the hospital in Cheltenham with Matty.'

'Your boy?'

'Yes; we had a bit of a scare, but fortunately they think he's just got measles.'

'Is that right?'

Jan thought she detected a touch of impatience in A.D.'s voice at being told about problems that had nothing to do with him and didn't concern him.

'I was ringing to tell you,' he went on, 'that I've arranged to send you my horses on August the sixth. I would like to come and see them the following day. Will that suit you?'

The suggestion posed no problems for Jan, and anyway, she sensed that A.D. wasn't giving her a choice, but she was grateful for the notice and the chance to plan for the horses' arrival.

'That'll be fine,' she said. 'I'm looking forward to seeing them.'

'And I thought we might have a little dinner at the Queen's Hotel in Cheltenham that evening,' O'Hagan added. 'Just the two of us. My horses are very precious to me and I like to get to know the people looking after them.'

Jan put the phone down, quivering a little and wondering what dinner alone with A.D. would be like. In all her dealings with him so far, his friends and gofers had always been hanging around, ready to implement the continual stream of instructions he issued.

She shook the stiffness from her limbs and saw that it was already eight o'clock. She went through to the living area of the caravan to find her bag. She rummaged in it until she pulled out a slip of paper with the phone number of Matthew's ward written on it. She dialled and waited nervously for a dozen rings, before her call was answered by a busy nurse.

'This is Jan Hardy, Matthew's mother. How is he?'

'Oh, hello, Mrs Hardy. He's fine; he slept well and he's looking much better already.'

'Oh, good. I'm just going to drop my daughter off at her granny's, then I'll be straight in. When will he be able to come home?'

'If all the tests are OK, I'm sure they'll let him go this afternoon.'

🐎

As it was a Sunday and there were no horses in the stables or any mucking out to do, Roz Stoddard wasn't supposed to be coming in.

Reluctantly, Jan rang her at home. Her mother answered and told Jan that Roz had already left for the day to take her younger brother to a horse trials in Wiltshire.

Jan put the phone down, wishing Annabel was around, but in her absence she dialled her other girl groom, Emma. Emma had gone with Roz and her brother for the day. So it looked as if Megan would definitely have to spend the day at Reg and Mary Pritchard's farmhouse in Riscombe.

4

Smarty was a silver grey Welsh pony, just eleven hands high, and he could be as tricky to load as any of the racehorses in the yard. Reg had given Jan the old single horse trailer he'd bought when she was a teenager, and she'd found she had to entice the pony up the ramp by rattling a large handful of nuts in a plastic bucket while coaxing him with a lunge rein fixed to one side of the trailer and pulled tight around his bottom. Jan hoped desperately it wouldn't take too long to teach him to go in more willingly.

It was only in the last couple of months that Megan had suddenly become interested in ponies, mostly as a result of her competitive nature and two other pony-mad seven-year-olds in her class at school. Jan had been so pleased when Meg announced she wanted to ride, and thrilled when she'd shown that she had a natural balance and suppleness that all good riders need.

Reg had taken it upon himself to find Meg her first pony. He'd travelled around the Cotswolds and had seen dozens of them before finding one good enough for his precious grand-daughter. Apart from Smarty's unwillingness to walk up into the dark and narrow confines of a trailer, he had a flawless nature. He was both athletic and beautifully schooled.

Reg loved it when Jan brought Meg and Smarty over to ride around the farm at Riscombe. Persuading Megan to spend a whole day with her grandparents had become a lot easier, especially since Reg had put together a small collection of oil drums, timber poles and pallets to jump in the paddock beside the house, where he was quite happy to spend the whole afternoon rebuilding them to make a circuit that would test the skills Megan had learned.

When the pony was finally in the trailer, Megan hooked the breeching strap behind him, leaving Jan to tie his head-collar rope before she came round to lift the heavy ramp.

'Got your tack, then?' Jan asked.

Megan nodded and skipped off to fetch the tiny saddle and bridle, which she had polished until they gleamed the day before. Jan had often told her she wouldn't be allowed to ride unless her pony and tack were kept clean, and after being refused one eagerly awaited session as a result of a muddied saddle and a dirty bridle, Megan had made sure it never happened again.

They put the tack into the back of the Land Rover, which was already hitched to the trailer. Then, with a wave to Joe Paley, who was on duty for the day, they drove down the steep track to the road.

As they crept up the long hill towards the top of the Cotswolds, the sun gleamed tantalizingly through the beech trees and burst on them in a glorious blaze at the top. Early on a Sunday morning was the best time to be driving along empty roads through the honey-stone hills that Jan had known since early childhood. At some time in her life, she reckoned, she must have hunted or ridden through every grassy hollow and sun-dappled coppice they passed. She still knew several of them by name, and she was happy that so little had changed and that Megan would share the same backdrop for her own childhood years. She just hoped it could be the same for Matthew.

🐎

Jan pulled up in front of her parents' house in a small green valley on the edge of Riscombe.

'How's the little fellow?' Mary asked as soon as Jan climbed out of the Land Rover.

'He's fine,' Jan said brightly, seeing the anxiety in her mother's pale blue eyes. The old woman was walking towards them, limping slightly from her arthritis. Her white curly hair blew in the gentle breeze that funnelled up the valley and softened the early heat of the sun, rustling the leaves of the mighty beech tree which stood beside the old stone cottage like a giant green parasol. Mary's cheeks glowed and her mouth spread into a big smile as soon as she saw Megan step down.

'Hello, Granny; how are you?' the girl shouted as she ran over to hug Mary, cheerfully unaware of the shadow cast by her brother's condition.

'I'm very well, darling.' Mary grinned, hugging her back. 'And all the better for seeing your lovely smiley face.'

'Thanks for having her, Mum,' Jan said. 'But don't let her drive Dad barmy putting up jumps. He's going to do himself a mischief if he goes on heaving those poles around all day.'

'Ah, but he loves it, don't you, dear?' Mary said, as Reg came out of the house.

'But Mum,' Megan justified breathlessly, 'Grandad teaches me, you know, and I give him one of my sweets every time Smarty knocks a pole down.'

The adults all laughed at this role reversal and Jan couldn't repress a quick surge of pride at her daughter's sunny personality.

'Don't you worry, Jan,' Reg said. 'Just you go and see Matty and bring him home safely. Now, let's get the pony off and unhook that trailor.'

🐎

'Mummy . . .'

Jan looked down at Matty, who was gazing up at her from his hospital cot with his eyes wide open. The smile on his chubby face instantly made up for all the anxiety of the last twelve hours.

'Hello, darling. Mummy's here. Are you feeling better?'

The little boy glanced from side to side. He studied the doctor for a moment, decided he approved and turned back to look at Jan. 'Want dink,' he said.

The doctor smiled down at him. 'Matthew will be very thirsty after the fever and all the tests he's been through.' He picked up a beaker of water from the table beside the cot and passed it to Jan. She offered it to Matty and watched him suck at it greedily.

'You can take him home now if you want. We're absolutely sure it isn't meningitis.'

'Thank God,' Jan said. 'How long will he have the rash?'

'For a few more days, I'm afraid, but he's over the worst.' He put his head to one side. 'Pity he didn't have the MMR, though; it might have saved you some anxious moments. And do remember to keep him away from anyone who could be pregnant.'

Jan drove back to Riscombe with Matty warmly wrapped up and strapped into his seat. The afternoon sun shone serenely in a bright blue sky, as if it were saying that the world would always carry on regardless of her personal problems.

As she parked her Land Rover on the patch of old cobbles and grass in front of her parents' farm cottage, Smarty's head was peeping over the bottom door of a stable in the stone barn. She looked behind her at Matty. He was soundly asleep and she didn't want to disturb him. As silently as possible, she climbed out into the quiet afternoon and saw that the old oil drums and timber jumps in the paddock had been taken down and neatly stacked by the fence. She walked around the house, through Reg's tidy garden of dahlias, sweet peas, lettuce, rhubarb and beetroot, to the sheltered rear, where Megan was sitting with her grandparents at a small wooden table beside the back door surrounded by pots of geraniums.

'How's Matty?' Mary asked at once.

'He's fast asleep in the back of the Land Rover,' she announced. 'And it's definite he's only got the measles.'

'Oh, thank the Lord,' Mary whispered, while Reg nodded and smiled.

'Does that mean Matty's coming home already?' Megan asked, sounding disappointed at the prospect of not having her mother all to herself as she had secretly hoped.

'Megan, don't be so unkind to your brother,' Jan scolded. 'Now tell me: how did you get on with Smarty today?'

'He was *brilliant*,' Megan said eagerly.

'He did go well,' Reg beamed. 'She's really got the hang of him now; you should take her to some little shows, like I used to with you.'

'I haven't forgotten, Dad.' Jan added in exasperation, 'But I'm going to be far too busy with the horses. The three from Fairyhouse should be turning up this evening. O'Hagan's are coming on August the sixth and I've got a feeling he's going to be watching me like a hawk.'

'I reckon he will; so you'll have to be on your toes. Has any of those others who said they'd be sending you horses come up with anything yet?'

'Lady Fairford's sent me a chaser called Young Willie. Actually, he's getting a bit long in the tooth, but he's still capable of winning a race, and Mr Bellamy sounded very pleased when I told him about the horse I'd bought for him in Ireland.'

'Did you hear any more from that Angie Sharp?' Reg asked.

'No, not yet.'

'I don't reckon you will,' Reg said with a shake of his head.

'But I thought you liked her. Anyway, I'm sure she will be in touch, even though she's already said there's no chance of me getting any of those horses off her parents.'

'I don't know about her, Jan, but I think you should have taken a bit more notice of Sean McDonagh. He seemed like a real, genuine sort of bloke.'

'What? Even after he put us off that Good Thyne horse, which went for no money to that big yard in Somerset? I don't know who was doing who a favour.'

'We'll see.'

'Anyway, I reckon Angie will come up to see the yard, and I'm sure if she can do anything about influencing her parents, she will.'

'So how many horses will you have for next season?'

'About twenty,' Jan started counting off on her fingers. 'Six of O'Hagan's, three for Toby Waller with his new one, Russian Eagle for Bel, two for Bernie Sutcliffe.'

'Is he still staying with you, after what happened with Russian Eagle?'

'He sold Eagle to Bel, thinking Eagle would burst a blood vessel again – I never asked him to, and besides, the horse he got in exchange is sure to win for him this season, and maybe Arctic Hay will too, that other one I got for him last year.'

'So what else have you got?'

'Colonel Gilbert's leaving one with me. And Frank Jellard's sending back three that could be useful, as well as the one we bought for him in Ireland last week. Then Penny Price's mum and dad have decided to come in with her and have a share in Arrow Star, so he's staying, and I'm positive I can find a good novice three-mile chase he can win. Then there's the horse I've bought for Bellamy, Lady Fairford's Young Willie, and August Moon, which I hope someone will buy off me before Lloyds Bank find they own more than one horse.'

'You can't sell August Moon when Mr Carey left her to you in his will.' Reg sounded shocked. 'Besides, she'd make a damn good brood mare – you could breed some lovely foals from her.'

Jan knew that he considered breeding your own horses was always preferable to buying yearlings or young stock, irrespective of the unsound economics involved.

'Well, I'm sure he'd understand, but needs must; though I won't sell her unless I really have to. But which should I put first, Dad, the horse or the house?'

For a moment, Jan found herself looking out over the riot of colour in Reg's garden and thinking of the last time she'd seen old Mr Carey. It had been when he was very near to death, though she hadn't realized it at the time, in his dark, gloomy room at Stanfield Court shortly after he had promised to put up her bond for the Jockey Club. Of course, the promise had died with him, but she was surprised to find how much she missed the old man and his wisdom now he'd gone. Leaving his high-class mare to her had been a wonderful gesture.

'Is twenty horses going to be enough to cover your costs, though?' Reg asked, still worried about the viability of Jan's yard as the only source of income for a woman alone with such a young family.

'Just about, though it won't leave any room for luxuries.'

'What if O'Hagan turns round and takes his away?'

'Then I've got problems – so let's hope he doesn't. But I've had a few other enquiries and I'm hopeful I'll have a couple more before the season gets going.'

'How many can you take altogether?' Mary asked, still unable to grasp the scale involved in Jan training with the professionals.

'When Gerry's finished the new run of stables I could have thirty, and maybe two more at a pinch if I move the feed store.'

Mary looked at her in disbelief. 'However would you be able to deal with thirty-two?' she asked.

'By making sure I've got good people working for me. Annabel's very knowledgeable and she's sensible. So's Roz, and even Joe Paley knows more about horses than most people learn in a lifetime.'

'But it seems such a responsibility to be charging people for keeping and training their horses, and then having so many to look after.'

'Mum, even if I had thirty horses, I'd still be one of the smaller yards. Some of the big trainers have got a hundred and fifty or more.'

Megan, who had been sitting hunched with her feet on her chair, shook her long blonde hair. 'And anyway, Granny, I'll be helping too. Mum says I'll be able to ride some of the horses when I'm bigger.'

Jan laughed. 'Not for a bit you won't, but you can certainly help with the feeding and mucking out at the weekends.'

'Oh, Mum!' Megan wailed with exaggerated anguish. 'I *hate* mucking out.'

'If you want to spend your life with horses, Megan, you'll have to get to like it.'

*

Jan mused on what she had said to young Megan as they drove home. It seemed to her that anyone who worked with horses for a living had to make some kind of sacrifice or compromise to do it. The simple truth was that the majority of people in the racing industry worked for significantly less than they could have earned elsewhere and that included the trainers!

Jan had often thought it quite bizarre that, of all animals, there was something particularly vocational about the horse.

The difference for her – she thought – was that, handling horses, however natural it had become, was just about the only skill she possessed, and she simply didn't know much about anything else or even want too. She turned and looked at Megan, curled up on her seat with eyelashes resting on her peach-down cheeks. *Maybe*, Jan thought, *it wouldn't be a bad thing if she didn't get too keen on mucking out.*

*

A lorry with Irish number plates was waiting by the yard gate when Jan and the children got back with Smarty. Joe came out to meet them in a state of high excitement.

'Them 'osses you bought in Ireland are here already,' Joe said excitedly. 'A couple of 'em's really nice.'

'I was expecting them,' Jan nodded. 'The transport people said they'd be here today.'

'The bloke who brought them wants to see you.'

At that moment a large, unfamiliar man rolled into view and walked towards them clutching a clipboard with a stack of papers, which he thrust at Jan.

'Hang on. I've got a sick child in the back of the car. I must put him to bed before I do anything else. And then I'll want to check the horses thoroughly,' she said, more coldly than she meant to. 'I want to make sure they match their passports and that they haven't been knocked about since I last saw them.'

'They're the right horses all right and they're in perfect condition,' the driver said, quite used to sceptical consignees.

Jan sighed and called to Joe to unload the pony. She opened the back door of the Land Rover and unstrapped a sleepy and still quite feverish Matty. She carefully lifted him over her left shoulder like a soft warm parcel and carried him up to the caravan.

Once she'd given him a drink and was satisfied that he was settled in bed with a story playing on his tape machine, she walked back down to the stables to inspect her new inmates.

This should have been one of the most exciting moments of her career – her first real quality horses, bought fresh by her, untainted by anyone else for the job she wanted them to do, and yet, after the shock of the previous day, the whole business seemed trivial beside the well-being of her small son.

In the stables, Joe strained over her shoulder as she looked at the animals and told him as much as she knew about each one. She was cheered by the fact that all three of them were every bit as good as she remembered. She particularly liked the big horse she had bought for Ray Bellamy.

When she was satisfied, she went out and gave the driver twenty pounds, then watched as he manoeuvred his big lorry out of the parking place and trundled back down the drive. When he was safely on his way, she turned to Joe. 'Right,' she said. 'We'd better get these horses settled in and find out what they're really like.'

The first thing they did was to take down the U-shaped metal grilles from the newcomers' stable doors. These were designed to discourage horses with a tendency to weave – a strange equine habit in which a horse would stand, shifting his weight constantly from one front foot to the other, waving his head and neck from side to side, causing undue wear and tear in his forelegs.

'Now they can have a good look around the yard,' she

explained, 'and we'll soon see if any of them are weavers. And we will need to keep a very close eye on them for a couple of days. Sometimes horses can get very stressed, especially on a long journey, and their digestive system slows down so any hay they eat gets balled up in their guts and gives them colic.'

'Aren't you going to put them out, then?' Joe asked, knowing that Jan liked to give her horses plenty of time in the paddocks.

'Not for a couple of days. In the meantime, I just want you to lead them out morning and evening for a pick of grass in the little paddock. You can also pull them some to have with their supper.'

While she was talking, Megan and Tigger appeared round the end of the barn and went to admire the new inmates. 'Mum, you said they were babies, but they're huge!'

Jan laughed. 'I meant they were young, but I didn't say they were foals. And this one's not so big,' she said, lifting Megan to see the horse she had bought for Frank Jellard.

'He's got a nice face,' Megan observed seriously.

'Yes,' Jan agreed. 'That's what I thought.'

Jan had fed Matty, settled him down again and was giving Megan her tea when she saw a small black Rover turn into the bottom of the drive and race up to the parking area.

She opened the door and waited to see who got out of the car. A tall man whom she didn't recognize emerged.

'Are you the doctor?' she called down to him.

The man nodded.

'Matthew's up here.'

'Coming,' he called, before leaning back into his car for his bag. He walked the fifty yards that separated them with an urgent stride.

Jan stepped down to meet him. She took in enough to be aware of a lean man, perhaps in his early forties, with strong features and steady grey eyes. When he reached her, she held out a hand. 'Hello, I'm Jan Hardy.'

'Tony Robertson,' he said as he took her hand. 'I've just started at the Winchcombe practice. I'm sorry I couldn't get here sooner. I was on an emergency call yesterday when you phoned in.'

'In which case you're a bit out of date. My son had a very high fever and a rash, and your surgery told me to take him to the A and E in Cheltenham. He was there overnight. They did all the tests for meningitis and he's fine; he's just got measles.'

'That must be a massive relief for you,' the doctor said with feeling. 'But at his age even measles can be pretty horrible. Anyway, I may as well take a look at him while I'm here.'

Jan stood aside to usher him up the step into the caravan with a friendly gesture, but when his eyes lingered on her a few seconds longer than was necessary she felt herself flush uncomfortably.

🐎

The next day, while Jan was having a quick snack up at the caravan, the phone rang.

'Hello, Jan?'

Jan recognized the hoarse, peevish voice of her mother-in-law, Olwen Hardy. She suddenly felt guilty that she hadn't rung her to tell her about Matty's illness, even though it had turned out not to be serious. Olwen had as much right to know as her own mother, she reasoned, but she knew it was the accusatory tone she always heard in the old woman's voice had deterred her.

'Hello, Olwen. How are you?'

'Not good.'

Jan winced. As the family of Olwen's only son, Jan and the kids were her nearest relatives. Quite frankly she dreaded having to deal with a failing mother-in-law as well as her own son and her fragile new business. 'Oh dear. Aren't you feeling well?'

'I feel all right,' the old woman croaked impatiently, 'but that crook you sold the farm to is making a lot of trouble.'

'Olwen, I didn't know I was selling it to Harold Powell and you know it. He conned me into it.'

'Hm,' Olwen grunted. 'You asked for it. Anyway, I've had a thing from the council saying he's applied to turn the lower field into a caravan park – holiday caravans or some such, dozens of 'em for townies to come and tear all over the place in their cars and motorbikes. And they'll completely surround my bungalow.'

'Oh, God,' Jan groaned. And she still hadn't told Olwen about Matty. 'I don't think there's anything I can do about it, but you can object, can't you?'

'There's all these forms to fill in . . .' Olwen didn't finish the sentence. The demand for Jan to come and deal with the problem was implicit.

Jan could see her, perched like an angry bird of prey on her telephone seat in the narrow hall of her bungalow, with her iron-grey curls neatly permed and wearing a spotless pink cardigan.

Jan took a deep breath. 'Send all the papers to me and I'll deal with it. I was just going to ring you to ask if we can come over next Sunday. Matty's been a bit unwell,' she added quickly.

Olwen picked it up right away. 'What? When?'

'When I got back from Ireland.'

'What do you want to go to Ireland for? See what happens when you go gallivanting all over the place and leave them. I never left my John for a single night.'

'Olwen, Matty would have got ill if I'd been there or not. My mum was here and she called the doctor.'

'What's wrong with him?'

'It's only the measles.'

'But that can turn very nasty if you're not careful. I told you he should have had that jab. I know John wasn't too keen, but . . .'

'Olwen, it's all under control. I am his mother, you know, and I love him too.'

By Thursday afternoon Matty was feeling well enough to sit up and play on the floor. Jan had just handed him a big new plastic digger when Frank Jellard phoned from his car to say he was on his way to Edge Farm to look at his new horse and wanted to discuss when his others would be coming in from the fields.

From an owner's point of view, deciding when the horses' summer holidays were over made quite a difference. While they were at grass, Jan charged only six pounds a day. As soon as they were moved back into their stables and began their training programme on a selected diet of hard food, more staff, bedding and the ancillary extras, her basic rate went up to twenty-five pounds a day, which still left very little for her own needs.

Frank Jellard's family had been growing fruit in the Vale of Evesham for generations. Ambitious and more entrepreneurial than his father, Frank had added value to his produce by processing it himself, bypassing the middlemen and marketing it as directly as possible.

Up until two years ago, people had told Jan, he had been utterly single-minded in his ambitions, but suddenly finding himself with more money than he'd ever imagined, he had succumbed to his wife's urging to spend some of it on things that would properly reflect their status in the district.

To Frank and his wife that had meant buying racehorses. Jan supposed he thought that by owning racehorses he could show people not only how much money he had to spend, but also how much he could afford to blow on a hobby.

Jan watched as Frank climbed out of his new Jaguar and closed the door with a resounding clunk. She didn't particularly want to talk to him in the caravan, so she went down to meet him. He was waiting for her with his hands on his hips, a big man, with a wide, flat face, wiry brown hair and dark, impatient eyes.

'So,' he said, without any pretence at small talk, 'let's have a look at him.'

'Just a mo. Let me get someone to go up to the caravan to keep an eye on Matthew.'

'Is that one of your kids?'

Jellard had known of Matty's existence and his name for at least a year. Jan wondered what he was trying to prove by appearing to be so ignorant of her private life. But she kept her thoughts to herself. She had long since realized her clients didn't pay her to give them lessons in personal charm.

She nodded and called to Roz to go up and keep an eye on the little boy.

She and Jellard walked through the yard. He muttered his approval of the surroundings – well-mown areas of grass were embellished with beds of marigolds and sweet peas were growing up trellises in front of the new timber stables.

The flowers were Reg's excuse for coming over most days. The previous year he had also planted neat little box hedges around the ends of each building and had started to train pyracantha up towards the gables. Half-barrels planted with flame-red geraniums stood between the stable doors and every piece of timber in the yard had been freshly stained or painted by Gerry.

'Have you thought about a name for him?' Jan asked conversationally.

'Not yet. Not till I'm sure I'm having him.'

Jan's heart sank; she needed the money for the horse as soon as possible, but she should have been ready for Jellard's habit of not committing himself and for making life as difficult as possible for everyone around him. She took a quick breath to control her irritation.

'You must let me know today if you're not,' she said. 'Because I bought him cheap, I've got other owners who'd be keen to have him and he'll have to start work before too long.'

Jellard glanced at her sharply. 'Don't you go telling people he's available until I say so. You bought him for me, and if there's a profit to be made I know who'll be making it.'

Jan sighed inwardly. It hadn't even occurred to him that she had just spent three long, unpaid days slogging around Ireland to purchase the horse in the first place. They had reached the entrance to the big barn, in which Gerry had built eight roomy stables the year before shortly after Jan had arrived at Edge Farm.

Jan had loosed the three horses from Fairyhouse into a paddock only that morning, planning to leave them out for five or six weeks to relax and settle in before she brought them back in to start their training. But when Jellard had phoned, she'd asked Roz to bring the smaller horse in again. They had given him a thorough grooming and he now looked superb.

'Here he is.' Jan led Jellard to the end box, kicked up the foot catch and drew back the bolt to go in.

When she'd first seen the horse at the sales, Jan had been struck by an interesting, slightly aloof air about him. At a full sixteen hands, he was slightly smaller than her ideal, but she had been impressed by his athleticism and conformation. He had a hardy look and she was confident that he would be a real workman on the gallops.

She hooked a rope onto his head-collar and led him out into the yard. Frank Jellard leaned against the wall of the barn and adopted the cynical face of a knowing buyer.

As if he knows what to look for! Jan thought as she held the gelding's head.

Jellard said nothing.

'Would you like to see him move?' Jan asked.

Jellard nodded.

Jan called to Joe Paley, who had been heaving bags of bruised oats into the feed store on the other side of the yard. She passed him the head rope and asked him to trot the horse along the track down the centre of the yard.

She and Jellard walked to one end to get a better look at the horse as he came towards them, Jan was again delighted with his beautifully balanced, athletic stride. Although any delay in getting the money to her bank could be extremely embarrassing, she'd been telling the truth when she'd told Jellard she could easily find another buyer. Without realizing it, she smiled and nodded her approval.

'Do it again,' she asked Joe.

She sensed Frank Jellard was struggling with an urge to ask for her reassurance and his desire to appear knowledgeable.

'OK,' he said gruffly. 'He looks pretty good. I can have him.'

'I'll need the money today,' Jan said quickly. 'I promised the bank.'

He nodded. 'I'll give it you now. Will readies do?'

❧

Jan realized as he drove away that a large part of running a yard with a public licence had little to do with horses and a lot to do with human relations. In the end, she thought, that was probably the case with most activities in life. She reminded herself, however, that the owners of the other two horses that had arrived from Ireland would certainly be more appreciative than Jellard. When she got back to the caravan, she was glad to hear that Ray Bellamy and Toby Waller had both rung to say they would be coming to see their respective new purchases the next day.

Ray Bellamy had originally written to Jan the day after the Jockey Club had approved her application for a public licence. He had been at Aintree on the day Russian Eagle had run and had been most impressed by the way the horse had performed over the testing course.

Jan rang him back at his hotel in Bath to say she'd be glad to see him the following afternoon. Then she phoned Toby Waller to invite him, too; in return he asked her if he could take her out to dinner after he'd seen his horse.

❧

The following evening Toby arrived punctually at seven.

'I really like him,' he told Jan with a delighted grin as they observed the horse in the field.

'Thank God for that!' Jan laughed. 'I think he's a good-looking fellow, but some owners are a bit apprehensive if there's not much black type in a pedigree; but he's got winners on the dam's side, and I've always felt a good mother is far more important than the father.'

'I trust your judgement implicitly – and your father's,' Toby added with a grin. 'The horse seems to have a super temperament, and I'm sure that can be a big help.'

'Of course it does, provided he has the basic ability and plenty of courage.'

They were still talking about the new horse when they sat down at a table beneath the old oak beams of the Fox & Pheasant.

'You'd better start thinking about a name for him,' Jan said.

Toby looked at the sheet of paper that she had pulled out of the catalogue so he could check the horse's details. 'By Gypsy King out of Balkan Ballerina,' he mused. 'I can't really call him something Dancer as I should think all those options have gone, with all those Northern Dancer descendants around the world, and anyway, it's not as though Northern Dancer figures among this chap's ancestors.'

'What about Balkan King?' Jan suggested, though she readily admitted she found it difficult to choose names. It was important – poor name, poor horse, she had often said.

'Too obvious,' Toby shook his head. 'I think, maybe, Flamenco.'

'Why?' Jan asked, making a face. 'What's that got to do with anything?'

'It's a sort of gypsy dance.'

'I know that, but it sounds as naff as anything I might have come up with, mind you, lots of horses' names can seem odd until they've run a few times. Then even the real horrors begin to sound good when they start winning.'

They chatted on about names until their food arrived. It was then that Jan discovered what Toby *really* wanted to talk about.

'Any news from Bel?' he asked lightly.

She looked at his podgy cheeks, his small mouth and eyes, and his thick, uncontrollable mop of dark hair. Jan was very fond of him; he was kind, clever and wealthy and he would almost certainly make some woman a good and loyal husband. But she knew how Annabel felt.

Annabel had tried. She trusted Toby utterly and his own slight sense of insecurity to some extent matched her own, but in the end, she'd confided in Jan, she didn't really fancy him.

'I got a card from her this morning,' Jan said. 'It sounds like she's having a great time in Italy, staying in some ancient castle.'

Toby nodded gloomily. 'I know the people who own it; their son'll be out there hunting her like a hound, I suppose.'

'Bel's never liked hounds – not the human kind, I mean,' Jan said. 'Anyway, I'm sorry you and she didn't work out.'

Toby made a grimace of regret. 'Me too. Still, I dare say she won't object if I take her out now and again?'

'I'm sure she won't. She's always enjoyed your company.'

🐎

Later, reviewing the day before she went to sleep, Jan thought about Toby and about Ray Bellamy, who had come to the yard earlier.

Ray Bellamy was altogether bigger and heavier than Toby, as a result of his career as a restaurateur, perhaps. He had more confidence and a flamboyant charm, too, though Jan didn't believe it ran as deep as Toby's.

He had already decided that the horse was to be named the Blue Boar, after one of his establishments. Jan had protested, on several grounds, but he was adamant.

The Blue Boar and Flamenco, she thought, *how awful!*

And God knows what Jellard was going to come up with for his. Still, at least he had coughed up the money, in time to cover her commitment to the auctioneers in Ireland without leaving her uncomfortably overdrawn at the bank. All in all, she was delighted that her first buying trip to Ireland's premier jumping sale had made three owners happy, at least for the time being.

❦

Driving over the Marches and the Welsh hills towards Stonewall Farm, which had been her home for eight years, Jan felt an unexpected twinge of nostalgia at all the memories they evoked.

When she pulled up in the lane outside Olwen's bungalow she wondered how on earth the old woman coped without being able to drive. Apart from the farmhouse, still unoccupied since Jan had moved out, there wasn't another dwelling for half a mile, but Olwen managed somehow with a rota of ancient acquaintances who dropped in, and younger women from the village who took her shopping in Hay twice a month. Even so, for ninety-five per cent of the time, she was on her own.

There was no doubt that she loved to see her grandchildren and the well-chosen presents she always seemed to have waiting for them had made her a firm favourite with Megan. When she opened the door in answer to Jan's knock, she greeted the children with a smile and a warmth she had never produced for Jan.

'Come here, Matthew, and let me have a look at you,' she chortled in her soft Welsh voice as she leaned down to the toddler. 'Say hello to your Nan.'

'Hello, Nan,' Matthew squawked obediently.

'There's some new farm animals set out for you in the front room,' Olwen said, straightening herself. 'And for you, Megan, there's something I think you'll like very much.'

She turned and led them all into the plain little bungalow, which had been enhanced inside with furniture and ornaments from the old farmhouse. Immediately on the right was a small and seldom-used sitting room, where, as she always did, she had laid out toys for the children, some old favourites and other new additions.

Megan immediately spotted her treat – a show-jumping game

with a circuit of jumps, horses and riders. Her face glowed and she was instantly on her knees beside it.

'Megan,' Olwen's voice growled behind her.

Megan took her cue and jumped up. 'Thank you very much, Gran. It's really lovely. Can I play with it now?'

Jan couldn't stop a quick smile at Megan's ready grasp of diplomacy and Olwen's determination to impose her own standards.

Once Olwen had made a thorough inspection of her grandson and the children had settled down to play, with a mug of orange squash each, she asked Jan almost reluctantly if she would like a cup of tea.

'I was hoping you would come over for lunch,' the old woman said pointedly.

'I'm sorry,' Jan said, 'but with everything going on at the yard, I knew I'd never be able to get away early enough.' She didn't add that she had always found the long, tense Sunday lunches of overcooked beef and soggy vegetables almost unbearable. 'I'd love a cup of tea and some of your chocolate cake, though.'

Olwen nodded curtly, and indicated to Jan that she should follow her through to the small dining room at the back of the house.

Once the teapot and the Royal Worcester china were on the table, Olwen sat down opposite Jan.

'Did you look at those papers?' she asked without preamble.

'Yes. He's up to his old tricks again, I'm afraid. He knows that field would be more valuable to us if it belonged to this bungalow.'

'More valuable to you, more like,' Olwen said sourly, reflecting the resentment she had felt since the day she'd learned that John had left her no property.

The bungalow, along with the farmhouse, buildings and land, had all been left to Jan, with the proviso that Olwen should be able to live in the bungalow for the rest of her life. In order to comply with John's instructions, Jan hadn't sold it, but now the land which enclosed it belonged to a company owned by Harold Powell and a business partner.

Jan didn't respond to Olwen's comment. 'Harold tried to get me to buy it last year,' she went on, 'after we'd made him pay compensation for selling the whole farm to himself too cheaply, but I wasn't going to be strong-armed into it. And, anyway, I didn't have enough money.'

'I reckon he knows this house will be worth peanuts if there's caravans all round it – on three sides of my garden!'

'He's not going to do this caravan thing – it's not his style. He's just trying it on, to put even more pressure on me to buy the paddock.'

'It's me that's getting the pressure, then.'

With a confidence she didn't feel, Jan reassured her, 'Don't worry. It won't ever happen.'

Olwen stared at her with eyes brimming with icy bitterness. 'Whatever you think about me, don't you ever forget I was John's mother, and I deserve your respect, not your pity.'

5

It was a little after seven on a warm but blustery evening when Angie Sharp's Range Rover turned off the lane and up towards the farm.

Pausing to watch, Jan found it hard to understand her own emotions. It seemed a little absurd that she should be excited about seeing a woman with whom she had spent just two and a half days a fortnight before. But during those few days in Ireland, when they had stayed in the same place, driven to the sales together, eaten together and swapped opinions, ideas and straightforward gossip about the people they had seen, she felt she had already become as close to Angie as anyone else she knew.

Jan knew she had a tendency to bond closely with female friends, perhaps because she had no sister of her own, but these friendships were different from the closeness she'd shared with her brother. Ben had suddenly decided to walk away from Gloucestershire, farming and everything else he'd ever known to pursue his passion for music. Since then Jan had received a phone call or a postcard from him every month, always warm, but brief and only superficially informative. So, when John had died and first Annabel, then Angie, had offered their friendship, she had been ready to grab it with both hands.

She was also conscious that Annabel's decision to go away for ten weeks had left her feeling lonely. As a result, her new friendship with Angie had grown, out of proportion to the length of time they'd known each other.

Angie had phoned the night before to say she was driving back down the M5 and would love to stop off and take a look at Edge Farm. Just before she arrived, Jan had given Matty his medicine and shooed Megan into bed. Now she was rushing around, preparing a meal, tidying things away, trying to make the caravan look as civilized as possible for her visitor. Angie had asked if she could stay the night, but Jan thought it would be far easier for someone of Angie's obvious sophistication to stay in one of the bedrooms above the Fox & Pheasant. Nevertheless, they would eat in the privacy of her caravan; flowers and oil lamps created an ambience which she was sure Angie would appreciate.

As Jan watched through the big window at the end of her mobile home, Angie stepped down from her Range Rover in a pale yellow linen suit that contrasted with her tanned skin and the rich dark brown of her hair. She opened the back door and took out a large bunch of flowers, a carrier bag and a bottle of champagne. Jan went out and walked down the hill towards her.

Angie smiled and her brown eyes shone. 'Jan! It's great to see you!' With her hands full, she leaned over the flowers and gave Jan a quick kiss on both cheeks.

Jan wasn't used to the habit, but did her best to do the same. 'I'm really glad you've come,' she laughed. 'I've missed all that gossiping we did in Ireland.' Thinking of Ireland, she'd been worried that the relationship they had made might change in a different context, but Angie seemed just the same.

'Me too. Still, we can make up for it this evening, can't we? I've brought a bottle of bubbly to help us along.'

'I saw that. What are we celebrating?'

'The first meeting in England between Jan Hardy and Angie Sharp!' They both burst out laughing in anticipation of the time they were going to spend together.

'Here,' Jan said. 'Let me take something.'

'Take the flowers; they're for Matty, but I don't expect him to appreciate them.'

Jan took the big bunch of carnations, knowing that of course the flowers were to comfort her. She was touched by her friend's thoughtfulness as she had mentioned Matty's measles only briefly when Angie phoned. 'Thanks very much,' she said. 'I'm sure he'll love them.'

'I can't wait to meet your kids,' Angie went on as they walked up towards the caravan. 'I feel I know them already after all you've told me. How is Matty?'

'Getting better. He looks less like a Dalmatian now. But it was pretty nasty the day I got back from Ireland.'

Angie's eyes filled with compassion. 'Oh, Jan, poor you. It must have been really awful. You thought he might have meningitis, didn't you?'

As they reached the caravan, Jan stopped and looked at her friend. 'It was, Angie, it's just so bloody hard to be rational about your own children.'

She pushed open the door and ushered Angie inside, where she put the flowers in a vase and just managed to squeeze the champagne into her cramped fridge.

Angie looked around her with a smile. 'It's amazing how nice you've made this place. When you said you lived in a caravan, I had visions of masses of plastic and Formica. But you've even got a wood-burner!'

'Yes, Eddie and Toby put it in last autumn and it certainly made the place a bit more bearable through the winter.'

'I would think it can get pretty cold and windy up here, though.'

'It sure can, and with little Matty prone to infection, I'm going to have to bust a gut to get the house finished so we can move in before next Christmas.'

'When am I going to meet him then?'

'He'll be asleep and I'm not going to wake him – even for you. But I think Megan's probably still reading.'

Jan went to the children's room and, as she'd predicted, found Megan lying on her front, propped up over a book.

'I heard you talking, Mum. Who's here?'

'A friend of mine; you can come in and meet her.'

Megan sidled into the room with a smile, half shy, half fascinated.

'Hello, Megan,' Angie said brightly. 'I'm Angie. Me and your Mum made friends at the sales.'

Megan nodded. 'She said; she said you were very pretty, too.'

Angie laughed. 'Not as pretty as you. And your mum told me you like riding, so I've brought you a little present.'

Megan's eyes lit up at the magic words, certain that whatever this magnificent woman had brought she was bound to like.

Angie picked up the carrier bag she had put on the table and pulled out a paper package, which she handed to Megan. 'Here it is.'

Megan took it and started to tear eagerly at the wrapping.

'Don't go at it like a lion with its dinner,' Jan ticked her off. 'You're scattering bits of paper all over the place.'

'Sorry, Mum,' Megan said breathlessly as she extracted a tiny pair of buckskin chaps from the mangled package. 'Oh, chaps! Just what I wanted, but Mummy wouldn't get me any.'

'Mummy probably had other things to buy,' Angie admonished gently.

'Mum, Mum. Can I try them on?' Megan's eyes gleamed with pleasure. Some of the older girls in her Pony Club had chaps, but no one her age.

'Go on, then,' Jan said. 'You shouldn't have,' she said to Angie as the little girl disappeared to put on her jodhpurs, 'but you couldn't have chosen better.'

By the time Angie left it was dark, the wind had dropped, the clouds had cleared and a bright moon hung over the Severn valley, lighting the back of the Malverns. Jan walked her down to the car and thanked her for coming. She asked if Angie could come up again the next day, after her night at the Fox & Pheasant.

'I wish I could,' Angie said, 'but I've got to leave first thing in the morning to make it down to a meeting in Bristol.'

🐎

Following their supper at Edge Farm, Angie came to see Jan every couple of weeks. At the beginning of August, she met Jan for lunch in Cheltenham and, driving back to Edge Farm, Jan thought how much she appreciated the support her new friend had given her since they first met.

In the meantime, Jan had brought in all the horses she planned to run before Christmas and had started light road work with them. She had several – Arctic Hay and Gale Bird in particular – that she thought might act even better on good National Hunt tracks than they had on point-to-point courses, but she knew she was going to have to get them as fit as they'd ever been to make any impression at this higher level.

The three Irish horses – Frank Jellard's had now been named Per Shore after his owner's home town – were still out at grass. They'd all had their first flu injections without any adverse effects, and Jan was happy to see them completely relaxed and putting on a bit more condition before they came in to work in the middle of the month.

It was a quiet Wednesday afternoon and a sultry heat lay across Edge Farm when A.D. O'Hagan's six horses arrived. They came in the most luxurious horsebox that had ever crawled up the hill to Jan's modest yard. The big maroon lorry was driven by one of the stud grooms who worked on the Aigmont estate in Ireland.

He stuck his head out of the window as he pulled up beside the yard gate. His hair was a crown of red curls and his hazel eyes glinted knowingly above sharp, freckled cheeks as he looked down at Jan, waiting in the parking area.

'Morning, Missis. Where should I put it?' he called.

Jan waved him towards the entrance to the yard and he skilfully manoeuvred the large vehicle into position. When he had parked and turned off the smooth-running engine, he and another two men jumped down and stretched their short legs.

'Sh'jaysus, that was a helluva good run! It'd normally take me four hours to get from the ferry to Cheltenham; I've just done it in three and a half.'

'I hope you haven't shaken those horses around too much,' Jan said.

'Hell no. 'Tis like riding in a Rolls-Royce for them.' He suddenly thrust a small, hard hand at her. 'I'm Albert Finnegan. I take it I'm addressing the guv'nor of this establishment?'

'I'm Jan Hardy, if that's what you mean,' she said.

The man lifted an eyebrow without saying anything, before walking around to the back of the lorry. With help from his mate, he unbolted the ramp and lowered it. Jan followed him and walked up into the lorry to find the six animals comfortably arranged in a herring-bone pattern of stalls.

The driver fetched the paperwork from his cab and helped Jan to identify each horse as the groom led them off, onc by one, to the stables that had already been prepared for them.

She checked each against its passport:

Anais is Arish
Erin's Jet
Emerald Isle
Wexford Lad
The Galway Fox
And last of all, *Tom's Touch*.

Tom's Touch was the five-year-old that A.D. had prepared at Aigmont, so he would be ready to run within a few weeks of arriving at Jan's yard. She couldn't deny that A.D.'s staff had done a grand job. The gelding looked magnificent and was carrying very little surplus condition. She was rather shocked by how superior this half-fit horse looked to the others already in her yard.

Jan was also impressed with the rest of the horses. Rather irritatingly, she had thought, apart from Tom's Touch, O'Hagan had never confirmed precisely which horses she was going to get, and having pored over the details of all his entries in *Horses in Training*, she concluded that this batch was as good as anyone could have hoped for.

'There's a few nice horses there,' she said, nodding and trying not to sound too impressed.

'He's not sent you any rubbish, that's for sure,' Albert Finnegan remarked dryly, conveying that he personally wouldn't have considered sending such good animals to a virtually unknown newcomer.

Jan had begun to get the feeling that the loyalty A.D. inspired in his workforce was strong enough to prompt a certain amount of jealousy of newcomers to the circle, especially if they seemed to be getting preferential treatment before they'd earned it. She decided that she had two choices: either she submitted to whatever initiation was required, or she marked out her territory now.

There had been a time when this would have been an easy decision for her, but she was beginning to get the idea that her usual frankness might not go down too well in a complex organization like A.D.'s.

'Albert,' she said, 'once we've got these horses settled, I hope you and your colleagues are going to come and have something to eat and drink before you head back to Fishguard. You obviously know a great deal about A.D.'s horses and it would be a real help if you could tell me everything you know about this lot.'

He glanced at her – to see if she was being sincere, she thought. After a moment, he smiled and nodded. 'I'd be delighted.'

❧

The next day Jan woke at five-thirty and went out to check that A.D.'s horses had survived their journey. Most of them had eaten up well, which was a good sign, but Erin's Jet, a small, flat-bred brown gelding, hadn't touched a thing. Jan mixed him an individual low-protein feed to tempt his taste buds and gave him a comforting pat to settle him down.

By half-past six, Jan, Roz, Joe and Emma were riding the four older horses out for a quiet walk, while Karen gave Matty and

Megan a little breakfast. And for the rest of the morning, she tried to prepare herself for A.D. O'Hagan's first visit to Edge Farm as a fully committed, multiple owner.

He arrived late-afternoon, with a small entourage in two chauffeured Mercedes. The first car to pull up contained A.D. and a tight-lipped woman in a dark green suit, whom Jan guessed was some kind of high-powered PA. From the second car emerged Eamon Fallon and Jimmy O'Driscoll, a famous old ex-jockey. At Fairyhouse, Sean McDonagh had told Jan that O'Driscoll was A.D.'s unofficial racing manager and frequent drinking partner.

The three men all shook hands with Jan and A.D. asked to be shown his horses. The woman wasn't introduced and barely spoke throughout the visit.

As they were all geldings, Jan had decided to keep them together in the run of timber and breeze-block stables which Gerry had put up the previous year. The boxes faced west across the yard and out over the Severn valley. All six horses had their heads looking out over their stable doors.

'Isn't that great!' Eamon remarked. 'They're all looking towards Ireland; they must be missing the place.'

'Because they had no work to do over there,' O'Hagan added, 'apart from Tom's Touch. Well, they certainly look happy enough. What are they eating?' he went on quickly, with a glance at Jan.

Jan didn't doubt that he knew what he was talking about and she gave him a detailed description of his horses' feed. She mentioned Erin's Jet's reluctant appetite and what she had done about it. A.D. didn't comment, which Jan took to be a sign of approval. And he didn't appear to need the name plaques Jan had already pinned up outside each box to identify the horses, from memory he was able to recite their individual racing careers as accurately as his horsebox driver had done from printed notes the day before. When she considered that he probably had at least a hundred horses in training in England and Ireland, Jan began to appreciate the sort of mind she was dealing with.

Jimmy O'Driscoll also decided to express his views. 'There should be a dozen or so winners from this little lot, provided they're kept fit and running,' he said menacingly.

Jan sensed that, like Albert Finnegan, the old jockey was keen to guard his place in the hierarchy of A.D.'s organization.

Eamon had evidently spotted it too. 'You needn't worry, Jimmy. Jan knows how to get a horse fit and hold it there. She's done a marvellous job with Dingle Bay, that good point-to-pointer I used to own.'

'Who did you sell him to?' Jimmy asked.

'One of Jan's young ladies.' Eamon grinned at Jan. 'She must be paying them too well.'

'Bel's got her own money,' Jan said quickly, to make sure O'Hagan knew there was nothing reckless about the way she ran her yard. 'And she bought him so she could swap him for Russian Eagle with Bernie Sutcliffe.'

'Why was she so keen to do that?'

'Because Bernie wouldn't let Eddie Sullivan ride Eagle in the Foxhunters'.'

O'Hagan shook his head. 'Jesus, why do people go in for all these ridiculous shenanigans? Ron Sullivan's boy rode a cracker of a race until he slipped off. That's why *I'm* here, for God's sake!' he laughed.

And I thank God you are, Jan said to herself.

'What's happened to Eddie now?' O'Hagan went on casually.

'I'm not sure,' Jan said, feeling her pulse quicken. O'Hagan knew that Eddie's father had ended up at the wrong end of a large loan from a bank with an unorthodox approach to debt collecting, which had caused the family to disappear suddenly, but Eddie had told Jan he didn't want a soul to know which continent they had fled to.

O'Hagan shrugged shoulders neatly tailored in pale blue mohair. 'I would have thought Ron Sullivan was a little long in the tooth to be ducking and diving like that, and it seems mightily unfair to involve his boy.' He flashed a penetrating glance at Jan. 'You must miss Eddie.'

Jan wondered what he meant. She had already gathered there was a subtext to most of what he said. 'We do miss him around the place,' she answered as lightly as she could.

After they'd inspected the horses and the yard, the three men were introduced to the rest of Jan's staff, except for Annabel, who hadn't yet returned. Her absence seemed to intrigue A.D., since he'd heard about her buying Russian Eagle. When they had seen as much as they wanted, Jan asked them up to her caravan for a drink, which the secretary, now identified as Miss Bennett, declined.

A.D. questioned Jan about his horses' proposed training schedule for the coming months, and when they'd finished their drinks they were all driven away in one of the cars, while the second Mercedes and its chauffeur stayed behind to take Jan to the Queen's Hotel for dinner in an hour's time.

Jan watched them go, wondering what on earth she should wear. Once the decision had been made, she changed quickly, not wanting to appear to have taken too much trouble; she still wasn't sure if A.D.'s interest in her extended beyond her ability to train racehorses. She knew that he was married to a much-admired Irish opera singer who would have satisfied the urges and egos of most men, but it was perfectly possible that he needed more. However, since she'd started taking an interest in him – as a new and important client – she hadn't heard any stories of affairs and certainly Miss Bennett, although undeniably attractive, seemed an unlikely candidate.

Jan thought her best course of action was to behave with A.D. as she might have done with old Mr Carey, although she acknowledged that would be difficult. For a start, A.D. was still an attractive man, with wit and a well-honed charm.

The Queen's Hotel was a classical, early Victorian building that impressed without daunting. It stood, comfortable in its prominence on the Imperial Gardens, at the south end of Cheltenham's Regency Promenade. The chauffeur dropped her right in front of the tall colonnaded portico. Rather apprehensively, she walked through the high doors, with the silk dress Eddie Sullivan had made her buy the previous Christmas swishing around her legs.

Get a grip, Jan, she chided herself.

She realized as soon as she asked for him at the reception desk that A.D O'Hagan was well known at the hotel.

A few moments later he walked into the lobby to greet her. 'Hello, Jan. My, you look well!' he said with a playful edge to his deep voice.

Jan hadn't been inside the hotel before, although she was aware that during the week of the Cheltenham Festival it was the watering hole for most of the big players who crossed the Irish Sea for the high point of the National Hunt calendar.

At other times, like now, she guessed, it was a more sedate place. Nevertheless, A.D. seemed to be immediately at home, and ushered her through to a high-ceilinged dining room, where a table in a quiet corner between two arched windows had been reserved for him.

When they'd sat down opposite one another, he allowed himself a few minutes to concentrate on ordering, which he did with a thoroughness that Jan had begun to recognize. He asked for details of anything which he considered unclear, and later sent back a bottle of wine which arrived with a different date from that marked on the list.

Once that was done, he put his hands on the table on either side of the cutlery in front of him and looked at Jan with steady, unblinking eyes.

'So, Mrs Hardy, I have just had consigned to your care half a million quid's worth of prime jumping bloodstock; I've agreed to underwrite any liabilities you might have, up to the tune of thirty thousand pounds in the event that your yard is a commercial failure. And you are a trainer who, since you were granted a public licence last April, has had precisely one winner. Do you think I'm mad?'

Jan wanted to gulp at this blunt statement of fact, but she held her breath and looked back at him with eyes as steady as his own.

'I certainly don't. In fact, I think you are exactly the opposite, Mr O'Hagan.'

'Would you call me A.D? Only the Irish tax people call me Mr O'Hagan. And please tell me why you think I'm not mad.'

'I'm sure you know perfectly well, but if you want me to tell you . . . First of all, you know I've trained successfully a horse that you considered unworthy to beat one of yours, which came from one of the best yards in Ireland.'

'Actually, it didn't beat it, but I'll accept it would have,' A.D. said quietly.

'Secondly, you know I've only had one winner since getting my licence because it was the end of the season and I'd more or less packed my team away for their summer holidays by then. Thirdly, you know I'll train a lot more, and as you're one of my first owners and you've backed me with your guarantee, you'll have first call on my loyalty.' She looked back at him, watching his reactions. She waited until his lips started to move before she went on, 'Provided, of course, *you* are always fair and loyal to me.'

A.D. conveyed his approval with a broad smile, the sincerity of which Jan couldn't begin to gauge.

'You're a bit feisty, Mrs Hardy,' he said, 'but I think we'll get on just fine.'

Jan grinned. 'As a matter of fact, so do I. And I want you to be the first to know, now your horses are here, that I've decided to hold an open day at Edge Farm in a month's time.'

She had to wait a second for A.D.'s reaction.

'I see,' he said icily. 'And why have you decided that?'

She blinked and wanted to gulp. 'Because I've still got room for ten more horses, and I need to fill the stables to make the sums add up.'

'Training horses isn't about sums adding up.'

Jan raised an eyebrow and tried to keep a tremor from her

voice. 'It is when you're starting out with no money and two children to raise.'

'Excuse me; I have personally guaranteed to pay the first thirty thousand pounds of any losses you make.'

'Of course you have, and I'm grateful for that, but if you don't want me to go bust and have your guarantee called in, I need to operate at a profit from day one.'

'All right, I'll grant you that, and there's no reason why you shouldn't get a dozen more horses in due course. When mine start winning, there'll be plenty of owners beating a path to your door.'

'But that will take a few months, and my staff need paying now.'

'Do you think throwing your doors open and inviting every Tom, Dick and Harry in off the streets is going to provide you with any more horses at all, let alone the right kind of horses?'

'It might,' Jan said with her eyes flashing. 'And of course I'm not going to take any old horse that's thrown at me.'

A.D.'s nostrils quivered. 'Jan, I really do not want you exposing yourself to this kind of public scrutiny – not while I have a number of horses in your yard. I sent them to you precisely because yours is a small, unknown yard which offers a bit of discretion. I'm afraid I really don't agree with this open day.'

Jan's eyes widened in amazement at his undisguised desire to control her activities. 'A.D., I'm sorry you don't like my plans,' she said as steadily as she could, 'but I really don't need your approval for anything I do in my yard which doesn't involve the training and running of your horses.'

The Irishman looked at Jan with unwavering eyes of arctic blue. 'I'm well aware of what you need and don't need. And right now you need my horses, so I suggest you act in a way that ensures you keep them.'

Jan stared back. 'Mr O'Hagan,' she said deliberately, 'naturally, I will take your opinion into account, but at the end of the day I have to make my own decisions about the running of my yard. I've made plans and I very much hope you'll be there to see the horses parade and to show you support my yard.'

A.D. didn't move a muscle in his face for a moment. He clicked his tongue. 'Right.'

For the rest of dinner he talked in his normal polite but enigmatic way about his horses. He didn't refer to the open day again, but Jan knew very well that the axis of their relationship had shifted markedly. She guessed that by now he was well aware that she had planned for his appearance to be the highlight of the day.

Later, leaning back in the soft leather upholstery of A.D.'s Mercedes while Daragh, his chauffeur, drove her back to Edge Farm, she realized that by reacting as she had, she had doubled the pressure on herself to perform. If O'Hagan had been prepared to put up with any excuses before, he certainly wouldn't be now. She shut her eyes tightly to squeeze back the tears and prayed that she would stay strong. Even if her biggest owner chose to shun her open day, she would survive, and on her own terms. She had to.

6

Jan was delighted a week later when Angie rang to say she was planning to bring her parents up to see the yard.

'But don't go getting your hopes up,' she added. 'I still don't think they'll move the horses from Martin Hunter's, but I've told them I might be keeping one with you. That could help change their minds.'

Despite Angie's warning, Jan couldn't help feeling just a little hopeful. She now had twenty horses back in training and had started their road work. Gerry had finished building the final eight boxes across the north end of the yard, but she was beginning to despair of ever filling them. This was the first time Angie had suggested that she might have a horse in training at Edge Farm, although they'd talked several times about the possibilities of her parents sending theirs.

She put the phone down in a better mood. As it happened, the yard had been running smoothly, despite the fact that they were short-staffed. As Jan hadn't intended to have so many horses in quite so early, Annabel wasn't due back for another fortnight, but Tom and Darren, two boys from the village who liked to help out at weekends, were only too eager to come up and work during their school holidays.

Early that evening she realized her optimism was still showing from Tony Robertson's reaction when he dropped in. After Matty's scare, the doctor sometimes phoned to say that he would call in since he was in the area. As usual, Jan offered him a drink.

Normally he refused anything except a cup of tea, but this time he joined her in a glass of cider.

He was always interested in the horses in her yard, and while they were sitting at Jan's table chatting Emma put her head through the door to say goodnight.

Jan asked her in and introduced her to the doctor.

'Emma joined us last summer, just after I started,' Jan said. 'She's one of the three best girls we've got now.'

'There are only three girls anyway,' Emma protested.

Jan laughed. 'And she's top babysitter, too.'

'So you look after the kids for Jan when she's out, do you?' Tony asked.

'Yes, they're ever so good,' Emma said. 'Especially that Megan,' she added, seeing Meg peeping round the door at the other end of the caravan.

'How do you feel about looking after them tomorrow night, then, while I take your boss out to dinner?' Tony asked.

Jan turned to him sharply to protest. But stopped herself. Despite the cheek of his invitation, it didn't seem fair to turn him down in front of Emma.

'Yeh, fine,' Emma said. 'I don't see why not. It's time she had an evening out.'

Tony Robertson finished his cider and stood up. 'Great – if that's OK with you, Jan?'

Jan smiled. 'That's fine. Thanks Emma.'

'I'll be off then,' Tony said. 'Bye. See you tomorrow, about seven-thirty.' He let himself out and Jan watched him walk back to his Rover.

'That'll be nice for you,' Emma said.

'I suppose so.'

'What? Don't you like him?'

'He's a perfectly nice bloke,' Jan said. 'Not my sort, though – even if I was looking, which I'm not: but I always enjoy a chat about the horses with him.' She looked at Emma and shrugged her shoulders. 'Anyway, I suppose there's no real reason why I shouldn't spend an evening with him. Poor man, he must be quite lonely.'

'I heard his wife died last year after an accident riding the cross-country course in a one-day event.'

Jan nodded. 'Up north, I think. They used to live in Yorkshire, but he wanted to move after that happened.'

'Can't blame him, can you? Not wanting to be reminded all the time, like. Did they have kids?'

'No, fortunately, though I suppose they'd have been company for him now. I don't know what I would have done without mine.'

🐎

Jan woke the next morning feeling far more relaxed about her date with Tony. She would make it clear that she wasn't available, and provided he took it the right way, she didn't see why they shouldn't have a good evening together. Her attitude to him was put quickly into perspective when she found a postcard from Eddie Sullivan in her letterbox which made her feel even more confident about her decision.

Given a choice of dinner with Eddie or Tony Robertson, she knew Eddie would have got her vote hands down.

His card showed a picture of a very basic, dusty race track with half a dozen horses leaning spectacularly into a tight bend. It had been postmarked in Queensland with the name of a town Jan had never heard of.

> Greetings from the Royal Ascot of west Queensland. No need to wear a topper here. Mum and Dad send their love. E.

Eddie's communications were, if anything, less informative than her brother's. But that wasn't the point, she thought. At least his cards showed that he was still thinking of the great times, the wonderful ups and downs he had been through with her during her first year at Edge Farm.

She'd met Eddie Doncaster at sales, where she'd advised him to buy Russian Eagle. As a result, he had become her most loyal supporter, although when his father had gone spectacularly bankrupt Eddie had been obliged to withdraw his financial backing, and their roles had become somewhat reversed. Shortly afterwards he'd been forced to sell Eagle, but Jan had done all she could to make sure he kept the ride on the horse in the big hunter chase at Aintree.

But during all that time their relationship had remained, at least on the surface, entirely platonic. If Eddie ever kissed her, it was only a peck on the cheek. Eddie had known, instinctively it seemed, that Jan would take a good while to get over losing John, the solid, dependable, quiet-mannered Welsh farmer to whom she'd been married for eight years.

In the end, she thought, Eddie was a bloody good friend; most women would have agreed he was also good-looking, witty and fun to be with, which was a huge bonus.

On the same day Jan had the satisfaction of seeing one of the most important projects in her personal life enter a new phase.

Gerry had pushed on with laying the block work that was the inner skin of her new house, and now he was well into completing the outer wall of irregular, golden stone. Within a week or two, he said, he'd be ready to start putting the roof trusses on, so what for over a year had been a vague outline and a pile of stones was now unmistakably a house, and she seriously hoped that she and the children might just be in there for the winter.

Somewhat prematurely, but with great persistence, Reg was already laying out a garden, working from the outer edges inwards. While Jan laughed at his optimism, she was grateful to him for understanding how much it meant to her and for helping in the only way he thought he could, although it didn't stop him spending a good deal of time sitting on a bale in the yard, observing the horses or talking to the staff. And inevitably he took a proprietorial interest in the animals he had helped Jan to buy in Ireland.

So it was with an increased confidence in her own future that she greeted Tony Robertson when he arrived that evening. Before he did anything else, though, the doctor sat down with Matty for a chat.

Tony Robertson took Jan to a pub with a small restaurant in a village about ten miles away, near Stow-on-the-Wold. Jan wondered if he'd brought her there in the hope that she wouldn't be known. If so, he was out of luck; the White Horse had been Eddie Sullivan's local for years, when his father owned the manor house a mile away, and then when Eddie had moved into the village's dilapidated mill house on a promise to the owners that he would do it up.

Jan hadn't been to the White Horse since Eddie had left the country, nearly five months ago now, and she felt a sudden pang as they drove past the long stone wall and tall, rotting gates that hid the mill house from the road.

Tony didn't seem at all disappointed or even annoyed when half the people in the bar greeted Jan by name and those in the know congratulated her on obtaining her professional licence. If they knew who Tony was, or were speculating about his motives for being with Jan, they kept it to themselves and left the two of them to sit down in a quiet corner of the restaurant.

Once they'd ordered, Tony leaned back a little in an old Windsor chair and looked at Jan with his habitual curiosity. 'Would you mind if I ask you about your husband?'

For a moment, Jan was taken aback by this blunt request, which she found particularly strange in these circumstances.

'No, I don't mind; in fact, I'd like to talk about him. It felt like there was a massive gap in me, as if someone had hacked out a part of my body the Christmas before last. But though the hole's still there, the wound's healing.'

'Where did you meet him?'

Jan laughed. 'At a show – the Three Counties, actually. I'd taken a horse of Colonel Gilbert's there to ride in the working hunter class. But there's always plenty of time to kill at those shows and I used to like wandering around looking at the livestock. Have you ever seen Welsh blacks, the small beef cattle they've always reared over the border?'

Tony shook his head.

'Lovely beef; nice cattle,' Jan said. 'Anyway, there was this tall, serious young bloke leading around a cow and calf. He was nice looking, though, and I caught his eye as he was walking past me, he gave me such a look that reached right inside me, it was as if he already knew everything about me. Anyway, I carried on watching and he actually won the class with his cow, then when he left the ring, he gave me a lovely big wink, so I followed him back to his pen and introduced myself. A bit forward, don't you think?'

Tony smiled at this evidence of Jan's forthright character.

'I asked him about the cattle,' Jan went on. 'He told me his name and where he lived and said if I wanted to see more of the cattle to come up to his farm, if I was ever in the area.

'I didn't have a clue how far it was to Radnor Forest where his farm was or anything, but anyway I went over there on my day off a week later. And that was that.'

'You mean you moved in?'

'God no! John wouldn't have had that, and his mother certainly wouldn't; she's a real old tyrant is Olwen. No, he came over here and took me out a few times, asked me up to the Royal Welsh Show and back to Stonewall for tea. He turned out to be older than he looked. I could see his mum was desperate to marry him off, but she wasn't at all happy about the daughter of a poor English tenant farmer from so far away. John was a very quiet, gentle man, but he could also be very determined, and when he said he wanted to marry me, I realized how much I loved him. For him, I reckoned I could hack being a farmer's wife even up in those cold hills and I thought at least he was big enough to keep me warm in bed.'

'Was it what you expected?'

Jan thought for a moment. 'No; it was a lot tougher and far more lonely. You'd sometimes go for days and see no one but the family, and that would be pretty unusual down here.'

Tony nodded. 'I used to come across some really isolated households when I worked up in Wharfedale. Sometimes you could see illnesses that were as much about loneliness or lack of human contact as anything else. But what did you do about his mother?'

'We tolerated one another for a while, then, fortunately, she decided to move out into a bungalow at the bottom of the drive. She refused to come into the house again until after John had died. She's still there now, although I sold the farm and everything else. But John's will said she could stop in the bungalow as long as she wanted. I expect she'll be there for a good many years yet, but she was furious when I sold the farm.'

'Why did you?'

'I'm no farmer, Tony. I don't know about sheep, but I do know about horses, and I was never going to earn enough on my own there to feed the family. I had to live where I had at least a chance of finding a few more clients. It was then I decided to set up the point-to-point yard here at Edge Farm.'

'So you didn't come here with the intention of taking out a licence?'

'It had never even occurred to me, to tell you the truth, but one of my owners, Colonel Gilbert, suggested it. His daughter had just been issued with one and she was bloody annoyed the colonel mentioned it,' Jan smiled. 'She could barely bring herself to speak to me as it was, especially when I beat some of the horses she sent pointing last year.'

They were briefly interrupted by a waitress asking them what they wanted to drink.

'Now, what would you like with your dinner?' Tony asked.

'I don't want a lot. I can't be late – I'm up at six in the morning,' Jan said, although she was enjoying the chance to reminisce.

'Fine,' Tony said. 'I understand. I'll get you back home and tucked up in bed nice and early.'

Jan gave him a quizzical look.

'On your own, of course,' Tony added hurriedly.

Good, she thought. *At least he knows the score and I'm not going to get any aggravation later.*

And with that knowledge, she felt more kindly disposed towards him.

When he said he wanted to know everything about her early days training pointers in Wales and her first year at Edge, Jan had the impression he was genuinely interested. She enjoyed talking about it all and appreciated his sympathetic understanding of just how difficult it was for a woman on her own with two young children to run a much bigger yard.

Their attitudes seemed so much in tune that she couldn't help warming to him, occasionally his eyes fixed on hers, dancing with good-humour and interest and she found herself smiling back happily.

'But, Jan,' he asked with a new, softer note in his voice, 'don't you sometimes feel that you're a little young to have to be doing this all on your own?'

Jan dropped her eyes and concentrated on the last spoonful of a delicious *crème brûlée*. She shook her head. 'I'm used to it; and I've got Annabel, who's a fantastic support.'

'I don't mean that,' the doctor said gently. 'I mean at night, when you're alone in bed, worrying about all the hundreds of things you have to do every day.'

Jan didn't look up; she sighed to herself. She didn't want this – at least, not yet; maybe not with Tony at all. And yet – he was thoughtful, practical, good-looking and considerate.

Now she lifted her chin, and faced him with a small smile – enough to say 'thank you' for the thought; not enough to encourage him too much. 'Just for now,' she said, 'I can cope as I am.'

❦

After dinner, Tony took Jan home at ten, as he'd promised. Emma left as soon as they arrived back, but he wouldn't stay for the drink Jan offered him. When the sound of his car had faded down the drive, she started tidying away the few things Emma had left out in the tiny kitchen. She was lost in thoughts provoked by the reminiscing Tony had encouraged when she was interrupted by the phone.

She picked it up, ready to be firm with any owner who had decided to ring at this time of night. She had made it clear to all of them, including O'Hagan, that she didn't want to take calls about the horses after nine, as she didn't want her children woken, and if she was to run her yard properly she liked to go to bed around ten in the summer, as they started work at six o'clock sharp each morning.

'Hello, Jan. I just thought I'd let you know I'm back.'

Annabel's soft, hesitant voice sounded strange to Jan after an absence of ten weeks. She was struck by how different it was from Angie's.

'Bel!' Jan shrieked with pleasure, realizing how much she had missed her friend. 'That's great. I thought you weren't coming back for another week, but we can certainly do with you.'

'Oh, good; you've missed me in the yard then, have you? I thought if you hadn't, you might not want me back after such a long time.'

'Of course we want you back! We've got twenty horses in already, and hopefully a few more to come. I've had Tom and Darren up here most days to help cover.'

'Oh dear; they won't be so pleased to see me then.'

'Don't worry, I can find plenty for them to do.'

'OK,' Annabel sounded more sure of herself now. 'I should be back at Stanfield tomorrow afternoon. I'll unload my stuff at the cottage then I'll come straight up. Will you be there?'

'I should be. See you then.'

In that contrary way nature has of turning a person's luck just when they are confident everything is under control, the following day started clear, blue and bright – and a mess. One of Frank Jellard's horses had got cast in its box during the night, and although Jan and Roz managed to heave the animal back onto his feet, it looked as though he'd twisted his back in the struggle to right himself. That would mean a good few sessions of expensive manipulation, which Jellard was certain to grumble about.

While walking out the first lot on the quiet lanes below the steep Cotswold edge, a large sheet of black plastic from a silage wrapper flapped in a hawthorn hedge where it had got caught, making one of the young horses shy and leap sideways, catching Emma, who was riding it, completely by surprise.

Emma hit the road with her shoulder first, followed by her head, which fortunately was encased in a new helmet beneath a woolly bobble hat.

Once they'd caught the errant horse and helped Emma back on her feet, they turned around and headed straight back to the yard, with Emma now leading her escapee and holding her painful arm close to her body.

Reg, evidently planning an early start on such a fine day, had just arrived as they turned into the yard. It didn't take him long to see what needed doing.

'I'll drive her to the A and E in Cheltenham, Jan, if you like.'

'Oh, *would* you, Dad?' Jan turned to him gratefully. 'As long as you know the way?'

'Course I do. I took you enough times,' the old man answered with a chuckle. 'Now, come on, my girl,' he urged Emma, 'just let me get you up into the passenger seat.' He'd already opened the door of his Daihatsu and was trying to see the best way of manoeuvring a slim, female body with a possible broken collarbone onto the seat.

Jan helped, grateful for her father's offer, though feeling a little guilty that she had accepted it so quickly, but knowing that they had twelve more horses to exercise before lunch and time was precious.

Annabel usually drove her black VW Golf at a speed that belied her self-effacing manner. The car shot up Jan's drive early that afternoon twice as fast as it could have done before the tarmac had been laid. At the top Annabel spun it into the parking place. She climbed out and stretched her slim, brown legs. Looking around with a smile at the familiar scene, she shook out her long, pale chestnut hair, which looked even lighter against her deeply tanned face.

Jan was already there to greet her; she had just strapped Matthew into his seat in the back of her Land Rover before setting off to Cheltenham with him.

'Hi, Bel,' she squealed with delight as they gave each other a long, affectionate hug. 'You're in a bit of a hurry, aren't you? I wasn't expecting you until much later, but thank God you're here; everything's gone wrong today. Right now I've got to go to the hospital in Cheltenham. Emma bust her collarbone this morning and they're sorting it for her.'

'Are you taking Matty with you?' Annabel asked, seeing him in the Land Rover. She opened the door and smiled at his big round face. 'Hi, Matty; how're you doing?'

Matty rewarded her with a broad grin. 'Had measles.'

'Matty,' Jan laughed, 'that was ages ago.'

'You look pretty good to me now,' Annabel said, and turned to Jan. 'I'll come with you, if you like.'

🐎

Jan ignored a faint sense of guilt she felt at enjoying Annabel's company so much for the half-hour it took to drive to the hospital. She knew the slight sense of disloyalty to Angie she was feeling had come about simply because she'd shared so much with her over the past couple of months and because Angie, with her strength of character, had a way of making her presence felt.

It was odd, Jan thought, that her two closest friends were so completely different; Angie was always taking the initiative, where Annabel tended to follow. But that didn't make Annabel's concern for Jan and her family any less genuine.

'And which doctor came when Matty was ill?' Annabel asked when Jan had brought her up to date with most of her news.

'The new GP at our surgery, Tony Robertson.'

Bel nodded. 'The good-looking one,' she smiled. 'I might have guessed.'

'Hang on.' Jan jumped in to defend herself. 'He took me out to the White Horse last night and I can tell you, he was very well behaved, and so was I. As a matter of fact, it confirmed I've still got very little interest in men. But he was fine about it. He dropped me back at ten and left without a murmur, just before you rang.'

'He seems like a really nice guy,' Annabel observed.

'Well, he is, and I suspect he's still suffering like hell from the accident his wife had.'

'I'm sure you're right,' Annabel agreed. 'At least you've got a good doctor you and Matty like. Anyway,' she said, changing the subject, 'although I had a brilliant time, you won't believe how much I've missed the yard and everything. Tell me what else has been going on since I've been away.'

For the rest of the journey into Cheltenham, and through the congested streets, Jan told Annabel all about the sales in Ireland, the horses she had bought, O'Hagan's horses, the dinner with A.D. and his opposition to the open day. She told her about the people she'd met – the suspiciously charming Sean McDonagh, and her new friend, Angie Sharp.

She was careful not to go on about Angie, but justified her obvious enthusiasm by describing the Sharp family as potential big owners.

'They've got quite a few horses – six or seven – with Martin Hunter, and he's getting nowhere with them.'

'Are they any good, though?' Annabel asked.

'I don't know.' Jan acknowledged Annabel's point with a shake of her head. 'I haven't seen any of them myself yet, but a couple have nice pedigrees.'

'It'd be no good taking them just to fill your boxes if they don't have a chance of winning; it would do you more harm than good in the long run.'

Jan thought about reminding Annabel that she didn't have a private income; she had a business to run, wages and a mortgage to pay, and she couldn't be too choosy. It even crossed her mind that Annabel was already jealous of Angie Sharp's influence. But she quickly rejected this, as she knew Annabel was right.

'Of course I won't take them if they're a load of rubbish, but if a couple of them have potential, I might just as well take the others. Anyway, I haven't been asked yet. Angie says her parents are very loyal to Martin.'

'I haven't had a look at my own horse yet,' Annabel remarked. 'Is he back in work with all the others?'

'Russian Eagle's back in, looking like an elephant; it's going to take a lot of steady work to get him looking like a racehorse again. I hope you don't mind, but I'm afraid that means he's back on full fees now.'

'No, I don't mind; I'm glad. I knew he'd need plenty of time to get rid of his big grass belly.'

'Sorry I didn't warn you, but I thought as we had to get on with A.D.'s, we might as well get on with all of them.'

'That's OK. And what does Billy think of O'Hagan's horses?'

'He hasn't seen them yet. But funny you should ask – he rang today to say he's coming back from his holidays late tomorrow and he'll be in to ride out the next day.'

Billy Hanks had ridden very successfully for the last three point-to-point seasons, including a number of winners for Jan. He probably should have turned professional a few years before, but his farming family had done everything they could to dissuade him. They said they needed him on the farm; they'd looked at the statistics and thought it unlikely he'd ever make any money riding racehorses. However, once he'd won the amateur championship, their arguments had fallen on deaf ears.

Billy had applied for a full licence and on the strength of his previous record had been granted it without question. Jan had asked him if he would become her stable jockey and he had readily agreed. This meant that she had first call on his services and, until he'd ridden fifteen winners, he could claim a 7lb allowance off the designated weight of any runner ridden by a fully fledged jockey – a considerable advantage for a competent rider.

Billy, at twenty-five, was eight years younger than Jan and a Cotswold lad. He had known her since he'd first started riding as an eight-year-old, and he'd watched with awe as she'd ridden a string of local point-to-point winners herself.

Since Jan had started training pointers, originally at Stonewall in mid-Wales and then at Edge Farm, she had given Billy a chance and a lot of winning rides, and they had developed a good working relationship. Recently, though, as Billy had become more successful, she had been disappointed to notice a growing arrogance in him, but she was hopeful that competing against tough, experienced professionals might just pull him down a peg or two.

At least Billy arrived in good time for his first visit to Edge Farm as official stable jockey. He had driven up in his battered Subaru, climbed out and looked around, surveying the area, and then stretched out his body like a preening bantam cock. To Jan, the change in his attitude was obvious; his whole demeanour seemed to say, *Now I'm a professional, you're bloody lucky I'm here.*

At five foot ten, Billy was a little tall, even for a jump jockey, but he looked lean and fit after a month of windsurfing and water-skiing in southern Spain. Above his flat, round face, sharp chin and snub nose, his fair hair was cut short and spiky, making him look more aggressive than he was.

Jan watched as he walked down the yard to join her. She sensed at once that something had changed between them and she was going to have to be careful in her dealings with him. However, she knew how ambitious he was, and there was no question that as long as he was riding for her they would both be working towards the same end – the winner's enclosure.

'How are you, Billy?'

'Fine, Jan, and you?'

Jan wondered if he ought to call her something more respectful, in light of her changed circumstances, though she didn't fancy being called guv'nor, like a male trainer. But she guessed she'd known Billy too long to expect him to start calling her Mrs Hardy.

'You look like you've had a good holiday,' she said.

'I did, thanks. How many horses have you got in?' he went on without a pause, glancing around the yard at some of the heads poking over the stable doors.

'Twenty-two.'

Billy didn't disguise his disappointment. 'Is that all? That's not going to keep me very busy.'

'You're perfectly entitled to ride for other trainers when I don't have any rides for you,' Jan said with deliberate indifference.

'Of course I am,' Billy said. 'But with only twenty-two, your chances of running real good horses aren't great, are they?'

Jan shrugged. 'I'm not keeping any rubbish here, and Mr O'Hagan's sent me six crackers.'

Billy's eyes warmed a little. 'Well, great. Let's have a look at them.'

'Sure, but there's only one of them ready to do any fast work – Tom's Touch, a really smashing horse that A.D. had worked on his own place for a month or so before he sent him over. He turned up looking like a Derby horse, he's fantastic. Ready to run in a couple of weeks, I should think.'

It was too early in most of her horses' training programme for Billy to ride any fast work, but Jan had thought if he rode out and saw some of the more promising animals have a canter, he'd begin to get an idea of what she had to run that season, besides A.D.'s. When her first lot set off that morning, with Billy and

Annabel riding beside her, Jan felt like she had in the old days at Stonewall Farm, despite her slight misgivings about Billy. Joe Paley, Roz and her sister, Karen, made up the string of six.

Without asking for too much, they all moved up the long grass gallop at a steady canter, almost to the crest of the ridge. It was a warm, still morning in the early sun, with a clear view from the top across the broad river plain. They walked their horses in a circle, blowing gently, while in the quiet air the sounds of a waking world drifted up the grassy slope towards them.

Jan turned to Billy. 'I know you couldn't tell a lot from that, but what do you think?'

'I can tell enough to see that you're doing the job right and if you can do the same with A.D.'s – if you get 'em real sharp, and manage to put 'em in the right races – you should get a few good winners.'

🐎

'Billy's changed,' Annabel said, echoing Jan's own thoughts a few hours later when they sat down for a coffee in the caravan after the third lot.

Before he'd driven off, the jockey had made disparaging comments about several of the horses that had stayed with Jan after her transition from amateur racing to the more competitive sport under National Hunt rules.

Jan nodded. 'I know. But he's right about some of the horses – even those that have won a few points. It's going to be much harder to find races that'll give them a realistic chance of winning. There are a couple that'll just have to go hunter chasing, which'll probably upset their owners.'

'But you couldn't tell them to take them somewhere else when they've been loyal enough to stay with you.'

'I know, but obviously I've had to put my fees up. I just hope Billy calms down a bit and gets off his high horse.'

'Yes.' Annabel nodded. 'Especially for the open day. It'll be bad enough holding it without our biggest owner if A.D. decides not to show up, so it's terribly important Billy comes across as a committed part of the team.'

Jan sighed. 'I'm beginning to wonder if I'm right to go ahead with this bloody open day.'

Annabel took Jan's hand and squeezed it. 'Of course you are! Don't be put off by one person's objections. If A.D.'s paranoid about publicity that's his problem. And don't worry about Billy. Once he's ridden against some of the top jocks and hit the deck a couple of times, he'll find out he's not quite so special,' she observed dryly.

'Well, I hope you're right. I mean, he's a dam good jockey, there's no doubt about it, but once he's ridden a few winners I know he's going to be unbearable. It's a shame really; he and I go back a long way.'

'Toby told me Billy's already been up to ride some of Virginia's,' Annabel said. 'Did he tell you?' Although she delivered the news casually, Jan couldn't believe she didn't realize the effect it would have.

'No, he bloody well didn't,' Jan snapped. She felt an instant, familiar knot in her guts. There was no reason why Billy shouldn't look at another yard's horses if he was asked, but nevertheless Jan felt betrayed that he hadn't had the decency to tell her.

Virginia Gilbert was Jan's closest rival as a trainer, at least geographically. Apart from being women and about the same age, they had little else in common. But Jan had known Virginia's father, Colonel Gilbert, for a long time. In her teens she'd worked with his horses; he was her father's landlord and he currently had a horse in her yard. The year before he had sent her a nice old pointer she'd won two races with. He had been delighted that his view of her skills had been substantiated and had urged her to train professionally, despite the intense competition that would create with his own daughter.

'What's the matter, Jan?' Annabel asked.

'I'm just disappointed Billy didn't tell me.'

114

'I should think he knew how you would react.'

'I hate it when people aren't honest with me. If he was straight with me, he knows bloody well I'd be straight with him. I'm really sorry for snapping at you, though,' Jan added. 'I'm just a bit pissed off, that's all.'

Annabel dismissed Jan's remorse with a wave of her hand. 'I understand. There's every reason why you should feel the cards are heavily stacked in Virginia's favour. She's got a lot more money, a lovely set-up with brilliant gallops on her father's place; she's got a load of rich friends who think it's nice to have a smart young Sloane Ranger like her as a trainer. But if it's any help, try and remind yourself that she's got about a tenth of your knowledge and talent with horses, and she knows it. So she's probably far more worried about you than you should be about her.'

'The main difference between me and Virginia is that she's doing the job for a bit of fun, whereas I'm doing it because it's the only way I know of supporting my kids, keeping food on the table and clothes on their backs.'

A week later Jan had the chance to observe Virginia more closely than she had for some time. She had been invited to judge the entries at a small children's show at Beauclerk Manor – one of the grandest Jacobean mansions in the Cotswolds. The chatelaine of Beauclerk was Lady Fairford, who was also one of Jan's owners. Jan had ridden the Viscountess Fairford's show horses for her, as she had for Colonel Gilbert and, like him, Lady Fairford had retained a healthy respect for Jan's abilities. Besides this, the mistress of Beauclerk had no interest in fawning social climbers. She loved Jan's directness and self-sufficiency.

On a warm Sunday afternoon in late August, beneath the spreading branches of a magnificent blue cedar, Jan was confident that she was as important as anyone else at the picturesque event and, unusually in this sort of situation, she was feeling entirely secure when the dreaded Virginia Gilbert appeared. Virginia was strolling across the lawn with one of her owners, who apparently had a daughter taking part in the show. She saw Jan sitting at her judge's table and came over.

'Hello, Jan,' she said with an uneasy smile. 'I haven't had a chance to congratulate you on getting your licence.'

Jan felt her hackles begin to rise, she wondered what was coming next and thought that if Virginia had been that keen to share her joy she'd had nearly four months to phone, or write, or call in at the yard. But Jan decided to be gracious. 'Thanks, Virginia,' she said, 'I hope I do as well as you.'

'I'm sure you'll do far better. I was just going to say, I know you aren't sending out any runners yet – I'm not sending out many myself with the ground still so hard – but if we're ever going in the same direction, we could always give one of yours a lift, if that would be a help.'

Jan looked closely at her rival to see if there was more to this friendly gesture than met the eye, but for once Virginia looked sincere.

Jan nodded. 'Thank you very much, Virginia. That might come in really handy.'

Jan noticed Annabel had come up behind Virginia's left shoulder, where she was standing with an expression of disbelief.

'Anyway,' Virginia said, unaware of what was going in, 'best of luck.' She gave Jan an enigmatic smile and moved on with her friends.

'What do you suppose she meant by that?' Jan asked Annabel, who had joined her.

Bel shrugged. 'Who knows? Perhaps she's finally realized that you're more talented than her and, as you said, her motives for being a trainer are a lot less serious than yours; maybe she's recognized that now.'

'She didn't say anything about our stable jockey going up to her yard, though.'

'Come on, Jan,' Annabel said. 'This is hardly the place. You're being a bit paranoid now.'

Jan took a deep breath and tried her best to relax. Even though Annabel was a lot younger than Virginia, Jan guessed she was in a better position to know how someone like her might think.

As Annabel moved on, Lady Fairford – a tall Wagnerian blonde of fifty or so – strode across the lawn towards Jan.

'All set to judge?' she boomed.

Jan nodded. 'I just hope I don't cross the wrong mother.'

'For God's sake, Jan, don't say that! The reason I asked you to judge this thing in the first place was because I thought you were beyond all that kind of nonsense. I could tell you about several friendships that have been ruined over the years and never recovered from questionable judging.'

'I knew there had to be a good reason why you asked me.'

'Jan, you also happen to be the most qualified person around here to judge,' Lady Fairford added.

Driving back later with Matty and Megan, who had both thoroughly enjoyed their afternoon, Jan thought about what her hostess had said. She didn't doubt that Lady Fairford had asked her to judge because she knew exactly what to look for in a horse and rider, or because she had no interest in local tiffs and squabbles. She was mightily relieved she didn't have to negotiate the shifting sands of the arcane social relationships people seemed to go in for in this wealthy corner of England. It all seemed a world away from where she had been two seasons before, training any old horse that came along to run in a few small point-to-point meetings in the furthest corners of Wales.

🐎

The next day was a quiet Sunday, spoiled only by Angie phoning yet again to say that her parents had decided not to come to the yard. She gave no reason, but promised she'd do her best to bring them to the open day.

In the evening, though, Annabel arrived to have supper with Jan. By the time the sun had dropped below the jagged line of hills to the west, they had already finished their pasta and wine. Jan gathered up the plates to take them indoors. She put them in the sink to soak and went through to the children's room to check on Matty. Happy that her children were safe for the night, she went back outside, hoping that Annabel might want to stop and chat for a while longer.

But Annabel was standing up peering into the fading light at an open-topped BMW, which had just driven up to the parking place. The only person in the car was just climbing out.

At that distance, all they could see was a man, very blond, medium height, slim and lithe, wearing jeans and a yellow T-shirt.

'Something to do with you?' Jan asked.

'No, I don't think so. Not yet, anyway,' Annabel laughed.

Jan shot a glance at her. It wasn't often Bel said anything to suggest she might be interested in a man.

Meanwhile the man, having looked around and noted that the caravan was the only human dwelling on the site, was walking up towards them.

The two women stood and waited, glancing at each other with bemused apprehension.

As he came closer, they saw that he was very tanned, as if he'd spent the whole summer in the open air. Suddenly Jan saw something familiar in the way he walked, and a fraction of a second later she was shrieking, 'Ben! Ben! Oh my God! What are you doing here?'

She ran the twenty yards that separated them while he stopped to absorb the impact when it came.

She flung herself at him, with tears streaming down her face. He laughed and wrapped his arms around her, hugging her like she hadn't been hugged for a very long time.

'Hello, big sis. How 'ave you been?'

'My God, Ben, you sound like something out of *Neighbours* with that Australian accent. What the hell are you doing, turning up like this out of the blue?'

'I've always liked surprises; don't you?' He laughed.

'God, it's fantastic to see you. You look so great, so bloody good-looking! What have you done?'

'Four years of debauchery and excess alcohol, I guess.'

'And quite a lot of hanging around on the beach, by the look of things.'

'A fair bit of that, too.'

They were walking up towards the caravan, where the lights in the windows were beginning to glow more strongly in the dusk.

Annabel was watching them, intrigued.

'Oh, Bel,' Jan said excitedly, 'it's my brother.'

'So I gathered.'

'Ben, this is Annabel Halstead. Bel, this is Ben Pritchard,' Jan said with a flourish.

Ben held out a hand to her. 'Mum and Dad told me about you, and so has Jan in her letters. She says you're the best lad she's ever had.'

Annabel shook his hand, grinning at the formal awkwardness of it.

'She's more than a lad now,' Jan said.

'I can see that.' Ben grinned.

'Bel, you'll just have to stay to celebrate Ben coming back. Let's stay out here,' Jan went on. 'It's so warm. I'll get a lamp and something to drink.'

When they were all sitting on folding chairs with a glass of wine, and Jan had set one of her old-fashioned oils lamps on the table, Ben stuck his legs out in front of him and lit up a thin cigar. He took a long drag and nodded slowly. 'This country may sometimes be cold, crowded, damp and crippled by antiquated social ideas and class, but on an evening like this it's bloody hard to beat.'

'Dead right,' Annabel agreed. 'There's no better place in the world.'

Ben turned to her and raised an eyebrow. 'Which bit's dead right?'

'All of it. I've just had a fabulous couple of months in Italy, too; and it was only the thought of Jan and the horses that brought me back.'

'But why should you mind about the old social divisions? I'm sure you must be a beneficiary of the system.'

It struck Jan that, along with his Aussie vowels, Ben seemed to have become much more articulate.

'That doesn't mean I have to approve,' Annabel said. 'My father's such a dreadful snob, in fact he's one of the most snobbish men I know and quite frankly I've got practically nothing in common with him. He seems to think he has a divine right to be as rude as he likes to anyone he thinks is his social inferior, then he sucks up like hell to anyone he thinks is higher up the pecking order than himself. It's just so nauseating.'

'So what does he think about you working for someone like Jan?'

'He thoroughly disapproves, but there's nothing he can do about it, and Mum's entirely on my side. She knows how much it means to me doing this job.'

Ben put his head on one side. 'Fair enough.'

'And, Ben,' Jan said, 'you must admit you didn't make Mum and Dad particularly happy when you turned your back on everything they'd hoped for you.'

'Do you think I don't know that? Do you think it was easy? I had strong feelings for the life I was leading over here. I loved the country, and I could have quite easily got into farming, if I thought I'd ever be able to farm my own land and not have to kowtow to an old codger like Colonel Gilbert.'

'He's not an old codger at all,' Jan protested. 'He's been incredibly supportive to me. He even encouraged me to compete with his own daughter, for God's sake.'

'So I heard, but maybe he's just trying to motivate her.'

'I don't think so!'

'All right!' Ben put his hands up in surrender. 'Maybe there are hidden depths to the old goat, but he still owns Dad's farm and calls the shots. Anyway, at the time I found I was getting a hell of a buzz from my music. It was the one thing I did where my background, my education – nothing like that mattered. All that mattered was that I could write a lyric and a tune – I was good at it, that's the reason people bought them.'

'But why did you have to walk out so completely?'

'I told you; there was a part of me that could have stayed and loved the farming, but I didn't want to end up being torn between the two and fudging it. When I reached Oz, I found a climate that was fantastic and a comparatively level playing field. People judge you there by what you can do and what you've achieved – not if one of your ancestors was Charles II's mistress.'

Jan nodded. 'I know what you mean. I've had to deal with quite a lot of stuffy old farts to get my licence, but, to be fair, in the end they judged me on my merits.'

'And because a few people like Colonel Gilbert put in a good word for you,' Annabel added.

'I'm sure that helped. Anyway, I take your point, Ben. But what's made you come back now?'

'To see you, and Mum and Dad, of course; anyway, I still missed the place. The trouble is, I've had such a good life where I've been, I've found England's lost some of the rosy glow I had in my memory.'

'Does that mean you're not going to stay?' Jan asked.

'No. I'll be here for a while – well, I'll be in London. I've got a contract from Brit Records as their top producer. I've just signed up for two years.'

Jan knew only vaguely what a record producer did, but Annabel was obviously impressed.

'My God! At Brit Records? That makes you one of the top producers in Europe.'

'Let's hope so.' Ben grinned.

'Jan never told me you produced. I thought you were some kind of singer song-writer.'

'Well, I was, but I kind of moved on, and I found I really liked the production side of things; there's as much creativity there as in the writing, probably more.'

Jan was amazed to see Annabel gazing at Ben with awe;

although Jan liked most music, Annabel knew far more about the who's who and what's what of the rock scene.

'Maybe we should open that bottle of champagne that Mr O'Hagan gave me,' Jan suggested, wanting to respond appropriately to the news of Ben's success.

'No,' he said. 'At least, not for me. I don't want to booze too much. I've got to be up early and head back to London at six tomorrow. My first band's due in the studio and I want to make sure everything's set up.'

'Where are you staying tonight?' Annabel asked.

'In my old room, of course. It's just the same as it was the day I left,' he grinned at Jan. 'Mum even made the bed with those Harley-Davidson sheets you gave me when I was eighteen and got my first bike.'

'She would. But will you come back before too long?' Jan asked, feeling cheated by her brother walking back into her life, then disappearing so soon.

'Of course I will. I want to come and have a real good look at your yard and all those horses in it. Johnny Carlton-Brown is dead keen on horses, especially jumpers. I might bring him down one day.'

'Who's Johnny Carlton-Brown?' Jan asked unimpressed.

'Jan! Don't you know?' Annabel exclaimed. 'He owns Brit Records; he started it and must have made an absolute fortune. And Ben's right, he's certainly into horses; George Gilbert told me he bought Miller's Lodge and sent it to Virginia.'

'Miller's Lodge, who won the Cathcart last year? Why the hell's he sent it to her?'

'I think his girlfriend was an old schoolfriend of Virginia's.'

'What a bloody silly reason for sending such a lovely horse to her.' Jan grimaced. 'Ben, you make damn sure you bring your boss down here – and make it as soon as possible!'

🐎

A week after Ben had turned up at Edge Farm, Bernie Sutcliffe drove his new Bentley into the yard.

Jan was on her own in the caravan with the children. She wished Annabel could have been there too, as Bernie was like a harmless jellyfish when she was around. But when Jan had told her he was visiting that evening, Annabel had suddenly found something else to do.

Jan couldn't blame her; they both agreed that Bernie was one of the most unattractive men they'd ever met. With his drab clothes, eau-de-nil complexion and thin, nasal voice, his saving grace, if he had one, was his considerable wealth. Jan had never discovered the real source of his affluence, though she knew from trying to contact him about his horses that he had interests in a variety of companies. He had originally come to the yard because his then girlfriend, a glitzy woman called Sandy, had told him that she wanted a racehorse, and Bernie, ever watchful of the purse strings, had heard that it was much cheaper to go point-to-pointing than to race under rules.

Sandy hadn't lasted more than a few months, but Bernie claimed he had developed a taste for the game, which was encouraged, Jan guessed, by Annabel's presence in the yard.

Annabel would have run a mile from Bernie, but had kept her composure until she'd managed to persuade him to part with Russian Eagle. Bernie had ended the season with two good horses: Dingle Bay, which Eamon Fallon had originally sent to the yard, and Arctic Hay, which Jan had bought for him from a big racing yard near Stow-on-the-Wold.

When Jan had first been granted her licence, she'd assumed Bernie would baulk at the higher costs and sell his horses, but after some protracted moaning he had decided to leave them, giving Jan six months to prove it was worthwhile.

Bernie clambered down from the big silver Bentley and picked his way fastidiously across the car park. A slight man in his forties, his lank grey hair and baggy eyes made him look ten years older. He was wearing his usual grey trousers and brown fleece, bought, Jan guessed, at some bargain store in the Black Country, where his business was based.

Jan quivered as she went down to meet him.

'Hi, Bernie. How are you?'

Bernie wrinkled his thin grey face. 'Mustn't grumble.'

'Business must be good, then?' Jan laughed.

'Actually, it hasn't been bad. I just bought a computer company.'

Jan couldn't imagine Bernie being involved in anything hi-tech. 'Oh, brilliant. I hope it makes you lots of money so you can buy a few more good horses.'

They walked into the stable yard, where horses' heads protruded over most of the doors.

'You seem to have enough here already,' Bernie answered.

'I could take another eight or ten with the block Gerry's built this summer.'

Bernie stopped and gazed around for a few moments. 'It looks really nice,' he said unexpectedly, 'with all these flowers, and the grass and everything. That's all grown since I was here last.'

'You can't stop them,' Jan said, and wondered what it was about Bernie that made her want to be facetious.

Bernie noticed. He gave her a pained look but said nothing. Since he'd taken her out for the most embarrassing evening she'd ever spent on Valentine's Day, when she'd had to make it clear that she wasn't a potential girlfriend, and particularly after his rejection by Annabel, Jan knew he had difficulty asserting himself in the yard in the way he did in his business life.

'So, Bernie, what can I do for you?'

'I wanted to have a look at my horses now the bills have gone up.'

'They're here, next to each other, where they were last year. They seem really happy.' Jan led him to the last two stables in the barn.

'Why aren't they in those nice new boxes you had built last year?' he asked suspiciously.

'These stables are just as good – probably better,' Jan said.

'Not as nice as those, though. Whose horses have you got over there?'

Jan sighed. 'A.D. O'Hagan's.'

'Who the hell's he?'

When Bernie said that kind of thing, Jan was reminded how little he knew about the racing scene. 'He's an Irish owner with a lot of horses. It was his horse that went on to win the race the day Eddie got bowled over by the loose horse in the Foxhunters'.'

'Oh, him. The flash git.'

'Most people think he's a pretty good owner,' Jan said mildly.

'Will he be at this open day of yours next Sunday?'

Jan hesitated. 'I'm not sure. He's a very busy man. He's got horses with five or six trainers here and in Ireland, and I think he might be racing over there on the day. But obviously we'd like him to be here.'

'Hm,' Bernie grunted. 'Swanning about, treating everyone like the poor relations, I expect.'

7

After a blustery week, to Jan's immense relief, Sunday 7 September dawned in bright sunshine, which was forecast to last all day. Every member of staff arrived by six to deal with the usual Sunday chores before starting on the preparations for their first open day.

Gerry had borrowed a large khaki scout tent, which he had put up at the far end of the barn to house all the guests for lunch. Mary Pritchard had worked solidly for the last few days to produce a traditional 'pub' meal of veal, ham and egg pie, sausages, baked potatoes, bread, cheese and pickles. To drink, there were red and white wine and a barrel of bitter, supplied by the Fox & Pheasant, with Julie the barmaid to serve them.

Reg had planted up two more large tubs of flowers and Roz, with an unexpected streak of talent, had made a ten-foot banner welcoming everyone to Edge Farm, which she had stretched between two poles at the bottom of the drive.

The open day had originally been Toby Waller's idea, and he'd willingly followed up his suggestion with a lot of practical help. Watching him get things done, Jan realized why he was such a successful banker. He paid great attention to detail, while keeping a shrewd sense of purpose. He had helped Jan to compile her guest list of potential owners, especially local ones, and had added the names of a few of his own friends and business associates who he thought could be interested in buying a share in a horse. They had also sent invitations to people in the racing media, leading jockeys whom Jan hoped might ride for them from time to time, as well as the vet and farrier Jan used.

Toby had organized the invitations, using a printing company who were his clients. He had also sponsored the production of an illustrated brochure about Jan and her yard, listing details of all the horses in it.

'Next year,' he'd said bullishly, 'we'll pay for it with advertising from your suppliers.'

Jan was still very concerned that A.D. wouldn't show up. As he was an important celebrity owner, other owners and the press would certainly be disappointed if he wasn't there, and it could lead to speculation about the strength of his commitment to her yard. Besides, Jan wanted A.D., more than anyone, to see just what she had done and planned to do with her yard and her plans for the future.

But Toby's attitude and everyone else's enthusiasm began to dispease Jan's worries about A.D.'s non-appearance and convince her that the open day was going to be a success with or without him.

Angie Sharp, on the other hand, had phoned to say she was definitely coming and she was still trying to persuade her parents to come this time. After the disappointment of her last attempt, Jan didn't hold out much hope of getting their horses. For one thing, as the season was well under way, Jan had been looking out for any reappearance of the Sharps' horses on the race track and Martin Hunter had already sent out two or three without success.

Nevertheless, Jan still needed at least six more horses to make the running costs of the yard balance. She could only hope and pray that the open day would help to provide them.

Toby Waller had stayed at the Fox & Pheasant the night before and came up to the yard shortly after nine.

'Good heavens,' he said, walking into the tack room, where Jan was on her own for a moment. 'I've never seen so many people around the place and there aren't even any guests here yet.'

'They've all been brilliant. Mum and Dad have been here for an hour already, getting the lunch set up. Even Roz Stoddard's mum came up with some flowers she's done for the tables.'

'I think it's great that you've got so many people on your side, Jan. Never underestimate the value of that sort of loyalty.'

'I don't: you've been a pretty loyal owner yourself.'

'If I am, I expect it's because there's something in it for me somewhere along the line.' He grinned. 'Are all your other owners coming too?'

'Yes, all of them, I think, except A.D.'

'What has he said about it?'

'I deliberately haven't asked him for any help because when I told him about it at dinner in the Queen's last month, he was very definitely against it.'

'So you said, but I don't see why.'

'He likes having horses in a small, obscure yard, he says. Don't ask me why, it's not as if he's not interested. He rings every few days to see how the horses are doing, but he hasn't mentioned the open day once.'

'It's a pity,' Toby said. 'I'd like to have met him, but there it is; it's not the end of the world. Bernie's coming, I suppose?'

'Too right. He was here last Sunday, grumbling that he was going to be treated like the poor relation now, with A.D.'s horses in the yard,' Jan said with a grimace. Then she went on guiltily, 'I shouldn't be too unkind about him; although he whinges the whole bloody time, he's always stuck to his word and he pays his account by return – which is a big help with all the bills and wages I have to pay.'

'Jan, you'll have to make sure he doesn't drink too much. Remember what happened last New Year's Eve?'

'Oh God, yes.' She frowned. 'You're right. We'll have to try and keep his mouth zipped. I'll ask Annabel to keep an eye on him; he always behaves when she's around.'

Toby looked miffed at the idea of Annabel being used as a

foil for Bernie. Jan had forgotten for a moment how keen Toby had been on Annabel, perhaps still was, so she added quickly, 'I'm sorry, Toby. It's OK, I'll look after him myself.'

The guests started to arrive at around eleven. As the regular parking place wouldn't hold all the cars they were expecting, Tom and Darren were directing traffic into the small paddock below the barn. Jan walked round, to see that it was filling up rapidly. She hoped everyone would have parked by the time she started the main item of the day, which was her presentation of the horses. While the spectators sat on straw bales around the edge of the yard to watch the horses parade, Jan was going to deliver a commentary over a PA system she had borrowed from the pub.

By midday, there was a good-humoured buzz of conversation in the air as people had a look at the stables and some of the inmates. Annabel and Julie had started to mingle with the crowd, offering coffee and biscuits, until Jan found herself standing in the middle of the yard, on her own for a moment, trying desperately to disguise a violent attack of nerves.

'You OK?' Toby asked, coming up to her with a glass of wine. 'You look as though you could do with this.'

'Hell, does it show that much?'

'Not to everyone. What's the problem?'

'It's just that I've never done anything in public in my life.'

'Of course you have,' Toby said. 'Every time you rode a horse in a race; every time you led in a winner as a trainer.'

'All right, but they weren't speaking parts. I just don't know if I'm up to this.'

'Jan, you're a natural. Trust me, I know. Just read the words; add in a few of your own if you feel like it.'

'And there's still no sign of A.D.'

'I've told you, Jan. It doesn't matter.'

'Not to you it doesn't. But two journalists have already asked me why he hasn't turned up.'

'There's no story in A.D. not being here. He's a very busy man; I bet he often doesn't turn up at functions, particularly when he's got runners.'

'All right, but I'm still pretty brassed off. He knows damn well how important it is to me.'

'In which case, you're going to have to get used to the fact that to someone like A.D. O'Hagan you aren't a major player; you're just a small part of one of his hobbies.'

'But he's taken so much interest in everything else.'

'I don't doubt that, but making phone calls is one thing – it probably never takes more than five or ten minutes to get all the information he needs. A trip out here would involve at least half a day. Like I say, he's a busy man and he knows how to use his time efficiently.'

Jan sighed. 'I suppose you're right. Still looking on the bright side, at least Bernie won't feel like the poor relation.'

'Bernie's far too busy chatting up Emma to worry about that,' Toby grinned. 'And by the way, I've just met your friend Angie Sharp; she seems very keen to get her parents' horses up here.'

'Yeah, she's tried to bring them before but apparently they don't want to do the dirty on Martin Hunter.'

'Very laudable, but you know what they say about eggs and omelettes.'

Cheered a little by Toby's down-to-earth analysis of A.D.'s attitude, Jan found Annabel and asked her if they were ready to bring the horses out for the parade.

Annabel nodded excitedly. 'It's great, everyone's been really positive. I even heard Lady Fairford telling your father how nice the yard looked – so you'd better get him a huge drink at lunch time.'

Annabel hurried off to take control behind the scenes. She had written a list so that each groom knew which horses they were in charge of and the order in which they were to parade.

Jan took a deep breath, braced herself, then went and stood in front of the microphone, which had been put on a base at the far end of the yard.

She cleared her throat before switching on the mike. 'Good morning, everyone – welcome to Edge Farm.' She was startled to hear her voice ricochet around the buildings. 'Thank you very much for coming. If you can all find yourself a bit of space on the luxurious seating we've provided, in a few minutes we're going to start showing you the horses, telling you a little of their history and what we hope for their futures. Of course, I won't go into too much detail, but if you want to know more just find me afterwards and I'll tell you everything I can about them.' Jan paused and heard a ripple of appreciative clapping.

Looking around, she saw two top-flight jockeys and, to her amazement, Virginia Gilbert, evidently with her father. A little more relaxed now, she stood back from the mike and smiled at the gathering of forty or more who had filled up the straw bales. She noticed two racing journalists from the national press she hadn't spotted earlier and wondered with a tingle what had brought them to her open day.

Jan was about to introduce the first horse when she heard the sound of more cars coming up the drive, fast. Tom and Darren had left their post by the paddock gate some time before, and the vehicles carried on until a moment later two large black Mercedes limousines swept into view. The crowd turned as one to see who was causing the interruption.

Jan already knew.

A.D. O'Hagan had decided to come.

With a feeling of relief, she realized that despite all his objections and other commitments, he had not only taken the time to come to her open day, he'd also brought his entourage to witness it, which surely must be a measure of how seriously he took her as a trainer, she thought.

She stepped back from the microphone, waiting for A.D. and his clan to find a space. She didn't feel that she should make a special point of greeting him, or show him any preferential treatment by finding him a seat at the front.

This approach appeared to suit A.D., who walked in as if no one had noticed him and settled on a spare bale two rows back.

Jan spoke for around an hour, introducing the twenty horses in her yard. Each one came out looking like a million dollars, with beautiful diamond patterns on its quarters and the best she had ever seen it. She felt tears of pride well up in her eyes and she wanted to hug her staff for doing so well.

Jan thanked Roz Stoddard by name as she announced Russian Eagle. Roz led him into the arena to a round of applause. Eagle reared and gave a couple of small bucks to show his appreciation. Jan didn't know if people actually remembered his magnificent effort in the Foxhunters' or whether they clapped simply because he looked that afternoon as if he was ready to go three times round Aintree.

Finally, when all the horses had made their appearance, without any obvious flagging of interest from her audience, Jan called Billy Hanks to join her.

As soon as he arrived beside her, she realized from the strong smell of alcohol on his breath that he'd already had a lot to drink. She gave him a warning look, to remind him of the notice in her tack room that said, 'Careless gobs cost jobs.'

But, to her relief, they had a quick, witty exchange, in which Billy managed to say that he felt privileged to be starting his professional career with Jan Hardy.

When Billy had finished his party piece, Jan said, 'Before I disappear, I want you to meet the rest of the staff who help me look after the horses. Several of them were already with me for the very successful point-to-point season we had last year, and our one professional winner – so far.'

Starting with Annabel, each member of the team came forward to be introduced by Jan before she eventually wound up her presentation to generous applause.

Then, as they had already agreed, Toby quickly came forward and took the mike from its base.

'For those of you who don't know me, I'm Toby Waller, one of Jan's band of loyal owners. Obviously, as far as I'm concerned, the two best horses we've just seen are Gale Bird and Flamenco, a lovely horse Jan recently bought for me at the Irish Derby Sale. But, I think you'll agree, you would have to go a very long way to see a yard full of such beautifully cared for and magnificently turned out animals.'

Jan felt herself flush as Toby's comments were greeted with another round of applause. It seemed quite unreal that so many people were prepared to come and listen to her talking about her job when she had barely run a horse on a National Hunt track. But, at the same time, she wished she could see A.D.'s reaction. Very much against her will, she'd found that all the time she was talking she'd cared more about what he thought than anyone else's opinion.

'So, on behalf of everyone here,' Toby was saying with his usual polished confidence, 'I'd like to thank Jan for inviting us all and putting on such a terrific show. If your horses perform half as well as they look, I think you should be in for a great season. Now, in case you hadn't spotted it already, there's a marvellous spread in the tent kindly loaned to Edge Farm by the Stanfield scouts, with food provided by Mrs Mary Pritchard, who also happens to be Jan's mother. Annabel and the team await you.'

He replaced the microphone. The spectators applauded again and began to get up from their bales to stretch their legs.

'I think that went brilliantly,' Toby said quietly beside Jan. 'Well done! I said you were a natural. If you weren't too busy training horses I would suggest you went around lecturing businesspeople on how to motivate themselves and their staff.'

Jan looked at him to see if he was drunk. 'Toby, don't talk such tosh!'

'I'm not, Jan. You've got a gift for inspiring people.'

'The only things I want to inspire are my bloody horses. Now, I'd better circulate.'

'Hello, Jan. Tim Farr, *Daily News*.' The man stood directly in Jan's path with the determination of a journalist who had been told by a lot of people where to get off.

'Hello. There's no need to look so wary. I'm not going to bite – I'm glad you made it.'

'Thanks. I wondered if I could have a quick word?'

'Sure.'

'I see from your brochure that you've got six horses for Mr O'Hagan. Can you tell me how long he's been a client?'

'I already told you that when I was at the mike, if you'd been listening. Something tells me you don't know a lot about racing, so why are you here?'

'To tell you the truth, I was staying the weekend not far from here with a colleague who's a racing writer and he asked me if I'd like to come along.'

'For a bit of free booze, I suppose?'

'Not just that. But now I'm here, my editor loves stories about people like Mr O'Hagan. So I just thought there might be some angle you could give me; you know, it would be excellent publicity for your new venture . . .'

'For one thing, I probably know a lot less about A.D. than you do and, for another, the only publicity I want for my yard is about the horses and my capabilities, not sneaking on my owners. I'm very happy to discuss my horses, but not my owners. So, if you'll excuse me.'

She could see in the man's eyes that he was considering making a stand but, after a fraction of a second, thought better of it. He nodded with a faint smile and walked away. Jan went on to find the object of his enquiries.

A.D. O'Hagan was in a corner of the scout tent, holding a glass of wine. Billy Hanks was standing in front of him, talking volubly, while the Irishman listened with a faintly quizzical smile.

Jan quickly walked up to join them. 'I see you've met Billy, then.'

'Yes, I've met Billy,' A.D. murmured.

Jan turned to her jockey. 'Billy, I wonder if you could find Angie Sharp and introduce yourself to her. Her parents are considering sending us some horses . . .' She stood and waited for Billy to take the hint. For a moment there was a defiant flicker in his eyes. Jan held her breath. The last thing she needed was a confrontation with an inebriated jockey in front of a client, and especially not in front of A.D.

But to her relief, Billy nodded. 'OK, what does she look like?'

'Very good-looking. Short dark hair, red chiffon dress.'

Billy's eyes lit up. 'I've seen her. Right, leave it to me.'

Billy made an attempt at a respectful nod in A.D.'s direction and turned jauntily on his heels to go about his mission.

Incensed, Jan watched him before turning to A.D. with an apologetic smile. 'I'm afraid the excitement of it all has gone to his head.'

'It's the wine that's gone to his head,' A.D. remarked dryly.

'He doesn't usually get like that,' Jan said defensively. 'And he's a hundred per cent reliable in terms of turning up to ride work or school, and following instructions in a race.'

'I've seen him ride. He's competent enough; he ought to win on the best horse in a race, but what makes a top jockey is the ability to win on a horse that's not best. I don't mind him having the odd ride; it's important for your yard that you're seen to use your stable jockey as much as you can. But I will want mine ridden by Murty McGrath when his stable doesn't need him; and I have an arrangement with him to that effect.'

Jan gulped. This was the first time A.D. had mentioned any special jockey arrangements and she couldn't help taking it personally; she felt it was *her* job to decide who would ride the horses in her yard. However, it wasn't unusual for an owner with such a large number of horses with several trainers to have his preferred jockey, and Murty McGrath was the reigning National Hunt champion, regularly scoring over a hundred winners a season. She couldn't blame the jockey. A.D. would be paying him a significant fee to have second call on his services after the original retainer. McGrath would also receive the basic riding fee and, when any horse he rode won or was placed, he would also receive, through official channels, a further seven per cent of the prize money.

Jan had to struggle for a moment to allow pragmatism to replace her pride. After all, however loyal she was to Billy, he was still an inexperienced claimer, and Murty McGrath would inevitably produce a higher proportion of winners for her yard.

She nodded co-operatively. 'That's fine. I'd love him to ride and it'll certainly keep Billy on his toes.'

'No doubt.' A.D.'s manner made it clear that was all he wanted to say on the subject for the time being. 'Now, I wanted to tell you, Jan, I think you're doing a grand job. My horses look splendid; I think you've got some excellent staff here, and that assistant of yours is truly dedicated, though God knows how you'll keep a lovely young thing like that hidden away down here.'

'She's done the bright lights and wasn't impressed. In the meantime, she certainly helps to attract the owners. She's a really good rider, too, and gets on great with the staff. I can be a bit demanding, but she always smooths the ruffled feathers.'

'It's a good combination. Nobody ever achieved high standards by compromising.'

Jan was relieved that at least they seemed to be talking the same language again. 'I'm glad you came today, although I know you were anti the whole idea.'

'I was and in principle I still am. A fine display is all very well, but in the end it's horses in the frame that count.'

'But A.D., I've already told you, I've got ten more boxes that need filling.'

'Maybe I should send you a few more, now I've seen how much you have to offer.'

My point exactly, thought Jan.

'That's very kind,' she said, 'but I'd rather you let me prove myself first with those you've already got here.'

'Fair enough, but as to this open day . . .' A.D. glanced in the direction of Tim Farr and his fellow journalist still lingering at the other end of the tent, 'I have to tell you, I've never, ever found the press do anything to help in the long term. The problem they have is that good news has a very short shelf life, whereas they can drag out stories of scandal and skulduggery as long as they want, simply by feeding the public's speculation. The art of dealing with the press is never to tell them anything too important and certainly not in confidence. Ah,' he said, his ever-vigilant eyes focused on the entrance, 'here's Eamon and some of the boys. You must let me introduce you.'

Jan chatted with O'Hagan's entourage for a few more minutes before excusing herself to go and look after her other guests. As she left the tent, she saw Tony Robertson for the first time that day. She watched him approach with a tingle which she wasn't sure if she should attribute to anxiety or pleasure. Before she could decide she realized she was smiling.

'I hope you don't mind me turning up,' he said apologetically. 'I must admit I've no intention of having any horses in training here or anywhere else. Not that I wouldn't like to.'

'I know, and of course I don't mind; I wouldn't have asked you otherwise. Anyway, you might have friends who'd like a horse, and we need a doctor here in case anyone gets kicked or goes down with food poisoning.'

'How can you say that?' Tony protested. 'The food your mother produced was delicious.'

'I know, I was joking. She's brilliant. Everyone's been brilliant.'

'I see even O'Hagan turned up, which you were worried about, weren't you?'

'Frankly, yes. He came and he's been fine – really supportive, so I can't complain. Even Billy's been great.'

'So far,' Tony said with a grin. 'He looked a bit worse for wear when I saw him just now. He was trying to get intimate with that sexy friend of yours.'

'You mean Angie? Do you think she's sexy?'

'In a rather obvious sort of way. Not subtly like you,' he added.

Jan wondered for a moment if she liked the idea of being subtly sexy. 'If you think you'll get anywhere with flattery, keep on trying,' she said.

'It's OK. I know you're not susceptible, but I do know you like a good dinner, so how about it?'

'When – tonight?' Jan asked doubtfully.

'No, you'll be too tired after all this. I thought maybe at the end of the week, if you've got a free evening?'

Jan looked at his warm, considerate eyes. 'I expect I can manage it,' she chuckled. 'Give me a call tomorrow.'

Around forty people had turned up to watch the parade of Jan's horses and most of them stayed on to eat, drink and enjoy themselves. Julie had plugged a CD player into the sound system, filling the yard with a real party atmosphere. Jan looked around at the people enjoying themselves, helping her to celebrate the launch of her new career as a professional racehorse trainer, and thought what a far cry it was from life up in the lonely Welsh hills with John.

Then, with a guilty twinge, she couldn't help thinking how much Eddie Sullivan would have been enjoying himself if he'd been here too. She wished there was some way she could find him to tell him all about it.

'Jan.' She heard an aristocratic voice over her shoulder. She turned to see Colonel Gilbert standing with Lady Fairford. 'Great show. I was very proud of Wolf's Rock,' he said. 'He looked magnificent. Let's hope he runs as well as he looks.'

Lady Fairford was wearing an emerald silk dress and a straw gardening hat over her mass of blonde hair. She nodded her approval. 'All very tidy.' She leaned a little closer to Jan, ostensibly for more privacy. 'But, my dear, you do have one or two very odd owners, which seems rather a pity.'

'They're all very nice,' Jan started to say defensively. 'Some are just a bit different.'

'I met a chap called Sutcliffe,' Lady Fairford went on, 'who asked me if I knew anything about horses, then it turned out he's some sort of scrap-metal dealer.'

Jan tried to laugh lightly. 'Oh, Bernie's fine. He knows practically nothing about horses, but he's very keen, and he's a bit more than a scrap-metal dealer. In fact, he's just bought a computer company.'

'Well, Jan, I'm not at all sure how helpful it is having those kind of owners.'

Jan looked at Colonel Gilbert for support. 'I think a proper, professional yard ought to cater for any genuine owners, if they're honest. Don't you, Colonel?'

The colonel smiled. 'Of course. Don't let Lady Fairford bully you, Jan. She's been doing it to me for years, but it's too late to stop her now.' Lady Fairford shot a glance at the colonel that expressed her amazement at both the idea and his disloyalty in expressing it, but he went on, 'And I also believe that a trainer should be the boss in his or her own yard. If anyone ever tries to tell you how to do your job, tell them to take their horses to a yard where things are done the way they want.'

Jan thought of A.D. telling her which jockey was going to ride for him, and she couldn't imagine asking him to remove his horses. But she knew what the colonel meant.

🐎

The crowd was beginning to thin out when Angie Sharp came into the tent to find her.

'Hi, Jan! At last. I've been wanting to talk to you since I arrived this morning.'

Jan realized this was the first time she had seen Angie the worse for drink. 'Hello, Angie. You look as if you've had a good time.'

'What do you mean?'

Jan was aware that some people became more sensitive when they'd drunk too much and she made allowances. 'Just . . . you look happy. I saw you being chatted up by Billy Hanks.'

'He's just a randy little bastard,' Angie chuckled.

'What did you think of the parade, then?'

'Great. Fantastic. I wish Mum and Dad had come. But I told you what they're like.' She shrugged. 'Anyway, Billy tells me he's riding this good horse of A.D. O'Hagan's, Tom something or other, in a few weeks.'

'Well, we might run him in a fortnight,' Jan said evasively. She didn't think now was the time to take Angie into her confidence over A.D.'s arrangements.

'And he says he's riding all the others. How do you think he'll get on?'

'I think he's a good jockey, or I wouldn't have retained him in the first place. He's a good horseman and he knows how to ride a finish.'

'In point-to-points,' Angie qualified, 'which are a bit different from the real thing.'

'He'll be fine, Ange. I'm not worried.'

Angie looked back at Jan. She lifted the glass of red wine she was still holding and drained it in a single swig. 'Yeah, I'm sure you're right. He'll be fine. We're going down the pub in a while. You coming?'

'I doubt it. I've got a lot of clearing up to do here.'

'We'll, see you there if you change your mind.'

Several hours later, when all the guests had departed, Jan, with her parents, Gerry, Toby and her staff cleared up the debris from the party and finished the evening stables.

Afterwards, Jan sat outside the caravan in the evening sun, drinking coffee with Toby, Roz and Annabel. They all agreed that the open day couldn't have gone better and two of Toby's guests had said they were definitely going to have a half-share each in a horse at Edge Farm.

'The only slight hiccup, as you might say, was Billy getting pissed,' Jan said.

'Yes,' Toby nodded. 'I did notice, and he was doing a serious chat-up line on your friend Angie Sharp.'

'I just hope he didn't push his luck too far,' Jan said, mostly to herself. 'Where's he gone now?'

'To the pub, I should think, with everyone else,' Gerry answered disparagingly.

'But isn't that his car?' Annabel said, pointing to the lower field, where two vehicles were still parked.

'He's probably gone down there with the lads,' Toby said. 'Whose is that Range Rover?'

'That's Angie's. She must have gone with them,' Jan groaned. 'I just hope she's got the nous to stay the night there. She'll never get back to Bristol with the amount she's had to drink.'

'Don't worry. I'm sure she'll be sensible,' Toby said, seeing Jan's concern for her friend.

'Yes, I hope so,' Jan nodded.

After all, she thought, Angie was a grown woman and it was none of her business.

🐎

Jan woke early the next morning, before her alarm had gone off, which always made her feel good at the start of the day. She lay in bed for a couple of minutes in a pleasant reverie, musing about the success of her open day. She was thrilled that A.D. had decided to come and she didn't feel there was anything more she could have done to have made it go better.

She got out of bed and made a cup of tea while she waited for Emma to arrive to look after the children. Sitting at the table looking out into a grey dawn, she glanced down at the lower field and saw that the two cars which had been there the evening before had now gone. She let out a sigh of relief at this evidence, which indicated Angie had recovered sufficiently to collect her car. She hoped desperately that her friend had returned safely to Bristol.

Emma was the first of her workforce to arrive, and as Jan walked down to the yard three more cars shot up the hill just in time to make the six-thirty deadline. Billy Hanks's Subaru wasn't one of them.

She waited for Annabel to park her car.

'I wonder where that sodding Billy is. If he doesn't make it in time for first lot because he can't control his boozing I'm going to be bloody livid. Everyone else has managed to make it so why can't he? Do you know what's happened to him?' she asked.

Annabel shook her head with a ripple of chestnut hair. 'No. I dropped in the Fox to see Julie on the way home, but there was no sign of him then.'

'Was Angie still there?'

'I didn't see her,' Annabel said in a way that suggested she didn't care one way or the other.

Jan and Annabel were walking into the yard as they talked. When they reached the tack room they focused on the job of organizing the first lot of horses that were to be ridden out.

'As Billy's not here, Bel, you can ride Tom's Touch.'

'Lord, do you trust me?'

'As much as I do Billy,' Jan sighed.

Ten minutes later the five of them were on board and ready to leave the yard.

As they were walking up the long incline to the gallops at the top of the ridge, Jan moved up to ride beside Joe Paley.

'Did you enjoy the open day yesterday?'

'Yes, Mrs H., I thought it went real good. The 'osses looked great, didn't they?'

'I think everyone was pretty impressed,' Jan nodded. 'Tell me, did you go down to the Fox last night with the rest of the gang?'

'Too right. We was all well lit up.'

'Did you see Angie Sharp there – the lady in the red dress?'

'Hell, aye!' Joe laughed. 'What a cracker! She was drinking with Billy.'

'Oh,' Jan said flatly. 'Billy was already pretty tanked up before he left. I hope he wasn't trying to get her drunk as well.'

'He wouldn't have had to try too hard, Mrs H. And, if you ask me, there was a bit more to it than that.'

'What do you mean?' Jan asked.

'Darren said he come back to get his bike after he left the pub, and he went back down through the fields by Billy's Subaru. He heard music coming from it and went to have a look, but he reckoned it was all steamed up, rocking around like there was an earthquake under it. And that Angie's car, well it was still parked up the top of the field.'

'Don't be ridiculous!' Jan said instinctively. 'Angie Sharp wouldn't mess around with Billy Hanks, especially not in the back of his rusty old car!'

'Suit yourself,' Joe said with an indifferent shrug. 'I'm just repeating what Darren said.'

Jan checked her horse a little, so that she fell behind Joe Paley's mount. She didn't want him to see the effect his words had had on her.

If what Joe had said really was true, Jan felt shocked by Angie's behaviour.

And she was absolutely furious with Billy. It was such a gross thing for a jockey to do – firstly to get drunk and then to seduce one of his trainer's potential clients!

For the rest of the exercise, Jan struggled to keep her rage under control. It was possible that Darren hadn't quite seen what he thought he had, or perhaps he'd made the whole thing up to impress his older colleagues. Maybe it hadn't been Angie in the Subaru with Billy.

Even so, Jan could hardly contain herself when they got back to the yard for breakfast.

Just before second lot, five minutes before they were due to pull out again, Billy arrived in his Subaru and parked by the yard gate. Jan watched through the window of her makeshift office as he climbed stiffly from his car, then managed to strut like a peacock across the yard towards Annabel and the others, who were waiting outside the tack-room door. He looked as though he'd spent the night under the hedge but, despite his puffy face and red eyes, he gave them a shameless grin and croaked a more affable greeting than usual, trying to bluff his way out of his late arrival.

Annabel's eyes narrowed. 'What on earth happened to you last night?'

Billy grinned. 'What do you think?'

'You threw up behind a hedge somewhere?' Roz suggested.

'Do you mind? I was working bloody hard on behalf of Edge Farm Stables.'

Jan braced herself. 'Billy,' she called through the open door. 'Come in here. I want to talk to you – now.'

Billy stepped through the door. 'Morning, boss.'

'Come in and close the door.'

The jockey heaved a shoulder and kicked the door shut with his heel.

Jan stared at him. 'Where the hell were you when we pulled out for first lot?'

'In bed.'

'For Christ's sake, Billy! What the hell's happened? What have you been up to?'

'I had a bucket load of booze at your piss up yesterday, you know, doing my thing for the yard, chatting up the punters and all that.'

'Yes,' Jan growled. 'I heard about your chatting up and, let me tell you, if you were screwing around with Angie Sharp, God help you!'

'Whether I was, or whether I wasn't, it hasn't done you any harm,' Billy said calmly.

'What are you talking about?'

'I reckon I've got you a few more horses to train.' Billy leered at her.

Jan froze. If by any chance he was making sense, and the Sharps' horses did come to Edge Farm, it wasn't going to help one iota if Billy thought he was responsible.

What the hell does Angie think she's playing at? Jan asked herself.

'Billy, we'll talk about this later.' Jan got up and went to the door, to find the rest of her staff still waiting. 'We've got work to do and you've got a horse to school when we get back, remember?'

'There'll be seven more to school soon,' Billy crowed.

'Whose?' Annabel asked.

'Vince Sharp's. I had what you might call a good session with his daughter yesterday, and I convinced her I was the right man for the job.'

'What!?' Joe Paley asked, doubly impressed. 'You sh—'

'Don't you dare!' Jan cut in. 'If you want to talk filthy, you can go and do it elsewhere. I won't have it around the yard.'

Billy beamed. 'You won't mind when you get seven more horses.'

'Angie had already said she was bringing her parents to look at the yard,' Jan said, wishing she hadn't let her herself get sucked into this sort of sparring.

'Angie said she needed to know how I was going to ride the horses first.'

'And her,' Joe tittered.

'Shut up, Joe,' Jan snapped. 'Billy, you'd better go and tack up Anais is Arish, right now!'

❧

Around noon, when most of the morning's work had been done and the staff were drinking coffee in Jan's office beside the tack room, the phone rang. Annabel answered it, before handing it to Jan.

'Angie Sharp,' she said.

Billy punched the air with a triumphant grin.

'Hi, Angie,' Jan said brightly, as if she were surprised to hear from her so soon. 'I hope you enjoyed the open day.'

'Yes, it was great, and I really liked Billy Hanks,' Angie answered without a hint of self-consciousness. 'I brought your brochure home and told my parents all about your open day and at last they've said they'll definitely come up and have a look at the yard. It's not surprising, really. Martin Hunter's going nowhere with the horses, and I've finally convinced Mum and Dad that they need a change of scene and you could set them alight again.'

'That's great news,' Jan said, trying to ignore Billy's smug gestures. 'When do you want to bring them?'

'How about next Sunday?'

When Jan put the phone down a few moments later, she couldn't ignore a surge of excitement at the prospect of seven more horses arriving. Determined not to succumb to wrangles over who had attracted them to the yard, she nodded at Billy. 'Seems like you were right, Billy. At least, Angie said she enjoyed meeting you and she's bringing her parents up here next weekend. I wonder what they're like.'

8

Jan's dogs, Fred, Tigger and Fly, didn't take long to make up their minds what they thought of the Sharps. As soon as they saw Vince and Dawn climb out of Angie's Range Rover just after midday, they raced across the yard and stood by the gate, barking furiously.

Jan shouted in a vain attempt to quieten them and wondered what their problem was as she walked down to meet her visitors. When she could see Angie's parents at close quarters, she began to understand why the dogs had gone potty. In contrast to their daughter, there was little that was attractive about the couple.

Jan judged they were probably both well into their seventies. Vince was short, slightly bent, with a face like a wrinkled prune and a big, fleshy nose. Dawn, in contrast to her name, didn't present a much better picture. Her clothes, although obviously expensive, hung off her like washing on a line. Her mousy white hair was heavily curled from excessive perming, and her alarmingly translucent skin was as grey-green as the River Severn in winter.

Jan overcame a natural prejudice against such an unappealing couple and smiled in welcome. They were, after all, her friend's parents, and Reg had warned her many times not to judge a book by its cover.

'Mum, Dad,' Angie said, grinning broadly and taking Jan's arm with one hand. 'This is Jan Hardy. Jan, this is my mum and dad.'

Angie stood back and Vince held out a bony hand on which

several chunky gold rings were crammed. 'Pleased to meet yer,' he grunted with an unwilling smile.

Jan took Vince's hand while Dawn inclined her head slightly. 'Angie's told us all about you.'

Jan nodded and smiled. She tried to see a connection between this awkward couple and their daughter. She couldn't understand how they could be so unsophisticated compared to Angie. They had clearly made a lot of money somewhere along the way and presumably were still. To keep seven horses in training at a yard like Martin Hunter's would be costing them well over a thousand pounds a week. Up until now Angie had only touched vaguely on the subject of her family's fortunes. They had a number of businesses, she'd told Jan, including a big hotel in Bristol and a small chain of clothes shops. Perhaps that was enough, Jan thought; although she had no idea what a big hotel was worth.

She would have liked to know what Annabel made of the Sharps, but she had sent her to pick up some new tack from the saddler's in Stow. She felt slightly guilty that she had done it deliberately because she felt uncomfortable when Annabel and Angie were around at the same time.

'Welcome to Edge Farm,' she said rather artificially, sounding like an air hostess. 'Would you like a cup of tea or coffee? I'm afraid I'm still living in the mobile home up there.'

'Nothing wrong with a mobile home,' Vince said without a hint of condescension. Jan had the impression that he too had lived in a caravan at some point in his life; perhaps it had even had a horse to pull it. At the same time, she tried to place his strangely clipped rural accent. 'We wants to have a look at the yard and your 'osses,' he continued.

'Fine!' Jan said, happy to oblige. She glanced at Angie, who was now standing behind Dawn.

Angie winked, as if to say, *Go for it!*

Jan led the small party into the yard. She took them into the barn first and told them about each horse, checking all the time for signs that her audience was getting bored, as some prospective owners might. But they appeared to be taking in everything she said, commenting knowledgeably and asking the occasional question about a horse's history or its owner.

Jan was impressed and puzzled. She had assumed that they had stayed with Martin Hunter simply because he had managed to convince them that their horses' lack of success was not his fault; yet it was clear they both knew enough about National Hunt racing to place the blame in the right place; in which case, she decided, their personal loyalty to him must be very strong.

But as they worked their way round the yard, eyeing up the facilities as well as the inmates, it became increasingly clear to Jan that their loyalty to Martin Hunter alone was not going to be enough to persuade them to leave their horses with him.

When they had finished looking at O'Hagan's hugely impressive string, Vince stood for a moment and gazed around at the buildings, taking in the clean cobbles and well-brushed concrete walkways.

'If I was to send you seven 'osses,' he said without looking at her, ''ow much would it cost?'

'I've got a price list with my brochure in the office,' Jan said, taken by surprise.

'Never mind brochures for now,' Vince said dismissively. 'We likes your set-up, but you'll 'ave to do us a price.'

Now Jan was beginning to see why the Sharps were with Martin Hunter, who would almost certainly be open to offering a discount on training a number of horses for the same client. And Angie had warned her in Ireland that her parents didn't like to be parted from their money.

Jan smiled. 'When I got my licence, I worked out the fairest price I could to train a horse and that's what I charge. I can't afford to drop that price for anyone, however many horses they send me.'

'So, what's that?'

Jan didn't doubt Angie had already told them exactly what the figure was, but she pretended they didn't know. 'Basic keep and training is twenty-five pounds a day, shoeing, veterinary treatment, transport and everything else is extra.'

'We'll pay you nine hundred quid a week, for the seven of them,' Vince said.

It took Jan a moment to work out that he was demanding a discount of three hundred and twenty-five pounds a week. At least she managed to smile and shake her head. 'I'll make you one offer, Vince, as you're Angie's dad, but that'll be my only offer. I'll do the seven for eleven hundred quid a week, plus shoeing and vets.' She looked at the pair of them and noticed Vince's wrinkled jowls grinding away nervously as he considered it.

'All right,' he said at last. 'Eleven hundred a week and we'll pay you in readies, mind; we don't want a bill or nothing.'

'If you don't mind, I run everything above board here,' Jan said, trying not to sound too prim. 'I have to, for the Jockey Club, the bank and the dreaded tax man.'

Vince glanced at his wife for the first time during the negotiations. To Jan's surprise, he waited until the frail old woman nodded, almost imperceptibly.

'A'right. Done.' He held out his ring-encrusted hand once more, and Jan, still surprised at the speed with which terms had been agreed, shook it.

'We'll have that cup of tea, now,' Vince went on.

'Isn't there anything else you want to see?'

'No.' Dawn said bluntly. 'We wouldn't have already said we wanted to send the horses here if there was.'

Jan led them up the hill, telling them about her plans for the new house as they passed the almost completed shell.

'You must come down to Overmere and see our place one Sunday lunch,' Angie said excitedly. 'Bring the kids, too, if you want to,' she added, knowing how Jan hated to be separated from Meg and Matty any more than she had to be.

In the caravan, Jan introduced Vince and Dawn to Emma, who had been looking after the children. They had been drawing and the table was strewn with the pictures they'd done.

Angie picked up one of a brown horse, done in crayons in a neat, childish way. 'Cor, this is good! Who did this?'

'I did,' Megan crowed.

'It's brilliant. Can I buy it off you?'

Megan put her head back and looked at Angie as if she was mad. She glanced at Jan.

'I tell you what. I'll give you a fiver for it,' Angie said and, to her father's obvious disapproval, she took a five-pound note from her purse and handed it to Megan.

Jan didn't know how to react. The transaction seemed false, as if Angie was dishing out charity. And yet Jan knew Angie wouldn't have meant it like that; she would be wanting to give Megan a present in a way which suggested the girl had earned it. She shrugged and gave Megan a quick smile.

'Thanks, Angie,' Meg said, no doubt calculating what she could get for her pony for five pounds, and what sweets she could buy if there was anything left over.

'Emma, could you just tidy away the rest of the drawings before Mr and Mrs Sharp buy them all?' Jan said quickly.

Emma nodded with a grin and cleared the papers away. Jan switched on the kettle and beckoned her guests onto the narrow upholstered benches on either side of the table.

Once they were settled, she poured the tea into the fine china cups she'd brought from Stonewall but seldom used. When they all had a cup, Jan passed a biro and pad of paper to Vince. 'Could you write down the names of the seven horses you want to send us, please?' she asked.

Vince stared down at the pad for a moment, without touching the pen. He gave Jan a quick, embarrassed glance and pushed the pad and pen over the table to his wife. Saying nothing, she started to write in slow, old-fashioned copperplate.

When the old woman had finished, she pushed the pad towards the end of the table. Jan picked it up and read it.

Lucky Charm
Vincent's Pride
Avon Supreme
King's Archer

Jenny Pitman

Moriarty
Overmere Lass
Bath Princess

She tried to imagine each name in the winner's slot with her name after it and she couldn't help smiling. She was fairly sure there were a few winners amongst them. If any turned out to be complete duds, as soon as she knew for certain she could always suggest to the Sharps that they send them elsewhere or sell them. There was little point in carrying passengers in the yard – even paying ones.

'Great,' she said, nodding her thanks. 'I'll go down and have a look at them tomorrow, to check them out and make sure they're sound, but there's just one thing – I won't take them from Martin Hunter until all his outstanding fees have been paid.'

Vince Sharp lifted his head with a jerk. 'Hang on,' he growled. 'That's our business, not yours.'

'Mr Sharp,' Jan said firmly, 'it's my business to stay on the best terms I possibly can with my colleagues, and I'd hate it if someone turned up here to take a load of horses away when the bill hadn't been fully paid. In fact, I wouldn't let them out of the yard; and maybe Martin Hunter's the same. Anyway, I thought it would be helpful for you to know how I operate, right from the word go. I'm sure you agree, the more up front we are with one another, the less room there is for any misunderstanding in the future.'

🏇

'I can't wait to meet these Sharps,' Annabel said gleefully. 'Vince and Dawn sound like a really bizarre couple.' She flicked a curtain of fine hair off her face while she hustled her car down the M5 as fast as the holiday traffic allowed.

Jan, leaning back in the seat beside her, grinned too. 'I doubt if you'll see them today and I'm not sure what you'll make of them when you do, but you should meet them soon. Angie's invited me to take the kids down to their place for Sunday lunch. I don't think she'd mind if I brought you along too.'

'Where do they live?'

'In a massive Victorian mansion, apparently, overlooking a lake about ten miles south of Bristol; not that far from Martin Hunter's yard, where we're going now.'

'It sounds a pretty weird set-up from the way you've described them.' Annabel shook her head, trying to get a better picture.

'I can't work it out myself,' Jan admitted. 'And I can't say I really took to Vince either. Let's hope he grows on me.'

'What's the mother like?'

'She's a small woman, frail as a bird, but much tougher than she looks. She doesn't say a lot. Vince does most of the talking, but I think she makes the decisions.'

'What about your friend, Angie? Does she have much say in the horses?'

'I'm not sure. I think she runs some of their businesses for them, but she's a bit cagey about it all. You can't blame her. But apart from that she's a really lovely person, nothing like her parents. I don't think we'd have become such good friends if she was.'

'I'll be most interested to meet her and I didn't get a chance to at the open day,' Annabel said without any obvious enthusiasm.

Jan felt a little guilty talking about Angie like this to Annabel, who had a far stronger claim on her friendship. Yet surely, as grown women, they didn't need to feel this kind of rivalry.

'I think you'll like her,' Jan said uncertainly. 'She's not like you – the opposite in most ways – but you know how opposites often attract. She's a bit—' Jan tried to find the right word, 'I suppose you could say she's flashy. She always looks like she's just walked out of the hairdresser's. She wears a lot of jewellery all the time; it's hard to tell if it's fake, and I can't imagine her getting her hands dirty with a muck fork. Even so, she's very kind-hearted. She's always bringing presents for the kids.'

Annabel nodded. 'Meg showed me the chaps.'

'I'm not really happy about how much she spends on them, but on the other hand it's Angie's way of showing she cares, and she must be able to afford it.'

'You said she might be sending you a horse of her own.'

'She did say she might a few weeks ago, but I suppose now her parents are going to send theirs she probably won't bother. That's OK, though. I've still got seven new ones.'

'You haven't yet,' Annabel warned. 'It's not like you to count your chickens.'

'You're right. They might be a load of lame donkeys, and if Martin hasn't been paid up to date, I won't collect them until he has. That's what I told Vince and I have no intention of backing down.'

'But will you take all the horses, even if you don't think they're much good?'

'You've already asked me that. I feel I owe it to clients to take any horses they offer to send me. At least that gives me a chance to have a good look at them and try them out. You'd feel a right idiot if you'd been offered an animal, turned it down on sight and then someone else got a win out of it.'

They turned off the M5 at the Weston-super-Mare exit and headed east, towards Cheddar and the Mendips. The rolling green hills looked soft and hospitable in the late summer sun.

'There are quite a few trainers in Somerset, aren't there?' Annabel observed.

Jan nodded. 'It's not a bad place to train, but it's quite a bit harder to travel to a lot of the better courses. The area's good in some ways, but the soil's quite heavy, and I would think that limits the use of grass gallops.' She looked down at the map on her lap. 'If you take the next left and go on for about three miles, we should end up at Hunter's place.'

They drove for ten minutes along a lane that narrowed progressively until the middle of the road gave way to a continuous strip of weeds. Through gaps in the high hedges, they saw that they were driving up a deep, grassy valley between small, round hills.

As the road petered out, they drove on between a pair of heavily listing gateposts and into a scruffy farmyard. Annabel stopped her car and turned off the engine. They wound down the windows and stared into a silence broken only by the occasional clop of an iron hoof on a concrete floor, and the warning *rit-it-it-it* of a startled blackbird. There was a festering muck heap at one end of the crumbling stone buildings and loose rotting straw lay all over the yard.

None of the usual things that kept people busy at a racing stables during the late afternoon were happening and there appeared to be no one around. A dozen horses' heads poked enquiringly over their stable doors.

'Do you think this is it?' Annabel asked doubtfully.

'We've followed the directions Martin Hunter gave us, and these look like thoroughbreds all right, whatever state they're in.'

The two women climbed out of Annabel's car and stood in silence for a few moments, gazing about them. Jan looked at Annabel and made a puzzled grimace.

She ignored a slight shiver of fear, and started to walk across the yard towards what might be a tack room at the far end.

'Hello?' she called.

Although she hadn't seen him for perhaps six or seven years, Jan recognized Martin Hunter at once from his raggedy black hair, which looked as if it had been shorn with horse-clippers and long square jaw, which hadn't been touched by a razor for several days. But where he had once had tough good looks that matched his prowess as a jockey, there was a worn flabbiness to his features now, which hinted strongly at too much tobacco and alcohol and not enough sleep.

He stood in the tack-room doorway and squinted at Jan through dark, baggy eyes, as if he'd just woken up. He had told her on the phone the night before that he wouldn't be at the races that day as he hadn't any runners. Given the number of horses in his yard, it wasn't too surprising, but she had expected to find him awake.

'Hello. I'm Jan Hardy. I phoned . . .'

He drew himself up. He had become a lot heavier since his race-riding days and a beer gut was visible beneath a grimy cotton shirt a size too small. 'For Chrissake! I know who you are. How many people do you think find their way up that poxy lane to this place? Not bloody many, I can tell you. It's like this place is a leper colony or something.' Suddenly his defiance left him and his face seemed to collapse. 'And I know why you've come.'

'Did the Sharps tell you?'

'Yeh,' he nodded.

'Have they paid you up to date?'

'No, but they said they will. Someone'll be over tonight or tomorrow.'

'Who did you speak to?'

'The lovely Miss Angie, of course. I've always dealt with her.'

'Well, I told them I wouldn't take any horses from your yard until you were paid in full.'

'How very sweet of you!' he slurred with vicious sarcasm, showing Jan that he was a lot more drunk than she'd realized.

She shrugged a shoulder. 'I just thought it's bad enough losing seven horses, without getting screwed for the fees as well.'

'I couldn't give a monkey's toss about losing the Sharps' horses – jumped-up little pykies. It's all a load of bollocks . . .' His voice trailed off and he looked desperate, until he appeared to notice Annabel for the first time. 'Who the hell are you? We don't often get gorgeous creatures like you up here.'

'This is Annabel Halstead, my assistant. We really came to look at the horses, to check out their condition before we decide if we definitely want to take them.'

Hunter looked back at Jan, his face like thunder, and shook his head. 'There's nothing wrong with any of them; course you're going to take them all, don't give me that crap, you can look if you want. That's them there.' He waved an arm at a row of dilapidated boxes on one side of the yard. 'All except the one at the end, which is my secret weapon,' he continued. His eyes glinted with a brief fire of optimism. 'Help yourself.'

He gave Annabel an unappetizing leer, turned and walked back up the yard.

'Hang on!' Jan called after him. 'How do we know which is which?'

'The stables are all named,' he said over his shoulder and carried on.

Jan and Annabel walked across to the row of stables he'd indicated, and found that a small card was fixed beside the door of each box with a rusty drawing pin.

'Is this worth doing?' Annabel asked.

'Too right it is. If there's anything wrong with any of them, I want to tell the Sharps tonight, so they don't start screaming at me as soon as I have to call the vet in. I'm not carrying the can for any problems they have already.'

🐎

All the sympathy Jan had felt for Martin Hunter before visting his yard quickly dissipated once she had looked into a few of the stables. It was clear that he was cutting corners at every opportunity. The place was obviously understaffed. The horses looked wormy, cold and uncared for and their bedding was an absolute disgrace.

Christ, Jan thought, *no wonder they don't win races.*

And yet, beneath the lustreless coats of the Sharps' horses, she could see quality. Martin Hunter, she concluded, had gone so far beyond the point of no return that, even with a couple of apparently compliant owners like the Sharps, he hadn't got the energy or the will to make anything of the horses they'd sent him.

She checked each limb on all seven horses and listened to their breathing. She stood and observed them for a few moments, and noticed a sad listless look in their eyes. Overall, though, she found nothing to give her any real cause for concern, although she was well aware more problems could appear later. However, Jan decided to check them all for signs of lameness, and asked Annabel to trot them up and down the yard a couple of times. She was amazed how well they moved, considering the state of their feet, with their shoes hanging off.

'What do you think?' Annabel asked as they put the last horse back into its dilapidated stable.

Jan shrugged. 'I can't see too much wrong with any of them that a bit of TLC and some decent grub won't cure, but that could all change as soon as they start doing a bit of fast work. None of them are fit to run as they are, but there are three or four nice horses, and the others . . . well, we'll have to see.'

'Haven't you seen enough yet?' Martin Hunter had reappeared and was leaning against the frame of the tack-room door.

'Yes, we have. We've just finished. I'll phone you tonight to make sure you've been paid and if everything's OK. I'll get someone back down tomorrow to pick them up.'

On the way back to Gloucestershire, Jan arranged to hire a large horsebox, since her own would take only six horses at a pinch and she didn't want to make two trips. Besides, the transport people would send their own driver, leaving Annabel and Roz free to travel in the back with the horses.

When they had got back to Edge Farm, and everyone else had gone home for the night, Jan asked Annabel to have supper with her. She opened a bottle of wine and took their food outside the caravan to an old rustic table. While they ate in the warm evening air, they gossiped and talked through the horses, much as they had the previous summer. Now, including the Sharps', there would be twenty-seven horses in the yard, with more owners expecting results, but the competition would be much fiercer than in point-to-points.

'I know it's a stupid question, but have you any idea how many winners you'll train this season?' Annabel asked.

Jan shook her head. 'To tell you the truth, I haven't a clue; if we were talking pointers, I'd have a fair idea, but this is such a different game. I suppose, with the Sharps' horses, assuming they've paid Martin and he lets them go, I'll have maybe fifteen or twenty capable of winning – in theory, that is. But in practice I don't know how they'll train. Some are bound to get problems of one sort or another. They might get flu, not be right on the day, meet a fence wrong, or strain a tendon – the list is endless.' Jan sighed. 'All the usual stories you hear trainers telling owners every day.'

'Just finding the right races for them can be tricky, I should think,' Annabel mused.

'I've already done a lot of homework on that,' Jan nodded. 'I've got the programmes book and I've been through the conditions of every National Hunt race between now and Christmas, marking which ones might suit a particular horse – at least from what I know of them so far. The trouble is, with some of the novices, I'm not going to know their actual distance until we've done a lot more work on them, sometimes not until they've raced for the first time this season. Obviously you can get some idea from how they are bred, but that's not written in stone. They're not machines.'

Annabel listened carefully to everything Jan said, nodding as she took it all in. Jan didn't underestimate how lucky she was to have an assistant who cared so much, who understood her ideas and would follow them willingly. Annabel had no axe to grind; she wasn't in competition with Jan; she didn't do the job for the money, she did it because she loved it, though Jan couldn't help wondering how long an unattached, attractive, twenty-four-year-old woman would stay so committed to the job. But she'd thought that last year and was glad Annabel was still there.

🐎

Martin Hunter phoned in the morning.

'The lovely Angie's been. She's paid me up to date in cash, but if I give her horses any more grub I'll be paying for it myself, so the sooner you can come and get them the better.'

With a tingle of anticipation, Jan immediately rang the

transport company to give them the go ahead and by the middle of the afternoon the Sharps' horses had arrived at Edge Farm. All the staff hung around to see the animals as they came off the transporter.

'Cor,' Roz said, 'they look a bit rough.'

In a moment of self-doubt, Jan found the same thought crossing her mind. She suddenly wondered if she'd been too hasty and overestimated the animals when she'd seen them the day before. 'We'll have to see what a bit of good grub and a nice warm stable can do,' she said, trying to sound as positive as she could. 'We'll put them all in the new block and keep them away from the other horses for the time being,' she continued.

Much later, when the staff had gone home, and the new tenants had been fed, watered and bedded down for the night, Jan and Annabel visited each of them for another inspection.

'What do you think?' Jan asked when they left the last stable.

'I think potentially there are two or three really nice horses,' Annabel answered. 'But you're the expert.'

'I agree. King's Archer's not got much wrong with him, although he looks pretty hard trained. Martin had already entered him for a couple of races. If he hasn't gone too sour, I'd be surprised if we can't get him winning again. In fact, I might give him a gallop alongside Tom's Touch next week.'

'And the filly, Overmere Lass, Martin said she had shown some ability on the gallops – she doesn't look too bad either and might be ready to run in a bumper in a few weeks' time.'

Jan nodded. 'He ran Vincent's Pride and Lucky Charm a couple of weeks ago, both finished mid-div.'

'So, what are you going to do with them?'

'I'll give them a few days to settle in, then we'll get them on the gallops and see how fit they really are.'

Feeling slightly more confident about the Sharps' horses, Jan was tidying up the tack room with Annabel when a BMW convertible cruised up to the yard gate and stopped, gleaming incongruously in the country surroundings.

A moment later Ben got out, followed by a tall, thin man

with long wavy grey hair, who was wearing a plum-coloured corduroy suit.

'Hi, sis!' Ben said, as she walked up to greet him. He took her in his arms and gave her a bear hug. 'How's it going? I've brought my boss to meet you.'

Over Ben's shoulder, Jan noticed the 'boss' wince at the description and immediately warmed to him.

She pushed Ben aside and held out her hand. 'Hi, I'm Jan Hardy.'

'And this is Johnny Carlton-Brown,' Ben said unnecessarily as the record company chief took Jan's hand and shook it.

'Hi, Annabel,' Ben said. 'Still letting my sister slave-drive you?'

Annabel smiled and nodded.

Ben went on, 'Johnny, this is Bel. She does all the real work round here.'

'I tell you what,' Jan said, 'if you two want to have a look around for a few moments, Bel can give you the tour while I go and sort out the kids. Then you can come up and have a drink.'

'Suits me. All right by you, Johnny?'

🐎

Twenty minutes later the men appeared at the caravan with the three panting dogs.

'Annabel's gone home,' Ben said. 'She'll see you in the morning.'

Jan nodded. 'OK you two, make yourselves at home. There should be something to drink in the fridge. Matty's feeling a bit queasy, so I'd better deal with him.'

'Oh, my God.' Johnny Carlton-Brown exclaimed in an old-fashioned, public-school voice. 'I'm so sorry. Would you like us to bugger off and come back later? I've got sisters of my own, so I know how inconsiderate brothers can be.'

'No, not at all,' Jan said. 'Everything's fine. It'll just take me a few minutes to sort out and get him and his sister into bed.'

Once she had tucked in the two children for the night,

without much hope of Megan staying put so early in the evening, she went back to join Ben and his boss. As they already had a beer, she poured herself half a glass of white wine topped up with sparkling water.

'How's Matty?' Ben asked.

'Fine. Apart from the measles, he hasn't been ill for ages.'

'He sounds as tough as his mum,' Ben said.

'I hope not,' Jan answered with a grin. 'Anyway, what's brought you over this way?'

'Johnny and I were checking out a recording studio in Bristol, and he wanted to call in and have a look at your yard. I'm sorry I didn't give you any warning, but it was a bit spur of the moment.'

'That's OK,' Jan said. 'Is there anything you'd like me to show you?'

'We had a pretty good tour with Annabel.'

'Ben says she's your assistant trainer,' Johnny added, as if he didn't believe it.

'Well, why shouldn't she be? This is an equal opportunities' business.'

'But if she could sing, I'd give her a contract on the spot.'

'Well, she can't, as it happens. She may look stunning, but she's far too modest for that game.'

'OK, OK,' the record company boss conceded with a laugh. 'It was worth a try! Anyway, she seems totally committed and she obviously loves the horses – especially her own. You should watch she's not giving him extra rations on the quiet.'

'She won't be; she's far too worried about his figure.'

'She doesn't need to worry about her own, that's for sure,' Johnny observed. 'And I wouldn't mind her looking after mine.'

'Your figure?' Jan tilted her head on one side.

'No. My horse.'

Jan tried not to look too excited. 'Are you thinking of getting another?'

'Yes, I am.'

'You've got one already at Virginia Gilbert's, haven't you?'

'Yes. But I thought if I had one with you, too, it might make you *both* try that little bit harder.'

Ben laughed. 'My God, Johnny, you're right! Nothing like a bit of naked rivalry to motivate a woman.'

Jan grinned. If ever she needed an additional incentive to win, there couldn't be a better one than the thought of beating Virginia Gilbert, especially for the same owner.

'Fine,' she said. 'If you let me know how much you want to spend, I'll start looking.'

9

A week later, as the Land Rover crested the last ridge before Stonewall, a blast of autumn wind was bending and flicking the scanty trees on the Welsh hills.

Jan wondered if Olwen had ever considered what a tiring trek it was for her to bring the children over, at a stage in her career when time was at a premium. But she had to do it – for John's sake, and for the children, who unlike her always looked forward to seeing their grandmother. They hadn't been for at least two months, but when Olwen had telephoned during the week Jan's conscience had been pricked.

When they arrived at the bungalow Olwen, in her usual way, made a great fuss of the children and had once again brought back a clutch of new toys from the shop in Hay. Jan had to give her mother-in-law credit for knowing how to manage her limited resources. But, with her, the old woman was as frosty and aloof as ever.

Over the customary tea in bone-china cups while the children played, Olwen fixed Jan with her pale blue eyes. 'You said you would do something about Harold Powell and his caravan park.'

'I have,' Jan protested, with a stab of guilt that she hadn't done more. 'I got the planning hearing put back a couple of months so that I can be there myself.'

'That's all very well, but it's the week after next, so what are you going to do about that?'

Jan looked out of the window to avoid the old woman's accusing eyes. She had meant to talk to Toby about it, but with all the activity in the yard since the horses had come back in, she had pushed the problem to the back of her mind. 'I'll be taking advice before it happens,' she said hastily, knowing that Olwen wouldn't be impressed.

'You don't care, do you, if I'm surrounded by townies and all their noise and rushing about?'

'Of course I care . . .'

'And so you should – for one thing, it'll knock thousands off the value of this place when you come to sell it after I'm gone,' Olwen muttered bitterly.

'That doesn't come into it.' Jan sighed. 'I'll do what I can and let you know.'

'Yes, well, it would be nice to hear about my grandchildren from time to time. How's Matthew been since that scare when you were away in Ireland?'

'You can see for yourself – he's absolutely fine.'

'You shouldn't be leaving your children like that.'

'Olwen, for goodness' sake – it was only measles, and it was only because my mother was so concerned for him that she thought it might be something much worse.' With an effort Jan tried to be conciliatory. 'But how have you been? How's the arthritis?'

'It'll be worse this winter, I expect,' the old woman said dismissively. 'What are you going to do about them children? Are they sill getting frozen in that caravan of yours?'

'The new house is coming on. Gerry reckons he might have the roof finished in a month or so – if I can afford the tiles, that is,' she added with a faint laugh.

Olwen gave her a withering look. 'It's not funny, taking chances with your children's health.'

Jan closed her eyes to stem the angry responses welling up in her. 'With a bit of luck, at least we'll be able to move in so that we can have Christmas there – in fact, I was hoping you might come over and join us this year.'

'Hgh,' Olwen grunted. 'And how do you think I'm going to get all the way over there – on the bus?'

'If the house is ready, I'll come and get you.' As she spoke, Jan asked herself why on earth she had issued a promise she would probably resent and find hard to keep. Guilt, she supposed.

🐎

A few days after Ben and his boss had been to Edge Farm, Jan sat in her Land Rover, a little away from the other cars outside the primary school in the next village. Megan had started there the previous autumn and, according to her teacher, was doing reasonably well. Jan knew several of the mothers who were either sitting in their cars like her, or chatting in a cluster around the main school gate as they waited for the release of the eighty children inside.

Jan felt guilty at not getting out and joining them; she'd known some of the women since her own childhood and had as much claim to being local as they had, but with the constant juggling of tasks involved in training nearly thirty racehorses she found it hard to join in all the talk about children which she guessed took up most of their time.

She couldn't help feeling a quick rush of motherly pride, though, as Megan emerged from the building, serenely indifferent to the streaming exodus of noisy children all around her. Although she was younger and smaller than most of the others, Meg's blonde head stood out, separating her from the crowd as she made her way across the playground to the furthest gate, where she knew her mother would be waiting.

'Hello, Meg,' Jan said with a big smile, as she climbed down and gave her daughter a hug. 'What have you brought home today?' She took Megan's tiny purple and blue rucksack and put it on the back seat, before lifting her up to strap her into the car seat.

'I did some drawings of Smarty,' Megan said. 'Going over all the jumps at a show.'

'On his own?' Jan asked with exaggerated disbelief.

'Don't be silly, Mummy. I'm riding him, of course!'

'Of course,' Jan murmured, as she climbed into the driver's seat. 'Right, we're off to look at some different sort of jumps this afternoon. We're meeting Bel and Joe at the race course in Worcester. We're going to gallop one of Mr O'Hagan's horses round the track with King's Archer.'

'Is that the one called Tom's Touch, which you said might go racing soon?' Megan asked. She took great pride in knowing the name of every horse in the yard.

'That's the one,' Jan laughed, impressed. 'I want to race him a week on Saturday, so I want him to get used to the course and I'm also going to check what the ground's like.'

'What do you mean, what the ground's like?'

'I'm going to enter Gale Bird to run at Worcester too, but I've never been to the course before, so I need to know if there are soft bits and harder bits. Then I can tell Billy where to go. We didn't have any horses racing during the summer because there's not been much rain and the ground's been dried up. Some horses don't seem to mind too much, though I'm not happy about it myself. Worcester's beside the River Severn, so they water the course and they say it never gets too firm there.'

In the forty minutes it took to get to the riverside course, Jan and Megan chatted continuously about the horses and school. When they arrived, Annabel and Joe Paley were already there with Tom's Touch and King's Archer still in the lorry. The clerk of the course had given them permission to gallop the horses, and as Tom's Touch had never raced on a proper track before or seen the paraphernalia that went with it, he was likely to be a bit spooked. Galloping with King's Archer, an experienced stable mate, would help to calm him and give Jan a chance to get his measure.

Tom's Touch came off the lorry with his head held high, ears pricked and eyes popping as he gazed around at the big, open expanse of green turf, the ominous looking dirty red-brick railway viaduct that strutted across one end of the course, the white rails cluttering the turf and the motley collection of buildings on the far side, where the crowds would be on a race day.

How he would react to the noise then Jan could only guess, but there was nothing more she could do about that until the day came. At least he would have seen the course and if he had galloped around it once without mishap, maybe he would approach the job with a little less fear than he might otherwise.

The gelding would be the first of O'Hagan's horses to run. At home he had shown he was fit enough to handle the more taxing conditions of a real race, and in a bumper – a National Hunt flat race, which he was about to run in – at least Jan didn't need to worry about his jumping ability.

Jan had also decided that, if the ground was right, the novice chase at the same meeting would suit Gale Bird, the good mare Toby Waller had bought from her the year before. She was almost ready to run and went best on good to firm ground.

Gale Bird and Tom's Touch would be Jan's first runners in her first full season as a professional trainer, so she wanted to start as she intended to carry on by leaving as little as possible to chance.

With Megan hanging onto her hand, she watched Annabel walk Tom's Touch up to the rails to let him have a good look and a sniff at them. When he had settled and got used to his surroundings, Joe Paley and King's Archer joined them for a short walk and trot before they broke into a canter. Eventually they set off at a good clip around the track. They went a good mile and a half, with Annabel riding Tom's Touch close to the rails when she could, so he'd learn they weren't a threat to him.

Joe, sitting quietly on King's Archer, did as Jan had told him and quickened the pace until his horse were really stretching over the final two furlongs, but Tom's Touch was still travelling well within himself.

'Whoa up! Brilliant!' Jan shouted excitedly as the horses started to ease down.

As they got back to the race-course stables, their riders jumped off. Jan was delighted, both horses still looked perfectly happy after the gallop. Annabel and Joe let out their girths and led the horses around for about fifteen minutes before Jan gave them each a small drink – six gulps and no more. She then took the bucket away, while Joe went and fetched an old milk churn filled with warm water, which they'd brought with them in the lorry. Jan hated the idea of washing down her horses with icy cold water when they were hot and sweaty.

Once the horses had dried off and been put back on the lorry, Joe stayed with them while the two women and Megan set off to look around the track.

'Why do you want to do this now?' Annabel asked.

'Because I might not get the chance the first time we run here – if we get held up on the way or something I intend to learn every bend, every hurdle and fence on each course that I'm going to run a horse on. I'm not prepared to tell a jockey what to do with just a bit of guesswork, then leave the rest to chance. No bloody fear!'

🐎

For the week following the race-course gallop and with just four days to go before her first runners of the new season, Jan was still feeling invigorated by the way Tom's Touch had worked. She had dropped off to sleep with a plan of Worcester race course firmly planted in her mind as she rewalked it in her dreams, but she woke suddenly, wondering if she would ever be able to find the restaurant where Angie Sharp had arranged to meet her for lunch.

It was a real problem, Angie insisting they should meet for lunch to discuss the horses, as if Jan had the time or even cared about having lunch in smart restaurants, but Angie had said she was far too busy to come out to the yard and would meet Jan in Cheltenham.

Setting off at half-past twelve, Jan was confident that she'd left enough instructions for the few small jobs that still needed to be done at the yard. She was in a state of heightened tension now she had committed herself to sending two horses out to race in just four days' time. She was determined that she shouldn't wreck the start of her first proper season by running horses in unsuitable races, when they were not properly prepared or being ridden by jockeys who didn't know them. She hoped Billy would be a little more co-operative when he was told what to do on the race course than he had been in the yard since the arrival of the Sharps' horses.

For the past few days Jan had been so preoccupied with her horses' imminent appearance on the race track that she hadn't given much thought to Angie Sharp. But as she drove towards Cheltenham's confusing town centre, she felt a twinge of resentment that Angie had hardly been in touch since her parents' horses had arrived. It was as if, now their relationship was that of trainer and client, there would be a new subtext to anything they said to each other.

To some extent Jan could understand this. Almost inevitably, when someone started to pay a friend a large amount of money to perform a service, that was likely to become the dominant influence in their relationship. But Angie Sharp was accustomed to her parents paying out this kind of money – evidently without too much pain – but, in one sense, Jan felt she had done her friend a favour by providing her with a very good reason to move their horses from a trainer who had quite clearly chucked in the towel.

She found Angie seated in a large, dimly lit restaurant, full of well-heeled lunchers. Angie looked up and smiled when she saw Jan weaving her way between tables towards her.

Angie was sitting with *Hello!* magazine and a bottle of mineral water on the table in front of her. Around her feet was a cluster of carrier bags with designer names.

'Hi, Jan. It's great to see you!' She stood to give Jan an airy kiss on each cheek and they sat down together.

Angie looked as composed as ever, her tanned features flawless, though a little extravagantly made up, and her lustrous dark brown hair freshly done. Jan tried to imagine her having sex in the back of an old estate car with Billy Hanks, but failed. Without thinking, she cringed.

'What was that for?' Angie leaned her head back with a bemused laugh.

'I'm sorry; it wasn't at you. I was just thinking I must look a bit of a mess.'

'So what? For God's sake, Jan, you've got plenty of other things to worry about. The only important thing in my life seems to be shopping. How sad is that?' Angie chuckled at herself this time. 'But I have got something for Matty which he'll like,' she said with the confidence of an experienced present giver as she leaned down to rummage in one of the bags at her feet. She came up holding a bright red self-propelled tractor with its own trailer and plough.

Jan smiled. 'Thanks, Ange. You're absolutely right. He'll love it. He's just at the age when he thinks tractors are the most important objects in the universe.'

'Good,' Angie said with satisfaction. 'But now, tell me how are the horses?'

Once again, Jan had the distinct feeling that the early foundations of their relationship had shifted. Maybe, she thought, it was realistic; when they discussed business they were subject to one set of rules, and for everything else there was another.

She had no qualms about describing to Angie, as a client, how her horses were doing. 'To tell you the truth, now we've had them just over a fortnight, I'm well pleased with them. We galloped King's Archer with Tom's Touch last week and they both went really nicely. He'll probably be ready to run in a couple of weeks. He's looking much better already and there's a race at Taunton that should suit him.'

Angie had taken a notebook from her bag and was writing in it. 'In future, Jan, can you tell me all the races you're thinking of entering our horses in and we'll let you know where we want to go.'

Jan felt a quick tightening in her stomach. She already knew the difficulties involved in owners wanting to plan their horses' campaigns themselves. 'The way I choose a race and decide whether or not to run in it depends on how I feel about it at the time. There are just so many things to consider: how the horse is and what the ground's like, and that can change from day to day, hour to hour, even. And I really only like to run them if the plus side is larger than the minus side.'

Angie looked back at her with a complicit grin. 'Of course you do, and of course Mum and Dad will listen to you. It's just that, as they're handing over quite a lot of money each week, they like to know exactly what the state of play is at any moment.'

'So they want me to ring up every time I might have any thoughts about whether or not to run a particular horse?'

'No, not *every* little thing, but if you could just jot down any changes and e-mail them.'

'I haven't got a clue how to do that; I haven't even got a computer and it's the last thing I intend adding to my shopping list.'

'Haven't you?' Angie looked shocked by Jan's frank admission of her lack of technical know-how.

Jan sneered. 'It won't make the horses run any faster. I'm a farmer's daughter who trains horses. Why should I need to mess around with all that sort of thing? You can't train horses by computer – they're not machines.'

'Maybe not,' Angie said, as if doubting that was true. 'But at least you could fax us a daily report on the horses and which races you're looking at for them.'

'I don't have a fax machine either.'

'We'll get you one then,' Angie said quickly. 'You might find it useful with other owners – like Mr O'Hagan. I'm sure he wants a regular report, doesn't he?'

'He said only when I think I have something worth saying,' Jan said pointedly.

'I'm sorry, Jan.' Angie tried belatedly to mollify her. 'Mum and Dad are getting on a bit and they came up the hard way, so they're very careful about any money they spend.'

Jan recognized an uncompromising firmness in Angie's manner. She wanted to resent it, but, in fairness, what Angie was saying was true. Her parents were committed to paying around fifty thousand pounds a year to Edge Farm Stables, and they had a right to know when and where the horses might be entered, if that was what they wanted.

'All right,' she said. 'If you get the fax machine and show me how to use it, I can do that.'

'I'm so pleased. Now let's just go through the horses one by one so you can tell me what you're planning to do with them.'

After an hour of detailed discussion over a meagre meal, which Jan barely noticed, Angie announced that she had to go, paid the bill and gathered up her shopping. They went out together and kissed each other on the cheek. Angie piled all her bags into her Range Rover, which she had managed somehow to park right outside without getting a ticket, while Jan went off to find her old Land Rover in a multi-storey car park.

Driving home, Jan was pleased she'd had the session with Angie. Looking at her position overall, she concluded that the shift in the balance of their relationship brought some bonuses. Although she was sure there was still a clear understanding between herself and Angie, being with Annabel would now feel a whole lot easier and at least she was beginning to learn how to deal with the Sharp family.

She was relieved, for one thing, to find out that she would mostly be dealing with Angie, which she hadn't realized at first. And once she'd accepted in her own mind that they wanted routine bulletins which didn't need to be over-elaborate, she would be totally frank with Angie about the horses' future.

There were only two horses in the Sharps' string who could be said to have any real quality: the rest might be all right as long as the races were moderate and favoured them. She had also gathered from Angie that Vince Sharp liked to have a decent bet occasionally. While Jan never bet herself – she had very little interest in that side of racing – she knew owners for whom gambling, and the possession of what they liked to think was inside information, was by far the most important reason for having a horse in training. *More fool them*, she thought. *If it's that easy, why are so many trainers standing on the gallops in the freezing cold and pouring rain every morning and living on a shoestring?*

As Jan had predicted, Matty was completely dazzled by the tractor. The next day he was playing with it in front of the caravan when Tony Robertson appeared after evening stables.

'Hi,' he said breezily, striding up from his car. 'Sorry I didn't ring. I was passing and I thought I'd just drop in on the off-chance you were here.'

'It's a pretty safe bet you'll find a mother with young kids in at this time of the evening.'

'I'll remember that.' The doctor grinned.

'But it is nice to see you.' Jan smiled back at him. 'And now I feel guilty that I never rang to thank you for that fantastic dinner you bought me – I can't believe it's two weeks ago! I'm really sorry. We've been just so busy.'

'That's OK.' Tony shook his head in understanding. 'I know what it's like.'

'I'd offer you a drink,' Jan said apologetically, 'but actually, Emma's just arrived and I'm going down to the Fox to have a drink with Annabel and to interview two girls there who rang and asked for a job.'

'Great!' the doctor countered. 'I'll come and buy you both a drink before they turn up.'

As well as seeing the girls, Jan specifically wanted to talk to Annabel about their runners at Worcester in two days' time, so while she always enjoyed Tony's company, she hoped he wouldn't hang around too long.

'All right,' she nodded. 'I'll see you there.'

Jan arrived at the pub before the doctor, and found Annabel already sitting at a table, leafing through *Horse & Hound*.

'Tony Robertson is on his way,' Jan said with raised eyebrows.

Annabel grinned. 'That's good. I think he really fancies you.'

'Maybe,' Jan said doubtfully.

'Come on, Jan,' Annabel admonished. 'Why on earth shouldn't he? He's been widowed for over a year; he's still young, fit and good-looking; and so are you.'

Jan felt a confusing pleasure at the words, as if it was the first time she'd considered the idea of a new relationship. Up until then it had been such an impossible concept that she had failed to register it at all. With Eddie, it had been something else – not platonic, more than brotherly, but definitely not a love affair.

'I really don't know about that,' she answered. 'But he's certainly young enough and good-looking – all that – and he's a wonderful doctor.'

Annabel laughed. 'The trouble is he's too much of a Goody Two-shoes for you.'

'I could get used to that. After all, John was a good, straight-forward sort of man and I was very happy with him.'

'Maybe, but I think Tony might not be tough enough for you. Although you don't take too kindly to people disagreeing with you, you don't like pushovers either.' Annabel put her head on one side. 'It's a narrow track, I can tell you.'

With a guilty grin, Jan acknowledged the truth of what Annabel was saying. 'I've just got high standards, that's all.'

'That's one way of putting it. Anyway, here's lover boy now.' Annabel nodded at the door as Tony walked in.

'Shut up,' Jan muttered under her breath as he strode across the bar with a broad smile on his face.

'Hi, girls! What do you fancy?'

'Two gin and tonics,' Annabel said promptly, smiling at Jan as Tony walked up to the bar.

He came back a few minutes later with the three drinks and sat down.

'So, what's cooking at Edge Farm?'

'We've got our first runners on Saturday,' Annabel said.

'What, first ever under rules?'

'No,' Jan said. 'We sent out a few at the end of last season and managed one winner. In a way, I wish we hadn't because it looks a bit naff in the record books, but I wanted to have a bash as soon as I had a licence.'

'What do you hope to score this season?'

'Don't ask,' Jan said. 'I don't want to tempt fate.'

'Well, best of luck on Saturday. Who's running?'

'One of Mr O'Hagan's, Tom's Touch, in the bumper, and Gale Bird in her first novice chase.'

'I seem to remember you won a couple of point-to-points with her.'

Jan nodded, impressed despite herself. 'I did; she's a decent mare, and Toby Waller, who now owns her, decided to leave her with me and try his luck under rules. I bought another new one for him in Ireland in June, though I think he only has horses as an excuse to come and see Bel.'

Tony looked at Annabel and grinned. 'You can't blame him.'

Annabel looked down and fiddled with her glass.

'And I think I've got another owner coming for the same reason.'

Annabel looked up sharply. 'Who?'

'Who do you think? Johnny Carlton-Brown, or JCB, as Ben calls him.'

'The head of Brit records?' Tony Robertson asked, impressed.

'Yes, Ben's my brother. He's come back from Australia and has just signed a production contract with Brit.'

'Your brother's a record producer?' the doctor replied dubiously.

'Yes, why shouldn't he be?'

Tony shrugged. 'No reason, I suppose; just . . . you seem so rural.'

'Thanks a lot,' Jan grinned. 'Ben and I, we're both very determined; he just happens to have followed his love of music, whereas I followed my love of horses. Anyway, he turned up here out of the blue last month. I hadn't seen him for four years. Then he brought his boss round.'

'Who's already got a horse with Virginia Gilbert,' Annabel added mischievously.

'And he rang today,' Jan went on, 'to say he's decided to buy August Moon and to ask me to get him another.'

Annabel stuck her chin out and stared at Jan. 'You never told me that.'

'I haven't had a chance, have I? He said he wants a proven young hurdler that can go on and make a top-class chaser. And he doesn't mind paying for the right horse.'

'That's fantastic!' Annabel burst out as her face flushed.

'What?' Jan chuckled. 'Getting two more horses or having JCB as an owner?'

'Both, I suppose,' Annabel admitted with a self-conscious grin.

🐎

Two days later, while riding out with the first lot through a crisp, sunny dawn, Jan tried hard to pretend it was just another normal day, but there was no escaping the buzz around the yard. Everything they'd been working for since the horses had come back into training two months earlier was about to come to fruition. From now until next summer, unless the yard fell victim to an outbreak of equine flu or some other virus, they would probably be sending horses out to race several days a week.

All the staff wanted to go to Worcester, but someone had to stay behind to look after the yard and the children until they got back from the races. Jan decided the only way to deal with it fairly was to draw straws. Joe Paley and Emma accepted their fate with good humour, especially now that Jan had the Racing Channel installed on the television in the office, which would allow them to watch the races live.

The novice chase was the second on the card, at two o'clock, and the bumper was the last race, due off at four. Jan, anxious that nothing should upset the day, instructed her staff to start loading both horses at ten-thirty. She wanted them to arrive at the course in plenty of time for them to be stabled, settle down, have a pee and get used to their surroundings. She also wanted to walk the course again, this time with Billy Hanks.

Billy had been up to the yard most days to ride out and was a little more subdued than normal. He'd already had several rides for other trainers, but usually on the second strings – horses that were only out for a school round; he said. He'd been in the frame a few times, but he hadn't yet ridden a winner.

Jan wasn't as worried about it as Billy. She was well aware that trainers wouldn't risk putting him up on their best horses until they'd seen he had what it takes to make the transition from being an amateur to a good professional jockey.

Looking through the list of runners for Gale Bird's race, she felt they stood a good chance of being placed, despite the bookies' predictions of 12–1 and more. Billy knew exactly how to ride Gale Bird, he had already won three races on her between the flags the previous season, and had regularly schooled her over fences during the last few weeks. As far as Jan could see, the mare was as fit as she could be for her first race of the season. But Billy was suffering from a crisis in his now very fragile confidence, so she asked Annabel to drive the lorry while she travelled with him in his Subaru.

'This is it, Billy,' she said, as they turned out onto the lane at the bottom of the drive. 'You and I have known one another and worked together for a bloody long time, but this is the big time, where the stakes are considerably higher at every level. I expect you're beginning to find that out now.'

'Of course I am.'

Jan nodded. 'On the point-to-point circuit you were a big fish in a small pond. Now you're one of the minnows, but don't let that get you down. In a way, it takes the pressure off. No one's expecting anything of you.'

'You are,' Billy grunted.

'Billy, I'm only expecting what I know you can do and, I can assure you, I'm not at all worried. Gale Bird will give you a great ride, she settles easily and she's totally genuine.'

'I know, I know, but there's a lot of bloody good jocks out there today.'

'It's the horse that wins, unless you do something to stop her from doing so.'

'Obviously I'm not going to do that, am I?'

'So just give us the best you can. You're very lucky to have the ride on Tom's Touch. If Murty McGrath hadn't been booked for his retained yard, he'd be riding him, but Mr O'Hagan says he's happy for you to have the chance this time.'

'Will A.D. be there?'

'I don't know,' Jan said, not entirely hiding her frustration. She had learned from Eamon Fallon that A.D. seldom committed himself to being anywhere because he hated to make arrangements he couldn't honour. 'Anyway,' she went on, 'Tom's Touch seems to have bags of ability, so provided you can get him settled early on, you should be all right.'

'Do you think he's got a chance?'

'He's a really nice horse and hardly any of the runners have ever been on a course before, so it's anyone's guess. I know A.D. thinks a lot of him and he's as good a judge as most.' Jan glanced at Billy and was alarmed to see he was as white as a ghost. 'For God's sake, what's the matter with you? There really isn't too much for you to worry about. Leave that to me.'

'I don't bloody know, Jan,' he mumbled. 'When my dad told me I was wasting my time turning professional and I'd never make any money out of it, I told him there was no way I'd be doing it if I couldn't make a success of it.' He stopped and bit his lip. 'But now I just don't know . . .'

'Billy, pull yourself together! You know damn well that you

can ride. You've proved it dozens of times. You just haven't had quality horses to ride since you turned pro. That's all. Today you've got two fit animals and you can do it. I *know* you can.'

Jan wished she felt half as certain as she sounded, but she knew she dare not let Billy detect any slight doubt in his current condition. She'd always known his ego was built on shaky ground, although she hadn't appreciated how much the lack of an early winner had affected his confidence.

When they arrived at the busy race course alongside the River Severn, there was no sign of Annabel or the lorry, which had set off some time before they had. Jan wasn't unduly worried. Annabel was a cautious driver with horses and they had plenty of leeway. But Billy was still looking as bad as ever, and she thought the sooner he had a little exercise and fresh air the better it would be for him.

'Right, you and I are going to walk the course,' she said, clambering out of his car.

'I've already walked it,' he muttered.

'Maybe you have, but today you're riding it for me for the first time. I want to discuss the approach to every fence with you, and find the best ground.'

'When it comes to it, I may not have any choice in the matter,' Billy said, disgruntled. 'And I'm not going to walk the bloody course again.'

Jan stopped in her tracks. Billy carried on walking for a couple of paces before he realized she wasn't with him. He stopped and turned.

Jan fixed him with an icy glare. 'Listen to me, Billy. If you want to carry on as stable jockey, I can tell you right now I'm not putting up with this crap. I've done everything *I* can to get these horses here in the best possible shape; I'm not having *you* let the side down just because you're feeling a bit sorry for yourself and you can't handle the fact that you're not the only star in the universe. When you're riding for me you do as I say, and if I say we're walking the sodding course, you and I are walking the course. Do you understand? Unless, of course, you haven't got the balls.'

Jan held his eye, hardly daring to breathe while she waited to see if the message had struck home. She had suddenly realized all too clearly that if she was going to make a stand, she had to do it now, and not a day later.

I need this fiasco today like an effing hole in the head, she thought.

But when she saw Billy's shoulders sag, she knew the message was on target.

'All right.' He sighed truculently. 'Let's get on with it.'

By the time they had walked a circuit of the track, Jan felt certain Billy had learned something from the exercise. He had changed his view of how to approach the open ditch and he'd seen for himself where the better ground lay coming off the bend into the home straight.

'OK, Jan,' he said. 'I'll see you in the weighing room.'

He strode off to collect his kitbag from his car. Jan watched and thought that he had regained some of his confidence as a result of their confrontation. She made her way across the course to the area reserved for horseboxes and in the distance she spotted her own navy and timber box. Annabel was already lowering the heavy ramp, helped by Roz and Karen.

Once the horses were off, with Tom's Touch having a thorough look at everything around him, the girls led them into the race-course stables, followed by Jan and Annabel, who handed over their security passes and signed the register.

'Any problems on the way?' she asked.

Annabel shook her head. 'None at all. I just took it slowly.'

'That's OK,' Jan nodded approvingly. 'I never got the chance to ask you what you thought of those two girls we saw last night.'

'They were fine, but I thought the doctor was never going to leave. He's a bit eager to please, isn't he? Which is rather odd, when he's so attractive?'

'Not all attractive men are selfish pigs with oversized egos,' Jan said defensively. 'I admit he's a bit submissive for me, but sometimes that's not such a bad thing.'

'No, I agree. Anyway those girls – Alice and Heidi; both ex-Cheltenham Ladies',' Annabel laughed. 'That's territory I know well; but I wonder if they'll actually stick the job when it comes down to it.'

'You did,' Jan observed.

'Yes, but I'd already learned a few lessons in life by then,' Annabel said. 'These two looked as if they'd pass out if you asked them to heave a bale.'

'You're no Arnie Schwarzenegger, but you manage all right.'

'You obviously liked the look of them,' Annabel shrugged.

'Provided they shape up and can ride.'

'We'll soon see when they come in tomorrow. We certainly need a couple more good riders. By the way, did you persuade Billy to walk the course?'

'Yes. Why?'

'Because he was grumbling when you mentioned it early this morning. If you don't mind me saying so, he's developed a bit of a rebellious streak.'

'Yes, well.' Jan sighed. 'That wasn't helped by what happened at the open day.'

'Do you think anything really did happen?' Annabel asked. 'I mean, from what I've seen of Angie, it seems pretty odd for someone like her to jump into bed with the likes of Billy.'

'It wasn't even bed, was it? Anyway, I don't know what happened, nothing, I hope. Angie hasn't told me and I haven't asked. But, as far as Billy's concerned, I told him he could either walk the course or sod off. In the end, I think he was bloody glad he made the choice he did.'

'How do you think we'll get on today?'

Jan shook her head. 'I don't know. I think Gale Bird could run into a place. Look at her – she's jumping out of her skin and really looking forward to it. Tom's Touch, I'm not sure. He doesn't know a lot, but I'm hopeful.'

'He looks pretty good and he's worked well at home.'

'Thanks, Bel.' Jan grinned at Annabel's proprietorial pride. 'Remind Roz and Karen to sign the register at the security office or I'll be in hot water before we get under starter's orders.'

🐎

When she was satisfied that all was well, Jan set off for the weighing room and caught a glimpse of the river, glittering under the sun as some swans glided across its placid surface. People were beginning to stream across the course and through the racecourse gates, filling up the bars and enclosures. Jan knew nothing would stop Toby from coming to see Gale Bird run, but she desperately hoped that A.D. would also put in an appearance.

When Jan finally reached the weighing room, she declared her two runners and checked with Billy's valet that he had both sets of colours. Several people called out a greeting or gave her a friendly nod. Worcester was in her home territory and for the first time since she had received her licence she felt that she wasn't a complete outsider.

With a little more spring in her step she made her way back to the stables to see how Annabel and Roz were getting on with their preparations. Gale Bird might only have been running in a novice chase for a prize of less than three thousand pounds, but Jan had told the girls she wanted the horse looking as if she was parading for the Cheltenham Gold Cup.

🐎

Forty-five minutes before their race was due to start, Roz led Gale Bird across the race course from the stables, with Karen carrying a bag of spare girths and a string cooler. While the preceding race was being run, Roz continued to lead her charge round the pre-parade ring to stretch her legs and loosen her up. Immediately the first race was over, Jan arrived from the weighing room with Billy's saddle and Roz led the horse into one of the saddling boxes.

Jan unbuckled the leather roller and draped it over her

shoulder, then she folded back the paddock sheet and buckled the strap of the breast girth over the horse's neck. Carefully she placed a chamois leather, a felt pad, the weight cloth, the number cloth and finally the saddle on Gale Bird's back. Roz swung the girth under the mare's belly to Jan, who buckled it up and threaded the straps of the breast girth under the saddle flaps to the girth. Jan then put a surcingle over the saddle and tightened it until she was confident it was secure. She then lifted each of Gale Bird's front legs in turn to stretch the skin out from under the girths and to make sure nothing was pinching.

Jan pulled the sheet back over the tack and put the paddock number on top, before securing it with the roller, while Roz took a sponge from a bucket of water and squeezed it inside Gale Bird's mouth to moisten it.

'Right, lady. You look wonderful,' Jan said.

'She does, doesn't she,' said Roz proudly. 'And look, here's her dad!'

Jan glanced up and was pleased to see Toby, accompanied by an elegant looking older woman.

'Hi, Toby! Glad you could make it.'

Toby leaned down and gave Jan a kiss. 'I wouldn't miss this for the world. I've even persuaded my mother to come and she doesn't usually race anywhere except Royal Ascot. Mum, this is Jan Hardy: Isabel Waller.'

Jan shook Mrs Waller's gloved hand and hoped she wouldn't leave it smelling too strongly of horse.

'Well, Toby, what do you think?' Jan asked.

Toby stepped back to get a better view of his mare. 'She looks amazing – even better than she did at your open day and a great deal slimmer. Maybe I should go on the same diet,' he chuckled.

'Only if you're prepared to gallop a mile and a half up Stanfield Bank every couple of days,' Jan warned.

'I'll pass on that. What do you think of her chances? The papers say twelve to one.'

'Fortunately she can't read newspapers, but I reckon that's good value. You know I don't give owners tips, and we really haven't got much to go on in a novice chase this early in the season. It all depends on how well they jump.'

'I think a bit each way, then, at that price and with sixteen runners.'

'Well, that's up to you,' Jan said, as she always did to gambling owners. 'Anyway, it's time to get to the parade ring. Are you and your mother coming in?'

'We certainly are.'

They made their way into the main ring, where Roz had already led Gale Bird from the saddling box.

'I see you're running a young horse of O'Hagan's in the bumper,' Mrs Waller remarked to Jan. 'I should think he's a pretty formidable man to train for.'

'So far he's been really nice. This will be my first runner for him, so I don't know what he'll be like if it doesn't win.'

'A.D.'s far too experienced to make a scene because a horse hasn't won,' Toby said.

'I know he thinks a lot of this one. Anyway, let's hope we won't have to find out how he reacts today,' Jan sighed. 'Actually, the horse is pretty impressive at home. When I galloped him here a week last Monday he went brilliantly, but I haven't a clue what the other horses in his race are like.'

'Bumpers are often lotteries,' Toby said, 'but best of luck. I shall certainly back him.'

They were now standing in the middle of the parade ring, where most of the horses competing against Gale Bird were being led round.

'Our girl's nice and calm,' Toby remarked, studying the other runners.

'A bit too calm, if you ask me,' Jan croaked, suddenly feeling rather queasy. Now there was nothing more she could do to help her runners, she could only hope and pray.

Billy Hanks still looked a little green, as he walked into the ring with a short, uncertain stride, wearing Toby's black and silver diabolos with silver sleeves and a black cap.

'Very chic colours, Toby dear,' his mother said.

'I'm glad you like them. Annabel helped me choose.'

Jan shot a glance at Toby, and at Annabel, standing next to her. This was the first she'd heard of it.

Billy shook hands with Toby and Mrs Waller, then stood facing Jan. 'What do you think, Mrs H?'

'As we decided this morning. She'll like the ground; but be careful of that boggy bit coming off the final bend, otherwise stay handy towards the inside – you don't want to get baulked by any of the others. I wouldn't be surprised if half this lot fail to complete.'

Billy nodded. 'She can jump all right.'

'And she's as fit as we can get her, so you just do your best.'

'Best of luck, Billy,' Toby added, with a friendly grin. 'I've got you doubled today.'

A few moments later there was a general commotion as all sixteen hyped-up horses were stopped and turned inwards by their handlers, and the jockeys were legged into the saddle. For another minute or two they jig-jogged around the parade ring, until they were led out onto the course one by one and freed to canter down to the start of the two-mile four-furlong chase.

Jan glanced at the stands, which were already packed. 'We might just as well watch from there, on the steps in front of the weighing room,' she said, trying to control the nervous quiver in her voice.

Jan lifted her binoculars to see Billy and Gale Bird quietly circling around behind the starting gate. Although in the parade ring she had been slightly worried that the horse was too calm, she was pleased it wasn't using up any more energy than necessary by pulling and fighting the jockey.

With such a large field of inexperienced runners, the starter took a while to call them into line and eventually let them go three minutes after the scheduled start.

As the runners made their way to the first fence, Jan saw Toby's silver and black colours on the inside lying around sixth.

Most of the field sailed over the plain fence without mishap, but one at the back of the field refused and 'carried' another outside the wing with it.

For the first half mile Jan guessed that they were travelling no faster than they would have galloped on an easy day along the top ridge at home, which would take very little out of Gale Bird. After they had swung round the long left-handed bend into the straight and passed in front of the stands, Jan was able to see clearly that Billy had the mare well placed and she was still travelling comfortably on the bit. As they turned away, down the far side, Gale Bird moved up and was now lying fourth.

Toby, standing beside Jan, put his head down towards her. 'What do you think?' he asked hoarsely.

'They couldn't be better placed at the moment. She's not under any pressure. But there are still six more fences to jump, a lot can happen from here on in.'

Jan was beginning to feel more confident than she dared admit. So far the mare hadn't made a single mistake at any of the fences. Billy knew her well and just how to place her. Even at this shorter distance it was obvious that she was still travelling really well as the black and silver colours moved up another slot.

The field was beginning to spread out now and there were only six in the leading bunch, which had gone ten lengths clear of the rest, going to the final fence in the back straight. Jan gasped. Gale Bird had stood off a full stride before the second horse; passing it in the air, she landed at full tilt and was now just a neck down on the leader.

Toby was already yelling madly. Jan glanced at the look of astonished excitement on his big red face, and it brought home to her what this business was all about. She just prayed his mare had the courage and stamina to get past the leader. Round the long curve towards home the horses raced head to head.

Jan held her breath. Gale Bird was just in front when a sudden interjection in the race-course commentary made her swing her glasses back a few yards.

'. . . *and Prussian Bear is making headway and closing fast.*'

Prussian Bear had started favourite, and had Murty McGrath, the champion jockey, on board.

'Billy, look out!' Jan yelled without realizing it.

Gale Bird reached the final fence just in front, but Murty McGrath had been playing his superior, nerve-racking waiting game and had known exactly when to produce his horse and with a classic surge he and Prussian Bear passed Gale Bird fifty yards from the winning post.

Early elation from the sudden promise of so much, only to have it snatched away in the final moment, left Jan limp with exhaustion and disappointment. She squeezed her eyes shut and tried despareately to come to terms with the drama that had just taken place, until she felt a pair of chubby arms around her in a massive, ecstatic bear hug.

'Jan – that was absolutely *fantastic!*' Toby chortled. 'I promise you, I nearly wet myself in the last furlong.'

'Toby!' Mrs Waller admonished.

'It's OK, Mother. Just a figure of speech. Jan, I can't tell you how delighted I am.'

'She did run well,' Jan said more calmly. 'I'm sorry she didn't win, though.'

'She bloody nearly did. But yer man, the champion, he did his usual trick. And I'm not blaming Billy one iota. He rode a super race!'

'Yes,' Jan agreed. 'He did, but he'll be bloody raging. He'll think he was caught napping.'

'Well, I'll tell him I'm very pleased, very pleased indeed! And I've got three to one for my place bet plus some prize money!' Toby crowed.

As Jan had predicted, Billy Hanks was furious he hadn't won, but it was clear to her that finishing so close had gone a long way to helping to restore his confidence, although Jan wasn't at all sure whether this would help his performance on Tom's Touch later in the afternoon. In the meantime, he had picked up a spare ride in the novice hurdle, the race before the bumper.

Toby and his mother had been overjoyed at seeing his horse in the second slot. Eventually Jan left them to go and have a drink while she went to make sure the mare was unscathed. Roz had sluiced her down with warm water, scraped off the excess and covered her with a string cooler before she walked her round to keep her muscles from stiffening up while she dried.

Jan checked that Karen knew what time to bring Tom's Touch over, then made her way back to the owners' and trainers' bar, where she had promised to rejoin the others.

'I'm sure,' Toby said, filling the glasses from the bottle he had just bought, 'there's some unwritten rule or taboo lurking in the folklore of racing that precludes the drinking of champagne when one's horse has only come second – but too bloody bad! I'd still have wanted to celebrate if she'd finished the course at the back of the field.'

'You do love your horse, don't you,' Annabel said affectionately.

'Of course I do! Wouldn't you?'

'I do. I've got my own, remember.'

'How could I ever forget Eddie Sullivan and Russian Eagle leaping over that last fence at Aintree? When will he be ready to run again? The horse that is, not Eddie,' he added with a slightly inebriated laugh.

'Not for a while; he got so big during the summer. But we really think we could go somewhere special with him this year, don't we, Jan?'

Jan nodded. 'After the way he went round Aintree. Do you know, A.D.'s horse won in a hell of a good time, and Eagle would have been a good couple of seconds faster.'

'Let's face it, ridden by a rank amateur, too. So, what do you think?' Toby pressed. 'One of the Nationals?'

Jan tilted her head to one side. 'Maybe. We'll have to see.'

'Well, come on, drink up! Here's to Gale Bird and Tom's Touch.'

Jan found she couldn't pay much attention to the next two races, although she was well aware that it was now part of her job to keep a sharp eye on the form of runners from other yards. But she couldn't help wondering if A.D. was going to turn up.

Somehow she had convinced herself that, if he didn't, it would mean Edge Farm, as Toby had already said, was just one of a host of interests he had. Still, at least he had come to the open day, and it was true he didn't attend every race meeting where he had a runner – especially as he often had them at two or three different race courses on the same day and in different countries.

She talked to Annabel about it, not for the first time since they'd both left home that morning.

'After all,' she said. 'this is my first runner for him, with a horse he seems to think has a great chance of winning. I think it would be damn rude of him not to turn up.'

'Stop getting in a state over it,' Annabel tried to reassure her. 'He's a very busy man; he's committed a lot of good horses to you as well as standing guarantor for your business. I'm sure, if it didn't interfere with his business activities or other things, he would come.'

Jan sighed. 'Yes, I know you're right. I just feel . . .' Jan tried to get a grip on her emotions. 'It really is such a big day for me – I mean, we've had quite a good result so far, but it's just so important we get A.D. off to a good start.'

'Of course it is, but it won't make any difference if he's here or not. It won't make his horse run any faster, and it'd probably only make you feel even more nervous – have you thought of that? Now, let's go and watch Billy riding in the hurdle race. Roz will be over with Tom's Touch soon.'

🐎

Billy Hanks rode as good a race as possible on a moderate horse, finishing fifth some twenty lengths behind the winner. Jan followed him to the weighing room. 'How do you feel?' she asked.

'OK,' Billy said neutrally.

'You rode that last race just fine. It was a moderate horse, that's all.'

Billy nodded. 'I'm well aware of that.'

'Well, at least you haven't got any jumping to worry about in this next one.'

'That never worries me.'

Jan gave up. 'Fine, Billy. You get your tack. I'll see you back here when you have weighed out.' She left and went to the pre-parade ring to see if their runner was there and settling down.

Tom's Touch was striding around the pre-parade ring beside Karen, looking around in the same way he had last time he'd been there when the course was empty. Jan was pleased to see that he seemed more fascinated than frightened; there was nothing in his movements to suggest he was feeling nervous. Satisfied, Jan went back to collect Billy's tack.

When Karen saw her with the saddle, she turned and led Tom into an empty stall. While Jan was putting on the saddle, she couldn't help feeling pleased with the condition Tom was in. Every muscle felt firm and there wasn't a pound of spare flesh on him.

Jan had checked his girth for the last time and was drawing the paddock sheet back over the saddle when she became conscious of a small group of people talking outside the box.

She glanced sideways.

'Hello, Jan.' A.D. said, studying the horse with a faint smile on his face. 'I knew this fella would make up. He's matured since I last saw him.'

Jan straightened her back and walked out to greet him. 'He does look good, doesn't he?'

Almost absently, A.D. leaned over and kissed her on one cheek. 'Has he been working well?'

'I told you about the gallop we did here. I gave him a piece of sharp work on Wednesday and it took nothing out of him.' Jan shrugged. 'He's in real good order so it just depends on what we are up against.'

'They're not a great bunch,' A.D. said quietly.

Jan didn't underestimate the research that lay behind the comment. It excited and terrified her at the same time.

If there really wasn't any strong opposition, there was a good chance Tom's Touch could win, but if he didn't A.D. would be very disappointed indeed.

There was a studied calmness in his demeanour that made her think he already had a lot of money riding on the horse, and no doubt, in view of the animal's visible fitness, more would be added.

'I hope you're right,' she said.

There was a sudden flare, almost instantly extinguished in the Irishman's eyes at the suggestion that there could be any doubt about the quality of his information.

'So do I,' he said mildly, as he walked up to the horse and fondled its nose.

Jan looked at A.D. more closely. He was wearing a yellow silk scarf around his neck, tucked into a spotless, pale, calf-length coat. His thick black wavy hair was as neatly trimmed and brushed as if he had just stepped out of a barber's. On his feet, the usual nut-brown brogues gleamed discreetly, untouched somehow by the muddy race course.

Standing back, also looking at the horse, were Jimmy O'Driscoll and a man Jan had never seen before.

Jan nodded at O'Driscoll. 'Hello, Jimmy. Just over from Ireland?'

'That's right, on the ferry.'

Jan remembered that A.D. wouldn't fly, which required him to be constantly chauffeured at high speed around the two islands. She guessed that meant his appearance at this race meeting really was significant.

'Where are you going after this?' she asked curiously.

'A.D. has business in London tonight.'

'I'm really glad he made it here.'

'He wasn't going to come, but we always have the racing on in the back of the car and when we saw your horse run in

second, and that jockey of yours put up such a good performance, he changed his mind.' O'Driscoll nodded once to underline
the significance of what he'd said.

A.D. meanwhile walked round the horse, giving it a thorough
inspection, then emerged from the box looking quietly satisfied.

'Right, Jan,' he said, 'it's time you had him in the parade
ring.'

There was a noticeable murmur of interest when Jan walked into
the parade ring with A.D. and Jimmy O'Driscoll. Jan was well
aware that a lot of punters might have thought it highly significant that A.D. had turned up at a small track like Worcester to
watch his horse run in a modest race. She guessed the bookies
had already marked Tom's Touch down a few points on the
strength of it.

When Karen led the horse into the main ring, Jan saw that
most people's eyes immediately turned to him. As she watched
him walking round, she didn't think there was another horse
there to match him.

Billy Hanks appeared, preening himself a little in A.D.'s
famous colours of blue and yellow stripes. He bounced over to
Jan's group and shook hands with A.D.

'You gave your horse a good ride in the novice chase,' A.D.
said, nodding his approval. 'But you let Murty sneak up on you.
If you want my advice, take the video home with you and watch
how he did it. You haven't to know just how to win races; you
need to know how to steal them too.'

For an uncomfortable moment Jan thought Billy was going to
say something to justify himself, but it appeared that even Billy
realized it would be unwise to bandy words with A.D.

'I'll get the video, sir,' he mumbled. 'Thanks a lot.'

'And now, give my horse a good ride, and he'll give you one
– OK?' A.D. gave the jockey a totally unexpected wink. 'Do you
have anything else for him, Mrs Hardy?'

'We talked the race through when we walked the course this morning,' Jan said and Billy nodded.

'Right,' A.D. said. 'Time to get going.'

🐎

Jan stood beside A.D., Jimmy O'Driscoll and the unnamed, as yet silent, third man on the steps in front of the weighing room.

She noticed that none of them seemed to have any inclination to speak, perhaps on the grounds that whatever they said could be heard and possibly used by the people milling around within earshot. She also realized that they took their racing very seriously and any light-hearted banter or gossip was out of the question.

They watched in silence as the horses made their way down to the two-mile start. As Jan raised her binoculars to her eyes, she found her hands shaking so much she could hardly see through them. She gritted her teeth and wondered if A.D. could sense her anxiety.

The starter called the eighteen runners into line and got them off quickly but rather unevenly. Tom's Touch was lying almost last as the field settled down. However, in the first two furlongs, Jan saw A.D.'s blue and yellow stripes begin to move steadily through the field on the outside, attracting the attention of the race-course commentator. Jan stole a glance at A.D. Not a muscle moved in his face as he stared through his binoculars.

On the wide outside, it was difficult to gauge how much ground Tom's Touch was making on the others. As they passed the grandstand for the first time, Billy had already moved up six or seven places.

'Steady, boy,' A.D. muttered.

Jan wondered what he expected Billy to do. He had managed to improve his position without overexerting his horse and he still had the whole of the back straight to use his horse's greater speed and get even closer to the leaders.

Billy did exactly as Jan had predicted and, by the time they had turned into the final bend, he had moved into fourth place.

He quietly tracked the leaders into the home straight, where he moved his horse out wide and without any fuss, leaning forward, he squeezed the horse's ribs with his legs, urging Tom's Touch to quicken. They cruised effortlessly past the leader and at the line they were twenty lengths clear of the second.

A huge cheer greeted the winner and Jan guessed the horse had been heavily backed in the final minutes before the off, and not only by A.D. She glanced at the owner and was immensely relieved to see a big, satisfied grin on his face, which she had never seen before – welcome proof that he was as human as anyone when his horses won.

After all, she asked herself, what would be the point of having horses in training if you didn't enjoy the victories?

10

Jan still hadn't come down from the elation she'd felt after their triumph when Annabel and Karen arrived at work the next morning.

It was policy on Sundays that only horses which were going to run on Monday or Tuesday were ridden out to exercise. While the previous day's runners were led out for a quiet walk, all the others still had to be mucked out, fed, watered and quickly tidied over. Jan had also arranged for Alice and Heidi, the two girls she and Annabel had interviewed earlier in the week, to be at the yard for nine so she could show them what the job entailed and see how well they rode.

But by half-past ten, when the work was finished, there was still no sign of them. Jan sat with Annabel and Karen in her makeshift office, drinking coffee and, for the umpteenth time, watched the video of Tom's Touch's winning race.

'It's a pity A.D. had to go off so soon afterwards,' Annabel remarked. 'I had a sneaky feeling he wanted to stay and celebrate.'

'But Jimmy told me he hadn't even planned to come, so I suppose we should be feeling really honoured – especially as we bloody won!' Jan added a triumphant whoop. 'Actually, it was nice to see him looking so human for a change.'

'My dad said he'd probably won about fifty grand,' the normally silent Karen said.

'Sure, he likes a bet, but I reckon it was seeing his horse win that mattered most.' Jan looked at her watch. 'Right, these girls

196

are well over an hour late. If they can't even make it on time for their trial, they can forget about working here.'

Annabel nodded. 'I didn't think they were very committed, but we still desperately need a couple more people.'

'I know we do. Only yesterday I was telling Jimmy O'Driscoll how hard it is to find capable riders and he said there's a couple of good lads at Aigmont who are keen to come and work in England. He said if I was interested to let him know.'

'Great,' Annabel said. 'I think it would be really nice to have a couple of Irish lads around the place.'

'Irish?' Karen said, screwing up her skinny face. 'I don't think so, they talk funny.'

'Well, you needn't worry, Karen. They won't eat you. In fact, you'll love 'em!' Jan laughed, then cocked her ear at the sound of a car coming up the drive. 'Here are those girls now.' She started to get up.

Annabel beat her to the door. 'It's OK, Jan, leave it to me,' she said. 'I'll tell them to forget it.'

🐎

At midday Jan strapped the children into the back of Annabel's Golf and they set off for Overmere, the Sharps' house in Somerset. The day after Jan had met her in Cheltenham, Angie had phoned to invite them to lunch, and said she thought it would be a good idea if Jan brought her assistant along as well.

Jan was pleased that Annabel was with her, despite her earlier doubts about how Bel and Angie would get on. She felt Annabel possessed the kind of subtlety that would be useful in dealing with oddballs like the Sharps.

'Where are we going, Mum?' Megan asked.

'I told you, to Angie's house, to see her mother and father.'

'They came to our caravan, didn't they? They looked very old and wrinkled.'

Jan chuckled. 'Shhh, don't you dare let them know you think so.'

'As long as they don't try to kiss me.'

'It's OK, I don't think they will.'

'I don't like old people kissing me, except I don't mind Grandma Hardy.'

Annabel smiled at Megan. 'Is she nice to you, then?'

'Yes, she gives us sweets and lots of toys.'

'Olwen's a canny old thing,' Jan observed. 'And she's amazingly good at knowing what they like.'

'Didn't you go over to Stonewall and see her the other day?' Annabel asked.

'Two weeks ago,' Jan answered. 'And this week Harold Powell's application to put a caravan park on the bottom field comes up in front of the planning committee.'

'What are you going to do about it?'

'I've spoken to Toby, and he's arranging for it to be adjourned again so that they can do some sort of "environmental impact assessment".'

'What will that do?'

'He says it might swing it in our favour. In the meantime he's offered to get his own surveyors to look over the application for me.'

'He's such a nice guy, Toby, isn't he?'

Jan looked at Annabel's perfect profile as she concentrated on the motorway ahead. 'He likes you too, Bel,' she said softly.

🐎

'This must be it,' Jan said an hour later, looking up from the map on her knees at the pair of massive black wrought-iron gates and bizarre neo-gothic gatehouse in front of them.

'It's very small,' Megan said disappointedly. 'You said it was a huge house.'

'That's not their house, Meg,' Annabel said. 'That's just the lodge. In the old days someone would have lived there, just to see who had arrived and to open the gates for them.'

'How the hell do we get them open today, though?' Jan asked.

'Look, there's some kind of entry-phone set in the gate post.

I'll go and press it.' Annabel got out of the car and walked up to a small stainless-steel panel set in one of the moss-clad stone pillars.

She spoke into the apparatus and a few moments later the gates started to swing open.

Annabel got back into the car with a grin. 'This is a bit like visiting the Addams family.'

She drove through the gates and onto a weed-covered drive, which snaked between walls of rampant rhododendron against a backdrop of towering Wellingtonias and Scots pines. After a hundred yards, they drove into parkland, railed with rusty iron fencing, and got their first view of a rambling Victorian mansion standing in front of a glittering lake.

'Ugh!' Megan wailed. 'It's grim! I don't want to go in there. It looks like a witch's house.'

'Don't be silly, Meg. It'll be fine inside, just you wait and see.'

Annabel grimaced. 'It does look fairly creepy, though.'

The strangely forbidding gothic house looked a little more down to earth when they pulled up in front of a cavernous porch beside Angie's Range Rover and a gleaming dark-blue Rolls-Royce.

Inside the porch, they stood in front of a tall, arched, oak door. With Matty standing beside her clutching one hand tightly, Jan tugged on the old brass bell pull beside the door and was answered by a distant tinkling.

The door was flung open by Angie, who beamed a welcome at them, immediately dispelling the vague sense of dread that was creeping over Jan.

'Hello, everyone!' she said. 'Glad you found us all right. Hello, Matty, how are you? And Megan. I've found some really nice toys for you to play with. And you can go swimming if you want to.'

'Where's the swimming pool?' Megan asked doubtfully, remembering the lake she'd just seen.

'It's in the old conservatory at the back of the house.' Angie turned to Jan and Annabel. 'It was the one thing I told Mum and

Dad they had to put in if they expected me to spend any time here.' She grinned.

She ushered them through the door as she spoke and they found themselves in a large, gloomy hall with a tiled floor cluttered with suits of armour, big oak coffers and chairs upholstered with armorial tapestry.

'Sorry it's a bit dark in here, but Mum and Dad won't change anything in this part of the house. It's a bit more civilized at the back.'

Vince and Dawn were standing by a blazing log fire, waiting for their guests in the long drawing room, which overlooked the park and the lake. Despite the gothic arched windows, the room was furnished with modern sofas and tables, a large television and a modern sound system.

Dawn seemed quite composed and surprisingly at home in the extraordinary house. Vince, however, looked distinctly uncomfortable.

He was wearing a loud tweed suit and a checked shirt two sizes too big for him with the collar hanging round his neck like a lifebelt.

Nevertheless, he made an effort to greet them as he shook hands with Jan and Annabel in turn. ''Ello, I 'ope you had a good drive down.'

'Fine, thanks,' Jan said. 'This is my assistant trainer, Annabel Halstead. She wasn't in the yard when you came to look round.'

'We read about her in the brochure.' Dawn spoke for the first time.

Vince nodded, but seemed reluctant to say more for the moment.

'You've already met my children, Megan and Matthew.'

The Sharps nodded at them without showing much interest.

'I'll show them where they can play,' Angie said, taking both children by the hand and leading them out of the room.

'Would you like a drink?' Dawn asked.

'Yes, please. A G and T,' Jan said.

'Just a tonic for me, please. I'm driving,' Annabel said with a martyred look.

'You get them, Vince,' Mrs Sharp ordered. 'I'll show them the pictures.'

Vince hobbled out of the room while Dawn walked up to a wall panel, which she pushed back to reveal an adjoining room. She beckoned Jan and Annabel through.

They found themselves in a room with tall, shuttered windows and a high, ornate ceiling. A dozen stags' heads on the upper walls were gazing down at them. Below these the walls were covered with around a hundred equestrian paintings of a bewildering variety.

Jan knew a little about fine art, from the pictures John had and from what Eddie had told her about his experiences as an art dealer. She found she recognized the style and quality of several of them.

'What a wonderful collection,' Annabel said, obviously impressed. 'Did you collect them all?'

'Vince has been getting them since he was a kid. His dad was a horseman and gave him a few, and he always had a good nose for 'em.'

'Some of them look really quite important,' Annabel said, trying to disguise her disbelief. 'That one looks like a Stubbs!' she added, pointing at a large canvas.

Dawn nodded. 'That's right. Worth plenty of money,' she said, leaning in confidentially. 'That's why we don't show them to too many people. I don't mind you seeing them, as you've got our horses, but don't go telling the world about them or Mr Sharp'll get very aereated.'

'No, of course not,' Jan said, more puzzled than ever by the Sharps' extraordinary set-up.

At that moment Vince Sharp appeared in the doorway holding two glasses, which he handed to his guests.

'D'you like 'em?' he asked, nodding his head around the room at his collection. It was obvious he was very proud of his pictures.

'They're really nice,' Jan said, feeling that was an inadequate description. 'Where did you find them all?'

Vince shrugged his skinny shoulders. 'All over. Sales, house clearances and such. And people sometimes bring them to me.'

Annabel was walking around the room, studying the paintings carefully. 'I can hardly believe it,' she said. 'Such a superb collection tucked away like this.'

'It's just for Vince's pleasure,' Dawn said, justifying their secretiveness. 'Anyway, you've had a look now. Come on back into the lounge.'

Somewhat unceremoniously, she shepherded them back into the other room, followed by Vince, who closed the door behind him.

'A mouse couldn't get in there without us knowing,' he said. 'We've got lights and secret cameras all around the house as well.'

'Why don't you sit down?' Dawn suggested.

Jan and Annabel looked at each other and lowered themselves onto a large sofa in front of the fire, while Dawn and Vince sat in their own individual chairs.

Jan wondered where Angie was, and wished she would come back and relieve the tension.

'How are the horses, then?' Dawn asked.

'I was telling Angie on Wednesday, we're pretty pleased with them. We've only had them about three weeks, but they're looking much better already. King's Archer should be ready to run soon, and the little mare, Overmere Lass, I reckon she should run in another bumper while we continue to school her over hurdles. Both of them look quite promising and the others could have a bit of potential.'

'They've got more than potential,' Vince growled. 'We never buy rubbish.'

'Who buys them for you?' Jan asked.

'We find what we want,' Dawn answered evasively. 'Angie's sending you the fax machine so you can tell us what you're doing with them.'

'Yes,' Jan nodded, 'That's fine. But I can't change my plans very easily. If I've decided to run a horse, I'll be gearing its training towards that particular race.'

'They're our horses, don't forget,' Vince growled, 'and we'll tell you where and when we want 'em to run.'

Jan sighed. There seemed little point in going over the technicalities of preparing a horse to race. Surely they must know about that already. She just hoped the Sharps were experienced enough to understand when it came to the crunch.

'OK.' She nodded slightly and wondered if she could smell trouble brewing.

Vince fixed her with a hard eye. 'Angie says you galloped King's Archer with that four-year-old of O'Hagan's at Worcester.'

'Yes, I did. I wanted Tom's Touch to gallop on the course with an older horse who knew the ropes. They both worked really well.'

'So you think you might find a couple of good races for King's Archer?' Dawn asked sharply.

'I would have thought so. If he holds his condition and doesn't mind a bit of cut in the ground, we might be able to get a few good wins out of him, that's if he doesn't get caught out by the handicapper.'

Vince nodded. 'It was a good race that Tom's Touch won yesterday. O'Hagan must have been 'appy.'

'Mr O'Hagan was delighted,' Jan agreed. 'And with the way our jockey rode his horse.'

'I reckon he's a good pilot, that boy,' Vince agreed.

'Me and Vince don't get to the races much ourselves,' Dawn said, 'but we watches it on the telly every day.'

'If you ever want to come, I'd be glad to . . .'

'Yes, yes, we'll let you know,' Dawn said with a touch of impatience. 'But our Angie'll always be there. I wonder where she's got to with those kids. It's time we had lunch.' The old woman winced as she rose creakily to her feet and went into the hall.

Jan, Annabel and Vince sat in silence as they listened to Dawn's shrill voice echoing around the house, calling for her daughter.

Soon they heard footsteps clattering on the broad flight of stone stairs which led up from the hall and Megan shrieking with laughter. A moment later Angie and Matty came into the room. He was sitting astride a plastic motorbike with a huge grin on his face as he legged it laboriously across the fitted carpet.

Megan came running in followed by a breathless Dawn, who looked in a mild state of shock.

'Mum, Mum, I slid all the way down the stairs on the rail, right from the top. Angie said I could.'

Angie glanced at Jan. 'It was OK,' she said. 'I was right beside her all the time – she was quite safe.'

Jan shook her head and smiled. 'That's OK. She certainly seems to have enjoyed it. Simple pleasures, eh?'

'Angie?' Dawn's voice rasped. 'It's time we had lunch.'

'Fine, Mother. It's all done. Come on,' she said to Jan and Annabel. 'Everything's ready.'

She led them all across the hall and into a barn-like dining room. At one end of an ancient oak table, at least fifteen feet long, six places had been laid, with a high chair for Matty. On a sideboard of equal antiquity stood a range of hot plates warming a number of serving dishes. At the end a big silver dome rested over a large oval meat platter.

Annabel looked at Jan, who raised her eyebrows in astonishment. At the far and of the room a small, dark woman seemed to appear from nowhere, evidently to serve the food. Vince sat at the head of the table with Dawn on his left, both of them seemingly intent only on eating. There was a bottle of wine in the middle of the table, which Angie offered around only once. Lunch consisted of a roast rib of beef and Yorkshire puddings superbly cooked, Jan guessed, by Angie; she couldn't imagine that it had been prepared by Dawn or the silent little woman with down-turned eyes who was serving them.

The meal passed in almost total silence. Megan, unusually for her, was completely subdued by the sombre grandness of the room and would only pick at her food. As soon as Matty had finished eating, Angie tactfully brought in the motorbike and left him scooting around the room, making the only noise in the place. When Megan asked if she could explore the garden, Angie told her how to find her way there and instructed the silent woman to keep an eye on her.

Jan was amazed that Angie seemed to accept this rather strange social occasion as normal and that she didn't make an effort to generate any conversation. Annabel and Jan knew they couldn't simply start up a conversation on their own, as if the others weren't there.

The embarrassing meal lasted little more than half an hour. Then, as coffee was served in silence by Angie, Vince leaned back in his chair and wiped his mouth with a large white napkin.

'Now then, Mrs Hardy,' he growled.

'Please call me Jan.'

'I'll call you Mrs Hardy, it's better. And I want to say something important, so make sure you listen. We've sent you seven really good 'orses, and we wants you to train them as best you can, but I want to remind you, whatever you said before we sat down for this meal, we – me and Mrs Sharp – we decide when and where the horses run.'

Jan felt the blood rise up her face as she realized that he had totally ignored what she'd said earlier.

'Now hang on a minute—'

'No,' Dawn cut in. Her wrinkled jowls quivered as she spoke. 'You hang on. We're paying you a lot of money; we've got more horses than anyone else at your place. We know you're only just starting up, so you needs good owners like us. But we always says what our horses do.'

Looking at the frail old woman, Jan was astonished by the vehemence of her delivery. 'Mrs Sharp, I'm not prepared—'

'If you're not prepared to do what we wants when we're

paying you to look after our expensive 'orses,' Dawn said, with quiet but unmistakable menace, 'we're not prepared to keep them with you.'

Jan gulped. She couldn't believe this was happening. She'd had the Sharps' horses less than three weeks, Angie had taken months persuading her parents to send them to her, and already they were throwing their weight around. They were right, she thought – too bloody right – when they said she needed owners like them, they knew damn well she couldn't afford to argue if it meant losing seven horses – not all at once.

In the silence following Dawn's uncompromising threat, Jan glanced at Annabel, who lifted her shoulders faintly to acknowledge the reality of their position.

Angie was studiously watching Matthew, who was pounding up and down the long room completely unaware of the drama taking place at the table.

Jan swung back to Vince, who was still leaning back in his chair, absently picking his teeth with a cocktail stick. She turned her gaze to the stone-faced old woman and met the icy blast of her eyes full on. But she had made up her mind there was only one way to deal with the Sharps.

'I've already told you why I have to make the final decisions about running the horses I train. There are very good reasons for it and I don't intend to make exceptions.' Deliberately, Jan rose from her chair. 'I'm not saying it won't be a blow to lose your horses, but there will be others.' She turned to Matty, who now sensed that something was wrong and had stopped dead still, sitting astride the motorbike while he looked quizzically at his mother. 'Come on, Matty, off you get.'

'Hang on, Jan,' Angie said, rising from her seat. 'I think we've got our wires a bit crossed here.'

'Angie, I wish we had, but if your mother and father want me to do things totally their way, then I'm afraid I can't. You've got a pretty good idea of how I operate. If it turns out it's the wrong way, so be it, but until then I'm not chopping and changing for anyone.'

By now Annabel had taken her cue and stood up too. Jan guessed her assistant would be very annoyed that she was risking so much. 'Sorry, Bel, but I think we've said all there is to say, so we might as well get off home. Let's find Megan.'

Annabel nodded, tight-lipped. Jan didn't look back at Vince and Dawn, but Angie followed them out of the dining room to the front door. As Jan opened it, she saw Megan swinging on the lower branches of a large blue cedar on the far side of the lawn and beckoned to her.

Angie pulled the door shut behind them.

'Listen, Jan, I know exactly how you feel; but don't worry. I'll tell them that you're going to keep the horses; that you'll let them know in plenty of time when you plan to run them in your daily fax reports. Please don't send the horses away, not when it's taken me so long to get them away from Martin Hunter's.'

'If you can guarantee your parents won't try and interfere in the way they are saying, that's fine; but I'd need their reassurance.'

'Jan, you've got it. Please believe me. There'll be a fax waiting for you when you get back confirming that you'll be making those decisions. Is that OK?'

'But, Angie, how on earth do you expect to influence them?'

'I know they're funny old things and fiercely independent, but I'm their only child and I've been working with them for over ten years, so believe me, I know what they're like. They're so suspicious and they worry about losing control of anything, that's all. Please, Jan, just try and forget what's happened. They like you and respect you, I know that, and I promise a fax will be waiting for you when you get home.'

Jan sighed. 'OK, if it is, that's fine. What can I say? I'm sorry I had to be so dogmatic, but you really can't train horses from an office.'

'Jan, it doesn't matter. Much better to get it out of the way now rather than later, eh?'

'Yes, I suppose so. Thanks, Angie.' She leaned forward and

they exchanged a kiss on the cheek. 'I'll ring you later. Come on now, you kids, into the car.'

🐎

Setting off down the drive towards the huge iron gates, Jan and Annabel didn't say a word, as if the Sharps could hear them through the elaborate surveillance systems surrounding the house. Jan didn't feel like speaking until the gates had opened to let them out and they had turned onto the road.

'Bloody hell, that was close!' Jan gasped.

'Too close for me,' Annabel said. 'I was sure you'd blown it, and it occurred to me that, even if you had agreed to do it their way, you could quite easily have organized things so they went your way in the end, simply by telling them a horse wasn't ready to run or was lame or something.'

'I wouldn't do something like that and it shouldn't be necessary. I need to know where I am, and if this fax arrives then I will, and that'll be fine. So, in the meantime, we'll just have to wait and see.'

'Fair enough,' Annabel agreed, 'but I'd never have been able to face up to that old witch.'

'Was she really a witch?' Megan asked excitedly.

'Well, not exactly.' Annabel laughed. 'I'm sure she doesn't do spells or anything.'

'Or she might do a spell against Mum!'

'Don't worry, Meg. She won't really do anything. We were only joking.' Jan sighed, 'But what a set-up!'

'Yes,' Annabel agreed. 'The house, the pictures, that awful lunch! I don't think I've ever sat through such a grim meal in my whole life.'

'Mum,' Megan said from the back seat, 'The garden was really nice. It had so many hiding places and everything.'

'And you never even got to swim.'

'But we saw the swimming pool,' Meg said excitedly. 'It was huge!'

'What did you really think of it all, though?' Jan asked. 'You know about big houses and paintings and all that sort of thing.'

'I've never been anywhere or seen anything like that,' Annabel protested. 'I can't think why on earth they ever bought the place – unless it's simply to have somewhere to put Vince's paintings.'

'They were pretty amazing,' Jan agreed.

'They're more than amazing. If those pictures are genuine, they are really valuable, as old Dawn said. Stubbs, Munnings, Herring – they're all there, as far as I could tell.'

'Perhaps he really does know a lot about them, but the extraordinary thing is I don't think he can even read or write. Maybe that gives him a better eye. But I wonder why they decided to show them to us,' Jan mused, 'when they're obviously paranoid about them being pinched.'

'I think the whole day was designed to make sure you know they've got an awful lot of money behind them – even if they do look like a couple of old scarecrows – perhaps it was done to convince you not to worry about your bills being paid and to persuade you to do as you're told, especially after that awful scene.'

'I guess you're right, though, as far as settling accounts goes, I've often found that the better off people are the worst. I've got one owner, Penny Price – you know, who owns Arrow Star – she's a secretary in Kington, and I don't think she has two halfpennies to rub together, she even worked night shifts at the chicken factory in Hereford all last year, just so she could pay the training fees. She is always one of my promptest payers. And now her mum and dad have taken shares in the horse to help with the higher running costs, and they always pay on the nail; so I'm not particularly impressed by lavish displays of spending.'

'The Sharps obviously thought you would be impressed.'

'Well, they certainly tried,' Jan chuckled. 'But I still can't understand how Angie copes with it all.'

'I don't know Angie, but I expect she goes along with it because she knows it's a waste of time doing anything else, and if, as you said, she runs their various businesses, I guess she wants to avoid any domestic squabbles.'

'I suppose you're right, but she certainly stuck her neck out for me just now, and she was marvellous with the kids, wasn't she?' Jan turned round to see Megan. 'Do you like Angie, Meg?'

'Yes, she's really nice. She gave me those lovely chaps and she always brings me sweets.'

'Angie, tractor,' Matty spluttered, anxious to get his views in too.

Jan turned to face the front. 'And she was extremely kind to me in Ireland. I know Dad was with me, but we were like fish out of water and we didn't know a soul until Angie took us under her wing.'

'Yes, and then she got her old fogies to send you their horses.'

'If they stay. Mind you, moving the horses was in their best interests too, given the dreadful state of Martin Hunter's yard.'

Annabel chuckled. 'It's all very odd. Still, like horses, owners come in all shapes and sizes, don't they?'

'They certainly do,' Jan agreed. 'But at least if the Sharps *do* leave the horses with us, I don't think they'll be going belly up, which is something you have to be very wary about these days.'

Riding out with first lot the next morning, Jan reasoned she was very fortunate still to have the Sharps' seven horses in spite of her display of bravado at lunch the previous day. It brought her out in a cold sweat just thinking of the risk she'd taken, but at the time she'd been so incensed by the Sharps' attitude that she genuinely didn't care if they took their horses away.

When she had got home with Annabel and the children the previous evening, the fax which Angie had promised wasn't waiting for her, but by the time she'd gone down to the office at nine o'clock that evening it had arrived. A brief but formally typed statement confirmed that Jan was authorized to decide when and where the Sharps' horses would run. It was signed by

Dawn in neat, old-fashioned copperplate and by Vince, Jan presumed, with an illegible squiggle.

Jan and Billy were at the rear of the string of eight they were exercising on the first truly autumnal morning of the year. The previous evening heavy cloud had glided in from the west to sit on top of the ridge, hiding it from sight, and this morning the world was shrouded in grey dampness.

'D'you know, I think old Vince could be right and we may be able to win a race with nearly all their horses?'

Billy nodded. 'They're looking a hell of a lot better already. They can't have been doing much work at Martin Hunter's, or getting much grub.'

'They did look a bit of a mess,' Jan agreed. 'Actually, they're quite fit now and will be ready to do a bit more work shortly. I reckon I'll get a run into King's Archer in a couple of weeks' time.'

Billy nodded. 'He'll be ready by then. I suppose you won't be getting rid of any of the others just yet?'

'No way, and I'm not just keeping them to fill up the yard, I can assure you of that.'

'It's weird that Angie and the old codgers haven't been to see them since they got here, though.'

'Oh, I wasn't really expecting them to,' Jan said lightly. 'From what they told me yesterday, I don't suppose we'll see much of them at the races either.'

'But Roz told me Angie was down here most of the time during the summer.'

'Maybe you scared her off, then.'

'No way! I got on really well with her, remember. It was me that made her mind up about sending the horses here – whatever you say.'

'Look, Billy, I'm not going over that again! I think you'd better let sleeping dogs lie.'

Billy was riding Lucky Charm, one of the Sharps' horses which had run from Hunter's yard six weeks before. Although the horse hadn't done at all well, Jan felt he had a lot more to offer and she was keen to know what sort of feel Billy would get from the gelding when he asked him to quicken.

The tilled gallop rose steeply at the top of the field, then curved ninety degrees to the left and levelled out along the ridge for another two furlongs.

'Go on, Billy,' she said. 'When you get to the top the others are going to pull up, but you carry on; get him to extend, but keep a good hold of his head. Let's see how he goes.'

The jockey acknowledged the instruction with a grin and started to make his way up the string.

The first two horses had reached the bottom of the gallop and broke into a sharp canter up the long incline, quickly followed by the others. Jan went last, with Annabel beside her on Russian Eagle.

Jan was riding Overmere Lass, a five-year-old mare who had won a bumper the previous season. Jan was growing confident that the mare would be fit enough to run again soon. Moving comfortably up the track on the well-balanced animal, she had a chance to study the horses in front, and glanced across at Russian Eagle. He had lost some of the excess weight he'd been carrying when he came in from grass in August, and was beginning to look more like the athletic chaser he'd been when he ran in the Foxhunters' the previous spring. Nevertheless, Jan thought she should wait a couple more months before she found a suitable race for him.

'All right?' Jan called.

'Brilliant.' Annabel laughed breathlessly.

At the top of the gallop, all the horses had pulled up except Lucky Charm, who was being pushed along by Billy. The rest of the string turned to watch how the horse would respond.

Jan trotted a little way back down the hill to give herself a better side-on view. She watched wide-eyed as the gelding eagerly stretched his neck and lengthened his stride after the long haul up the hill.

Great, she thought to herself. *That will do just fine.*

Later in the week, as Jan was watching the second lot leave the yard, she felt pleased that she was now more at ease about leaving Annabel in charge of the straightforward exercise.

'Come on,' she said to Meg, who was swinging on the yard gate with her small purple and blue rucksack on her back. 'It's half-past eight; you'll be late for school if we don't go now.'

'I've been ready for hours, Mum. Can I just give Smarty his carrot before we go?'

'Yes, if you hurry.'

The little girl leapt off the gate, collected a carrot from the feed store and raced round to the paddock, where Smarty was standing by the gate waiting for his treat.

Jan smiled, remembering how she had been at that age, and climbed into the Land Rover. Megan scrambled in beside her, breathing hard, and pulled the door shut.

'Seat belt, Meg.'

'Dolores Wilson's got a new thirteen one. She says it's the best pony in the Vale Pony Club.'

'Who on earth is Dolores Wilson?' Jan laughed.

'The new girl, Mum. I told you. She's always got new things. Her mum's got a car like Angie's.'

'She sounds a bit spoilt to me.'

Megan didn't answer at first. After a moment's thought, she asked, 'Mum, are we really poor?'

'Well, we're not rich. That's why Mummy has to work so hard with the horses. If we can look after them well, they can win lots of races and then more people will want to send horses to us.'

'But that's stupid, Mum. Where would we keep them?'

'If they came, we'd find somewhere, don't you worry.'

'Would we live in a house then?'

'Our house should be ready in a month or so, at least some of it. Gerry's got on really well. He says he will finish the roof as soon as I get the tiles, and maybe I can buy them with the money we get for August Moon.'

Please God, she added to herself.

Eventually, with no let-up to Megan's questions and views on the other girls in her class, they reached school with the main surge of mothers. Jan watched her daughter rush in, with a quick backward glance as she reached the door.

Jan waved, wheeled the Land Rover round and set off back to Edge Farm.

As she turned in at the bottom of the drive, she found a local taxi preceding her up the hill. She followed it curiously and, when it reached the top, parked beside it.

She climbed out just as two young men were letting themselves out of the back of the taxi. One was tall and thin with lank fair hair. The other, Jan was amused to see, was almost the opposite – short and stocky with dark, wavy hair.

'Hello,' she said.

'Morning, missis,' the shorter one said, while the other helped the taxi driver with the bags from the boot and paid him off.

'We're lookin' for Mrs Hardy.' There was an unmistakable Irish lilt to the small man's voice.

'You've found her,' Jan smiled.

'Great!' the short man said. 'We just got over from Ireland.'

'I guessed. You must be Declan and Connor.'

'That's it,' the short one said.

'That's right,' the other confirmed. 'I'm Dec; he's Con.'

'Glad you made it. Bring your bags down to the office. I'll make you a cup of coffee.'

They followed her down and shuffled self-consciously into the cluttered room.

'So, how was your journey?'

'Oh, I thought 'twas fine,' Dec, the tall one, said, 'but Con was sick as a dog on the ship.'

'Are you all right now?' Jan asked Con.

'Sh'jaysus, yes – soon as I got off that feckin' boat.'

'Right, we'll have this coffee and, if you're ready, my second lot will be back shortly; then we've got four more to take out, so you can ride and I'll come with you to see how you get on.'

🐎

Jan rode back into the yard with Dec, Con and Karen after forty-five minutes on the more backward horses, satisfied there was nothing wrong with the Irishmen's riding.

'I'll have a look at you doing some fast work tomorrow, but now there's a couple that need schooling. Have you done much?'

Jan knew that both lads had ridden in a number of point-to-points in Ireland, but that was no guarantee of sound jumping skills.

However, after half an hour with Russian Eagle and Dingle Bay in the long field, where she had a run of three good-sized schooling fences alongside the hedge, she was confident that both her prospective lads would be a huge bonus.

At the end of the session she rewarded them with more coffee and a doughnut in the office.

'Right, you'll do. I was pleased with this morning's exercise. But as I told Jimmy O'Driscoll, you're here on a month's trial, and if either of you step out of line you'll both be straight back on the ferry. Understood?'

They stared back at her and nodded slowly.

'And no messing around with the girls, at least not while you're in the yard and in my time. And however wrecked you get on a Friday night, arriving here late on a Saturday morning is a mortal sin, if you know what that is.'

'We know,' Con nodded.

'We sure do,' Dec confirmed.

'As far as accommodation's concerned, Roz's parents live in the village and they have a caravan in one of their fields, which they've got ready for you. That'll give you somewhere to kip until we decide if you want to stay. Their two girls work in the yard, so you won't have any excuse for being late.'

'OK.' They both nodded again.

'Right, if you're happy with what I've told you, I'll introduce you to the rest of the troops.'

'I can't wait,' Con said with a broad grin.

Jan left the lads sharing sandwiches with Annabel, Joe Paley and the girls. Their initial reactions had seemed all right. She had been worried that Joe, who was used to being the only adult male around the place, might have his nose put out of joint, but he looked frankly relieved at the prospect of some male company in the team.

Karen had obviously dealt with whatever preconceptions she might have had about Irishmen and was giggling happily at Con's description of his ferry trip.

Frances Walters, Jan's new help, was in the caravan giving Matthew his lunch when Jan came up. She still felt a twinge of guilt that she wasn't performing this basic task herself, but even her old-fashioned mother had told her not to worry – little boys don't care who gives them their food, as long as they get it. It's the hugging, playing, chatting and story-telling that really matter.

A full-time child-minder had been Annabel's idea, and Fran had turned out to be a real treasure. Permanently good-humoured, small, plain and forty-five, her only child had moved away from home five years before, leaving her alone with her husband, leading a very quiet life in a council house on the edge of the village. Coming up to Edge Farm every day, she said, had given her a new lease of life.

'Hello,' she said brightly, looking up from the spoon she was about to ease into Matty's mouth. 'You just missed a phone message. The doctor called. Did you get the flowers he sent after your win last week?'

Jan winced guiltily. 'Thanks, Fran. I did get them.' She nodded at the large bunch of roses in a vase on the table. She knew she should have acknowledged them, but she'd been so busy it kept getting put to the bottom of the pile. Poor Tony. She really didn't treat him at all well, she reflected.

Remorsefully, she rang the mobile number he had left, and thanked him for the flowers, and after some persuading she agreed to have dinner with him at the White Horse the following evening. She put the phone down, relieved that her apparent indifference hadn't put him off asking her out again. Some men wouldn't have bothered. But she felt Tony understood her priorities and didn't blame her for them, and she was actually a little surprised to find how much she was looking forward to seeing him.

After eating a quick lunch and reading a story to Matty while he lay down for his rest, Jan went back down to the yard.

Dec and Con were watching the racing with the others in the office and seemed to be quite at home already.

'Bel,' Jan said, 'while it's quiet let's show our new lads the horses. We can tell them all we know.'

'Sure,' Annabel said, easing her slim hips off the bean bag she had settled into to look at the TV.

The two lads came out willingly, both of them Jan noted, watching Annabel's movements with fascination.

Jan led them next door to the first stable in the block opposite the barn. A large chestnut head with a narrow white blaze was looking over the door. Jan kicked the bottom latch over and slid back the bolt.

'Come on, Willie. Back you go,' she urged as she pushed the horse from the door and led the others into his box.

The Irishmen stood with their backs against the wall as they looked enthusiastically at the big gelding.

'Irish bred,' Jan announced, 'like a lot of the others in this yard.'

'Good-looking type,' Dec said.

'Useful,' Con added.

'This is Young Willie. He's a nine-year-old and he's won eight races, six of them over three miles plus.'

'Is he a good lepper?' Dec asked.

Jan took a moment to interpret before she answered. 'Oh yes, he's a great jumper. Lady Fairford, who owns him, says he's never fallen.'

'So, he looks very well in himself,' Connor said. 'Is he ready to run yet, would you think?'

'Very nearly. I think I'm going to enter him in a three-mile chase at Cheltenham in three weeks' time, and if he goes well

Lady Fairford's very keen for him to run in the cross-country race there in the middle of November.'

'I've seen that race on the television. He looks the sort. What distance is that?'

'Just under four miles. The track's improved a lot over the years and some of the live fences there are pretty big now – the laurel hedge has a six-foot drop to it. So it's quite demanding and because of all the turns you need a nimble horse, which he is, although he's quite big.'

'So you'll be wanting him to do a bit of fast work next week?'

Jan nodded. 'That's right. Bel worked him yesterday. Tell the boys how you found him.' She turned to Annabel.

'Super. He's not the fastest horse in the yard, but he loves the job and doesn't wait to be asked he's so enthusiastic.'

'Right, let's look at some more.' Jan led them out and opened the next box.

'This is Dingle Bay.'

Declan looked hard at the handsome bay as he searched his memory. 'I saw him run two or three years ago. Eamon Fallon had him, then he came over to some little place I never heard of. Who owns him now?'

'A chap called Bernie Sutcliffe, who comes from a place we call the Black Country. It's an industrial area to the west of Birmingham. Bernie's a bit of an amateur owner, but we're teaching him, aren't we, Bel?'

'And he's learning,' Annabel added.

'The horse looks in great nick,' Con said.

'He is,' Jan agreed. 'I've already entered him to run at Taunton, a week today. One of you can ride him work tomorrow.'

As she talked, both Irishmen ran experienced hands down the horse's big strong legs.

'Great!'

'There's nuthin' wrong with them.'

Jan led them out and across the yard to the block at the far end.

'This is a very tasty lookin' little mare,' Connor observed as they walked into a box occupied by a compact, tough-looking individual.

'She's called Overmere Lass,' Annabel told the Irishmen. 'She's coming together. We're probably going to run her at Stratford on Saturday week. She's one of seven horses in the yard belonging to some people called Sharp.'

Jan took over. 'Their daughter's a friend of mine. We've only had them for three or four weeks, but we're much more pleased with them now. I don't think the Sharps pay much money for their horses, but they certainly seem to know what they're buying.'

Jan was pleased to see the lads were listening intently and taking in everything she said; she knew how important it was that anyone who worked in a yard should feel they had an idea of what was going on and who owned what. Besides, it impressed the owners if the staff knew which horses belonged to which owner.

When they'd looked at all the Sharps' horses, Jan led them over to the barn. 'Now, you won't need an introduction to any of these chaps.'

Although Jan had no runners the following Saturday, she was really looking forward to the weekend. On Sunday Johnny Carlton-Brown and a girlfriend were coming down with Ben to have lunch with her. JCB wanted to finalize his purchase of August Moon, the grey mare Victor Carey had left to Jan in his will when he died the previous spring. He was also going to decide how much he wanted to spend on a new horse, perhaps at the November sale in Newmarket, as he wanted a horse that was ready to go racing straight away.

Jan would have liked to entertain her brother and his boss at home, but she knew this wasn't possible in the mobile home. She so wished her house had been ready, but although Gerry had managed to felt and batten the roof, he had run out of tiles and Jan didn't have any spare cash to buy more until the deal with August Moon was completed. She asked herself fleetingly, in light of her father's strong views on selling the mare, whether she was right to swap a potentially nice brood mare for a lorryload of roof tiles. In the short internal debate that followed, the tiles won hands down.

When she told Annabel she was going to ask the pub if she could use the small room behind the main dining area, Annabel had insisted that, as assistant trainer, it was perfectly reasonable for her to host the lunch at the pretty eighteenth-century stone cottage she rented from the Stanfield Court Estate.

'Are you sure you don't mind, Bel?'

'As long as you don't mind me muscling in on the lunch.'

'Of course I don't, but what's your interest?'

'The good of the yard, of course,' Annabel grinned. 'And I rather liked your brother and his boss.'

'JCB is bringing a girlfriend, don't forget.'

'I know. That's fine. What do you think? Are we agreed?'

'I think you're a gem; that would be brilliant and, if I ask Fran, she'll come and take the kids for a walk while we talk business.'

'Perfect,' Annabel crowed.

After the Sunday morning stable duties were over, Jan drove down to the village and dropped off the children, and arrived at Annabel's to find her putting the final touches to the leg of lamb she was going to cook.

Ben and the Brit Records boss turned up soon after with a studious, rather hippy-looking girl in large sunglasses, which were designed to disguise her stunning good looks, without completely obliterating them.

'Hi, good to see you,' Johnny said in the unassuming manner Jan remembered from his last visit. He leaned down and gave her a quick peck on the cheek. 'This is Vanessa.'

Jan was shaking hands with the woman, trying to look at her more closely, when she suddenly realized she was welcoming a leading British film actress. She wondered for a moment why Ben hadn't told her the full story, but on reflection she was very relieved he hadn't.

Glancing at Annabel, she saw that her friend had also recognized her.

Before lunch, they had drinks in Annabel's small but exquisitely decorated drawing room. Jan noticed that Ben was completely at ease with the film star, talking to her about music and films. Only now did it occur to Jan that her brother probably spent most of his working life, and presumably quite a lot of his leisure time, with musicians and singers who were household names, and that when he was in the studio with them, as the producer, he was also their boss.

Vanessa turned out to be less full of herself than Jan might have expected, and after a while she almost forgot how important she was. Over lunch Johnny wanted to discuss the horses. He had seen August Moon briefly on his last visit and he wanted another look. He was particularly interested in breeding from her. He also fancied the idea of racing her, perhaps for another season or two, with the aim of getting a little more bold type onto the pages of her progeny.

After lunch Johnny and Jan went through the catalogues of past and forthcoming sales, while Ben, Vanessa and Annabel let themselves out of the back gate for stroll across the parkland which Mr Carey had loved so much when he was alive.

'It seems to me,' Johnny said, when he felt he had a good fix on the market, 'to find what I want, I'm going to have to go to about fifty grand, or maybe more. What do you think?'

Jan tried not to let him see how much she was quivering at the thought of spending so much money on a horse. She had been a nervous wreck spending just ten thousand at the Derby sale.

'We'd get something suitable for that, I'm sure, or a bit less if we take a chance and go for something less exposed.'

'But I like having winners. That's why we all go racing. The only point in buying cheaper horses is if you haven't got the money to buy the better ones. Luckily for me, I have, so with your help we should try for the best.'

Jan was aware that JCB had paid a lot more than fifty thousand for Miller's Lodge, who had won a big race at the Cheltenham Festival the previous year and was now in Virginia Gilbert's yard. 'Fair enough,' she said. 'I'll let you know what I think we should bid for. Will you come to the sales?'

'If I can, but right now I'd like to come up to your yard and look at this mare you're so keen for me to have. If I like her, I'll give you a cheque today.' *I really hope you do*, Jan prayed.

11

Tom's Touch was entered to run for the second time of his career in the bumper at Towcester on Wednesday 15 October. On this occasion, Murty McGrath was available and had been booked to ride.

A.D. O'Hagan telephoned Jan while she was in the lorry on the way to the course and explained that he was in Barbados so would be unable to be at the track on this occasion. He would, however, be watching on the Racing Channel.

'Very best of luck, Jan,' he said. 'I have every faith in you and don't let Murty boss you around. He knows he's to follow your instructions.'

Jan had never met Murty McGrath, although she had a thorough knowledge of his riding style. She'd also heard he had a reputation for being a little too self-confident at times and she wasn't much looking forward to their first meeting. However, she wasn't going to be intimidated, and in one respect she held the trump card. Tom's Touch had won so easily last time the jockey would have trouble blaming the trainer if it didn't win again.

🐎

Murty McGrath strode into the parade ring, well accustomed to wearing A.D.'s blue and yellow stripes. At thirty, he was as fit and hard as he'd ever been and his jawline reflected his aggress-ive, Machiavellian riding tactics.

He bounded straight up to Jan. 'Mrs Hardy.' He nodded curtly.

'Hello, Murty.'

'Anything I should know?' he asked.

Plenty, she thought, but decided to be gracious.

'You finished behind this horse at Worcester,' she replied, 'but I expect you saw how Billy Hanks rode him, so do the same today; keep him in touch, around third or fourth, but don't ask him to go on until you've passed the two-furlong marker, and we should be OK.'

'Let's hope your horse is as good as he was at Worcester.'

'Oh, he is, Murty. He's probably better, so you just do your best.'

'Mrs Hardy, I always do my best,' the jockey countered.

Jan watched him mount her horse and prayed that engaging the country's leading jump jockey would be successful.

In the race, despite the softer ground and the undulations of the Northamptonshire track, Tom's Touch disposed smoothly of the other runners and repeated his performance of ten days earlier, although by a lesser margin of ten lengths.

Having removed her muddy boots, Jan was lying back in the passenger seat of the lorry with her feet on the dashboard as Annabel drove. She was wondering if A.D.'s office would give her his number in Barbados when she heard the muffled tone of her mobile phone, buried under her fleece.

'Hello, Jan,' a mellow voice echoed along the airwaves. 'Well done!'

'Thanks, A.D. He's a very good horse, you know.'

'That doesn't take anything away from you, so don't be too modest. How was he after the race?'

'Absolutely fine,' Jan said. 'To be honest, he didn't look as if he'd run one. He was as bright as a button.'

'How are the others coming on?'

'Erin's Jet has really caught up. I think he might be ready to run next, or Wexford Lad. They've both been schooling really well.'

'Wexford Lad would be like the fella who won today.'

'Yes,' Jan agreed. 'He's the same type. What was the bumper like he won last year?'

'You look it up, you'll see there's some useful form.'

'I will. There could be a novice hurdle suitable for him at Cheltenham on the twenty-ninth.'

'Two weeks? You reckon he'll be ready by then?'

'I think so.'

'Good. Keep me posted. Maybe I'll come. 'Bye, Jan.' Without waiting for an answer, A.D. cut off.

'I wonder if our palates are getting jaded by the taste of success,' Annabel said as the lorry rumbled down the M5 to Taunton the next morning. 'Of course, it was really exciting to win yesterday, especially with the "champ" on board. But it doesn't feel quite so fantastic as our first win, does it?'

Jan was driving. She turned to Annabel with a quick grin. 'It still feels pretty good to me. It's a bit like a dream, though; I know Tom's good, you have to ask yourself how long he can keep it up. Of course, we'll have to send him hurdling sooner rather than later, and there's no reason why he shouldn't be just as good at that, if not better, since he jumps so well.'

'How are you feeling about the two in the back?'

Jan shook her head uncertainly. 'Well, the way King's Archer worked with Tom's Touch should make him pretty good. The rest of the field doesn't look too special, either, so, maybe. As it's our first runner for the Sharps, I really hope so, but having said that, after their experience with Martin Hunter, their expectations won't be as high as A.D.'s.'

'When did they last have a winner?'

'Not since early last season. They had a little run of winners just before Christmas, I seem to remember, when I looked up their form, then they all seemed to go off the boil. Of course, that may have been about the same time Martin was hitting the rocks, or maybe he had a virus in the yard and just never told them.'

'Billy's quite confident,' Annabel said. 'Riding that winner for Virginia the other day perked him up no end.'

'I just wish it had been for anyone but Virginia,' Jan growled.

'Oh, Jan, don't be so vindictive.'

'But she's been so bloody nasty to me over the years. I really would like to rub her nose in it.'

'Anyway, didn't Billy say the work he'd ridden on Archer last week was the best he'd ever done?'

'Yes, I was watching. But I don't want to turn up today too full of myself and not pull it off. The mountains you meet in life are hard enough to climb without building them higher yourself.'

'Yes, I'm sure you're right, but what about Dingle Bay?'

'To be honest, I think the trip might be a little short for him, but Bernie's ever so keen to see him run, and,' Jan shrugged, 'it'll certainly be interesting to see how he copes at this level.'

'Bernie's been rather sweet, hasn't he, the way he's been ringing up every day to ask how the horse is?'

'I expect he just wanted an excuse to talk to you,' Jan chuckled.

'No, he didn't,' Annabel protested. 'Anyway, he knows there's no point.'

'A cat can look at a queen, you know.'

'Thanks, Jan – like Tony Robertson with you.'

'That's not quite the same,' Jan protested. 'As a matter of fact, when he took me to the White Horse last Friday he was such good fun we had a really nice evening.'

'Things *are* looking up for you – a man who's fun and a house that's almost got a roof!'

'It *will* have a roof by the end of next week – I bought the tiles on Monday and Gerry's absolutely promised we'll be in before Christmas.'

'Great!' Annabel exclaimed. 'That's going to make a massive difference to your life.'

'It'll certainly make a hell of a difference not having to dodge cement mixers and piles of stone, or pull Matthew off the builders' sand. The mess of it all's really beginning to get me down, never mind the extra bills for the materials.'

'Oh come on, Jan,' Annabel chided her. 'It'll be worth it.'

Jan nodded with an apologetic smile. 'Yes, of course it will.'

🐎

After they had arrived at the race course and unloaded and stabled the horses, Bernie was one of the first people Jan saw going into the bar.

'Hello, Jan,' he said with unusual friendliness. 'How's Dingle?'

'He's fine, Bernie. Raring to go, as always.'

'How do you think he'll get on?'

Jan sucked her teeth. 'First run of the season, it's hard to say, but I hope he'll run a big race,' she replied, trying to be realistic.

'That other one of yours won first time out, that one of O'Hagan's.'

'Yes, but they'd been preparing him in Ireland for some time before he came over, so he was a bit further ahead than the rest of them.'

'So, should I have a bet?'

'Bernie, I've told you dozens of times, I never give betting advice. He might win and he might not. But he'll certainly be doing his best.'

'I hope that Billy Hanks isn't getting above himself,' Bernie went on, identifying something else to grumble about.

'He's only ridden two winners since he turned professional,' Jan said patiently. 'When he's ridden ten more and loses his claim, he'll probably get a great deal worse.'

'How many does he have to ride before he loses his seven pound allowance then?'

'Unfortunately, his three previous hunter chase wins count against him, so with the two this season, that's five out of the fifteen he's allowed. Anyway he'll still claim five pounds until he's ridden those winners.'

'There's your friend over there,' Bernie said suddenly, pointing at the entrance to the members' enclosure.

Angie Sharp was just coming through the gate, looking as

chic as ever, even on a blustery wet day on the Somerset hills. She was wearing a sable hat and a long dark-brown suede coat with a sable collar. Jan couldn't begin to imagine how much the outfit cost. She waved, and Angie hurried over.

'Hi, Jan!' she beamed. 'Well done yesterday.'

'Oh yes, I forgot,' Bernie chimed in. 'You had the champion jockey on board, didn't you?'

'We'd have won with Billy on. In fact, Bernie, we'd have won with your granny on.'

'I reckon you would,' Angie said. 'Anyway, have you got time for a quicky before you start getting busy?'

Jan made a face. 'Sorry. No, not really. I've only got Bel and Declan today.'

'Is he one of your new Irish boys?' Angie asked.

'Yes, lovely bloke, beautiful hands on a horse, so gentle. None of this yanking about.'

'Where did you find him?'

'He was working at Aigmont.'

'A.D.'s place?' Angie asked with a hint of a raised brow.

'Yes.'

'My God!' Bernie blustered. 'O'Hagan's making bloody sure he keeps his eye on you, isn't he?'

'For heaven's sake, Bernie, he's not planting spies! They're just a couple of lads who want to work in England for a while. It was Jimmy O'Driscoll who recommended them; I doubt if A.D. even knows who they are.'

'I hope you're right,' Bernie said, unconvinced.

'Well, anyway, I've got to go and declare, so I'll see you around later, Bernie. You and Angie go and have that drink; it will help calm you down!'

Jan hurried off with the horses' passports, thinking, not for the first time, that she didn't need stroppy owners telling her how to do her job or, at least, that they could be more considerate.

🐎

Billy was in the weighing room. Jan hadn't seen him since Tom's Touch had won the day before with Murty on board.

'Well done,' he grunted.

'Oh come on, Billy, you know the score. For what it's worth, I told A.D. we'd still have won with you up,' Jan added, trying to remember if it was A.D. she'd said that to. 'And you've got a really good chance today.'

'Not on Dingle, I haven't.'

'You could have and we're not going to know until you get out there and give it a go. Anyway, don't let Bernie see you're so pessimistic, or he'll think we don't care about him and he's not important.'

'Tosser!'

'Shut up, Billy. He's a good owner, even if he is a bit of a pain in the arse sometimes. And without the the owners,' she went on, feeling guilty about her earlier thoughts, 'you and I don't have a job. So get your arse in gear and go out and do what they pay you to do.'

🐎

Billy's predictions about the result of his two rides for Jan were borne out when Dingle Bay ran a reliable though somewhat one-paced race to come fourth, twenty lengths behind the winner of his race, while in the two-mile handicap chase, King's Archer, carrying nearly top weight, came home easily in pole position.

'I didn't even pick my stick up!' Billy boasted as Jan walked alongside the horse to the winner's enclosure.

'He looked like he had plenty left in the tank,' Jan agreed. 'Well done, I'm so relieved. Here's Angie, she'll be chuffed.'

Angie was beaming. 'Oh, Billy, what a fantastic ride,' she said rapturously.

As far as Jan knew, when Billy had walked into the parade ring before the race, it was the first time he and Angie had met since the well-rumoured but unconfirmed sexual dalliance in his car after the open day. Nevertheless, Jan thought she could detect a distinct frisson of intimacy between them.

Billy raised an eyebrow and leered at Angie. 'I always give a fantastic ride.'

After a quick celebratory drink in the bar with Angie, while Billy was riding in the last race, Jan left and was on her way back to join Annabel at the stables when a gravelly voice stopped her.

'Well done, Jan.'

Jan didn't miss the caustic edge to the comment and turned to find Martin Hunter following her.

'Thanks, Martin. No doubt your preparation helped.'

'No doubt. Is Miss Sharp pleased with the win?'

'Yes, of course. She's chuffed to bits.'

'That's all right then. How's the others doing?'

'Not bad. Overmere Lass runs in the bumper at Stratford on Saturday, and Lucky Charm will probably go to Chepstow next week.'

'Best of luck, then. I hope the Sharps treat you right.'

He turned and headed off towards the car park without expanding on his last statement. For a few seconds Jan watched him go, wondering if there was more to it than mere sour grapes. While she had no problems with Angie, she had to admit that, since that rather bizarre lunch she'd had with the Sharps in their gothic mansion, the only thing she could say with any certainty about Vince and Dawn was that they were eccentric and she should be prepared for the unpredictable.

Glancing back towards the stands, she noticed Angie walking towards her, still looking as glamorous as she had when she had arrived, with not a hair our of place.

Jan waited for her, wondering how she managed it.

'Sorry, Jan, I've got to get off,' Angie said, when she was close enough to be heard over the noise of the race that was going on. 'I was coming to say goodbye and to thank you.'

'I'm glad you could be here today and I'm really pleased he pulled it off for you.'

'Billy?' said Angie quizzically.

'Well, I meant King's Archer, actually, but Billy, too.'

'Mum and Dad will be so pleased. They'll have watched it on TV. They might even come to Cheltenham in a couple of weeks if you have any runners there.'

'I probably will,' Jan said. 'It's a lovely track and so near home.'

'They'd like that. By the way, was that Martin Hunter I just saw you talking to?'

'Yes.'

'Oh. What did he want?'

'Nothing really. He just said well done. I think it was only sour grapes from the way he said it, though.'

'Yes, probably,' Angie nodded. 'But he can't complain; he had his chance.'

It was twelve days since King's Archer's win at Taunton and today was the first of the two-day meeting scheduled to take place at Cheltenham. It was mid-morning as Jan set out for Prestbury Park with her two runners on board the lorry.

The race course was about thirty-five minutes away by car, but in a lorry on a race day Jan decided to allow an hour. On the way, with the two Irish lads in the cab, she was almost quaking with excitement. She'd never had a runner at the course before, not even in a hunter chase, but she was looking forward to it with her usual quiet optimism.

Since Taunton she'd sent out twelve more runners and clocked up two more wins. Toby had been overjoyed when Gale Bird had come in first at Chepstow and Jan had scored her first double when another of the Sharps' horses, Lucky Charm, had won his race that same afternoon.

However, the horses that she'd taken to Kempton Park the previous weekend had run moderately, leaving her feeling rather deflated as she'd driven back home that evening.

As they dropped down the hill towards Cheltenham, Declan interrupted her thoughts. 'Jan, is it five winners you've had so far this season?' he asked.

'So far,' she nodded.

'And is it seventeen runners you've sent out?'

'That's right.'

'I reckon that gives you around twenty-nine per cent winners – which is one hell of a strike rate!'

Jan laughed. 'I'd worked that out, too, but I'd be pretty naive if I thought I could keep that up for much longer. Anyway, it's all very well, but it also builds up owners' expectations so it can work against you.'

'Are we going to win today, then?'

'Not being a fortune teller, I really don't know, but we've got two decent animals on board.'

Today's runners were for two of Jan's local supporters – Young Willie for Lady Fairford and Wolf's Rock for Colonel Gilbert.

With her determination to leave nothing to chance, Jan and her team arrived in plenty of time for her to walk the course with Billy Hanks before the start of racing. Although Billy had ridden round the Cheltenham track several times before, he evidently didn't think it worth objecting and added to Jan's understanding of the course by recounting his personal experiences as they walked round.

Jan was struck by how much more pronounced the undulations of the track were in reality than they appeared from the stands. Billy said the fence at the top of the hill was like jumping into the sky, before the track dropped away to the left. By the time they had walked the steep hill from the turn for home to the winning line, she fully appreciated why Cheltenham was generally considered one of the most testing tracks in British steeplechasing.

Jan filled in the next half-hour by wandering around. She knew it was important to familiarize herself with the surroundings. Most of the officials, including the clerk of the course and the clerk of the scales, seemed to know who she was and were very helpful. There was also a scattering of faces she knew from the pony club and local hunts which she'd been involved with before she married John Hardy and went to live in Wales.

The only face she wasn't happy to see was Virginia Gilbert's. Cheltenham was as much Virginia's local course as her own and, inevitably, she was also keen to run horses there. She had brought three today and was scheduled to run another two the next day.

Jan managed to force a smile for her rival while praying that Wolf's Rock would perform well for Colonel Gilbert and vindicate his decision to keep a horse in a yard that was in direct competition with his own daughter's.

Wolf's Rock was a talented horse, who'd lost his novice tag at the end of the previous season. Jan was confident that she had him trained to his peak. He had been working well at home with Tom's Touch, who was one of the quickest horses in the yard.

The colonel strolled into the parade ring with his wife. He was wearing a tweed suit of large brown checks with a brown trilby. He looked the typical English owner. If he was being presented as a species of wildlife, Jan thought with a grin, you would say that this race course was his natural habitat.

Mrs Gilbert, whom Jan barely knew, gave her a polite smile and glanced around at the other owners in the ring, while her husband gazed approvingly at his horse.

'I don't think I've ever seen him look so well, Jan. That piece of work I saw him do last week was very impressive.' He took a long breath. 'I don't want to feel too confident because so many things can go wrong, but I certainly feel hopeful, and the bookies seem to agree. How about you?'

Jan gave a cautious smile. 'There are one or two horses here with better form,' she said. 'But I walked the course with your jockey this morning and we planned how Wolf should be ridden. Billy's proving quite reliable in carrying out his instructions and hopefully there shouldn't be any pilot error. So, all being well . . .' Jan shrugged her shoulders.

'Here he is now,' the colonel said as the fifteen jockeys entered the ring in a burst of colour, like a troupe of medieval entertainers. Once the riding plan had been reiterated to the colonel and his wife, Jan legged Billy into the saddle.

In the stand reserved for owners and trainers Jan stood on the step behind Colonel Gilbert and remembered during the previous spring, before she had been granted her licence, how she had looked longingly at the people qualified to be there – now she was one of them!

As the field charged away from the starting gate, she watched her first-ever runner at the famous course with her binoculars glued to her face. Billy was placing his horse well at each fence and they were jumping them beautifully. Passing the stands for the first time, they were lying in the middle of the field, exactly as they had planned. She watched Billy's head glide smoothly alongside the running rail as he crouched calmly, unmoving, over the horse's withers.

'Rock looks very comfortable,' Colonel Gilbert leaned back and grunted in Jan's right ear.

She nodded, fearful of voicing her opinion and tempting fate. Billy and Wolf's Rock were still jumping fluently on the far side of the course, and were moving up the incline more easily than most of their rivals. Turning left after they had flown the fence at the top of the hill, the horse remained balanced and they cruised easily down towards the third from home. He was now in second place.

Jan's heart was beating so loudly she was sure that the people standing close to her must be able to hear it.

Suddenly the horse in front of them was checking, something had made him take a second look at the fence. He faltered, tried to shorten his stride and never took off with any impulsion. He ended up straddled across the solid birch obstacle, directly in the path of Colonel Gilbert's horse.

Billy was already committed and had no time to change direction. Wolf's Rock, in a desperate bid to avoid a collision, swerved instinctively to the inside.

Through her binoculars, Jan saw a shape in coloured silks and white breeches hurtle through the air and hit the ground on the far side of the fence. The horse quickly scrambled to its feet, looking rather bewildered.

'Oh dear,' the colonel said quietly. 'Ah, good! Billy's sitting up.'

'I'll go and check the horse,' Jan said, squeezing her way past him, pushing through the crowds to the track, almost oblivious to the hullabaloo that was going on as two horses raced up the hill neck and neck.

Wolf's Rock was hacking up the hill towards her, trailing the reins around his feet. An onlooker had almost cornered the horse when Jan came running up to grasp the dangling leather.

'That's a shame,' the man said. 'He was going really well until that happened. I thought he was the winner.'

'It wasn't his fault,' Jan said grimly. She could accept being beaten fair and square, but to have been taken out by another horse through no fault of their own was so bloody unjustified!

She gave the horse an affectionate rub on the nose. 'What a bugger! You all right, old lad?'

She was worried that he might have picked up an injury, but when she gave him a thorough inspection there didn't seem to be anything wrong. Mightily relieved he was in one piece, she gave him a pat and led him from the track, past the enclosures and up behind the big display board to the stables.

Suddenly she remembered the jockey and wondered if she should have checked on Billy too, but the colonel had been quite definite when he said he'd got up. Besides, if Billy was in trouble, the ambulance tracking the race would have picked him up by now and taken him to be examined by the race-course doctor.

Colonel Gilbert had made his way to the stables, and was waiting outside when Jan arrived.

'How is he?' he asked, with the concern of a genuine horse lover.

Jan gave him a wry grin. 'He's fine. Just brassed off a bit, like me.'

'And me!' The colonel grunted sympathetically.

'I know you can never tell what's going to happen on this course, but our chap looked so well placed coming into the fence I'm sure he'd have finished in the first three,' concluded a down-hearted Jan.

'That's what I thought,' replied the colonel. 'He certainly doesn't look tired. Anyway, there it is,' he went on philosophically. 'I'm looking forward to seeing him run next time.'

'We'll see how he is in a day or two. I'll get him a race as soon as I can, Colonel. Perhaps we'll be able to run him here in a fortnight, on Countryside Day?'

'I'd like that very much, Jan, if you think the race will suit him.'

Half an hour after the incident, Jan's two Irish lads were still fuming at the incompetence of the horse that had fallen in front of theirs.

'Jaysus, he let it come tumbling into the fence on its nose! He should have pulled him up as soon as he felt the animal wasn't travelling well.'

By now, Wolf's Rock had been checked by the vet and given a clean bill of health, and Jan was concentrating on her next runner, Young Willie.

'Come on, you two leprechauns, I want this horse looking like it's just won the Championship at the Dublin Horse Show.'

The lads knew every trick in the book for making a horse and its tack gleam, and when the time came Declan led Lady Fairford's horse into the parade ring, showing off its exquisite physique to great effect.

Lady Fairford, standing beside Jan in an ancient mink coat, squinted big aquamarine eyes that she was too vain to assist with spectacles. 'My goodness, Jan,' she said. 'He looks absolutely terrific.'

Jan couldn't deny that she felt pleased when people appreciated how hard she and her staff tried to produce their horses, looking as well as they possibly could. For although a certain amount of presentation was on the surface, a horse had to be well inside to look really well on the outside.

'Thank you, Lady Fairford. He's feeling pretty full of himself, too, though being the kind of horse he is, I think he's going to need all of this three and a quarter miles to make any impression. Mind you, none of the others have won at this distance either.'

'If he does come home comfortably, I really would like to run him in the cross-country race.'

Jan nodded. 'So would I.'

'That's lucky,' Lady Fairford said with a smile, one strong-minded woman recognizing another. 'I'm delighted young Billy Hanks wasn't hurt,' she went on. She had known Billy since he was an eight-year-old pony-clubber. 'It looked a very nasty fall from where I was watching.'

'Yes, he was lucky. The doctor said the only thing wrong with him is a bruise on his backside. Still, he won't get time to sit down in this race, so that shouldn't bother him,' Jan said, and the two women chuckled as Billy walked gingerly into the parade ring with a little less bounce than usual.

🐎

Young Willie lived up to his magnificent appearance in the paddock and stormed up the hill to the winning post with his ears pricked on his big chestnut head. Four lengths further back came his nearest rival.

He came into the unsaddling enclosure to a great reception and Jan realized that he was just the sort of old-fashioned steeplechaser the Cheltenham crowd adored.

Jan was thrilled with the result – her sixth win so far – and was equally touched by the owner's reaction; she had never seen the stately owner so moved. Large, glistening tears were welling up in Lady Fairford's eyes and, in her excitement, she hadn't noticed that a thick tress of blonde hair had broken free from her chignon and was dangling over the collar of her dark fur coat.

'Jan, thank you so much,' she said, grasping both Jan's hands in hers. For a moment, Jan thought she was going to be showered with kisses, until Lady Fairford suddenly relaxed her grip. 'Let's go and celebrate!' she said, like a naughty schoolgirl about to get into mischief.

🐎

The next day Jan was running another of A.D. O'Hagan's horses. As A.D. had indicated, Wexford Lad had beaten several good horses in his bumper in Ireland the previous year.

Jan wasn't in any doubt that the horse was ready to run; whether he would perform well over hurdles first time out wasn't so clear, but A.D. had phoned that morning to say he would be at Cheltenham, and had invited Jan to join him in his hospitality box if she had any time to spare.

Jan's only other runner was one of the Sharps'; Avon Supreme had finished fourth in a race somewhat above his class the previous week.

Jan decided it would be prudent to spend a little time in A.D.'s company before lunch. As the ground conditions hadn't changed since the previous day, she didn't need to walk the course, and at midday she was able to slip up to his box for a while without feeling she was neglecting her duties.

For a change, today it seemed that A.D. wasn't tearing from one mega-deal to the next and had come in plenty of time to enjoy lunch with his usual band of cronies, and Miss Bennett in attendance, who seemed on permanent standby to take a letter or make calls.

Wexford Lad's race was the novice hurdle, the first race on the card, due off at two o'clock. A.D. had estimated that he and his guests would have finished eating by then. Jan had made it clear she wouldn't be able to dine with them and said she would be leaving the box at one to make sure Annabel had everything under control.

At dead on half-past twelve Annabel burst into the box with a look of horror on her face.

'Hello, Bel,' Jan said, somewhat alarmed, knowing that only something serious could have produced this reaction in her assistant. 'What's wrong?'

'I'm not sure,' Annabel said in a strangled voice, glancing at A.D.

'Is the horse all right?' Jan almost barked.

'Yes, yes. The horse is fine, but when I went up to the weighing room to declare, I noticed on the form they'd ticked the little box by his name saying "passport required", so I went to the lorry . . .' Annabel stopped and lowered her voice, although Jan knew that A.D. was hearing every word, 'and I can't find it.'

'Whose passport's missing?' Jan hissed.

'Wexford Lad's.'

Jan didn't turn to see O'Hagan's reaction. She looked at her watch. 'We've got until one-fifteen to find it before the declarations close! I'll come with you.'

Before she left, Jan had to turn and face A.D., who was looking at her with a studiously blank expression on his face. 'I hope there's not a problem, Jan,' he said quietly. He waved a hand around the room and out at the course beyond the private balcony. 'I won't be too amused if I've come all this way for nothing. It would be most embarrassing in front of my guests.'

Outside, in the corridor that served the private boxes, Jan faced her friend and stared at her.

'Bel, please tell me you haven't lost it.'

'Jan, I haven't a clue where it is. I assumed you'd put it in the folder with Avon Supreme's, like you usually do.'

Jan's heart was pounding like the bass track to the relentless house music Karen played all day in the yard.

'Is Avon's there?'

'Yes, that's all fine.'

Jan closed her eyes and tried to cast her mind back a few hours to the time when they had been getting ready to leave in the morning.

She could see the two passports on the table in the office. She remembered putting one into a folder, then there'd been an commotion, some minor crisis in the yard which had brought her rushing out of the office with the folder in her hand. They'd loaded the horses and gone.

Wexford Lad's passport was still sitting on the table, where she'd left it.

Jan squeezed her eyes shut.

'Shit!' she gasped. 'Shit, shit, *shit*! It's all my fault. I don't think I put it in the folder! They won't let the horse run without its passport.'

'Are you sure, Jan – if you explain?'

'No way. No passport, no race. A.D. will be absolutely fuming!'

'When do you have to get it in by?'

Jan shook her head. 'Forty-five minutes before the race – one-fifteen.'

'Do you know where it is?'

'Yes, I think so,' Jan hissed. 'On the table in the office.'

Annabel looked at her watch. 'It's twenty to one. If we ring Roz now, she could bring it!'

'Bel, don't be crazy! She'll never make it.'

'She might. Jan, it's got to be worth a try!' Annabel grabbed Jan's shoulders.

Jan stared at her for a fraction of a second, prepared for the moment to believe in miracles. 'OK.' She pulled the mobile from her bag and stabbed in the number of her office.

The answer-phone cut in with its usual message. 'This is Edge Farm Stables. I'm sorry no one . . .'

She cut off. 'Damn! She must have gone for lunch.'

'Try the caravan then,' Annabel urged. 'She sometimes goes up to see Fran.'

Shaking as the pressure mounted, Jan wildly punched out her own number.

Fran answered.

'Fran, it's me. Is Roz there? It's an emergency!'

'No, Jan, she's not. She may be down at the pub.'

'Thanks, Fran.'

Jan cut off again. She looked wildly at Annabel. 'Do you know the number at the Fox?'

Annabel screwed up her face in an effort to remember. 'I should do, I often ring Julie. I know,' she gasped suddenly. 'Eight two zero, six three six!'

Once again Jan tried carefully to enter the numbers, and misdialled twice before she got it right.

Julie answered.

'Julie, Julie, it's Jan. I must find Roz. Is she there?'

'Yes, she's right beside me.'

Jan's knees trembled with relief when she heard Roz.

'Hello, Jan. What's the trouble?'

'Jan, I've left Wexford Lad's passport on the office table. Have you got the office key on you?'

'Yes.'

'Have you got your car there?'

'Yes.'

'Thank God! If you fly, there's just time. Go up to the office, grab the passport and bring it here to the weighing room, right now.'

'Where's the weighing room?'

'Right in front of the parade ring. You can't miss it – glass doors.'

'What time do you need it by?'

'One-fifteen, not a second later or they won't let us run Wexford Lad.'

'Jesus!' Roz gasped. She knew as well as Jan what that would mean. 'I'll do my best.'

'Go for it, Roz! But for God's sake, don't kill yourself.'

'I won't. See you in the weighing room.'

She cut off and Jan stared at the phone for a moment and prayed that Roz would be all right. Logically, though, she knew there was very little chance of her making it.

She looked at Annabel and breathed out with a sharp hiss. 'She's on her way, but she's got to get from the pub to the yard, and then here in,' she glanced down at her watch, 'just over thirty-five minutes.'

'I could do it in that.'

'Yes, but she hasn't got a souped-up Golf, and she doesn't drive like an orang-utan with a death wish, unlike you.' Jan grimaced at the thought of Roz haring through Prestbury.

She looked round and realized that several people were hanging about obviously listening to the drama. She smiled wanly at them and decided there was no point in going back to see A.D. until she had something more positive to tell him.

'Come on, Bel. Let's go and make sure nothing else has gone wrong.'

They walked quickly down to the stables and once Jan was satisfied that Wexford Lad was all right and ready to go, she left Annabel in charge and made her way through the swelling crowd back to the weighing room. In the bustle around the clerk of the scales' desk, and the coming and going of stewards and officials, Jan saw some of the head lads and trainers with horses in Wexford Lad's race arriving to hand their declarations to the efficient-looking woman in the declarations office, to the left of the main door.

'Has your passport arrived, Mrs Hardy?' the woman asked.

Jan looked at the big clock on the wall behind the clerk of the scales. Its large second hand swept jerkily around the face while the big hand clunked ominously forward a notch for every minute.

It was five to one.

'Not yet,' Jan replied.

'You only have twenty minutes left to produce it,' the woman warned.

242

Jan tried to guess how far Roz had got – had she found the passport and left the village yet?

A few people said 'hello' to Jan as she stood and waited just inside the door. She responded with a vague, preoccupied smile as her eyes focused again on the clock. Her heart pounded harder each time it clicked to the next notch.

By ten past one, she began to feel sticky with cold perspiration as she rehearsed how she would tell A.D. O'Hagan that Wexford Lad wouldn't be running. She couldn't stop condemning herself for putting all A.D.'s support and sponsorship into jeopardy through just one bloody simple mistake.

It was exactly the costly sort of mistake that she constantly drummed into her staff not to make. And now she would have to live with it in front of them. She felt humiliated by the experience and she knew that telling herself she would never, ever make the same mistake again would do nothing to lessen the catastrophe of losing A.D.'s belief in her.

At twelve minutes past one Jan wanted to die and be swallowed up by the floor. It seemed impossible to her that Roz could have got back to Edge Farm, found the document and driven through all the traffic fast enough to be there within the next three minutes.

But refusing to be defeated, she approached the declarations window, and tried to put on a light smile.

'Wexford Lad, number six. My assistant will be here with the passport any minute.'

'Are you all right, Mrs Hardy?' the woman behind the window asked solicitously. 'I noticed you standing by the door; you look very pale.'

'Oh, I'm fine,' Jan blustered. 'I'm just beginning to wonder what's happened, you know.' She tried to smile, involuntarily glancing over at the clock once more. The sweeping hand was fifteen seconds away from the deadline.

Jan knew she had blown it.

She wanted to go to the lavatory; she felt ill.

She heard the minute hand clunk forward and closed her eyes, half expecting the building to come crashing down around her ears.

Half a minute passed. Nothing happened.

Suddenly, above the murmured hubbub of the room, she heard steps running.

She grasped tentatively, then desperately, at the possibilities they offered.

She looked at the door as Roz burst through, waving the passport in her hand.

'Roz, here!' Jan shrieked.

Roz changed course, almost crashing into Jan, who grabbed the document and hurled it through the window. 'Here it is,' she gasped.

The woman looked at her for a moment, before glancingp up at the clock. Jan held her breath, quivering with trepidation.

'That was lucky, Mrs Hardy. Just in time.'

Jan walked from the weighing room, her legs weak and the whole of her body quivering, feeling drained, but with relief that she could now face O'Hagan, knowing his horse would be allowed to line up at the start.

🐎

'Everything all right with the paperwork, then?' A.D. peered at Jan with a gimlet eye from beneath one lowered, glossy black brow.

'Oh, that was all fine,' Jan said, adding with a faint laugh, 'False alarm.'

'Good. I'm really looking forward to seeing this horse run. He's one I bought myself, against my agent's better judgement.'

Jan looked around at the other people in the parade ring and thanked God once more for Roz's help. 'You bought a nice horse,' she said truthfully. 'He's certainly got speed, but he's not a natural jumper. He may need this run to show him what the job's all about, but I'm fairly hopeful.'

Jan's prognosis proved right. Wexford Lad made a complete hash of the last two hurdles before Murty McGrath drove him up the hill into second place.

To Jan's relief, A.D. appeared perfectly satisfied with the result.

'I thought it was a bit too soon to back him,' he murmured to Jan, as they waited for the horse by the second slot in the unsaddling enclosure. 'But he should get there next time, if you find the right race. What's this horse you've got in the handicap chase?'

'Avon Supreme. The Sharps own him. He's not a bad sort. He ran for Martin Hunter a couple of months ago and looked fairly ropey when he came to us. We ran him for the first time early last week. He didn't do too badly, but was a bit outclassed. Hopefully, he'll do a bit better today.'

'Who are these Sharps?'

'Vince Sharp's a businessman, based in Bristol,' Jan replied, conscious that this was a rather vague description.

'Hmm,' A.D. grunted thoughtfully. 'Well, best of luck with them and thank you for what you've done for me. I expect you know I'm sending a horse over from Ireland to run in the Murphy's Gold Cup, so I shall be here for that. You've nothing entered for me that day, have you?'

'No, there isn't a suitable race for us. Well, not that we'd have a chance of winning, anyway.'

'Fair enough. I'm not interested in having runners just for the sake if it. But I'd be delighted if you could join me for lunch in the box. Would twelve o'clock be all right?'

'Thanks very much,' Jan said. 'I'd love to.'

Jan said her goodbyes and left the winners' enclosure to follow Wexford Lad back to the stables. As she passed the weighing room, someone called out to her.

''Ello, Jan.'

She had to search around for a moment before she spotted Vince and Dawn Sharp standing by the entrance to the parade ring.

'Hello, Mr Sharp,' she said brightly. 'I didn't think any of you were coming today.'

'We weren't,' Dawn said, 'but I changed my mind.'

'Well, it's great to see you. We're in the race after next, but you're welcome to come to the saddling boxes, if you want.'

'That's all right. We'll see you 'ere when the 'oss comes in.'

🐎

Jan was surprised to see the Sharps, since Angie had told her they didn't like going racing and preferred to watch their runners on the box. She had to admit they looked a bit out of place. But there was no reason why they shouldn't enjoy their horses, more especially since they'd produced three individual winners for Edge Farm already.

In fact, the more Jan saw of their horses the better she liked them, and she had to give the Sharps credit for having bought them in the first place.

But she had allowed herself to become rather too confident about the horses and was disappointed when Billy Hanks and Avon Supreme only finished third.

The Sharps are taking it surprisingly well, she thought.

'Don't worry. You've done a marvellous job, dear,' Dawn croaked at Jan as they patted the horse in the unsaddling enclosure. 'We're very pleased with the winners you've got us so far.'

After Dawn's icy display at Overmere, Jan was surprised and relieved by her enthusiasm. She was in no doubt that happy owners were much easier to deal with than miserable ones.

'You've got some super horses, and though I'm sorry we didn't win with Avon today, I'm sure we will soon, and with Moriarty. He's worked so well at home.'

'Good. Well, you keep those fax reports coming and we'll let you know.'

'Fine,' Jan nodded, fleetingly annoyed to be reminded of the handcuffs. 'I'm surprised Angie's not here today.'

'Busy,' Dawn said, with a sudden return to her normal evasiveness.

'Oh well. Give her my love, won't you?'

Dawn nodded.

'Cheerio then,' Vince said, and the strange old pair waddled off towards the car park.

Annabel joined Jan in the ring.

'I wonder if Vince drove up here in that old Rolls,' she said with a grin.

'I just don't know what to make of those two,' Jan said and she repeated her conversation with Dawn. 'I've got a gut feeling something doesn't quite add up.'

'There's no particular mystery,' Annabel said. 'They've obviously come up from pretty humble beginnings – I should think that Vince's family were probably horse dealers. And Dawn's background must have been similar. What *is* a puzzle, though, is how they produced a daughter who's so good-looking and sophisticated – well, at least on the surface,' Annabel added.

Jan shrugged as they strolled back to the stables. 'Still, they sent us seven nice horses; they pay their bills. Why should we be bothered how they got their money? It really is none of our business.'

12

Racing with Johnny Carlton-Brown at Ascot the following Saturday was an entirely different experience. Like A.D., he didn't mind what he spent on his leisure activities. At the same time, Jan didn't have to contend with the mind games A.D. played constantly. Johnny seemed to have no need to exert his influence over everyone around him, yet there was a much more subtle strength to his personality.

He had particularly asked Jan to run his new mare, August Moon, in a novice chase. Jan had advised against it, but he was keen to see her run. Business commitments meant he wouldn't be able to go racing for several weeks and there was no pressure on her to win.

Jan didn't like sending out runners on this basis, but Johnny had asked her so politely and with such enthusiasm that she had reluctantly agreed.

Although the mare was outclassed, she ran creditably and didn't disgrace herself. As far as Jan was concerned, it was a useful exercise in gauging the right level of race to pitch her in the next time she ran.

On the same day, however, Jan had also sent Moriarty to Hereford with Annabel, and almost didn't believe the result when she saw it on Channel 4's racing results. The horse had provided a third victory for the Sharps and a seventh for Edge Farm.

When JCB saw the result, he gave her an enigmatic smile. 'Your Irishman must be rather pissed off that your tinkers are getting such a lot of winners from just seven horses.'

'I don't suppose he minds,' Jan said. 'There's a good chance most of his will win too, once they start running. They're a bit behind the Sharps' in their training, that's all. Anyway, the Sharps' horses had such poor form until I got them that it's like picking cherries.'

'Well, I still think he won't like it,' Johnny said. 'He's the sort of chap who likes his dominant position clear-cut. That's why I'll never have more than two or three with you, as long as he's there. Talking of which, I was thinking, rather than wait for the sales, maybe you could start sniffing around to see if anyone wants to sell anything privately? I'm sure some good horses must come onto the market that way.'

'Here,' Jan nodded. 'Or in Ireland?'

'I don't mind. Both, if you like. Do you know much about the Irish scene?'

'To be honest, I've only been over there once, but I was really impressed – it's such a great source of jumpers. I made a few contacts while I was there, too,' Jan added, thinking of Micky Byrne and his chums, and Eamon Fallon.

'Good,' Johnny said. 'Give them a call. See what you can unearth.'

🐎

Driving home in the lorry after the races, Jan found the idea of visiting Ireland again quite appealing. She was more confident about what she could achieve there than she would have been a few months ago.

For one thing, she was definitely more of a presence in racing now. The number of winners she'd managed to achieve from such a small string had been covered well by the racing media, although she resented their tendency to dwell on her age and the colour of her hair rather than her horses and her ability as a trainer.

Roz, with lots of tittering, was reading out a piece along those lines from the racing pages of one of the nationals.

'Do you know, I find it bloody insulting,' Jan said when she'd finished. 'They would never refer to a male trainer as bouncy and blonde, even if he were. They wouldn't mention the size of his private parts, either, would they?'

Roz sniggered. 'Cor, I wouldn't worry if I was you,' she said. 'At least it gets you noticed.'

'It's a double-edged sword,' Jan replied, still feeling rather irritated.

That night Jan couldn't decide who to phone.

She trusted Eamon Fallon. He'd always been totally straight when he'd had his point-to-pointer with her last season, but she couldn't overlook the fact that he now relied on O'Hagan for his bread and butter. After Johnny's convincing analysis of A.D.'s desire for control, she guessed it might be hard for Eamon to be impartial or point her in the right direction without referring to his boss.

The old jockeys she'd met at the Derby sale she had liked very much, but she couldn't deny they were unlikely to have any worthwhile contacts of their own in the current market. Micky Byrne probably knew a few breeders who'd had strong racing connections in his day. But that might be more of a hindrance than a help now. He might feel more obligated to them than to her.

She leaned back on the bench in her caravan and pulled the catalogue of the Fairyhouse sale from her bookshelf. In the back of it she had written notes, recording her impressions, useful information and, most importantly, the contacts she had made.

When she saw his name, she wondered why she hadn't thought of him at once. Sean McDonagh.

The picture of him in her mind's eye was reassuring. And yet – what had it been about him that had made her doubt his sincerity?

He had told them not to bid for a horse; he'd heard a rumour it had already been tried at home, despite the description in the sales catalogue. A big, handsome horse, she remembered, bought cheaply by Arthur Pickering, a trainer with a big yard in Somerset. Somebody undoubtedly thought they had gone home with a bargain.

But . . . had they?

She took down another book, *The Directory of the Turf*, and found the phone number of the West Country yard.

She looked at the Swiss clock her mother had given her as a wedding present, mounted perilously on one of the caravan's walls.

It was nearly ten. Arthur Pickering had had runners at Ascot but, like her, he would be back home and tidied up by now.

She dialled his number. The phone was answered after a few rings by a man's voice.

'Hello?'

'Hello, it's Jan Hardy here. Is that Mr Pickering?'

There was a moment's silence before the man replied. 'Yes. What can I do for you?'

'I'm looking for more young stock.'

'Pulling the punters in, are you?'

'I've had a few enquiries,' Jan answered evasively. 'And I remembered a horse I liked very much at Fairyhouse, but I missed him going through the ring. In the sale report, they said you'd bought it.'

'Which was that?'

'A big bay by Good Thyne, around Lot One-Ninety, I think.'

'I know the one. What about him?'

'I wondered if by any chance he might be for sale?'

'He could be.'

'Who owns him, then?'

'I do.'

'How much would you want for him?'

There was a moment's silence. 'Twenty grand.'

'Oh, that's more than I thought. Sorry.'

'Hang on. What would you pay?'

'I was thinking nearer five or ten.'

'Well, we may not be too far apart.'

'I'd have to come and see him first,' Jan parried.

'Hmm. Let me know when you're coming, then.'

'I will.' Jan said goodbye and put the phone down.

She leaned back on the bench with a thoughtful smile. If Arthur Pickering was prepared to lose the horse from his yard at this stage of the season, it was very likely a dud.

If he was prepared to let it go for the kind of money they'd talked about, it was unquestionably a dud. Which meant the advice Sean McDonagh had given her was entirely genuine.

🐎

After the long day at Ascot, Jan spent a lazy Sunday afternoon at home with the children. Megan jumped Smarty in the paddock, while Matthew played with the tractor Angie had given him. Jan wandered around the echoing spaces of her half-finished house, wishing, now that the roof was on, she had the money which Gerry needed to go ahead with the floors and ceilings. As often happened with her, she found the prospect of finally moving into the house had galvanized her into action.

Later she walked down to her office, where she could still keep half an eye on the children and found the business card Sean McDonagh had given her in Fairyhouse.

'Well, well, Mrs Hardy,' Jan heard him say, when she introduced herself. 'It's good to hear from you. I see you've got off to a grand start.'

'We've had a bit of luck,' Jan agreed. 'And we've been sent some pretty nice horses.'

'It looks like it, attracting the right horses is as important as training them. So, what can I do for you?'

Jan smiled at Sean's soft Irish voice and tried to remember his blue eyes and handsome Irish face.

'One of my owners wants to buy a young star that's already proved itself either pointing or over hurdles and is ready to go novice chasing – something with a bit of class.'

'Do you want to buy through the ring?'

'Not necessarily. There may not be anything good enough at this time of year.'

'No, you could be struggling. How much will yer man pay for the right horse?'

'Up to fifty thousand, sterling.'

'OK. Leave it with me, Jan. I'll get back to yer in the next few days.'

'Do you think you may be able to find something?'

'I'd say so.'

'Thank you, Sean. I'm glad I phoned you.'

'Why did you, now, after such a long time?'

Jan gave an embarrassed laugh. 'I rang Arthur Pickering and asked him about that horse you warned me and Dad off at the Derby Sale.'

Sean chuckled. 'What did he say?'

'He couldn't wait to get rid of it.'

'Well, there it is.'

'Yes. Thanks again, Sean. I'm sorry to have rung on a Sunday.'

'It doesn't matter at all. I'll be in touch.'

🐎

During the fortnight following her conversation with Sean McDonagh, Jan was sending out runners several days a week. If they were at different courses she used her own lorry and the local horse transport company. She could have hitched a lift with Virginia Gilbert on a few occasions, but couldn't bring herself to phone and ask the favour.

By the time Countryside Day at Cheltenham arrived – a Friday in the middle of November – Jan had produced another winner for the Sharps and an unexpected win with Erin's Jet over two miles for A.D. O'Hagan, bringing her total to nine.

Apart from Young Willie in the cross-country race, she was a bit disappointed that she had no other runners over the three days of the Murphy's Gold Cup meeting. It just happened that none of the other races were suitable for her horses.

She wasn't feeling at all comfortable about going on her own to A.D.'s lunch on Saturday at Cheltenham while Annabel took Avon Supreme to Haydock, but she knew she had no alternative.

A.D. greeted her warmly and introduced her to Dermot O'Hare, the legendary Irish trainer, who had brought his horse over for the big race.

Dermot was a tall, handsome man in his mid sixties. When A.D. moved on, the Irishman offered to fill up Jan's glass. 'That was a nice result for you in the cross-country yesterday.'

Jan nodded. 'I thought the race would suit our horse. He ran really well here two weeks ago, over three and a quarter miles, and I knew he wouldn't mind those banks and ditches.'

'Some of those natural hedges have grown a bit since I last ran a horse over them,' Dermot chuckled. 'Just remind me, who owns Young Willie?'

'One of my locals, Lady Fairford from Beauclerk Manor.'

'And who are these other people you've been having such a good run for?'

'Vince and Dawn Sharp. They come from Bristol.'

The names obviously meant nothing to Dermot. 'Aha?' he grunted. 'And are you happy with Billy Hanks?'

'Yes, very. There've been a couple of races he probably should have won if he'd been more on the ball and ridden them differently, but he's learned a lot this season.'

'I watched him yesterday. I know he's not Irish, but he's not bad,' Dermot grinned. 'Anyway, the very best of luck to you. I'll watch out for you if you ever send any runners across the water.'

'I hope to sooner or later,' Jan said. 'I went over to buy a horse for a client the other day.'

'I heard. Supercall is a very grand sort of horse. You were lucky to get him.'

Jan got the impression that Dermot would have liked the horse for himself, but she said nothing.

'Who put you in there?' he asked.

Jan tensed. She felt she'd told Dermot enough already. 'A friend of mine,' she replied enigmatically.

Dermot had got the message. 'We'll meet again, no doubt,' he said with a wink and turned to talk to another of A.D.'s cronies.

At lunch Jan found that she had been placed next to her host. She wondered, not for the first time, why A.D.'s wife seemed never to be present on these occasions. It was odd, she thought, but there was never anything in the newspapers about A.D. philandering.

Perhaps he didn't play the field; or perhaps his close relationship with the owners of the major newspapers was such that his activities were not on their agenda. Looking at his clean-cut features as he sat beside her, Jan was fascinated to consider that this was a real possibility.

He turned, his blue eyes fixed on her. 'So, Jan, we're not doing *too* badly, are we?'

Jan thought of what Johnny Carlton-Brown had said about A.D.'s view of the Sharps and wondered if now, in his mind, he was comparing their tally with his own. 'We've run three of yours and won with two. I suppose you could say that wasn't too bad,' she agreed with deliberate understatement. 'Wexford Lad will win shortly, I hope; so, once the others have run, we might even get a full house.'

'That would be way beyond my expectations,' A.D. said. 'There's bound to be the odd injury and one or two off-colour at some point. But so far, Jan, I'm delighted with what you've achieved. Let's hope one day we might be able to send out a horse to compete in the Murphy's.'

He looked inquisitively at her, before glancing at Dermot O'Hare on the other side of the table.

'In the meantime, I'd really like you to come over to Aigmont and have a look at the set-up. I'm off to Australia at the end of the month for a bit of racing and then I'm in the Far East for ten days. But there's a meeting at Leopardstown on the twentieth of December. Come over, have a look, and stay for a couple of nights.'

Jan was aware that A.D. wasn't canvassing her opinion on the arrangement; he was telling her that he expected her to visit.

Jan pulled her diary from her bag and thumbed through it. 'We're racing at Ascot that Saturday, but I can catch a flight when racing's finished and be over for the evening.'

'That would be fine. That's settled then!'

🐎

As Jan walked from the course to the car park, she was extremely apprehensive and wondered how it would feel to enter the lion's den – or perhaps, she thought, the spider's web was a better analogy. Whichever, she found she couldn't rid herself of the image of A.D. as a predator and she was seriously questioning the wisdom of getting too close to the enigmatic Irishman, despite the fact that, apart from his initial frostiness over the open day, he had so far only been supportive of her. However, she was committed to the visit, so she would just have to go and make sure she didn't drop her guard.

She was dragged back to the present by someone shouting her name. She turned to find Tony Robertson jogging to catch up.

'Hi, Jan, I was looking for you earlier.'

His big, open smile came as a relief after the session with A.D.'s guarded pleasantries. 'I saw that you'd become one of the course doctors – one way of getting free tickets, I suppose,' Jan said with a laugh.

'Actually, there was a bit of work to do this afternoon.'

'There weren't any bad falls were there?'

'No, but an old lady passed out in the Silver Ring. I don't know if it was excitement or what, but I thought she was a gonner for a couple of minutes. Her husband's just taken her off. She seems quite happy now, so that was a good result. Only trouble was I missed the big race.'

'I was in A.D.'s box when his horse won. They went wild.'

'Were you, indeed? Well, I've got an even better invitation for you – dinner at L'Escargot in Middle Swell.'

Jan looked blank. 'Is that good?'

'It's got a Michelin star, for God's sake, and François, the owner has offered me dinner for two tomorrow night.'

'Why – have you been supplying him with drugs or something?' Jan laughed.

'No, but I cured his mother-in-law's irritable bowel.'

'Sounds like a fair swap.' Jan giggled. 'I'd love to come, but let me check I can find someone to look after the kids first. And I won't want to be out too late – I'm up at six on Monday morning.'

🐎

Jan's Land Rover bounced out of the car park and she headed up Cleeve Hill to Winchcombe, where she turned off for Riscombe; she had promised her parents she would drop in on her way home as, for once, she hadn't any horses with her.

Reg and Mary, as usual, questioned her about progress on the house; Mary was almost as adamant as Olwen that the children shouldn't have to spend another winter in the mobile home.

'Mum, I don't think we'll have to, but if we do it's not the end of the world. They did it last year and thousands of families live in them all the time.'

'Yes, but after last year I keep worrying about poor Matty. I'm sure he's not as tough as Megan.'

'Mum, it looks like Gerry'll have enough done to let us move into part of it by Christmas, so let's aim for that. You and Dad can come over with Ben for Christmas Day, if you like.'

'That would be wonderful,' Mary said fervently. 'I'll help with the cooking.'

'No you won't,' Jan said. 'I can manage.'

'But how do you find the time?'

'I don't know. But we don't starve. As a matter of fact, tomorrow night I won't have to cook at all – I'm having dinner at some amazing place I've never heard of called L'Escargot at Middle Swell.'

'Bloody hell,' Reg grunted. 'I hope you're not paying. They say it costs an arm and a leg to eat there.'

'Tony Robertson, the doctor, has asked me; apparently he's been offered a free meal for two, so that's all right.'

'And he's taking you?' Mary asked, wide-eyed.

'Why not? It's not the first time he's taken me out to dinner. He must have asked me half a dozen times since he came to see Matty – you know, the chap who called when you were there.'

'Of course I know who he is. Why didn't you tell us before, love?' Mary asked, settling down and pouring herself another cup of tea.

'Because I knew you'd read too much into it, like you are now, Mother.'

'Have another cup of tea, dear. You don't have to rush off just yet. Tell us.'

Jan gave a wry smile and sighed reluctantly as Mary refilled her cup. 'There isn't anything to tell. He's a nice bloke, quite funny, thoughtful, good-looking, I suppose, and much too nice for me.'

'What?' Mary looked shocked and disappointed. 'Don't be silly, why should he be too nice for you? All right, he may be public school and all that, but that doesn't matter – not these days.'

'No, of course it doesn't; it's not that. It's just, well, he always treats me as if I was sort of . . .', Jan shrugged, searching for the right word, '. . . fragile.'

'Isn't that nice?'

'But Mum, I don't want to be put on a pedestal; I'm not a bloody saint.'

'Well, your dad and I think you are, with all the hard work you've put in for those kids and looking after all those people who work for you.'

'I have to look after them, Mum, or they wouldn't work for me,' Jan chuckled at her mother's view of her self-sacrifice.

'Look, I've already thought carefully about going out with Tony, and I'm slowly getting used to the idea. The only reason I'm going tomorrow is because he doesn't pressurize me.'

'Has there been much what you might call romance yet?' Mary asked tentatively.

'No, it's purely platonic. I don't think I'm ready for it to go any further. In the meantime at least he makes me laugh, and he's taken me to some really good places, which is nice.'

'Well, Jan,' Reg said, thoughtfully stuffing the bowl of the pipe he occasionally brought out if a serious discussion was taking place, 'he's widowed, and not too old. You could do a lot worse, you know.'

'Dad, please. You know that I'm not very good at compromise – and "could do a lot worse" is definitely a compromise.'

'That's all very well when you're young,' Mary said. 'All those romantic ideas and principles, but you've got those children to think about, and don't you forget it.'

'I don't, Mum; I promise you I never will.'

Supercall, the rising Irish star Jan had recently acquired for Johnny Carlton-Brown, arrived at Edge Farm on Sunday morning. Jan had bought the horse from a frail, tweedy Anglo-Irish woman from West Cork who had been breeding old-fashioned jumpers for over thirty years.

It had been many years since Margaret Berrington had sold her young horses at auction for a price she thought worthwhile, and when she had watched one of the best colts she'd ever bred fail to attract a bid higher than seven thousand pounds, she had defiantly refused to sell the animal. She'd had it gelded and sent into training to run in her own famous colours.

Also her daughter was married to a charismatic but penniless leader of a ceilidh band and wanted to buy a bungalow in Kerry, so Margaret considered it was the right time to cash in the animal for something like its real value.

Supercall had been really successful as a four-year-old hurdler.

He had run with impressive consistency during the next two seasons and now, at six, he was potentially one of the best novice chasers in his country, well bred and built like a Sherman tank.

He was exactly what Johnny Carlton-Brown wanted. And Sean McDonagh was the only bloodstock agent in Ireland whom Margaret Berrington trusted.

When Sean had introduced Mrs Berrington to Jan, the old lady was sitting in a wicker chair in the soft, damp air of her crumbling conservatory and looked long and hard at her for an interminable thirty seconds.

'Tell me, Mrs Hardy,' she had asked eventually in a strange, Victorian English with an Irish lilt, 'if you were to buy this horse, where do you think he would end up?'

'He looks to me,' Jan said without any hesitation, 'like a classic Gold Cup horse.'

The old lady smiled. 'I like dreamers,' she said, 'especially those with a really good eye for a horse. Do you think your owner would go to seventy-five thousand Irish for him?'

Jan battled with herself for a few moments. She ought to be bargaining. But she wanted the horse and she knew he was probably worth more than was being asked; she sensed the old lady wanted her to have him. And Jan didn't doubt that Sean would have another customer if she quibbled and didn't make up her mind there and then.

'Yes, I think he would,' she had answered. 'If I recommend him.'

As the horse was led off the lorry, Jan couldn't stop smiling. The thrill of seeing him standing in her yard made her feel as if the sun was bursting out through her body; Supercall was simply one of the best-looking, best-made horses she had ever seen. She thought she must be dreaming, it seemed crazy that an animal like this should be coming to live with little Jan Hardy, the farmer's daughter from Gloucestershire.

The Irish lads and Annabel had waited after morning stables for the arrival, and there was an air of sheer delight in the yard as, like Jan, they took on board the possibilities that the horse had to offer. 'I think I'm in love,' laughed Annabel.

Jan was still entranced when Tony came to collect her that evening.

'Sounds like your first top-class horse,' he remarked.

'Yes, though I have got three others I think could be as good in time.'

'Well, I hope you're right. It strikes me that until you start sending out quality runners, you'll never do more than scrape a meagre living with an awful lot of hard work.'

Jan glanced at him as he focused on the narrow lane ahead. It was the first time he had ventured a view about the blunt realities of her way of life; and she wasn't sure she liked it. 'Yes, well, I knew it wasn't going to be a picnic.'

He turned to her quickly, to read her face. 'I'm sorry,' he apologized. 'I know it's none of my business, but I am very pleased that you've reached this new stage in your career, when people are prepared to send you better horses.'

For the rest of the evening, as they ate a memorable dinner in seductive surroundings, Jan was aware that, for Tony, their relationship had moved onto a new level. In some ways she was flattered by his interest and concern, but since John's death she had become used to making her own decisions and running her own life; she was out of the habit of sharing its details with anyone else. Even Annabel she told only as much to as she felt her friend needed to know.

Nevertheless, patiently and without any pressure, Tony was slowly breaking down her reluctance to confide, and he had already combined his love of horses with a well-informed view of the racing world which he enjoyed sharing with Jan.

'Do you know what?' she said, as they were finishing their dessert. 'You've managed to drag more private thoughts out of me than my own parents have recently, and I'm not sure if I like it.'

'You mean, like those Amazon Indians who think they're having their souls stolen if someone takes a photograph of them?'

'Something like that,' Jan smiled. 'But don't ask me any more questions. I've been bloody lucky so far since I've had my licence, and I don't want to rock the boat by changing my methods at this stage.'

'I wasn't questioning them,' Tony said gently. 'I thought I was helping you to plan a long-term strategy.'

'Thanks, but this season my only strategy is to get as many winners on the score sheet as possible, never mind the quality. I'll concentrate on the better races in a few years' time.'

❧

Jan's irritation didn't run deep, and as Tony drove her home she forgave him for prying too far into her affairs. She wondered what he would suggest when they arrived back at Edge Farm.

When they pulled into the parking place in front of the yard gates, Tony sat for a moment before he undid his seat belt. 'I'll walk you home,' he muttered.

He strode round the car to open Jan's door, but she was already out. As they walked up the hill, he gently took her arm. When they reached the step to the caravan, Jan was asking herself if she should invite him in and let Emma go home. He turned to face her and gripped both her arms just below her shoulders. In the dim light through the reeded glass door, she saw a question in his eyes. Then he leaned down and, for the first time, kissed her on the lips. 'Night, Jan,' he said as he stepped back and walked away to his car. Jan lay awake wondering if she had really liked being kissed by Tony, or just liked being kissed.

❧

The last day of the month was crisp and clear. Sunlight flooded through the freshly glazed windows of the new Farm House. Jan picked her way carefully across the screeded floor as Gerry escorted her through the ground-floor rooms, pointing out what remained to be done.

'I suppose you *could* move in next week. It'll be a bit of a squeeze,' he said doubtfully, in answer to Jan's question.

'But would we be in the way of you finishing off?'

'A bit, but I could get the floors down in a couple of the bedrooms. Nothing would be decorated.'

'I know, I know,' Jan said impatiently. 'But if I'm in here already, I can't help thinking the whole thing will move a bit faster. I might even be able to do some of it myself.'

'What, with all the horses to do? I don't think so,' Gerry said as firmly as he dared.

'Let's have a look upstairs,' Jan instructed excitedly.

Resigned, Gerry led her up the timber staircase, which had been installed two days before. 'Just you you be careful. If you step off the joists, you'll go straight through the plasterboard and we'll be back where we started.'

'Don't worry, Gerry. I won't let the kids up here, either.'

Jan couldn't keep the excitement from her voice. Even in this unfinished condition – floorless, bare plasterboard, with doors leant against the walls waiting to be hung – at last her new house felt more like a home, and she could walk through rooms which until a short while ago had existed only in her mind. It was less than two years since she had first come to look at the motley collection of extremely dilapidated buildings that was called Edge Farm, but much had happened and the house had risen out of the ground so slowly that it felt a great deal longer.

She breathed in the smell of raw, sawn timber and glaziers' putty as she inspected the bathroom fittings, which were due to be installed the following week.

'I really think, once a house has a bathroom, it's habitable, so we'll start moving in the basics next weekend, then with a bit of luck it'll be all right for Christmas, even if it's not actually finished.'

'OK, Jan.' Gerry gave a small sigh. 'What do you think of it, then?'

'Oh, Gerry! I haven't thanked you, have I? Well, thank you, thank you, thank you, very, very much.' She leaned up and kissed his cheek and watched his grey-brown eyes cloud over with emotion. 'You have been absolutely fantastic – a real star – I'll never be able to repay you for what you've done for me and the children.'

'That's all right,' Gerry mumbled, embarrassed now by the scale of Jan's gratitude. 'I wanted to do it, I've enjoyed it.'

'And you've done it brilliantly.'

'I've had some good blokes to help, mind.'

'But you were in charge, making sure everything's right.'

Through the window of what would soon be her bedroom, Jan looked out across the sunlit valley and saw a gleaming car creeping up the drive.

For a moment and from a distance, Jan thought it was Tony Robertson and felt a little shiver of anticipation that she couldn't explain. Perhaps, she told herself, it was simply the fact that she hadn't heard a word from him since he had kissed her outside the caravan after their dinner at L'Escargot.

But when the car stopped she realized quickly, with a mixture of disappointment and relief, that it wasn't the doctor's at all but Toby Waller's.

'Here's Toby,' she told Gerry. 'He said he'd be up for a look round. Do you mind?'

'Course not. He's a good bloke is Toby. He told me where to go to get these funny old-fashioned baths you wanted.'

'Did he? He's amazing, isn't he? He always seems to know where to get things.'

An hour or so later Toby and Jan walked up to the caravan to have a drink and a chat before he took Annabel to lunch at Colonel Gilbert's.

'Do you suppose Virginia will be there?' Jan remarked.

'I doubt it.' Toby chuckled, 'Not if she knows your assistant's going too.'

'Well, I'm not sure,' Jan mused. 'It's the sort of thing the colonel likes to do to keep Virginia in her place.'

'Oh, for God's sake,' Toby said, 'you women! Talking of

tricky women, have you heard from your mother-in-law about Harold Powell's application?'

'She phoned about a week ago and said she'd heard they were still considering that report your surveyors commissioned.'

'Good. I meant to check. I should have heard back about their findings, if they have any. I'll give them a prod. In the meantime, don't worry. We'll make sure the old biddy doesn't get crowded out.'

'And that Harold Powell doesn't end up making another bloody great profit out of our old farm.'

'I don't think he's serious about it anyway. Like you said, he just wants to persuade you to buy it.'

'Hgh,' Jan grunted. 'It's all I can do to pay for the last bits of material to finish the house.'

'But, you're very lucky, you know.' Toby turned and indicated the house as they reached the caravan. 'Your Gerry has done a really excellent job. This is going to be a very tidy little set-up when it's all finished – anyway, if the worst comes to the worst, your mother-in-law could always move in with you. You'll have bags of room.'

Three weeks after Supercall had arrived from Ireland, Jan asked Annabel to let the gelding into the small paddock beside the barn. She wanted him to stretch his legs before he was loaded onto the lorry for his first appearance in Johnny Carlton-Brown's colours at Sandown.

Jan had decided to run the horse in a couple more hurdle races while she schooled him over some small fences to prepare him for his steeplechasing career. If all went well, he could start his novice campaign in the New Year.

Checking entries in the office, she heard Annabel calling.

'Jan, Jan, come here!' Clearly there was a note of alarm in her voice.

Jan leaped to her feet and rushed outside. Annabel was by the barn, beckoning her.

'Quickly! Come and have a look at Supercall; he's hopping lame!'

Jan felt a ripple of fear pass through her body, bringing home to her how much she had been looking forward to the race today as the start of a whole new stage in her career. Heart thumping, she raced across the yard. Rounding the corner at the end, she saw the gelding standing morosely in the far corner of the paddock with his ears back and his tail twitching.

'Bel, get me a handful of nuts in a bucket.'

The familiar rattle of delicious food was enough for Supercall to overcome his reluctance to put pressure on his sore foot. With a whicker of expectation, and heavily favouring his off-fore, he hobbled across the turf towards the gate where they stood.

Jan opened the gate into the paddock while Annabel took the bucket and held it close for the horse to delve with his nose. Jan bent down and lifted the foot that was causing the trouble. She cradled it in her hands and immediately noted the heat. 'It feels like it's on fire,' she said to Annabel, turning it skywards to clean the frog with a hoof-pick, hoping to find the problem.

'It's no good, Bel,' she said desperately. 'We'll have to get him in and give it a good wash out.'

Ten minutes later, the sore was obvious. 'He must have trodden on something, or maybe the farrier pricked him when he was having his racing plates fitted yesterday. Whatever, it's gone septic. It'll need a poultice, damn it! And he won't be doing any work for a good few days!' Jan was almost shaking with anger and frustration. 'Why the farrier didn't notice and say something about it, God only knows!'

For the rest of the morning while she drove to Sandown, Jan couldn't shake off her depression. In her experience, the problem with Supercall's foot might take some time to clear up and, if it persisted, she wouldn't be able to exercise him at all and inevitably, while he was confined to his box, he'd be losing his fitness.

As they came nearer to London, Jan had brightened a little. They still had a chance of bringing home a winner. The Sharps' horse, Lucky Charm, was running against moderate competition; since his first win for her, he'd scored a third and a fourth in much better company than today's race and the trade papers were predicting odds of even money which reflected his chance.

Billy knew the course well; he and Jan had walked it the first time he'd ridden there for her and he'd worked out how to deal with the three tricky railway fences on the far side of the course.

Angie was the only member of the Sharp family to come and support their runner. She met them in the paddock, looking as well turned out as usual, and gave Billy an encouraging smile, while Jan confirmed their tactics for the race.

Lucky Charm was a horse who preferred to see plenty of daylight and didn't like to be crowded. As soon as the runners had surged away from the starter, Billy sent his horse to the front as he and Jan had agreed. Passing the stands for the first time, he was running keenly – a little too keenly, Jan thought. They already had a ten-length advantage over the others.

Jan winced and Angie noticed.

'It's all right, isn't it?' she asked. 'Lucky likes to be up front.'

'Yes, but not that far. When they catch him, he'll have nothing to fight back with. He's on too high a burner for this stage of the race.'

'But Billy looks as if he's in control and the horse isn't under pressure.'

'He soon will be,' Jan muttered, seeing the rest of the field swiftly gaining on her horse as they approached the three tricky fences.

By the time the field had jumped the last of them, Lucky Charm had been caught. When they reached the home straight, he was lying fifth and rapidly running out of steam.

'Shit!' Jan gasped. 'Billy, you bloody fool!'

'But it's not Billy's fault, surely?' Angie protested.

'Yes it is. He still hasn't learned how to ride a front runner.

They need pacing, he's let this chap run away for two miles and he's completely run out of juice.'

'Well, obviously, it's a shame,' Angie understated, 'but don't take it out on him. He'll realize what he's done, won't he?'

'I bloody hope so,' Jan said through gritted teeth, watching her big hope for the afternoon trail in last of the ten runners.

🐎

Jan waited for Billy in the weighing room.

'What the hell were you doing?' she asked in a throaty whisper.

'What do you mean? I done my best. I tried to ride him out, didn't I? But there was nothing left in the tank.'

'You know bloody well what I mean. Of course there wasn't anything left – you knackered him by going so far ahead of the pace.'

'He was quite happy; that's what he wanted to do.'

'You're the bloody jockey, Billy. You're supposed to tell him what to do!' Jan shook her head. 'D'you know, sometimes I find it very hard to believe that you don't know how bloody stupid you're being.' She glared at him for a moment before turning abruptly on her heel and striding out of the building.

🐎

The following day, Saturday, didn't even yield a place from the two runners Jan sent out. Bernie Sutcliffe, who had hyped himself up into thinking Dingle Bay might at last realize his potential, had marched off the course filled with discontent.

Back in the caravan that evening, and with Supercall still limping around his box, the only thing to brighten Jan was the thought that tomorrow Gerry was arriving to help her start moving into her new house.

🐎

This is not before time, either, Jan thought the next day. Clear signs of Jack Frost's artistic talents were appearing on some mornings inside the windows of the mobile home, even when the wood-burner was stoked up.

Even though there were no carpets or curtains in the house, or even floors in some of the bedrooms, and the kitchen floor was just concrete, the plumbing had been finished and there was oil in the fuel tank, so the central heating was on. To Jan and the children, although unfinished, the house would be like a palace after a year and a half in the pokey mobile home.

From the start, Gerry had had a very good idea of what Jan wanted in Edge Farm House – a home that would blend into the hillside, built of the same honeyed stone that was just below the surface of the thin soil covering her sloping pasture. She had wanted a house that looked as if it belonged, as if it had been on the site as long as the barn, which was the only original farm building still standing. By using the reclaimed stone, timber and tiles which Eddie Sullivan had gathered for Jan the previous year, Gerry had achieved exactly that effect and although he probably knew in his own mind that he and Jan would never be the item he had wanted them to be, his devotion to her was as strong now as when he'd first committed himself to the project.

The house had a large kitchen with windows facing south and west, and Jan planned to spend most of her time here. A reconditioned Aga found by Gerry took pride of place in the large chimney breast and there was still plenty of space for the long pine table that had come from Stonewall.

⚘

By mid-afternoon, the table, chairs and a large oak dresser had been installed – the kitchen was transformed and looked amazingly comfortable and ready for use, despite the lack of a floor covering and bare windows. Although two of the four bedrooms were still unfinished, the children were thrilled at the prospect of living in a real house. Megan remembered a little about Stonewall, but Matthew nothing at all.

Annabel helped them to make their beds and arranged their toys before disappearing to her cottage, only to reappear half an hour later with an assortment of curtains that she had brought from her parents' house when she first moved to Gloucestershire.

Roz and Karen Stoddard turned up with a huge casserole they had made for supper – a sort of house-warming, they said, and Julie and the two Irishmen arrived from the pub with four bottles of wine.

Even with Gerry, Emma and Joe, they had no trouble in fitting around the big table to raise their glasses and wish Jan every success with a great deal of affection. So, for the time being, she was able to push Supercall's septic foot, Lucky Charm's lousy run and Bernie's scathing criticism to the back of her mind.

🐎

It was most fortunate that Jan had moved in when she did as the very next morning she woke in her undraped bedroom, opened the window and found a fierce frost had gripped most of the country.

Outside in the first light of day the Severn valley was as white as the Arctic, while the Malvern Hills were covered in a mantle of snow like icing on a cake.

Jan saw the glistening ice on the drive, where the water that trickled down it the previous evening had frozen into a sheet. Annabel and the rest of the staff didn't even try to drive up the track. They were forced to park their cars on the verge at the bottom of the hill and walk the rest of the way to the yard.

Jan greeted them with a fatalistic smile. 'We're certainly not going to be able to use the gallops today and we'll have to deal with the track before we try and exercise any horses down the lane. Joe and Con, there's some bags of salt at the top there. And two shovels in the tool shed.'

While the others were getting on with their stable duties, Annabel and Jan went into the office.

'This is all we need after the way Lucky Charm ran last week,' Annabel groaned.

'Yes. I'm afraid it doesn't look like we'll be able to run Russian Eagle at Hereford on Thursday either.' At this stage in the season and as he was a horse who was slow to come together, Jan had entered Eagle in an undemanding novice chase to sow the seeds for his new campaign.

'Oh, no!' Annabel wailed. 'I suppose we won't. And I was so looking forward to it.'

'Well, there's nothing we can do about it, we're in the lap of the gods. Anyway, he's entered for a similar race at Fontwell next Monday.'

The thermometer didn't rise much above freezing until Thursday morning, so it was inevitable that the clerk of the course at Hereford would announce that the meeting was abandoned. But at least Jan had kept her horses on the move and as they were already fit her plans to have two runners the next day at Ludlow weren't affected.

Overmere Lass was due to run in another National Hunt flat race, and Arctic Hay was having his first run of the season for Bernie Sutcliffe in a two-mile novice chase. Following the overnight rain, Jan thought the soft ground would suit Bernie's horse, but not the Sharps'. Nevertheless, on the strength of her last win and the lack of any worthwhile form in the rest of the field, the filly was likely to start favourite. Jan could only hope she wouldn't let her and the punters down, as Lucky Charm had the previous Saturday.

❦

None of the Sharps came to Ludlow, which was a relief to Jan when Overmere Lass failed to get in the frame. Jan had phoned them during the morning to say she thought the going would be against their mare, and now she hoped they would accept her explanation. Privately, she wasn't at all pleased with the way Billy had got the filly shut in on the rails behind the leading bunch as they turned for home, leaving her no way through: she'd appeared full of running at the time.

'Jan,' he protested. 'I hadn't got any choice. If you try to take her wide, she doesn't like it. Anyway, she wasn't going to quicken, however much daylight she had.'

'OK, Billy.' Jan sighed. She felt as if she'd been nagging him constantly for the last few weeks and she really didn't want to be unfair or affect his confidence and blunt the extra edge needed to drive a horse home first. 'Arctic Hay might get a bit wound up down at the start, but once they're running he should settle. At least you know this course well enough,' she grinned encouragingly.

She and Billy had won their first hunter chase at Ludlow on Harold Powell's Rear Gunner. It had been a little less than two years ago, but now it seemed like another era.

'I ought to,' Billy grinned back, sharing the memory of that triumph.

Bernie Sutcliffe had been hanging around all afternoon, but Jan didn't have a chance to say much more than 'hello' until he was standing beside her in the parade ring.

'I bloody well hope your jockey focuses on the job a bit better than he did in that last race.'

'Bernie, the horse had run out of steam. If you'd ever ridden a racehorse yourself, you'd understand. When the fuel gauge is on zero, there's no point knocking seven bells out of it, or you'll wreck it.'

'Bernie, I'm really sorry,' Jan was saying twenty minutes later, after they'd watched Arctic Hay come fourth, having received a very hard ride from Billy. 'There were some good horses in that race. Perhaps we were aiming a bit too high.'

'He's won better races than that.'

'I know, but that was two years ago, then he went a bit sour. That's how we managed to get him for the price we did, if you remember. At least he's improved physically since he came to us.'

'I'll grant you that,' Bernie said, 'but I still think that little bugger, Billy Hanks, isn't pulling his weight.'

'Bernie, if you're suggesting my jockey isn't doing his best on your horses, I should warn you I won't keep them in my yard and you'll have to find another trainer.'

Bernie looked at her straight in the eye for a moment, to judge her resolve.

She didn't blink.

'All right, Jan,' he conceded. 'Forget I mentioned it.'

Billy Hanks had yet another chance to prove himself at Cheltenham the next day, when Murty McGrath was claimed by his stable to ride in Yorkshire. A.D. O'Hagan telephoned to say Billy could have the ride on Erin's Jet. He apologized and said that as he would be watching his horses in Ireland that weekend he wouldn't be coming to Cheltenham.

Once again, Jan anguished as she watched the little horse battle its way up the hill, desperately trying to catch the third horse, and failing by a short head. *He gave him too much to do*, she said to herself and felt like bursting into tears. After such a magnificent October and November, when it seemed she only had to send a horse to the start for it to succeed, it was now over three weeks since she'd had her last winner, although she'd been sending out more horses and there had been no sign of illness in the yard to which she could attribute their poor performance.

'What the hell's gone wrong?' she muttered to herself as she went to greet her horse.

Now she started to feel sorry for Billy, too. Perhaps he didn't understand what was going wrong any more than she did; he had even been in to ride work and school more often, and there weren't that many times when she could categorically say he should have ridden a race better than he had.

Roz had gone to lead in the horse while Jan walked slowly across the paddock to the unsaddling enclosure.

'Oh dear,' she heard a familiar female voice say behind her. 'Somebody seems to have lost the magic touch.'

Jan turned around to find Virginia Gilbert, dressed in her usual Sloane Ranger coat, looking down her long, spiky nose.

'Oh, hello, Virginia.' Jan gave her a wan smile. 'Well, if you ever manage to find it, let me know, won't you?' She didn't wait for an answer; she really didn't care what Virginia Gilbert thought or said. She knew she could always produce a fitter, better-schooled horse. But she did care very much what A.D. O'Hagan thought.

Jan was well aware that, immediately after racing at Ascot on the following Saturday, she was going straight to Ireland to stay at Aigmont for the first time. She had been hoping to go over there in a blaze of glory, or at least with a few recent winners to bolster her confidence.

Still, at least Tom's Touch was entered to run at Ascot in a novice hurdle and she was hopeful of his chances. He was an exceptionally talented horse, who had continued to work well at home.

Driving morosely back to Edge Farm that evening, she prayed that nothing would happen to interfere with the horse's preparation or to stop the Ascot meeting going ahead. But the week started badly. After three days of continuous rain, the meeting at Fontwell was abandoned and Russian Eagle had missed his chance to race for a second time.

'Oh God!' Annabel groaned, when Jan told her the news. 'What's the next race we can put him in?'

'I did enter him tentatively for a novice chase at Ascot on Saturday. But I wasn't seriously considering it.'

'Why not?'

'I'm desperate to get a race into him, but frankly I think it'll be too competitive for him. It's a top-class race and there are sure to be some very good horses entered.'

'But, Jan, he's no slouch! You know that. He did Aintree in a hell of a good time.'

Jan shook her head. 'But that was a very different ball game –
it was only a hunter chase.'

'Even so, I'd love him to run. If he doesn't win, it doesn't
matter. I'm not going to blame you.'

Jan smiled wryly. 'We've been having such a lousy time lately,
I don't suppose anyone will notice one more loser,' she said,
dejectedly.

'For God's sake, Jan, don't go thinking like that, or we'll be
beaten before we get under starter's orders!'

'Of course I won't, but I can tell you I'll be bloody annoyed
if Tom's Touch doesn't do better than the others we've run
recently.'

'You're off to see A.D. straight after racing, aren't you?'

'Yes, I'm absolutely dreading it. There hasn't been much to
please him recently, not from our yard – though he's been
getting quite a few winners from elsewhere.'

Jan, Annabel and Declan made the journey to Ascot with Tom's
Touch and Russian Eagle. It was a fine morning, which would
have normally put Jan in a buoyant mood, but another failure –
this time by King's Archer at Uttoxeter the day before – had left
Jan feeling extremely unnerved. She almost wished that she
hadn't had so much success earlier in the season, when winning
had seemed quite normal. Now, by contrast, she was feeling a
failure.

Most of her owners, however, had been totally supportive.
A.D. had said very little that could be taken as negative and even
the Sharps, for whom she had done so well to start with, seemed
philosophical about the situation. Jan found herself wondering
if there was something peculiar about their horses, which made
them good for the first few weeks of the season and then go off
the boil, as this was the pattern that had been seen previously
when Martin Hunter was training them. Frank Jellard had only
had a few runners so far, but Jan knew that if she didn't get him

something to boast about he would soon start grousing. Meanwhile Bernie Sutcliffe was becoming increasingly vociferous and his criticisms were more pointed every time he phoned.

Jan started to feel a little more confident when she saw Tom's Touch coming down the ramp from the lorry. Alert as always, he was a real eye-catcher, and there was nothing about him to suggest he wasn't at his peak. Having studied the form of the other runners, she was almost tempted to have a bet on Tom's Touch herself, until she saw the best price on offer was eleven to eight on.

Jan and Annabel were standing in the parade ring without an owner when Billy sauntered out of the weighing room with the other fifteen jockeys but with none of his usual vigour. He could hardly bring himself to look Jan in the eye as she went over his instructions. 'And Billy,' she added. 'No cock-ups this time. I'm seeing A.D. later and he knows damn well this horse is capable of winning today, I'd be surprised if he hasn't put a pile of money on it already – so please, give me a good weekend, right?'

Two miles with eight tiddly hurdles to jump should have been a piece of cake for Tom's Touch. From where Jan stood with Annabel, watching through quivering binoculars, he got away from the start well and settled down in seventh or eighth place, where he stayed. But as the field swung out of Swinley Bottom three horses made a break, leaving Tom's Touch stuck in the pack about ten lengths behind. As hard as Jan prayed and willed Billy to pull out and go round, they were hopelessly trapped on the rail behind a solid wall of horses with nowhere to go.

When they raced into the home straight, the field fanned out. But it was too late.

Eventually Tom broke free, but he could only make up five of the fifteen lengths; when Billy realized he had an impossible task on his hands, he just stopped riding.

Jan put her binoculars down, closed her eyes and began trembling.

On all known form, her horse should have won this race quite easily, but he'd lost it. She just couldn't begin to imagine what she was going to tell A.D.

Annabel saw her distress. 'Jan, it's OK. They did their best.'

Jan shook her head. 'That was an effing disaster! He never had a chance!'

'Let's go and see what he says.'

Jan bit her lip and nodded. They hurried down to the course, where they met Declan on his way to lead Billy in.

Declan, too, looked pale and distressed.

'Did you put a lot of money on that horse?' Jan asked.

The Irishman nodded. 'I thought there's no way he could get beat.'

Jan smiled grimly. 'You, me, and probably his owner, too.'

By this time Billy was jogging back from the track towards them. Jan turned to the other two. 'I'll lead him in. I want a word with him while his memory's still fresh.'

Annabel understood and turned to go back to the stables, while Declan lagged behind, ready to take the horse when Jan had delivered her thesis.

'Right, Billy,' she said as the horse and jockey came within earshot, 'what happened?' She looped a lead rein through the bit and clipped it on the other side.

'God, Jan, I'm sorry.'

She heard a quiver in his voice and glanced up at him. The man was almost in tears. 'Billy, please just tell me, why the hell did you lay this horse so far out of its ground?'

As she spoke she inspected the horse more closely. He was hardly blowing and looked almost as fresh as he had in the parade ring.

'I was held up, in Swinley Bottom,' Billy sniffed. 'Got trapped on the inside.'

'I could see that was going to happen from where I was standing, you were behind a wall of horses. Why the hell didn't you move out? A blind man could have seen you were never going to get through there!'

'I did try, Missis, but by the time I got out, there was too much work to do.'

'You didn't try very hard did you? You stopped riding as soon as you got any daylight.'

'He was a bit rough in the wind, Mrs H. Roaring like a bloody lion!'

'What the hell are you talking about, Billy? That's the first time anyone's ever mentioned anything to me. Listen to him now, nothing. He wouldn't blow a candle out, he looks as bright as a button.'

'I promise you, he was making a noise out there. I couldn't push him no more. Anyway, he's still come fourth.'

'Don't talk such rot, Billy. Do you think that's going to please Mr O'Hagan? I very much doubt it.'

While she was speaking, the PA announced: *Mrs Hardy, would you please come to the weighing room.*

'Do you hear that, Billy? Now the stewards want an explanation. The horse started odds on favourite. They're going to want a very good reason why he didn't win.'

'I've already told you why, Mrs H., and I'll tell them, too, if they like.'

Jan sighed. 'You've got a ride in the next race, haven't you? Well, you'll have to try and convince the stewards before that, and, Billy, you haven't convinced me yet.'

It was the first time Jan had ever been called before the stewards of the Jockey Club to explain the running of one of her horses. Before she went into the stewards' inner sanctum beside the weighing room, she made a supreme effort to compose herself. She had already been informed that her horse was subject to a routine dope test.

Five men in tweed suits faced her across the table, reminding her of the po-faced, sombre trio who had interviewed her when she had applied for her professional licence. They listened carefully to what she and Billy had to say, accepted that the horse did get boxed in and had been subject to a respiratory problem when put under pressure. The stipendiary steward pointed out that this was Jan's first appearance in front of any race-course stewards.

After a short confab, they noted her explanation and wished her well with her runner in the novice chase later that afternoon.

By the time she had calmed down and walked back from the stewards' room, Billy was already in the parade ring, about to be legged up onto the horse he was riding in the handicap chase. Thoughtfully, Jan watched him jog out onto the course before she made her way to the pre-parade ring to find Annabel and Declan.

Declan was still grieving. Jan guessed he must have piled all the money he had onto Tom's Touch. She prayed that A.D. hadn't invested as painfully.

Jan shook her head. 'I just can't imagine what happened. Billy swears he was making a roaring noise.'

'He's never made a noise in his life, not when I've ridden him work anyway, Mrs H.,' Declan said.

'Maybe not, but these things do sometimes happen when a horse is under pressure. Anyway, the stewards accepted it as a good enough reason for Billy not riding him out. So who am I to argue with them?'

'How were they?' Annabel asked, with a small grin.

'Same gang of pompous old farts!' Jan replied with a touch of irony in her voice.

'I'm sure "gang" isn't the right word,' Annabel mused. 'What do you think the collective noun is for a group of Jockey Club stewards?'

'A "flatulence" I should think.' Jan burst out laughing, glad to lighten the gloom a little. 'Right, let's go and see how Billy gets on in this race. If he wins, I'll be fuming!'

On one of the television monitors outside the weighing room, Jan and Annabel saw Billy part company with his mount, slap bang on top of a fence, before falling off the other side, while the rest of the field galloped straight over him.

'Oh my God!' Annabel gasped. 'That last horse kicked him right in the face!'

Jan gritted her teeth and nodded. Even though she wasn't too pleased with Billy Hanks right now, no one deserved a hoof in the face. 'Let's get to the first-aid room and see how he is.'

'I hope he's OK,' Annabel said guiltily. 'If not, who's going to ride Eagle?'

Billy was far from OK, but at least he walked into the medical room on his own two feet. He was clasping a thick wad of lint to his face.

'Billy, are you all right?'

The ambulance man following him shook his head. 'If you wouldn't mind, ladies, leave him for the moment. I think he's broken his nose, and that can be very painful indeed.'

'Is there anything I can do, Billy?' Jan asked.

Snuffling like a Pekinese, Billy waved her away and sat down, burying his face in his hands.

Jan turned to Annabel. 'Looks like your jockey's gone for a burton, Bel.'

'But it's only his face, Jan. He might be all right in a while.'

'The doctor'll come and have a look. He'll soon say. We'll see you later, Billy,' she said more loudly.

They went out and hurried towards the weighing room. 'I think it's highly unlikely he'll be riding again today, although I know he can be a bit of a jessie and inclined to make a fuss about nothing.'

'Jan! How can you be so unsympathetic?'

'I'm sorry. But I'm struggling to find any sympathy for Billy bloody Hanks at this present moment. Now we'd better see who we can find to ride your lovely horse.'

Fourteen runners were declared for Russian Eagle's race and, at first glance, Jan saw all the top jockeys were booked to ride in it.

'I know Eagle hasn't got a great chance of winning, but that will diminish even further if we put up a claimer,' she said gloomily.

'Look,' Annabel said excitedly, staring at her race card and clutching at Jan's sleeve. 'Murty McGrath's riding in the next and he hasn't got anything in the novice chase!'

Jan inspected the programme Annabel had shoved under her nose. The next race was a valuable three-mile hurdle, and Murty was riding the likely favourite. But Annabel was right, he hadn't got a ride in Russian Eagle's race, though he did have one in the race following it, so he wouldn't be rushing off home early.

'Murty may be picky about what he rides in novice chases,' Jan mused. 'He's in the fortunate position where he doesn't have to take any old ride if he thinks it's too risky and it doesn't jump well enough.'

'But you could ask him!' Annabel said, fortified by the prospect of the champion jockey riding her horse.

'OK,' Jan nodded. 'If the doctor's stood Billy down, we'll ask Murty.'

'Great! Do you think he'll take the ride?'

'He's already ridden a couple of winners for me.' Jan shrugged. 'But he may not be too impressed with our recent record.'

'Remind him how well Eagle did at Aintree – he jumped so well and he would have won if there hadn't been that barging match.'

They waited until Murty had weighed in after he'd won the hurdle race. Jan caught him before he disappeared into the jockeys' changing room.

'Hello, Mrs Hardy,' he said, friendly enough. 'How's Billy?'

'Not too bad, but he's broken his nose and has been stood down.'

'And you want someone to ride yours in the next?'

Jan nodded with a questioning grin. 'Yes please.'

'Remind me what it's called.'

'Russian Eagle. He'll probably be a bit outclassed, but he's a great jumper and needs a good school round.'

'Oh yes. I remember, I watched him run in the Foxhunters' last spring; unlucky not to have beaten that horse of Mr O'Hagan's. Sure, I'll take the ride. Thanks,' he added as an afterthought.

'Thank you, Murty,' Jan replied, making no pretence of who was doing whom the favour.

🐎

Three of the runners in Russian Eagle's novice chase had already won decent races and looked like daunting opposition, regardless of the extra weight penalty they had to carry. Murty looked as confident as he always did when he marched into the parade ring, wearing Annabel's colours of pale blue and green hoops.

'So, Mrs H., I see this horse belongs to your assistant,' he said with a nod at Annabel. 'Maybe she'd like to tell me how to ride him?'

'Oh, no,' Annabel protested. 'That's Jan's job.'

'Of course,' Murty grinned. 'Only joking.'

'He's a very genuine horse and he's got a big, bold jump, so you can use it if you have to,' Jan instructed. 'Drop him in five or six lengths off the pace so you can get a lead. You know the rest; you've been around long enough.'

Murty nodded as he watched Declan leading Russian Eagle round the parade ring.

'He looks well. Right, I'll see what I can do.'

🐎

Once Russian Eagle and Murty had left the ring and were making their way to the start, Jan and Annabel climbed the steps of the stand to watch the race. Jan noticed that, despite being ridden by the champion jockey, their horse was being offered at thirty-three to one. The bookies and the public had either forgotten or were totally ignoring Eagle's performance at Aintree.

'I've just got to have a bit on at that ridiculous price,' Annabel said.

'You might as well, but don't put on your whole inheritance.'

Annabel rushed off to find a bookie and rejoined Jan a few minutes later as the field was lining up behind the starting tape.

'How much?'

'Fifty quid each way.'

'Good God,' Jan laughed. 'I hope you can afford it.'

'Come on, Jan, you're my trainer; you're supposed to be telling me the horse has a great chance.'

'Bel, that's not fair. I never tell owners their horses have a great chance if they've got very little. But then again, I don't usually run them when they haven't got any.'

Annabel bristled a little. 'Well, Jan, all I can say is I've obviously got more faith in him than you have.'

The three-mile chase got off to a slow start, with several of the horses jumping rather deliberately. After two miles, three had already fallen, while Murty McGrath was sitting quietly on Russian Eagle in fourth place, seemingly unperturbed.

Annabel leaned and whispered in Jan's ear. 'He looks good value at thirty-threes now, doesn't he?'

Jan nodded, not taking her eyes off the race. Russian Eagle was still travelling well within himself. He put in a massive jump at the big open ditch coming out of Swinley Bottom and touched down in third place.

Annabel nudged Jan excitedly. 'Did you see that?'

'Murty's doing a great job,' Jan murmured.

'So's Eagle,' Annabel hissed indignantly.

Suddenly, there was a marked increase in the pace, which quickly split the runners into two groups. Russian Eagle was still in the leading bunch with three others. At the next fence, he jumped into second place, three lengths down on the favourite, who was under no pressure and looked as if he only had to jump the last two to win.

Jan glanced at Annabel and saw the knuckles gripping her binoculars were completely white, then her eyes were quickly drawn back to the race by a loud groan from the crowd. At the last fence the leader had pecked badly on landing, tipping his jockey out of the side door. A split second later, Eagle's head appeared on the far side of the fence with his beautiful big ears standing bolt upright. He tucked his front feet close to his body and cleared the fence with a foot to spare.

Murty, crouching down low to his horse, took a quick look over his shoulder. Two other runners were still chasing after him, being ridden hard. Jan's heart pounded, she could see Murty asking Russian Eagle for more effort and the big horse responded immediately. At full stretch, he galloped towards the finishing post, without letting his rivals gain another yard.

He had gone halfway round the next bend before Murty could pull him up to a rather subdued cheer from the handful of people who had backed him – and completely wild, ecstatic shrieking from his normally self-conscious owner.

Jan turned and flung her arms round her friend with a beaming smile and saw tears were streaming down Annabel's face as she shook with sobs of joy.

'Bloody hell, Jan!' she gasped. 'That was the most exciting thing that's ever happened to me.'

Jan wondered if that really was true, and guessed, just at that moment, it probably was.

She felt pretty ecstatic herself. Russian Eagle had provided her with the most unlikely win of her career to date, and, as it happened, her first for over a month. For the time being, it replaced in her mind the disappointing result she'd had with Tom's Touch.

🐎

Annabel was still bubbling with excitement as she drove Jan to Heathrow to catch the six-thirty flight to Dublin.

Jan had protested at the arrangement. 'How will I get back from there on Tuesday?'

'I'll come and get you. Then you'll be able to tell me everything that's happened on the way home.'

'You may not want to hear.'

'Jan, stop worrying. A.D.'s a big boy. He knows there's no such thing as a racing certainty – at least, not with horses, and Eagle's win shows you haven't lost your touch.'

'Thank God. But I can still hardly believe it . . .' Jan sighed. 'You were just *so* excited! I suppose you're going to resign, now you've won all that money.'

'You know I don't work for you for the money. Though that doesn't mean I'll do it for nothing,' Annabel added quickly. 'And, anyway, it was hardly the lottery. Ten thousand prize money and just over two thousand from the bookies – not a bad day's work.'

'I should think they were happy and paid with a smile; after all, the favourite got stuffed.'

'Do you think Eagle would have got up to beat it if it hadn't unshipped its rider?'

'We'll never know, but to be honest, probably not. Still, jumping's the name of the game.'

'He did beat some good horses today, though.'

'Yes,' Jan readily agreed. 'We'll aim him at a similar race next time. I wonder what Eddie would think if he knew what's just happened. He really loved that horse, you know.' Jan shook her head affectionately at the memory of her first encounter with Eddie Sullivan. He'd been standing in the parade ring at Doncaster sales, when he had spotted Megan in serious danger from a careering horse and had effectively saved her life by scooping her out of its path. After that Jan had helped him to choose a horse suitable for him to ride in hunter chases and Russian Eagle had not caught the eye of many buyers at the sales that day.

'Maybe he still gets to read the English racing results, wherever he is?' Annabel probed subtly.

'I bet he does,' Jan nodded, not wanting to give anything away.

13

On the short flight from London to Dublin, Jan struggled to get herself into the right frame of mind to cope with the trip to A.D. O'Hagan's.

Come on, for God's sake – he's not going to bite you, she told herself.

She really did not like travelling on her own, but at least she knew her children would be happy while she was away. Fran had moved into the new house to stay in the third bedroom, which Gerry had worked hard to finish in time and she was going to stay there until Jan arrived back, four days before Christmas.

At Dublin airport Jan was met by Daragh, the young chauffeur who had driven her home from the Queen's Hotel in Cheltenham after her dinner with A.D. He greeted her with his usual friendly smile.

'Sh'Jaysus, how are you doing, Mrs Hardy? You look marvellous,' he said as he took her bags and led her to the black Mercedes waiting outside.

Daragh continued to rattle on as he whisked her around the edge of the Irish capital. Jan only half-listened, cocooned in her own thoughts and the quiet warmth of the big car. She felt she needed to prepare herself for the meeting with A.D. Despite Annabel's assurances, she was sure he would be annoyed with the way Tom's Touch had run. In the end, she reasoned, 'I can only tell him what happened and hope that he will be reasonable about it.' But mentally she braced herself for the worst.

They headed south, past the small town of Naas and down

the Kilkenny road. It was a clear, moonlit evening and when the Mercedes turned off the main road to head east Jan could just make out the craggy bulk of the Wicklow Mountains ahead. The big car sped on, along narrow lanes between high hedgerows, past dark clusters of houses and an occasional well-lit bar. After ten miles, and without any warning from Daragh, the big car swung off the lane and towards a pair of wrought-iron gates hung on massive stone piers. A security guard stepped forwards to check the car's occupants.

As the gates closed behind them, the car swept down a long drive, which switch-backed in gentle curves through open ground, until it brought them face to face with a discreetly lit Georgian mansion.

The Mercedes drew up in front of a high-pillared portico and Daragh jumped out to open the door for Jan.

'I'll bring your bag,' he said, and stood back to allow Jan to walk up the steps to the front entrance. 'Give the bell a pull when you get to the top,' he continued.

Jan followed his instructions and waited on the top step in front of a pair of glazed double doors. A moment later a small brown-eyed man in a white cotton jacket appeared and opened one of the doors to let her in.

'Good evening,' he said in an Italian accent.

'Hello, I'm Mrs Hardy,' she said nervously.

'Mr O'Hagan is expecting you.'

In the entrance hall, above a floor of polished stone, an enormous crystal chandelier cascaded from three floors up and beautifully reflected the flickering flames of the log fire burning in a white marble fireplace.

A.D. seemed to appear from nowhere. 'Welcome to Aigmont,' he proclaimed with a proud smile. 'What do you think? Not bad for a village lad from the Reeks, eh?'

'It's amazing,' Jan said. She knew it was a feeble response, but she couldn't think of a better one at the time.

'Did you have a good journey?'

'Yes, thanks. It was really kind of you to send your driver.'

'No problem.' A.D. dismissed it with an airy wave. 'Come and have a drink, then I'll have Mrs Massey show you up to your room.'

He led Jan through a doorway to the right of the entrance, into a large, perfectly proportioned drawing room, furnished entirely with very good antiques. The room was lit more intimately than the hall, with wall lights, table lamps and another fire flaming lazily in a large iron grate.

Three men were standing there with drinks in their hands. One of them she recognized as A.D.'s Irish trainer, Dermot O'Hare.

'We were racing today at Leopardstown,' A.D. said, 'so we've a small house party. Now, you know Dermot.'

Jan shook hands with the trainer and A.D. turned to his other guests.

'Gentlemen, you haven't met Jan Hardy. She trains half a dozen horses for me in England, conveniently close to Cheltenham. Jan, this is Lord Hatherop, whom you'll know, and Cyrus Huffer the Third, who has a lot of horses in Kentucky, and a few more at Newmarket.'

Jan knew Huffer by name as the owner of an English Derby winner and Lord Hatherop by sight, as a Jockey Club steward.

She shook hands with both men and wondered what on earth she had in common with or could talk about to these two racing bigwigs, apart from horses. Perhaps, in the circumstances, that would be enough.

'What would you like to drink, Jan? There's freshly made martini cocktail here.'

'That would be great,' Jan said, although she'd never had a martini cocktail before and prayed it wouldn't be too strong as she'd only eaten a sandwich since breakfast.

A.D. picked the shaker up from the drinks trolley and gave it a final rattle. He filled a glass and handed it to Jan. She took a sip and unconsciously nodded her approval.

'Glad you like it.' A.D. smiled. 'Now, I wonder where the other ladies are. I'll just go and check with Mario.'

As he left the room, his heels clicked across the hall floor and faded into the distance.

Lord Hatherop was a tall man of about seventy, with thick white hair slicked down on his head. He was wearing a tweed suit, which failed to disguise the fact that he was a stone or more overweight. So far he'd only said, 'How do'you do?' to Jan. Now he cleared his throat as he turned to her. 'I watched a very nice horse of yours win at Ascot.'

'Thank you,' Jan said. 'He ran really well, didn't he?'

Dermot O'Hare grunted. 'A.D.'s runner didn't do so well, though, did it?' he said in a soft tantalizing voice.

Jan felt her hackles rise, but she didn't move a muscle in her face; she wasn't going to give the oily old creep the satisfaction. 'Not this time, unfortunately,' she answered mildly, knowing he would be fully aware that Tom's Touch had already won twice from her yard.

Lord Hatherop appeared not to have noticed the exchange. 'Who owns him?' he asked thoughtfully.

'Russian Eagle?' Jan asked. 'He belongs to my assistant, Annabel Halstead.'

'Halstead? Is she Bunny Halstead's daughter?'

Jan had never heard that Annabel's cold and distant father was known as 'Bunny'. 'I don't know, I'm afraid,' she said. 'They live in Wales, not far from Kington, I think.'

'That's him, Bunny Halstead. Knew him when I was still in the Blues and Royals. His daughter's a pretty girl, isn't she? I seem to remember meeting her at the Guards Polo Club once.'

Jan nodded. 'You might have done; she's very pretty.'

Cyrus Huffer broke his silence with a loud herrumph. A large man, his walrus-like face and moustache matched the noisy breathing of a seriously overweight older man. 'Must make quite a team, then, two pretty girls,' he guffawed.

Jan felt a flush move up her face like a wave. The American was ogling her unashamedly. Stifling her indignation, she wondered why on earth A.D. had asked her to join these old gits for dinner and she was hugely relieved to hear the sound of more people approaching the room.

She turned to avoid having to answer Cyrus Huffer, and looked expectantly towards the door.

A moment later, A.D. ushered two women into the room.

'Jan, I'd like you to meet Lady Hatherop, and Siobhan Fitzgerald, my wife.'

Although Jan wasn't an opera fan, she recognized the famous singer immediately, and wondered why A.D. hadn't introduced her as Siobhan O'Hagan.

Lady Hatherop looked to Jan like a stereotypical English racing aristocrat – grey-black hair pulled back into a chignon, with an understated, navy blue, knee-length silk dress, a single row of pearls and a brooch depicting a horse and jockey in gold and tiny precious stones.

A.D. had been followed into the room by Mario, the butler, who set about making a fresh shaker of dry martini.

Finding herself next to Lady Hatherop, Jan did her best to chat about the prospects for Cheltenham. But she couldn't help picking up snatches of other conversations going on in the room. One comment pulled her up sharp.

Cyrus Huffer was standing with Dermot O'Hare a little to one side, where they thought they couldn't be heard. The American was constantly glancing in Jan's direction. 'What's the story with the chick?' he murmured.

'Work away!' O'Hare chuckled.

Jan tried hard to concentrate on what Lady Hatherop was saying, but she was boiling with indignation.

She excused herself and walked across the room to her host. 'A.D.,' she said quietly, 'would you mind if I went up to my room to freshen up?'

'Good God, no. I'm sorry, I should have thought of that sooner. Come on, bring your drink and we'll find Mrs Massey.'

Out in the hall, A.D. stood and shouted, 'Mary!' and a moment later a small, grey-haired woman, with the softest blue eyes Jan had ever seen, appeared through a door at the end of the hall.

'Would you ever show Mrs Hardy to her room, please, Mary?'

'Of course I will.'

A.D. disappeared, and the little woman smiled at Jan. 'This way, Mrs Hardy.' She led Jan up the sweeping curve of stairs to a wide-railed gallery, where she turned along a corridor, where the walls were covered from top to bottom with equestrian paintings, reminding Jan of the Sharps' extraordinary collection.

Mrs Massey stopped outside a door, opened it and stood back to let Jan into a beautiful room exquisitely decorated. Her bag was already there, resting on a trestle.

Jan could see into the large ensuite bathroom.

'Mrs Massey, do you think I've time for a bath before dinner?'

'Sure'n you have. Dinner's not to be served till nine. You help yourself and enjoy it!'

🐎

Jan lay back and soaked for twenty minutes, preparing herself mentally for the coming ordeal. So far A.D. hadn't mentioned Tom's Touch, but Jan was certain he must have discussed it with O'Hare. Even though the trip to Aigmont had been planned some time ago, long before Jan's fallow patch, it was turning out to be a great deal less enjoyable than she had originally imagined.

Well, now is not the time to weaken, she told herself later, as she flicked a brush through her hair. Ten minutes later, when she heard an old-fashioned gong sound in the hall, Jan descended the stairs, relieved she had changed into a smarter dress.

Dinner was laid in a room similar to the drawing room, on the other side of the hall. Jan was placed on A.D.'s left, with Cyrus Huffer beside her and O'Hare opposite. She sat down, dreading the meal. She couldn't think what on earth she had to say that would interest these people.

As they were eating their first course, A.D.'s wife leaned across Cyrus Huffer to ask Jan a few polite questions about her family. Jan knew that the O'Hagans had no children and this was evident from the singer's vagueness about child-rearing. Still, Jan thought, at least she had made an effort.

As the dinner proceeded, it became evident that the only common denominator among the party was horse racing, which took up most of the conversation. Dermot O'Hare took it upon himself to make several pointed comments, and Jan thought less of him each time he did. She did well to hold her own, while A.D. did his best to boost her confidence, without once referring to the miserable run she'd been having recently.

During the dessert, just as Jan was congratulating herself on getting through dinner satisfactorily, she felt one of Cyrus Huffer's chubby legs squashing up against hers. As subtly as she could she moved hers three inches to her right. A few moments later, the American's leg was against hers once more, followed by distinct pressure on the top of her thigh. She froze for a moment, until a set of podgy fingers began to squeeze through the flimsy material of her dress, making their way towards the top of her leg.

Jan looked around the table in despair. There were two other conversations going on; she couldn't catch A.D.'s eye; she didn't know what she would say if she did.

Summoning up courage that had been fortified by the martinis and a few glasses of wine, she turned to Cyrus Huffer III. Quivering, she looked him straight in the eye and spoke in as steady a voice as she could manage.

'Excuse me, Mr Huffer, would you please take your hand off my thigh?'

Huffer's hand shot away as he stared at her in disbelief.

In the seconds that followed, Jan realized that this was probably the first time anyone had reprimanded him for his groping.

The conversation around the table ceased immediately; everyone was staring at her in shocked silence.

Look at him, for God's sake, she thought indignantly, *not at me.*

Huffer gave her a steely glare, while Dermot O'Hare leered across the table.

After a moment's silence, A.D. burst out laughing. 'Cyrus, you randy old devil, will you not let your physical urges get the better of you! I don't want Mrs Hardy distracted while she has horses of mine to train.'

Looking back on the incident, Jan realized A.D. had worked out what he considered the quickest way to diffuse any embarrassment.

She wondered how much damage she had done herself in his eyes by exposing the randy billionaire's groping habits. Well, that's too bad, she told herself. In the end her function in A.D.'s life was to train his horses as honestly and well as she could, and she had no intention of putting up with the humiliating treatment his guest had shown her.

A.D., looking less than pleased, took the party back to the drawing room for coffee and brandy. When the men settled themselves into a huddle on one side of the fire to talk about world affairs, Jan baulked at the prospect of trying to make conversation with the two women. She decided to bite on the bullet and stood up.

'Will you excuse me, A.D.? I've had a long day, and I'm really very tired.'

A.D. glanced at her. She couldn't read what was going through his mind, but he nodded. 'Of course. You go to bed, Jan. We'll see you in the morning. Get up whenever you like, there'll be breakfast when you want it.'

He sounded nothing but charming and considerate. If she had annoyed him by denouncing his billionaire friend, he wasn't revealing it.

Jan went upstairs with tears in her eyes; feeling vulnerable, she locked her door.

She lay in bed, fighting off the image of Huffer's mean, lecherous, piggy little eyes and O'Hare's spiteful laughing face. She knew she still had to face the post-mortem A.D. would undoubtedly want, and she half wished it was over and done with already. In the end, she fell fast asleep and to her surprise woke the next morning feeling better than she had for some time. At home, she always woke early, tossing and turning, wondering when her alarm would start to buzz.

She walked to the window to pull back the curtains. The morning sun was behind the house, casting its light obliquely on the misty landscape in front of her. A broad expanse of open pasture and parkland trees swept down a gentle slope towards a long stone wall almost half a mile away at the bottom of the valley. It was a serene and beautiful setting and she could see now why A.D. was so proud of his home.

She turned back into the room and looked at her watch. It was just before nine on Sunday morning. Decisively, she washed and dressed in cords and a fleece. She made herself up sparingly and let herself out of the room.

She walked along the corridor with its horse paintings, across the galleried landing and down the broad stairs to the hall.

She tried to open the glass doors onto the portico, but they were locked. Tentatively, she headed for the door at the back of the hall from which Mary Massey had emerged the evening before.

It opened into a service passage, which she followed until she heard sounds of activity and a moment later emerged into a large light kitchen, where Mary was busily preparing breakfast and Mario sat drinking coffee and reading an Italian football paper.

'Good morning, Mary.'

'Good morning to you, Mrs Hardy. Would you like breakfast?'

'Not yet, thanks. I thought I'd have a quick walk first – it's such a lovely morning. Maybe I can have a peep at the horses. Are the stables nearby?'

'Yes, a couple of hundred yards, through there.' She waved at a half-glazed door.

Jan let herself into a courtyard at the rear of the house. Heading the way Mary had indicated, she walked through a gap between the main house and the old dairy and emerged onto a back drive.

A little way down the hill the slate roofs of more buildings protruded above a high hedge of rhododendron. She guessed this was where she wanted to be and strolled down towards them, happy to feel no pressure, and for the time being pushing the disaster of Tom's Touch and Cyrus Huffer's sexual harassment to the back of her mind.

The stables were a classic four-square construction, with an archway and what clearly had previously been accommodation for coaches, horses and their handlers. Jan walked through the arch and found a quieter version of what activity she would have seen at home.

Here the horses, mostly brood mares and young stock, still had to be fed, watered and mucked out, but the staff spent far less time than her own riding out.

'Good morning,' she called to the nearest back disappearing into a stable.

A man turned. She recognized him as the groom who had come to Edge Farm with Albert Finnegan to deliver A.D.'s horses.

'Hello, Mrs Hardy,' he said. 'How are you doing? The boss said you were coming over.'

Jan walked towards him. 'Ups and downs; usual stuff,' she grimaced.

'Yes, well,' the groom said without a hint of malice, ''osses can't tell us what they want or how they're feeling, can they?'

'I was so disappointed with Tom's Touch yesterday,' Jan said.

'To tell you the truth, so were we. Albert had a right bet.' He winced. 'He's not here at the moment, so that's all right. Would you like to have a look at one or two of the mares?'

'Thanks, I'd love to,' Jan said.

After half an hour or so, Jan began to feel guilty. 'I think I'd better leave you to get on,' she said. 'You've been so helpful. I've taken up too much of your time already.' Jan rummaged through her pocket for a ten-pound note she knew she had there.

'You shouldn't,' the lad grinned. 'It was a pleasure. Say hello to Dec and Con for me.'

Wrapping her fleece more tightly around herself and still feeling relaxed in the soft December sun, Jan strolled out through the arch and back up towards the house.

'Good morning, Jan.'

She turned to find A.D. striding up the drive towards her, with a pair of Irish setters gambolling around him.

'Morning, A.D.' Jan smiled. 'What a lovely day. I went down to have a look at the horses.'

'Good. I'm glad I caught you. I wanted a word. We can walk on past the house and up the hill a little. The views are even better up there.'

O'Hagan and Jan took a path which climbed through the woods behind the house. The air was heavy with the scent of damp woodland and the ground was carpeted with leaves of rusty beech and golden oak.

'I'm sorry about the business with Cyrus last night. I fear he hasn't taken it too well,' A.D. said, after a long silence.

'I didn't mean to embarrass you. I'm not a prude, but I just can't stand men who are so arrogant that they think a woman won't mind their foul behaviour.'

'I understand, but perhaps,' A.D. shrugged, 'you could have been a little more discreet.'

Jan felt the blood rush to her cheeks. He was blaming her for making a fuss. What the hell did he expect her to do?

She felt her body tense and stole a glance at him as they walked side by side in the dappled winter light. He didn't look annoyed. But she was used to the fact that A.D. never showed what he was feeling.

With a struggle, she stifled what she wanted to say. 'Perhaps I could,' she answered blandly.

'It's OK,' A.D. said in a way that meant the subject was closed. 'I spoke to Murty last night. He was pleased to have had the ride on Russian Eagle yesterday.'

'He gave the horse a smashing ride,' Jan said.

'Yes,' A.D. murmured thoughtfully. 'The horse belongs to your assistant, Annabel, doesn't it?'

'That's right. Originally Eddie Sullivan bought it, then he ran out of funds and had to sell it to Bernie Sutcliffe, another of my owners.'

'I think I met Mr Sutcliffe at your open day,' A.D. nodded, widening his eyes.

'Well, Bernie wouldn't let Eddie ride the horse for some reason, so Bel persuaded him to sell him to her.'

'It's not hard to imagine how,' A.D. commented.

'She did no more than go out to dinner with him a couple of times. I can assure you of that, A.D.'

A.D. laughed. 'I'm only teasing, you don't have to defend your friend's honour. She bought the horse so young Sullivan could ride it in the Foxhunters', is that right?'

'That's right.'

'A noble gesture.'

'They're old friends.'

'But now young Sullivan's disappeared who knows where, so why does she still keep the horse?'

'She found she loved the experience, but she can only just afford it and finds it a bit of a struggle.'

'Do you think she might be interested in selling him?'

Jan looked up sharply at A.D. The question had caught her completely unawares. 'I . . . I really don't know,' she said.

'You must have some idea, though?'

'I suppose she might, but I very much doubt it. She was absolutely thrilled when he won yesterday. And of course the prize money was a big help. She won a bit when she backed him, too.'

A.D. chuckled. 'He was a hell of a price. Did you think he was going to win?'

'No, not really. I told Murty to look after him, I thought he might come in fifth or sixth. I only ran him because Bel was keen to and we'd missed two other races with the weather being so awful.'

'I guessed so. Well, I'll have to ask her myself, won't I? So Murty gave the horse a good ride. Do you think Billy Hanks would have done the same job?'

The question was delivered in A.D.'s normal silky smooth timbre with no cynical undertones, but Jan wasn't under any illusion about where the conversation was heading.

'Err,' she hesitated. 'Probably not, given his recent record.'

'That's what I thought. D'you know what the problem is?'

'I wish I did. Somehow he's lost the edge he had earlier in the season. I realize you must be bloody annoyed by Tom's Touch yesterday,' she went on quickly. 'I was gutted. Before the race I was really confident we'd win. I told Billy exactly what to do, but he got boxed in and then he said the horse made a roaring noise and couldn't get his wind.'

A.D. stopped walking and turned to face Jan. 'Do you believe him?'

Jan tried for a few moments to withstand the intensity of his blue eyes, but she gave up and dropped her gaze to the leafy ground at her feet.

'I've got no real reason not to, but I'm not sure,' she said. 'And that's the honest truth.'

A.D.'s nostrils quivered as he sucked in a lungful of crisp air.

'I love horses,' he said slowly. 'I've been around them all my life. I love winning and I don't mind how much I spend doing it, but I only like winning fair and square. So, when I feel someone's interfering with the true running of my horses, I'm liable to get very, very annoyed.' He gazed at Jan for several seconds without moving. 'Now, it so happens I believe you when you say you have no idea. But would I believe Billy Hanks? I don't think so.'

'But, A.D., I tackled him again and he got very upset. In fact, he was nearly crying when he came in on Tom's Touch yesterday.'

A.D. sighed sharply. 'His face wouldn't be wreathed in smiles if he'd just pulled your horse, would it? Jan, I'm telling you straight, it's not just race-track gossip. Murty passed him coming out of Swinley Bottom and he told me Billy had a real good hold of the horse's head. In fact he said he was strangling it and making no effort to get out from behind the other runners. Jan, someone's getting to him. Look at all the other horses in your yard that were winning a month or two ago. Not just for me but for those tinkers of yours. What's happened to them now?'

'A.D., I've been asking myself the same question over and over again for the last few weeks,' Jan blurted, 'and I just don't bloody know any more. But I'm not convinced it's Billy. How could it be? He and I go back a very long way, you know.'

'Well, let me put it to you bluntly, which I didn't really want to do. If you want to keep my horses in your yard, you're going to have to sort the problem out. There's no point you putting all your knowledge, your time and your considerable talents into training horses if your own jockey's deliberately losing races for you.'

'Look, A.D.,' Jan said desperately, wondering why she was resisting, 'let me give him another chance, and I'll find a way of proving it one way or the other. If you're right, the minute I have proof, I promise you, I'll have him out the yard so fast his feet won't touch the ground.' Jan stared at A.D. 'But I can't do it just on suspicion and rumour – I owe him that.'

O'Hagan was still looking at her. He lifted his shoulders. 'You fight your corner, Jan, I'll give you that. But fine, you set it up so you can see beyond doubt that he's cheating you.' His eyes narrowed. 'And then sling him.'

🐎

A.D. walked back to the house with Jan in silence and left her to have breakfast with Lady Hatherop, who told her Dermot had left for home in the early hours of the morning, and Cyrus Huffer had gone off with her husband to shoot on a neighbouring estate.

After breakfast Mario approached her. 'Mr O'Hagan, he have to go with Madame Fitzgerald. He say the chauffeur take you to the airport.'

Jan felt a moment's panic. She had thought she'd been invited to stay until the next day, but maybe, now he had said to her all he had to about Billy Hanks, A.D. thought it a waste of her time to hang around any longer.

Anyway, she thought, although there was no racing in England until Boxing Day, she'd be glad to get away from Aigmont and back to her horses and the children and to start preparing for their first Christmas in the new house.

Daragh appeared at noon. Jan had already packed her bag and placed it by the front door. She had said goodbye to Lady Hatherop and Mary Massey, who were the only people she could find in the house. On the way to the airport, she chatted to Daragh about his family and how he enjoyed coming to England, especially for Cheltenham Festival, when he always drove the boss. They talked about Russian Eagle's win, and the race he should have won at Aintree.

'When the boss was at the races in Australia, he saw that fella's father,' Daragh said.

'Who?' Jan asked a little too sharply, flushing suddenly.

'The father of the fella who rode your horse, Edward Sullivan.'

'You mean Mr O'Hagan saw Ron Sullivan in Oz?'

'That's what I heard him saying on the phone in the back of the car when I picked him up from the airport the other day.' The chauffeur chuckled. 'The boss was in a bad way. He *hates* flying.'

'Yes, but are you sure? Did he say he actually saw Ron Sullivan?'

'Yes, I'm sure he did. I can remember the man myself. He used to have some good horses a few years back. He'd a building firm; I knew a few blokes who went across to work for him. He went bust; in a big way, they say.'

'Yes, that's right,' Jan almost whispered, thinking how small the world was, that the man in whose house she had been staying in Ireland should have travelled twelve thousand miles across the world and ended up meeting Eddie Sullivan's dad.

14

Ben Pritchard looked out across the Severn Valley from one of the big windows in Jan's new kitchen. 'If we lived on top of those hills over yonder, we'd be having a white Christmas,' he remarked.

'We haven't had one of them for years.' His mother smiled, ensconced in a rocking chair by the Aga. She felt comforted by the return of the Gloucestershire lilt to her son's voice.

'Well, it looks like we're having a sodding freezing one now,' Jan sighed, as she stood by her brother and surveyed the bleak landscape in the fading light. 'I bet the temperature hasn't risen all day.'

'Don't use that kind of language, Jan,' Mary said in reprimand.

Ben grinned at Annabel, who was still sitting at the table, where they had just finished the turkey and Christmas pudding Jan and her mother had cooked. 'Looks like you'll have a day off tomorrow, then.'

'A day off – at Edge Farm?' Annabel laughed. 'You must be joking. Jan's brilliant at finding things to do even if the ground's like iron.'

'You certainly won't be racing, though. Where were you going – Kempton?'

'No, Leicester, and Newbury on Saturday.'

'It might have cleared by then.'

'I bloody hope so,' Jan said, exasperated.

'But you haven't got a jockey at the moment, have you?' Reg said from the comfort of the high-backed carver at the head of the table.

'No, he'll be off until the second week of January,' Jan said, wishing she didn't have to wait so long to prove that A.D. was wrong about Billy. 'But I shouldn't think I'll have too much trouble finding jockeys in the meantime. Murty McGrath said he'll ride for me when he can – and not just A.D.'s horses. Now,' she went on with a change of tone, determined to forget that she was a racehorse trainer, at least for today, 'if you can put up with the bare floor we could have a coffee with mother-in-law in front of the fire in the drawing room.'

'As long as you don't wake Olwen or interfere with Megan's Lego castle and Matty's farmyard,' Ben said. 'I went in there just now to see how they were getting on, and got a right rollocking for treading on two saddleback sows.'

'Maybe it would be better if we stay here,' Annabel said, 'especially if we're going to have some of this dodgy cider brandy Ben's brought.'

'It's the best Calvados you can get,' Ben protested. 'JCB gave it to me and he's a real connoisseur.'

'He would be,' Annabel grunted.

'Ooh, hark at her!' Ben teased.

Annabel blushed and Jan wondered, not for the first time if her friend was really interested in Johnny Carlton-Brown, sometimes it seemed to her that it was Ben she liked seeing most. When Annabel had told her that Major and Mrs Halstead were going to the States for Christmas, Jan had invited her to spend the day at Edge Farm; only when it emerged that Ben would also be there did Annabel finally commit herself.

Olwen had been even more noncommittal than Annabel about visiting Edge Farm House for Christmas. She had only just been persuaded in the end when Annabel offered to drive over early in the morning to collect her. The old woman insisted on going to church with her grandchildren, although Jan doubted that she had been inside a church since John's funeral. Annabel had arrived back at the house with the dour old woman in time for them all to troop down to the service in the village, which they had been to the year before.

As soon as Olwen had finished her lunch, which she had eaten without joining in any of the conversation, she left the table, announcing that she would 'look after' the children while they played in the sparsely furnished drawing room. Dutifully, twenty minutes later, Jan also left the table and went through to talk to her mother-in-law.

When she drew up a chair on the other side of the fire, Olwen allowed one eyelid to rise.

'Oh, it's you,' she said.

'The others are all trying some drink my brother brought, so I thought I'd come and see how you are.'

'I'm all right.'

'I'm pleased you've come over to see the house.'

Olwen opened the other eye and tuned her head a little to gaze around the bare walls and unpainted windows. 'I'm surprised you've visitors with the house in this state.'

'They don't mind, and they're all family, well, practically. What do you think of it?'

'T'ain't a bad house,' Olwen conceded.

'I'm glad you like it because I wanted to say that if this scheme of Harold Powell's to set up the caravan park at Stonewall ever happens, I want you to know that you'd be very welcome to come and live here.'

Jan held her breath, until Olwen shook her head disdainfully.

'I couldn't live so far from Wales. It was bad enough moving from home when I married John's father.'

Jan tried not to let her relief show. At least she had made the offer, established that she would make the sacrifice, if necessary – and she would have done, she told herself.

'It hasn't happened yet,' Jan said, 'and my friend Toby Waller reckons there may well be reasons why Harold will never be able to get his way. I've given Toby's surveyors all the papers and we're waiting to hear. In the meanwhile, he's had the meeting postponed three times, so Harold must be going mad. Mind you, I think he was just waiting for me to make him an offer to buy the field – as if I had any money to spare after doing all this.' Jan swept a hand around the room.

'Well, Jan,' Olwen said in a more conciliatory tone than Jan had heard from her in years, 'it was kind of you to offer, even if I knew you wouldn't have wanted me to say "yes".'

Olwen looked at her shrewdly through pale blue eyes and Jan knew there was no point in denying what she'd said.

🐎

Much later the whole party except Olwen and the children were sitting around the table in the kitchen, cautiously sipping the contents of Ben's bottle as the conversation automatically reverted to horses.

'Have you heard about the offer Bel's had for Russian Eagle?' Jan asked her brother.

'No, who's that from?'

'Mr O'Hagan, no less.' Annabel preened.

'Presumably as a result of Eagle's race last Saturday?'

She nodded.

'You're not going to sell him, though?' Reg Pritchard said fiercely.

'No, of course I'm not.'

'But, Bel,' Jan said, 'he's made you a huge offer, six times what you paid for him.'

'I know that, but I think he's worth ten times that at least.'

Jan had already expressed her view to Annabel that she should take the profit while it was offered. Although Annabel had some money of her own, Jan was fairly sure she couldn't afford to own a sixty-thousand pound horse, but now wasn't the time to pursue it. 'Annabel was so excited when he won at Ascot, she was screaming and howling her eyes out – I've never seen her like that before,' she said in defence of her friend.

Ben looked affectionately at Annabel. 'Aaahh,' he murmured. 'So, you'll never sell him?'

Annabel shook her head.

'I'm not so sure,' Jan observed. 'I think A.D.'s one of those people who never takes "no" for an answer.'

New Year passed and the frost still hadn't eased its grip. With the three blank days before Christmas, there had been no racing anywhere in Britain for nearly a fortnight. Jan, like every other trainer in the country, was beginning to feel extremely frustrated, but with the help of Reg's old Ferguson tractor and a fertilizer spreader she had managed to salt the yard, the drive and public lane, so they would have a safe surface on which the horses could at least trot.

The track down from the yard was treacherous every morning until it had been resalted, and the yard itself was covered with used straw from the stables to stop the frost getting into it and prevent the horses slipping on the icy surface.

The only respite from the gloom had been a New Year's Eve party at the Fox & Pheasant, where Toby Waller had booked a room for the night. Bernie Sutcliffe turned up, as he obviously had nowhere else to go. When Jan saw him in the bar, she hoped there wouldn't be a repeat of the awful scene he had made the previous year at Eamon Fallon's club, but he seemed content to be known as someone who had an association with an increasingly well-known local racing stable.

A more unexpected arrival at the informal party was Angie Sharp, which delighted Jan. Although they had spoken on the phone regularly, and Jan had kept up the faxed reports on the condition of the horses and their racing plans to her parents, she hadn't seen Angie since Lucky Charm had failed to live up to his promise at Sandown nearly four weeks before.

Angie was full of sympathy for Jan's plight and asked after Billy.

'He hasn't shown up yet,' Jan said. 'As it wasn't actually an Edge party, he thought he might go to some other do at Stow.'

Angie nodded. 'Is he mended yet?' she enquired with concern. Jan was still baffled by the conjecture surrounding Billy and

Angie. 'He should be able to ride again next week. He could have started back a bit sooner, I suppose, but there's been nothing for him to do up at the yard at present.'

'What the hell are you going to do if this frost keeps up?'

'There's not much I can do, but everyone's in the same boat and I suppose we have to grin and bear it; it's driving me absolutely nuts!'

At midday, two days later, an unfamiliar silver car turned into the drive and slithered wildly up the unpredictable surface, spraying grit and slush over the verges.

Jan didn't have a clear view of the parking place from the new house, since it was partially obscured by one of the stable blocks. She carried on preparing the children's lunch while she waited to see who would appear.

Wearing a red baseball cap with a suede peak, and a bright red fleece jacket, Billy Hanks bounced into view and made his way up to the house.

'Hi, Jan. Happy New Year!' he called as he walked in through the kitchen door. There was still a plaster stuck across the bridge of his nose, although the bruising that had accompanied the damage had almost disappeared.

'Hello, Billy. Did Father Christmas fall in love with you or have you won the lottery?'

'What are you talking about?'

'The sporty silver number that only just made it up the track.'

'Oh, that. There's times when I miss my old four-wheel drive, but the Toyota's fantastic – it don't half attract the birds!'

'Aren't you the lucky boy, then.'

'Yeh, well, I've been saving money like mad for three years, and after I had that smash I thought it was time to splash out and cheer myself up.'

'And does the doctor think you'll be able to ride next week?'

'Provided I don't fall off and bang my nose,' Billy snuffled.

'Seriously, though, when do you think there'll be any racing again?'

'Your guess is as good as mine. The forecast this morning said there's no end in sight it's the north-easterly that's bringing all the cold.'

'What form are the horses in?'

'Going a bit stale, like me.'

'Isn't there an all-weather gallop you can borrow from someone?'

'Not that's usable round here. We're all in the same boat. Virginia can't do anything and Jim Hely told me that they're badly frozen up; all his horses are stood in their boxes. There isn't a single gallop open at Lambourn either and the West Country's just as bad.'

Billy sighed. 'Well, I hope it ends soon, or I might start running out of money and have to sell my new car.'

A week later there was still no sign of an end to the frost and snow, and an air of desperation hung over Edge Farm like a dark cloud. The only consolation, Jan felt, was the fact that she'd moved into the house before the snow started. The intense cold would have been unbearable in the caravan, and she didn't know if Matty could have coped with it.

After exercising three lots of horses by monotonously trotting them up and down the gritted lane, Jan was sitting in the office with Annabel, going through the motions of entering horses in the hope that they'd be fit enough to race when the frost finally relented when the telephone by her elbow rang.

'Hello, Jan.'

Jan experienced the nervous tingle she always felt when she heard A.D.'s voice and automatically straightened her back.

'Good morning, A.D.'

'I wanted to ask if you would pass on a message to that good-looking assistant of yours.'

'She's right here beside me. Do you want to talk to her?'

'No, that's OK. She'll want to discuss it with you anyway, I dare say.'

'Discuss what?'

'My increased offer for an interest in Russian Eagle. She's told me since the horse won at Ascot she's not interested in selling any part of it, even if I offered her fifty grand.'

'Eagle's worth more than that.'

'Maybe you're right, which is why I'm prepared to offer her the same for a two-thirds share.'

'She won't accept that, I can tell you now; though maybe she would for half the horse.'

'That's no good. I'd want the horse to run in my colours and to have the final decision on races and jockeys.'

'She might agree to that with a fifty per cent share,' Jan suggested doubtfully.

There was a brief silence at the other end of the line. 'All right,' A.D. growled. 'Put it to her, but she would have to sign a partnership agreement giving me those rights.'

'I'll see what I can do,' Jan replied cautiously.

'Let me know, soon as you can.'

As usual, he put down the receiver before she could say 'goodbye'.

Jan looked up at Annabel. 'A.D.'s just offered you fifty grand for half your horse,' she said with a grin.

'Hmm.' Annabel pondered, refusing to be over-impressed. 'Do you think he'd go to sixty?'

'He's overpaying at fifty, Bel.'

'But with sixty thousand pounds and what I've already got, I could afford to buy Glebe Cottage without a mortgage. The executors of Mr Carey's estate have just offered it to me. If A.D.'s prepared to pay over the odds at fifty, I think he'll go to sixty.'

'He wants you to agree that the horse will run in his colours, with his choice of jockey and also the races he runs in.'

'As long as I still own half, I wouldn't mind that.'

Jan hadn't thought that Bel would agree, even though it was

undoubtedly the most sensible course of action. 'Great! I'll ring him back.'

Two minutes later Jan put the phone down with a triumphant grin on her face. 'Congratulations, Bel. Sixty thousand and the horse is still half yours, but Murty McGrath rides whenever he's available and not Billy Hanks.'

'Oh Lord,' Annabel murmured. 'I hope I've done the right thing.'

'Bel, you can't go back on it now,' Jan said quickly.

'No, OK, but just give me a little time to get used to the idea.'

'All right,' Jan said, understanding. 'Let's get back down to earth. Some of these horses are putting on too much weight, but I daren't cut back on their feed.'

Annabel nodded. 'Eagle's beginning to look distinctly tubby. It looks as if Mr O'Hagan will be getting more horse than he bargained for.'

Jan laughed. 'So you're getting used to the idea already?'

'Yes, so now you'll have two ecstatic owners to deal with every time he wins,' Annabel chuckled.

'Or two bloody miserable ones when he doesn't,' Jan added. She took a deep breath. 'I'm going to have to sort out this Billy business. This damn frost couldn't have come at a worse time from that point of view. A.D. thinks Billy's up to no good.'

'So does Bernie,' Annabel broke in. 'He went on and on about it in the pub on New Year's Eve. Angie got really annoyed with him.'

'Frankly, I'm not too worried what Bernie says. He's had it in for Billy ever since he went off with that tarty girlfriend of his. But I am worried about A.D. He's my most powerful owner and he knows what he's talking about. I've looked back over all the races Billy's ridden in which we felt he could have won, and there's not one where I could honestly say he did anything specifically wrong. I mean, on Tom's Touch at Ascot he *did* get boxed in – I saw that with my own eyes.' Jan shook her head. 'But I've promised A.D. I'll make absolutely certain, one way or the other.'

'How do you propose to do that?'

'I'll run a couple more horses in races where they have a good chance and see how he gets on. If he loses both of those, I'll enter King's Archer into something well below his level, and see what happens then.'

'But, Jan, even that wouldn't be conclusive.'

'I know, but it's the only way I can think of discovering the truth without actually putting thumbscrews on him.'

'I don't envy you. I know you're fond of Billy, even though he can be a complete prat at times.'

'Yes, well, it's all rather academic at the moment, isn't it? If I don't get a bit more work into some of these horses soon,' Jan said, 'we'll never get them fit enough to put A.D.'s theory to the test.'

'But if there isn't a gallop we can use anywhere, there's not a lot we can do about it.'

'Actually, there is. I've been thinking. When I was back in Wales and it was frozen up, I sometimes took the horses to Pembrokeshire, and galloped them on the beaches. There's a huge space you can use at low tide, and it does their legs good to have a bit of a paddle in the sea afterwards.'

'Didn't old Ginger McCain gallop Red Rum along the beaches in Lancashire?'

'That's right.'

'But Pembrokeshire's hundreds of miles from here.'

'I'm not suggesting we go there, but I've had a good look at the map and I think we could get to Burnham-on-Sea and back inside a day. They've got ideal beaches there; I've checked.'

'Great, let's do it!' said Annabel, hugging her friend.

🐎

Two days later, after a forecast for a bright but continuously cold day, Jan drove her lorry cautiously down the track from the yard at six o'clock in the morning. At the bottom she stopped and jumped out to lower the ramp. The girls and lads led five horses down through the field to load them. Roz, Declan and Connor then piled into Roz's car, while Jan and Annabel climbed back into the cab of the lorry.

Jan wound down the window before she pulled out into the lane. 'Roz, make sure you stay behind us, in case we have a problem and need your help.'

Following a tricky drive on the country roads Jan was relieved to reach the M5 at Tewkesbury, where there had been enough gritting to keep the lanes clear of snow and so they settled down for an easy run.

'How was the doctor yesterday?' Annabel asked, aware that Tony Robertson had called to take Jan out for the first time since the dinner at L'Escargot.

'OK, though I was a bit annoyed that he hadn't been in touch since the last time. He said it was because he was worried he might scare me off by showing too much interest, so I told him I'd rather he was straightforward about it.'

'But, in a way, he did the right thing. I mean, Jan, I know you. If he'd pressed harder, you would certainly have backed off.'

Jan sighed. 'Maybe, at least I can think about having a boyfriend now. I'm not a nun and there are times when I feel I would like to have a man with me.'

'But only if it's the right man,' Annabel added quickly.

'Of course. Anyway, it was OK, and he didn't even try to kiss me this time.'

'Did you mind that?'

Jan nodded slowly. 'Yes. A little. It makes me wonder just how much of a man he really is.'

'You can't have it both ways, Jan – expecting him not to get too keen, but hot to trot as soon as you give him the nod.'

'I know – pity, isn't it.' Jan chuckled.

Around two hours after leaving home, they reached the seaside town, where the beach was windy and deserted. In an empty car park, they unloaded the horses and put on their exercise tack, which Jan checked carefully. When they were all ready, she climbed into Dingle Bay's saddle and led them in single file onto the beach.

The sand at the top, seldom covered by the sea, was soft and yielding, and the horses' hoofs sank in to their fetlocks, but as they walked through the flotsam and jetsam flung up by the briny at the last high tide the sand grew firmer, until at the edge of the water it was an almost perfect surface on which to canter.

As soon as the horses felt the shallow sea beneath their feet, they began to show their mettle, arching their necks and sticking their long tails skywards. When they eventually broke into a trot behind Jan, it was all the lads could do to hold onto them. Tom's Touch put in a huge buck, which had Declan throwing his hand in the air like a rodeo rider, desperately trying to stay in his saddle. Annabel was almost ejected by Erin's Jet in a series of exuberant plunges.

'Keep his head up,' Jan shouted as she led them into a canter for a mile along the beach. The strong tang of seaweed, the salty air and the spray from waves breaking ten yards out whipped through her hair and made her feel more alive than she had for weeks.

As they approached a spit of rocks marking the end of the beach, Jan slowed to a walk. They turned their horses' tails to the wind and gave them a breather.

As the horses blew, their jockeys were whooping with the sheer exhilaration of the exercise.

'If you lot are feeling like that,' Jan shouted above the wind, 'think what these horses must be feeling.'

'Did you see my lad trying to deck me?' Declan shouted back.

'He wasn't trying to deck you – he was just letting off steam. You did well to stick to him! Bel you had a bit of a rough time, didn't you?'

'Well, I'm still here.'

'Thank God. I wouldn't fancy trying to catch a loose one on this beach – especially if they got it into their heads to take off, which they probably would after they've been cooped up for so long. Hopefully they won't do it again today, but we'll have to watch out when we bring the next lot down here.'

'Are we coming again?' Con asked eagerly.

'I should say so,' Jan answered, 'or we're soon going to have a lot of disgruntled owners on our hands.'

Toby phoned on Tuesday evening, after he knew Jan would have finished putting Megan to bed.

'Good news,' he said.

'What about?' Jan tried to think which of Toby's horses was making him excited.

'Your bungalow at Stonewall. It looks as if Harold Powell's shot himself in the foot.'

'How come?'

'The only access to the field from the road is up the drive to the farm. When the plans were drawn for the original auction, the first bit of the drive beside the bungalow was lotted in with it and excluded from the sale, so you still own it. Without your permission, people can't even get up to the farm, let alone hundreds of caravaners.'

Jan felt an enormous wave of relief flood over her. As he continued, she rummaged through the drawers of John's old bureau for her copies of the relevant documents. She found the plan that had accompanied the sale. 'My God, you're right! I can see how it could have happened if Harold was doing it in a hurry and wasn't concentrating properly. Serve him right, the incompetent fool!'

'If you're feeling really vindictive, you could easily squeeze a good bit out of him to allow access to the farm. A bit of a result, I'd say!'

'Toby, you're brilliant!'

'It wasn't me who spotted it,' he disclaimed.

'No, but somehow you always manage to pull something out of the hat. Thank you very much.'

'Don't mention it. Just get my horses back onto the race course and winning as soon as possible.'

'If you have as much influence over Jack Frost as you seem to have over everything else, maybe you could use it there.'

Toby laughed. 'I'll see what I can do.'

🐎

Jan took four more loads of horses to Burnham-on-Sea before the rain arrived the following weekend and the frost and snow disappeared as suddenly as they had arrived.

She woke on Monday morning and recognized a different quality in the air as soon as she went to the window. The wind had eased and was back to its normal south-westerly direction, bringing the soft, warm rain with it. She dressed quickly, went out, climbed straight into her Land Rover and drove up to inspect the tilled gallop on the side of the long field and the turf gallop at the top of the ridge. She stuck a well-used walking stick into the ground and came back to the yard to announce that they were usable at last.

'Oh fiddlesticks, I'll miss the beach!' Roz wailed.

'I just wish I'd started using it sooner,' Jan said. 'Anyway, it's business as usual and we've got a massive amount of work to do if we want to be running horses by the end of the week.'

🐎

Despite all their concentrated effort, Jan realized they wouldn't have a horse ready to run for some days. Billy came in and rode all the early prospects for her, but she couldn't escape the evidence of her own eyes that the month's lay-off had set the horses back considerably.

Finally, nine days after the end of the big freeze, Billy rode Wolf's Rock and King's Archer at Leicester, where both horses finished unplaced.

Jan didn't get a chance to talk to her jockey alone until after racing. Whatever A.D. O'Hagan had said or heard, she was determined to be fair to him. She arranged for Roz to drive the lorry home while she got a lift back with Billy in his new Toyota.

'So, tell me about them,' she asked as they left the race course.

Billy shrugged. 'They've been off a long time.'

'So have everyone else's.'

'But some of 'em's got all-weathers they've been able to use.'

'Not many.'

'Well, whatever.'

'Billy, that's not bloody good enough.'

'Jan, are you accusing me of something?' Billy asked angrily, swerving onto the verge for a moment.

'Take it easy, Billy. What I'm saying is that your attitude isn't good enough. Just to say, "Whatever", as if it didn't matter a damn. Well, I reckon Wolf's Rock was as good as, if not better than, most of the others, but you never had him in a decent position at any stage during the race.'

'He didn't want to know, Jan. What else can I say?'

'And what am I supposed to tell the owner?'

'Don't ask me. You'll think of something,' he replied weakly.

🐎

At home that night the fact that Billy had defended himself so feebly seemed to indicate to Jan that he wasn't covering up any dishonesty, but she was extremely upset when Colonel Gilbert telephoned, starting his conversation with an apprehensive clearing of his throat.

'Jan, I don't really know how to say this, but your jockey didn't look as if he was trying too hard today.'

'I'm sorry, Colonel. I said exactly the same to him in the car on the way home and he assured me the horse just wasn't giving him any sort of feel.'

'Do you think that's right?'

'I can't be certain, but Billy didn't make any of the usual excuses you'd expect him to if it wasn't.'

'So you feel confident he's not up to anything?'

'Yes, Colonel. I'm as sure as I can be.'

'All right, Jan, I must accept your assurances, but next time we run Wolf's Rock, I'd like to try another jockey. I'll let you know who. I hope that's all right?'

'Yes, of course, Colonel.' She put the phone down, sighed and shook her head in despair at the uncertainty of it all.

By contrast, on the following Saturday there was jubilation at Edge Farm.

Jan had taken A.D. O'Hagan's Wexford Lad to run at Sandown Park. It was now nine weeks since the passport fiasco at Cheltenham. On that occasion the horse had muffed the last two hurdles but still managed to finish in second place. Since then Billy had spent a lot of time carefully reschooling the horse until he and Jan were convinced he'd completely got the hang of it and, as Murty McGrath was free, he had been booked to ride the horse.

Jan telephoned A.D. on her way home.

'I saw the race, he jumped beautifully. It was a grand piece of training,' he said. 'And superbly ridden.'

'Yes, I was really pleased with the way Murty rode him.'

'No progress with yer man then?'

'The last few rides he's had haven't proved anything one way or the other. But there've been a couple that maybe he could have won.'

'Yes,' A.D. cut in. 'Those two at Leicester. And I see one of those belonged to those Sharp people.'

'I'm running another of theirs at Fontwell on Monday, as well as Erin's Jet for you.'

'So I see.' A.D. always checked the entries when he spoke to Jan. 'As Murty's committed elsewhere, Billy can have the ride, but, Jan, don't tell him it's his last chance. If he blows it this time, he'll never ride another horse for me again.'

'I won't say a word.' Jan understood his inference.

Angie Sharp met Jan at Fontwell Park and watched in stony silence as Overmere Lass failed to make any impression on a field she should have galloped into the ground.

Jan was flabbergasted. She was sure the mare was in good order; she had been working so well at home and even Billy had seemed optimistic. Jan couldn't look Angie in the eye.

'God, Angie. I don't know what happened. I just don't know what Billy's playing at.'

'It wasn't Billy's fault, Jan. Let's face it, you're just not getting these horses on song. You had them going wonderfully at the start of the season, then something went wrong, didn't it?'

'Angie . . .'

'Look, Jan, you and I are friends. We're not going to fall out over this, but Mum and Dad are getting a bit fed up. They stuck with Martin Hunter longer than they should out of the kindness of their hearts. I worked hard to persuade them to move the horses to you and when you got off to such a good start, they were delighted, but now . . .' Angie shrugged her shoulders.

'I don't know what to say, Angie, I really don't. You're such good owners – the last thing I want to do is upset you. I swear I've done everything I know to get these horses to win races.'

'It's not as though it's only ours. It hasn't been going too well for your other owners, has it? Isn't Mr O'Hagan getting a little pissed off?'

Jan didn't want to talk about A.D. with Angie, and she thought it was very wrong of Angie to drag him into this.

'What I talk about with any of my other owners is confidential,' she said frostily.

'Sorry, Jan.' Angie tried to soothe her. 'I accept that. I hope Erin's Jet runs well for you, but I'm going now. I may come up to watch King's Archer at Hereford next week. He'll be a bloody short price, but at least he should win, eh?'

Jan nodded weakly. She'd entered King's Archer in a race well below his class. Unless he fell, which was unlikely, there was no reason why he shouldn't win doing the proverbial handsprings.

On the card, Erin's Jet had been a clear favourite, but like Overmere Lass he failed to deliver and finished a remote fifth.

Again there was nothing precise to condemn in Billy's riding and, once again, he blamed the horse for feeling lifeless.

Jan was in turmoil, trying to work out what was happening. She had been on tenterhooks since the visit to Aigmont and also during the cold snap, knowing that she was on probation as far as A.D. was concerned. This final defeat could be the last straw for him.

But she didn't tell Billy that his days of riding A.D.'s horses were over. She thought it wiser to wait until after King's Archer's race at Hereford, which she would have to treat as conclusive.

It was five days since King's Archer had run at Hereford. Roz drove Russian Eagle and Lucky Charm to Warwick races in the lorry, while Jan went with Annabel in the Golf a couple of hours later.

'I'm afraid to say,' Annabel said, 'I'm rather relieved that Murty's riding Eagle today and not Billy.'

'I can't say I blame you after what happened at Hereford. How Billy slipped off at that fence, I'll never know,' Jan sighed.

'He told me King's Archer put in a short one that took him by surprise, so he was unbalanced when they landed. Still, at least he was all right.'

Jan grunted. 'I'm getting a bit pissed off with Billy's lame excuses. There's nothing wrong with the horses. I've had them all checked over by my vet and blood-tested. The results of the tests are excellent. I'm sorry, Bel, I've defended Billy's riding till I'm blue in the face. Well, this is D-Day and now I'm bloody angry. So we might see some changes after this,' she added mysteriously.

Russian Eagle had worked off all the surplus condition he had put on during the freeze and was looking happy and workmanlike

as Declan led him around the parade ring before the big steeplechase of the day.

With just one win in a novice chase under rules to his name,
Russian Eagle was low in the weights for this competitive
National trial over three miles and four furlongs.

'It's sad not to see him in my colours,' Annabel murmured
beside Jan. 'I'm sure carrying A.D.'s blue and yellow stripes has
knocked a couple of points off his odds as well.'

'It will have done,' Jan agreed, 'but you have got Murty on
board and he seems delighted to have the ride.'

'He must think a lot of him,' Annabel surmised.

'Well, A.D. wouldn't have considered buying the horse if
Murty hadn't recommended him.'

'No, I suppose not. Anyway, the good news is it feels just as
exciting owning half the horse as it did owning all of him.'

Jan smiled. 'Well, let's hope we'll be ringing your co-owner
with some good news in a quarter of an hour or so.'

🐎

To Jan's surprise, A.D. wasn't available when she tried to contact
him after the race, and she couldn't think where he might be.

'I'm sure he'll ring us back,' she said. 'I bet he watched the
race, wherever he is. He's bound to be chuffed.'

'Not half as chuffed as I am,' Annabel said, with eyes still
damp with the emotion of seeing Russian Eagle storm past the
finishing post before the second horse had cleared the final fence.

In the unsaddling enclosure after the race, Jan asked Murty
for his views.

'That is one hell of a good animal. You could go a long way
with him,' he beamed.

Coming from the champion jockey, and one famous for
understatement, Jan knew this was serious praise. Russian Eagle's
win had given her back complete belief in her ability and had
put her in a much better frame of mind to deal with Vince and
Dawn Sharp before Lucky Charm's race.

Although their horse hadn't run since finishing last at Sandown in December, his previous win at Chepstow hadn't gone unnoticed by the punters and a couple of tipsters had selected him for today's race.

Jan's troop had worked hard to produce a horse that looked outstanding as he strode around the parade ring. As she stood with the Sharps and Annabel in the middle, she noticed Vince was wearing a baggy mac at least a size too big, which looked as if it had come from an upmarket charity shop, while Dawn was clad in a limp musquash coat. They were watching the horse carefully and so far the conversation had been rather strained.

Jan braced herself for Billy's entrance.

He bounced up to them in a way he hadn't done for weeks. She guessed it must be for the Sharps' benefit, and smiled to herself.

'What shall I do today?' he asked Jan with a smirk.

'I'll tell you what you can do, Billy,' Jan replied grimly. 'You can please your effing self because that's precisely what you've been doing for the last three months. Every single horse I've put you on that's stood a chance you've ridden exactly how you bloody liked, and I'm not putting up with your crap any longer.' She stared at him without blinking as he quailed under the onslaught, and tried to regain his composure.

'Hang on, Jan!' he blustered.

'Mrs Hardy to you!'

'Bollocks to that! What the hell are you talking about?'

'That's enough!' Jan snapped. 'I know bloody well what you've been doing! It must be a dozen times at least that you've pretended you didn't know what I was talking about when I've bollocked you for not riding properly – and you've done it deliberately every time, haven't you? Since last autumn you've stopped every horse you've ridden for me that's had a winning chance. You get them boxed in – like Overmere Lass at Ludlow, and Tom's Touch at Ascot – you never moved on him when you claimed you'd been riding out a finish. The horse was as fresh as a daisy when he came in – remember? You deliberately screwed up Lucky Charm, bursting him at Sandown. There've been loads of times. I don't have to go on, do I?' Jan glared at him. 'In my book, there's only one reason why jockeys behave like that. You know it. And so do they!' She snapped her head round to face the Sharps.

Vince's face was quivering with guilt. He had turned a purplish brown and was making a strange choking noise. Jan had always suspected he was the weaker of the two.

Dawn's wrinkled lips were also trembling, but she could still use them. 'Just what d'you think you're saying?' she snapped shrilly.

Jan turned to Angie, who was looking on in utter disbelief. 'I'm sorry, Angie. I guess it's not your fault.'

'Listen 'ere,' Dawn croaked again. 'What d'you think you're doing?'

Jan took a deep breath to steady herself. 'You can get all your horses out of my yard because this is the last runner you'll be having with me! Bel, you leg him up.'

Jan turned on her heel and headed straight for the exit. She didn't look back and carried on until she was well away from the arena. Shaking with fury and pent-up emotion, at that moment she didn't care where she was going.

She was aware that a lot of people had witnessed the scene in the parade ring, and hoped the stewards had been out of earshot. Maybe she shouldn't have done it there and then, but she didn't care. Guilt was written all over Vince's face and it was clear from Dawn's reaction that they had been colluding with Billy over the running of their horses and others in her yard. Why they had done it and and what was in it for them, she had no idea, but she thought that somehow it had to be linked to the betting.

How Billy could have done such a thing, and gone on and on doing it, hurt her more than anything else at this moment, she knew she would never forgive him for his treachery. It was a complete nightmare.

Suddenly she heard the course commentator announce that

the runners were down at the start. Without any real interest, she made her way to the stands and huddled in a corner to watch the race.

It felt utterly pointless when Lucky Charm ran an almost perfect race and finished second, beaten by a short head.

Jan was the first to reach Billy and Lucky Charm as they made their way to the unsaddling enclosure.

'You tried a bit harder that time,' she growled.

'I always bloody try,' he hissed. 'If you think we've been up to something, you're bloody mad; you don't want to lose seven horses, do you?'

'Just shut up, Billy. And I'd keep well out of my way, if I were you.'

Jan left Roz to lead the horse in. 'Tell Annabel I'll see her back at the stables; she can look after the owners.'

'Right,' Roz nodded knowingly.

Jan guessed the story of the parade ring bust-up would spread like wildfire around the course.

🐎

Annabel had already arranged to make a detour on her way home, to see a friend in hospital at Leamington Spa, so Jan travelled back in the lorry with Roz, Con and the horses in almost complete silence. The grooms were well aware of the day's drama.

Jan hadn't been in the house five minutes before the phone rang. She hoped it might be A.D. to talk about Russian Eagle's win.

But it was Billy.

'Can I come up and see you?'

'What for?'

'I want to tell you what's been going on.'

'I know what's been going on, Billy. You've been stopping my sodding horses.' Jan felt her voice rise and begin to shake. She really didn't want to go into this again, she was exhausted, but now there was no way out. She took a deep breath. 'Listen, Billy, I've had a chance to think about it on the way home and I'll tell you what conclusion I've come to. I've worked my arse off to build up this business from nothing, working seven days a week, all the hours God sends; I've battled to get a professional licence and a backer. I've done everything I know to produce fit, well-schooled horses. That's what I set out to do; I've had a good run of success, and I'm not having some double-dealing little toerag like you take the piss and screw the whole thing up. Is that clear enough for you?'

There was silence at the other end of the line. 'What the hell do you expect me to do?' Billy whimpered finally.

'I expect you to come here, collect all your stuff and then stay well away from my yard.'

Annabel had purposely dropped in on her way back from Leamington. Although she was still hyped up by her horse's victory, she understood the implications of the drama that had taken place a few hours earlier at Warwick. She was still taken aback, though, when Jan told her she had sacked Billy.

'Bloody hell, Jan. Are you absolutely sure that's the right way to deal with it? I mean, losing seven horses and your stable jockey in one hit.'

'As it's impossible to win races with either, I don't feel I had any other choice.'

'But what about the fees?'

'Bell, if I hadn't sacked Billy, we'd have lost a lot more than the Sharps' horses, I can assure you. A.D.'s been getting very touchy, as well as the colonel – let alone Bernie Sutcliffe, so, as you can see, it was him or me!'

Annabel sighed. 'You're probably right. Actually, I feel a bit guilty. I heard Billy having a rather odd conversation ages ago, before Christmas. He was on his mobile phone and I didn't think anything about it at the time, but he was arranging to meet someone at the services on the M5. It's only just crossed my mind, it isn't somewhere you'd go for a social drink, is it? Perhaps he was meeting old Sharp there.'

'Probably,' Jan agreed. 'I still feel sorry for Angie. I can't believe she had any idea about what was going on. She was so pissed off when Overmere Lass didn't win at Fontwell, even though I'm certain now Billy stopped her.'

'It looks as though Angie's parents have used her as well. Maybe they did the same with Martin Hunter. After all, he must have been in the same boat. He had a little run of winners early last season, didn't he?'

'You're right,' Jan nodded, 'and he said something to me when I saw him at Taunton which could have hinted at it. I should have taken more notice – I think he was probably giving me the gypsy's warning, but dared not say more because he didn't want to incriminate himself if anything ever came out.'

'Do you think it will?'

'I'm not going to lodge a formal complaint; there's no point as I can't provide hard evidence. And I don't suppose anyone else will do anything unless Martin Hunter decides to come out of the woodwork.'

'Jan, I'm afraid a lot of people heard what went on today. I should think everyone in racing knows about it by now. The jungle drums will be doing overtime.'

🏇

When Annabel had left, Jan was leaning back in the rocking chair in front of the Aga in the kichen. She was trying to collect her thoughts after the drama of the day and trying to get used to the idea that the Sharps' horses really were going to leave the yard, when the silence was broken by the telephone. Jan looked at the clock. It was nearly eleven. She hoped it wasn't another of her owners, demanding an explanation of the happenings at Warwick.

'Jan, it's Angie.'

Jan's heart sank. She hadn't been looking forward to dealing with Angie. After her initial reaction that Angie couldn't possibly be involved in whatever scam it was the Sharps were running, she had reluctantly deduced there was no way they could be doing such a thing without Angie knowing about it.

And she hated the inevitable conclusion that Angie had been duping her all these months.

'Hello, Ange. I'm sorry about the scene today,' she said, still giving her friend the benefit of the doubt.

'Not half as sorry as we are,' Angie replied coldly. 'It's my parents you should be apologizing to. You must be off your trolley, threatening to chuck seven good horses out of your yard.'

'I wasn't threatening, Angie, they're going.' Jan felt the beginnings of a red mist before her eyes. 'I don't know what your parents are up to, but I'm not training their horses while they're still doing it.'

'You're mad. You can't afford to lose their horses. You'll have to sack at least two of your staff; you only just have enough horses to break even as it is. And you've still got all your bills to pay. Jan, I *know* how tight it is for you, with your new house and everything, remember? If you've got any sense, you'll apologize to my parents and tell them the horses can stay.'

Jan found it impossible to believe that someone who knew her as well as Angie did was saying this to her – how could she? But now Angie was talking like a total stranger, not the friend with whom she'd shared so many jokes and private thoughts over the past six months.

'Angie,' Jan interrupted with icy calm, 'your parents, and you too, it seems, were colluding with my jockey to stop your horses from winning, and not only your horses, but several others that should have won from this yard – I know Billy was picking up money for his services, and I know where.'

'Listen, Jan, you don't get it, do you? You're a new trainer with very little money behind you; you need to keep your yard full of horses. The way we want our horses to run is our affair. You're paid to train them, that's all. And any arrangements we may have made with Billy needn't concern you.'

Jan held the phone away from her ear and looked at it, shaking her head before she spoke again. 'I can't believe I'm hearing this. But you're right about one thing – your arrangements with Billy have got nothing to do with me any more because I've just sacked him. He'll never ride another horse from my yard again.'

'You've sacked Billy?' Angie gasped.

'Why are you so surprised? Because I've sacked a jockey who was being paid to lose on my horses? Now, let me tell you what's going to happen. I'll be making up a bill for keeping your horses until tomorrow, and after that it'll cost you twenty-five pounds a day per horse until the bill's paid in full and you collect them. If they're still here at the end of the month, I'll get a lien against them and send them to public auction to recover the debt. I hope that's clear. I'll send the bill on your fax machine, which you can pick up when you collect the horses, right?'

Jan banged down the receiver, feeling a whole lot better for having got some of the anger and frustration off her chest.

🐎

Annabel had been spot on when she'd said the story of the row would spill out all over the place. It had even leaked onto the racing pages of one or two of the Sunday newspapers. Mrs Sharp was quoted as saying she had no idea why their trainer, Mrs Jan Hardy, had asked them to quit her yard. The paper stated that it seemed an extraordinary action to take, given the number of winners Jan had got from their horses and the considerable support the Sharps had given her in her first full season. It looked as if the gentle old couple from Bristol were being cast as the victims and Jan was the villain.

Jan threw the papers onto the kitchen table with a groan. 'Oh God. From the heights to the depths in under six months. I suppose the phone will be ringing before long.'

'Rubbish.' Ben looked up from where he was reading another paper while he ate breakfast. 'If you're right, and the Sharps were getting Billy to pull your horses, you can settle down now and watch your horses run competitively again. After all, Russian Eagle and Murty did prove the point yesterday.'

'Sure, but it'll take time to repair the damage, and you can't get away from the fact that the Sharps did have one or two nice horses. That's what's so weird. You'd think they'd want them to win as many races as possible.'

'Well, maybe it'll all come out in the wash. But you're determined to stick to what you've said, are you?'

'Ben, do you need to ask? I don't have any choice. Especially after the way Angie's taken me for a total mug. Do you know she had the gall to look completely mystified when the balloon went up yesterday?'

'What happened after you walked out of the ring?'

Jan grimaced. 'Poor Bel. I feel really bad about it now; I dropped her right in it, and without any warning. But she just got on with it and legged Billy up – she even heard him ask Dawn what he should do, and she said, "You'd better win if you can." Angie had hurried off to find me, apparently, but I'd tucked myself into a corner to watch the race. Anyway, afterwards I couldn't face seeing them, I'm afraid, and I left Bel to deal with it all.'

'What a drama, eh? Well, I'm pleased you've sorted it before Supercall runs. When do you think he'll be ready?'

'By next week, I hope. That blasted septic foot set him back a few weeks, but he's coming on now and looking really great.'

'JCB can't wait. By the way, he was asking after your lovely Annabel the other day.'

'What about the film star?'

'They come and go with him. They only get a short-stay ticket'

'Then I don't think I'll encourage Bel. Anyway, I thought you fancied her – and vice versa.'

'Did you?' Ben asked blandly, turning back to his paper.

Jan gave up with a grin. She liked having Ben to stay now and again. He brought a glimpse of another world with him, which she found very refreshing. She had also been nursing a secret fantasy, in which he and Bel got together, but she knew that she couldn't put any pressure on him. Still, it would be interesting to see how they got on when Annabel came round for lunch.

Jan benefited from the therapeutic qualities of cooking as she prepared their meal, she was quite relaxed and a great deal calmer than the previous day when A.D. phoned just after noon.

'Jan, well done!' he crowed.

'For winning with Eagle or outing the Sharps?'

'Both,' A.D. laughed. 'But have you sacked the jockey too?'

Jan breathed a loud sigh. 'Yes. I had no alternative.'

'I'm afraid I was right, was I not, Jan?'

'So it would seem,' she admitted, though she deduced it wouldn't be wise to tell the likes of A.D. that they were right more than was absolutely necessary.

'OK, well, you can get on with turning out a few more winners now, and as for Russian Eagle, if your lovely assistant is agreeable, I think we should aim him at the National.'

'What!?' Jan gasped, appalled at the idea of running the inexperienced Russian Eagle in the world's toughest steeplechase. 'The Grand National?'

'No, no, of course not,' A.D. said impatiently. 'The Irish National, here at Fairyhouse on Easter Monday.'

Jan almost fainted with relief, although she had no idea what the course at Fairyhouse was like. 'Do you think he'd stand a chance?' she asked. 'I know very little about the race.'

'I wouldn't have suggested it if I didn't think he had, and I've spoken to Murty. So get him entered and bring him over.'

'Don't you think we ought to put him in another National trial over here first, just to be sure? I've already found a suitable race at Sandown on March the seventh.'

'Hell, no!' A.D. laughed. 'He'd stroll up and earn a penalty in the National. The horse is still well handicapped and I know he's up to the job. And, what's more, I'll put you and my co-owner up at the Shelbourne. We'll have a great *craic*, even if he doesn't win. Is that OK?'

Jan caught some of his infectious enthusiasm. 'It doesn't sound as if we've got much choice,' she laughed.

'No,' A.D. agreed. 'I'll try and phone Annabel, but if I don't get to her first, will you inform her?'

'That's OK, I'll see to it, A.D.'

When Annabel arrived for lunch, Jan couldn't resist the chance of a quick tease.

'A.D. phoned,' she said.

'Great! What did he say?'

'He was over the moon with the result yesterday. He thinks you've got a real star on your hands, and wants me to enter him for the National.'

Annabel, in the course of taking off her coat, dropped it on the floor.

'W . . . what!?' she stammered. 'The Grand National? For God's sake, Jan! He can't be serious.'

'Well, that's what he told me, and I have to say, I was pretty doubtful too, until he told me he was talking about the *Irish* National!' Jan burst out laughing at the look on Annabel's face.

'Jan,' Ben said, looking up from his paper, 'that was a very nasty trick. Look at Bel. She's as white as a ghost.'

'Shut up, Ben,' Annabel ordered. 'Jan, you're a cow! What's the Irish National like?'

'All I can tell you is that your co-owner is very enthusiastic about it, and so, apparently, is Murty McGrath. A.D. wants to put us up in some swish hotel and have a bit of a *craic*, whatever that is.'

'You'll find out soon enough,' Ben said. 'I'm sure you'll have a great time.'

Although Jan had no runners at the Cheltenham Festival, she treated herself to a day out and went to watch the Gold Cup on the Thursday.

Dermot O'Hare had sent over a fancied runner for A.D. O'Hagan, and once again Jan was invited to join the Irishman in his box for lunch.

There was a great deal less tension than there had been on earlier occasions. Jan had scored a couple more winners for A.D. recently, as well as her first success with Supercall. Although faint rumblings had followed the fracas with the Sharps, once she'd given a guarded interview over the telephone to one journalist she hadn't been approached again, and the story died down.

Jan hadn't seen the item in the newspaper until one of A.D.'s guests pointed it out to her during lunch.

Underneath the unflattering photograph of Vince and Dawn Sharp was a caption:

Elderly Bristol Couple Arrested for Fraudulent Tipping Line Operation

And in one of the tabloids:

West Country OAPs in Tipping Line Scam

above a picture of Overmere Manor.

Neither piece referred to their disagreement with Jan five weeks before, but she had an uneasy feeling it was only a matter of time. She read the scant facts behind the headlines and realized that the police had chosen to release very little information at this stage. There was no mention of Angie, who was managing to keep out of the limelight somehow.

Discreetly, she showed the news items to A.D.

He cast a quick, experienced eye down them. 'Well, now you know – if these people have got their facts right, which, of course, they may not have. It seems inevitable that you'll get a visit from the police and Jockey Club Security. Billy, too, I expect. Fortunately, even if the Sharps try to point the finger at you, your actions show that you were never implicated. However, I should make sure you brief your lawyer at once, and if you think he's not up to it, get one that is. You can't afford even the hint of a scandal hanging around your yard at this stage in your career – you may never shake it off. In any event, you can be sure of my support, one hundred per cent.'

15

Jan thought about A.D.'s support a week later, as she and the lads loaded Russian Eagle onto the horsebox for the first leg of his trip to Ireland.

He had helped her with lawyers and professional PR advice. He had publicly stated his own complete confidence in Jan Hardy as a trainer and as a friend. To prove his point, he had sent two more horses to Edge Farm to be trained by her. As a result, since the announcement of the Sharps' arrest, all references to her in the press had been favourable, and previous speculation about her indifference to the Sharps had been modified.

Johnny Carlton-Brown, whose name had appeared as one of Jan's high-profile owners, had sounded impressed the last time he'd phoned.

'Amazing publicity you're getting,' he'd said. 'I wish some of our bands found it that easy – and none of it bad.'

'Not lately.'

'That's fine. It's only the latest news that counts. And I'm bloody glad A.D.'s come out so publicly on your side. The only person I've heard saying anything nasty about you is your favourite neighbour, Virginia Gilbert,' he chortled. 'I wasn't very impressed. I think Miller's Lodge may be due for a move soon.'

'Don't start putting me in promise land, Johnny. You know I don't like bullshit.'

'Yes, I've learned that much about you. So, no bullshit. Miller comes to you next season, but don't tell anyone until I've told Virginia. OK?'

'Brilliant.' Jan let out her breath.

🐎

Roz was to drive Russian Eagle to Luton airport, where he would be loaded onto a purpose-built cargo plane and flown with ten other horses to Dublin. Declan was travelling with the horse and would be responsible for him at the other end.

'Don't forget,' Jan said, before he climbed up into the passenger seat, 'when you get to the race-course stables, give him a little lukewarm water, one of the electrolytes, then dress him over and rug him up carefully. When he's settled, take him out on a long lead and let him have a pick of grass in one of the paddocks.'

'Right, Mrs H. I'll look after him like he was my own granny.'

'You do that. Now, have a good trip and we'll see you tomorrow evening. You've got your mobile charger, I suppose.'

'Mrs H, I've got everything but the gallops tractor.'

Jan and Annabel stood and watched for a moment as the lorry crept down the drive and turned into the lane towards the motorway.

'Well, we're committed now,' Jan said.

'It feels extraordinary sending off a horse – *my own* horse – to run in a race like the Irish National.'

'Do you remember what it felt like almost exactly this time last year, taking him up to Aintree for the Foxhunters'?'

Annabel nodded. 'It feels weird, looking back on it. So much has happened since then – I mean, I felt we hardly knew what we were doing then, and sending a horse to run at a major meeting was really strange. But now, only a year later, well, we've won a few good races, haven't we – none of the major ones, but on big courses, beating horses from famous yards.'

'I certainly never expected to run a horse in a National, not in my first year,' Jan said. 'Let alone one that I'd just bought for a few grand for a friend to go hunter chasing on.'

🐎

After lunch on Easter Sunday, Jan packed her bags and took them out to Annabel's car. She leaned down to kiss the children, who had followed her outside to see her off.

'Goodbye, sweethearts,' she said. 'Be very good for Fran, won't you?'

'I'm always good for Fran,' Megan said.

'And be *very* nice to Grandad when you go there tomorrow.'

'We will. But, Mum, will we be able to see Eagle on the TV?'

'Yes, they're showing the race here on Channel 4.'

'But will you be on television?'

Jan laughed. 'I doubt it, unless we win.'

🐎

On the way to Birmingham airport in the Golf, Jan and Annabel felt like a couple of schoolgirls going off for a mad weekend.

'Are you sure you've brought enough luggage?' Jan giggled, seeing Annabel's two large bags.

'I like to have a choice just in case, that's all. I mean, suppose we did win; there'd be a bit of a celebration and, as it's half my horse, I'd want to rise to the occasion. On the other hand, if we don't come anywhere, I'll want something a bit more casual.'

'But you can only wear one outfit for the actual race.'

'Well, that depends on the weather.'

Still bubbling with excitement, they were met at Dublin airport by Daragh in the Merc.

'Hello, again, Mrs Hardy,' he beamed. 'Mr O'Hagan says I'm to look after you for the next two days.'

Jan introduced him to Annabel and noticed the young man flush a little. It was extraordinary and quite endearing, she thought, that her assistant didn't seem to realize that she often had this effect on men.

On the way into Dublin, they gave in to the unstoppable flow of Daragh's obvious enthusiasm. The big race the next day was top of the agenda, and to have the trainer and an owner of a fancied outsider in the car was obviously a chance he wasn't going to pass up.

The Shelbourne on St Stephen's Green in the centre of the city was a grand hotel of the old school. Early on Sunday evening, when Jan and Annabel walked into its big square lobby, it was filled with people sitting around taking tea among tall mirrors and comfortable sofas by a massive open fire.

They were expected and were quickly shown up to a pair of large, beautifully furnished rooms, each with its own marble bathroom.

Jan wandered through into Annabel's room.

'This is a bit of all right,' she said, watching Annabel unpack half a dozen different outfits.

'It's very generous of him to put us both up like this,' Annabel observed. 'This must be one of the smartest hotels in town.'

'It certainly looks like it,' Jan agreed. 'I suppose, if Eagle wins, you could always pay him back out of your half of the prize money.'

'I'd even pay for you,' Annabel laughed. 'So, what's the plan now?'

'Daragh can drive us out to Fairyhouse to have a look at Eagle. When I spoke to Declan this morning he said he'd just taken him out for another pick of grass and he was quite happy.'

Sixteen miles north-west of Dublin traffic was streaming away from Fairyhouse under a warm spring evening sun at the end of a busy day's racing. The race course was on the opposite side of the road from the bloodstock sales and Jan remembered the route well from her first trip out in the minibus with Mickey Byrne and his friends.

Daragh dropped them by the main gates, where gypsy women stood behind trestle tables selling bags of fruit and chocolate bars to the departing race goers. Whole families – mothers, fathers, children, babies and grandparents – had come out for their day at the races and there was a festival atmosphere about the place as they headed home.

Jan and Annabel walked through the gate, then spotted the secretary's office and went in to ask where they would find the stables.

Beyond the modern glass and brick weighing room and behind the saddling boxes stretched a long run of stables, in which the last of the day's runners were being made ready for the trip home. There were several horses from England and more distant parts of the Republic who, like Russian Eagle, were due to run the following day.

Jan got directions to their horse's stable, where they found Declan lounging on a hay bale by the door, gossiping with a girl.

He jumped to his feet as soon as he saw Jan.

'Hello, Missis.'

'Hi, Declan. How's our boy?'

'He's as happy as a nun in church. He knows he's back where he came from and he likes it. I just gave him his supper.'

Jan remembered how Declan loved to tell people that most of the horses he looked after in England had been born in the Emerald Isle, like him.

Jan let herself into the stable, followed by Annabel. Russian Eagle looked up from the manger in which his nose was buried, recognized them with a cursory glance and returned to his food.

She unbuckled his rug, whipped it off and ran a hand over his ribs. He felt wonderful, silky warm and in excellent nick.

'He's a lovely, docile chap, isn't he?' she said.

'Excuse me!' Annabel said indignantly, patting his neck. 'You'll be like a lion tomorrow when the chips are down, won't you, Eagle?'

Jan laughed. 'Yes, of course he will, but it's a big relief to see he hasn't suffered any setbacks from the flight. Some horses loathe it, and there's very little you can do about it, only observe.'

Russian Eagle had reluctantly raised his head again, and Annabel was busy rubbing his nose and murmuring endearments to him.

'Don't get too soppy, Bel, or he might forget he's supposed to be a lion.'

🐎

When they arrived back at their hotel, a porter sidled up to them.

'Is one of you ladies Mrs Hardy?'

'That's me.'

'Mr O'Hagan is in the Horseshoe Bar and would like you to join him there.'

They found A.D. in the hotel's largest bar, which was busy with a broad cross-section of Dubliners, from rugby internationals to Trinity students to Irish grandes dames, and tourists from around the world.

A.D. was sitting at a table with his wife, the opera singer, and two good-looking teenagers, instead of his usual henchmen.

He stood up with a smile and beckoned a waiter to bring up two more chairs.

'Jan, Bel! It's great to see you. We were at a family baptism this afternoon – you know, Easter Sunday.' He lifted his brow. 'These are my niece and nephew, Orla and Kilian. Siobhan, this is Annabel Halstead, who has the other half of Russian Eagle.'

As Siobhan Fitzgerald shook hands with Annabel, she made a quick appraisal of her husband's co-owner.

Jan smiled at her. 'Hello, Mrs O'Hagan.' She wondered if the singer ever worried about her husband's fidelity, but had the impression that she felt no insecurity on that score.

After a few enquiries about the flight and the comforts of the hotel, Annabel and Siobhan started discussing music, while Jan could sense that A.D. was longing for a bulletin on his runner in the premier Irish steeplechase.

'We've just been to see Eagle he looks fine. Quite relaxed,' she summarized.

'Will you exercise him tomorrow morning?'

'Yes, about seven.'

'Great! I'll be there.'

'How did Murty get on today?'

'Have you not checked the results yet?'

'Actually no. As soon as we'd had a look at Eagle we came back into town.'

'He'd a good winner today, but not for me – I'd no runners. But he's got three rides for me tomorrow.'

'Does he fancy his chances on our horse?' Jan asked.

'He didn't say, but I think he could do well.'

'I hope you're right.'

'I was right about those Sharps and Billy, wasn't I?'

'Yes, but why have you brought that up?'

'It was on the teletext – did you not see? They've been charged with fraud.'

'All of them?' Jan asked hoarsely.

'Yes, all of them – parents, the glamour girl and your ex-jockey.'

'Angie?' Jan gasped. 'They've charged her too?'

A.D. raised his hands. 'Don't blame me. I'm only telling you what it said.'

'No, no, I'm delighted. I thought she was going to keep out of it somehow because she hasn't been mentioned before. Do you realize,' she looked up at A.D., not really expecting much sympathy, 'I trusted her completely? I didn't want to believe she was involved until she rang me that night. Shit!' Jan took a deep breath. 'Oh, I'm sorry, Mrs O'Hagan, but it's just a bit hard to take.'

'Why is that, Jan?' Siobhan asked gently.

'Because when I met her she deliberately befriended me, at the sales last spring, and we got on really well. There was a great spark between us. She was a strong woman running a big business on her own – so I thought – and I was on my own, trying to get my new yard off the ground . . . Oh, God!' Jan moaned. 'When I think how she must have singled me out, like a cat stalking a mouse, she must have identified my little yard as the best one for her purposes – and me just starting off too inocent to question too much!'

A.D. was nodding his head. 'That is what it looks like and that's what I concluded,' he said.

'Thank God I dumped them when I did.'

'Amen to that,' A.D. intoned.

🐎

Jan was pleased, and a little surprised, to find Daragh and the Merc waiting for them outside the hotel at half-past six the next morning.

By the time they reached the race course, there was a promising hint of pink in the sky and the watery sun was slanting across the gentle undulations in the land.

In contrast with the previous evening, the race-course buildings were deserted and silent. Only in the stable yard were there any sounds of activity.

Declan had already tacked up Russian Eagle.

'Right, let's get him out,' Jan instructed.

Declan came out of the box with Eagle, who was wide awake and on his toes.

'Ooh, he looks great!' Annabel said with delight. 'How *are* you, boy?' She gave his lower lip an affectionate tickle.

'Come on, Bel, he's got work to do.'

Annabel stood back while Jan legged Declan onto the horse. 'Aren't you going to wait for A.D.?' she asked.

'This session is for the horse's benefit, not A.D.'s. If he lies in bed and misses it, that's too bad.'

They followed Eagle along a woodchip walkway, past the end of the oval parade ring, and went across the track to where the schooling gallops ran through a patchwork of fields in the middle of the course.

'Hello!' a voice called out.

They were startled and turned to see A.D. getting up from a

seat in the nearest stand. They waited while he crossed the course at a leisurely pace with a large cigar clenched between his teeth.

'Morning, A.D. I thought you'd come to the stables.'

'Not with this,' he said, taking the cigar from his mouth with a flourish.

'I don't know how you can smoke a disgusting thing like that first thing in the morning.'

'Maybe it's last thing at night for some of us,' A.D. chuckled.

Jan glanced at him more keenly and saw signs of sleep deficiency in the bags under his eyes. He was also wearing the jacket and fawn trousers he'd had on the previous evening. 'I see,' she said.

'Cards,' he offered by way of explanation. 'Now, let's have a look at this horse.'

'Right, Dec,' Jan called to where Russian Eagle was impatiently pawing the ground at the start of the gallop. 'Walk him to the top, then trot him back for about a quarter of a mile to loosen him up, then canter him gently back to us.'

As they trotted along the shallow skyline, A.D. produced a pair of compact binoculars and clapped them to his eyes. When the horse broke into a canter, curving gradually back towards them, he nodded his approval.

'He looks in great shape. Are you going to give him any more to do?'

Jan shook her head. 'Nope. That's it. A tiny breakfast, a bit of a drink, and he should be spot on for this afternoon.'

A.D. came back into Dublin with them, but Daragh drove him on after they had dropped the two women at their hotel.

Jan and Annabel walked into the dining room, but when they sat down at a table laid for a full Irish breakfast on snow-white linen Annabel made a face.

'I think if I eat anything it might end up at my feet.'

'Oh come on, Bel. It's six or seven hours until the race. You'll feel awful if you don't eat before then – especially if you're going to be drinking champagne afterwards,' she added with a grin.

Annabel laughed. 'Good point. All right. Juice and muesli, but that's it. None of that bacon, black pudding and sausage malarkey.'

After an equally frugal meal, Jan spent an hour helping Annabel decide what she should wear before the front desk phoned to say Daragh was waiting for them downstairs.

*

Dublin had an unmistakable holiday air on Easter Monday morning as they drove down through College Green and across the Liffey. Jan tried to recognize the little guest house where she and Reg had spent their first night in Ireland after the ordeal with their Land Rover.

'It's there in O'Connell Street,' she nudged Annabel and said, 'that's where those retired jockeys picked me up in their minibus.'

'Who was that?' Daragh asked, unabashed at listening in.

'A bloke called Micky Byrne.'

'Micky Byrne! He's one of the greatest old characters in racing.' Daragh laughed. 'I bet he had a few stories to tell you.'

'He did. I had a running commentary from here to Fairyhouse, and all the way back.'

'Those old fellas, they're the backbone of racing. Of course, it's marvellous that gentlemen like Mr O'Hagan can put a lot of money into the game, but it would be nothing without all the little people in it.'

It's quite true, Jan thought. *All the lads, work riders, farriers and race-course staff are as important a part of the scene as the big owners and powerful trainers with two hundred or more horses in their yards.*

There were the punters, too, who would be descending on Fairyhouse today in their tens of thousands: some to back their judgement with money they couldn't afford to lose; others gambling more light-heartedly, bringing their families for the sheer joy of seeing beautiful animals perform at peak fitness, displaying their skill and courage, and of course the professional gamblers like A.D.

Today, Jan thought, she was providing two important players in this spectacle, which would be seen not only at Fairyhouse, but also on televisions all over Ireland and Great Britain.

As they drew closer to the course, with more than two hours to go before the first race, there was plenty of other race traffic on the road – cars, buses, horseboxes and four-wheel drives with trailers. You name it, if it had an engine they turned up in it.

The car parks were already starting to fill up as Daragh drove them round to the front of the lorry park and dropped them a short walk from the stables. The security men on duty recognized Jan and Annabel from their early morning visit and waved them through.

Declan was still at his post, self-importantly guarding a runner that was attracting a bit of interest.

'Everything OK, Declan?'

'Just fine, Missis,' Declan replied.

'Good. We're meeting Murty at twelve to walk the course. We'll be back later to give Eagle the once-over, but if you need me, try the mobile. I'll be just over in the Powers marquee. If it doesn't work, Mr O'Hagan's got a private suite at the top of the stand, overlooking the course.'

'OK, Mrs H. I'll see you later.'

❧

Murty McGrath was waiting for them by the weighing-room door, chatting in his customary undertone with some fellow jockeys.

He extracted himself from the group when he saw Jan approaching.

'Morning, Murty.'

'Good morning, Mrs H. And a fine one it is too. How does the horse look?'

'Pretty good. He's travelled well. Declan rode him out and gave his legs a bit of a stretch this morning. No problems.'

'Well, that's a fine start. Right, now – you want a guided tour, is that right?'

'Yes, please.'

Murty led Jan and Annabel past the parade ring and out onto the track the way they'd gone with Russian Eagle earlier that morning.

As they passed among the early crowds congregated around the buildings, people instantly recognized the Irishman who was champion jockey in England, and hailed him like a returning conquering hero.

The course had been described to Jan as a lop-sided 'O' with a flat bottom: it was one mile six furlongs round, with a two and a half furlong straight in front of the stands. Moving away from the stands, the ground rose steadily and deceptively to a fairly tight bend, before falling gradually until the turn for home.

Once they had started up the track proper, Murty kicked into the turf with the sharp toe of his Chelsea boot.

'That splash of rain during the week has brought it just right. It was a little too yielding yesterday, but it feels about spot on to me today. Your boy would favour a wee cut in the ground, would he not?'

Jan nodded. 'Yes, but I'll tell you what's worrying me. What do you think he'll make of these aprons in front of the fences?' she asked, as they approached the first obstacle on the far side.

Until today she'd never seen a steeplechase fence like it, where birch was laid on the ground between the guard rail and the upright of the fence itself, forming a platform, four and a half feet wide.

'Oh, he'll be all right,' Murty declared. 'You know he likes to stand off his fences. Some horses do put in a short one and take off from the apron, but it's no problem.'

'Amazing,' Jan said. 'You learn something every day, but I wish someone had told me about them. We could have made one and schooled him over it at home.'

'There it is – you'll have to get used to the funny ways over here if you're planning on sending more horses across,' Murty laughed. 'And one other thing you'll have to remember is that there's only rails twenty metres up to each fence and on the corners; that can sometimes faze a horse that's only run on English tracks.'

'Do you think it'll be a problem for Eagle?'

'No, not at all. He steers very easy.'

As they walked the rest of the course, Jan had a good look at all twelve fences – ten plain, two regulation ditches – and tried to get a feel for the track. But in the end, on this occasion, she knew she was completely in Murty's hands.

'Thanks for coming with me,' she said when they arrived back at the stands. 'What can I say? You know the horse well, and the course is in a bloody sight better nick than me at present, so I don't think there's anything I can tell you.'

Murty smiled. 'Never mind, Mrs H.,' he said, 'you'll get your chance, I'm sure. Now, if you'll excuse me, I have to get into the sauna for an hour or two if I'm to make ten stone two on your horse.'

He headed back to the changing room, while Jan and Annabel took the lift up the back of the main stand to find A.D.'s private suite.

They only had to mention the name 'O'Hagan' to be whisked like celebrities along the corridor and into a large, airy room. A long table was laid to seat twenty people for lunch, and a floor-to-ceiling window opened out onto a private balcony with an almost perfect view of the whole track and just fifty yards short of the finishing line. It was after midday and several people, whom Jan could easily identify, were already standing around the table with drinks in their hands.

A few minutes later Dermot O'Hare walked into the room. Jan knew that Dermot had three runners today, two of them for A.D., but none in the National. She hadn't spoken to him since her visit to Aigmont just before Christmas, and she still hadn't forgiven him for what he'd said to the repulsive Cyrus Huffer III.

Dermot was eyeing up Annabel before he noticed Jan.

'Hello, Dermot. Work away,' Jan said loudly. 'You might not get as far as your friend Cyrus, though.'

The tall trainer swung round, trying to preserve his dignity. 'Oh, hello, Jan. How're you doing?'

'So far so good. Learning a lot. Have you met my friend Annabel Halstead? She's co-owner of Russian Eagle.'

Jan was gratified to see O'Hare do a quick double-take. 'Good Lord,' he said. 'A.D. never told me he was in partnership with such a young beauty.'

'I wonder why,' Jan said. 'Well, here he is,' she went on, seeing the tycoon enter at a brisk walk, in a fresh set of clothes since the morning.

He looked surprisingly alert for a man in his fifties who hadn't slept for over twenty-four hours. He beamed at Jan and Annabel and, for the first time since she'd known him, greeted them with a kiss on both cheeks.

'A big day, eh, Jan? Are you looking forward to it?'

'I'm halfway through it already and I still can't get my head around being here,' she laughed. 'But I've done everything I can so far. I've just walked the course with Murty.'

'Have you indeed? Good. Now the plan is to have lunch before the races, so everyone has the chance to do their own thing, if that's what they want. Obviously, you'll still have plenty to do. You've remembered his passport this time, have you?' he added with a wink.

Jan flushed hot and cold for a moment as she tried to think where it was, then remembered: of course, she'd given it to Declan.

'Don't do that, A.D.,' she laughed.

'OK. Let me know if there's anything else you need, and we'll have another chat about the plan in the parade ring.'

🐎

Jan, like Annabel further down the table, found it impossible to eat anything at lunch. Although the food looked wonderful, the tension was making it totally unappetizing. Nor did she dare have a drink. She guessed she would be highly susceptible to alcohol in her current state, so she stuck to water. She tried to talk to her neighbours, conscious that, as the trainer of the host's runner in the big race, she was guest of honour, despite the presence of such a renowned trainer as Dermot O'Hare.

She was more than ready to leave by the time most people had finished their dessert, and with a quick nod in A.D.'s direction, she beckoned Annabel to follow and went down in the glass lift to the bustle around the parade ring.

'Sorry, Bel, but I'd dried up and completely run out of conversation. Nerves, I suppose, though they were really nice and friendly.'

'They were, weren't they. The Irish seem so much more relaxed than us lot.'

'Anyway, I thought we'd check the horse and give Declan a hand putting on the final touches as I want him to have a good long walk before he comes into the ring.'

❧

A rather nerve-racking hour and a half later, Declan led Russian Eagle into the main parade ring, which was lined with spectators eight or ten deep. Speculation over the outcome of the race had been rife, as always. Journalists in the newspapers and on television had pronounced in minute detail on the chances of the twenty-four horses that were competing, and Jan guessed that the betting public had spent millions of man hours trying to predict the winner.

Jan was standing with Annabel and A.D., watching the horses walk round, as if the whole event were some kind of fantasy. Thousands of people had their eyes focused on the runners and their connections in the middle of the arena. A few yards from her a commentator was discussing the runners with one of the older trainers, which was being relayed over the PA system. Jan heard them talk about Russian Eagle, mentioning his wins at Ascot and Warwick but, while admiring the look of him, they were unwilling to endorse his chances.

'Suits me,' A.D. chuckled, with his eyes still firmly fixed on his horse.

Inspite of A.D.'s famous colours and the significance of Murty's trip from England to ride and the stone and three quarters they were receiving from the top weight, Russian Eagle's previous successes still weren't enough to convince the bookies or the general public of any worthwhile success and he was still being offered at sixteen to one or more – a long price for an O'Hagan runner.

'You see,' he said, 'there are advantages in sending out runners from an unknown yard.'

'Thanks,' Jan said drily.

After the jockeys had mounted and the horses were leaving the ring, Jan half followed for a few yards as Declan led Russian Eagle and Murty along the walkway out onto the course.

'Just go for it, Eagle!' she whispered to herself. Silently, she pleaded, 'God, please let him do it and keep him safe!'

'Come on, Jan,' she heard A.D. say behind her. 'Let's get up and watch from the balcony.'

Jan would rather have been on her own somewhere quiet, but she turned and tried to look willing as her host ushered her and Annabel back into the lift.

By the time they reached the balcony at the front of A.D.'s suite, all the horses were out on the course, being paraded in front of the stands. Their lads released them in turn and they cantered back to the start, to the left of the stands at the bottom of the incline.

Jan peered through her binoculars at the horses as they milled around behind the starting tapes while the starter's assistants checked their girths. As the clock ticked closer to the start time, the jockeys pushed and jostled to get into a prime position. Murty had Russian Eagle well placed standing steady on the right of the track.

The starter stepped up onto his rostrum, raised his hand to the lever and a second later the tape flew across the track and the field of twenty-four stormed away to a tumultuous roar from the crowd.

With three miles five furlongs and twenty-three fences to cover, the runners galloped at a reasonable pace steadily up the hill. As the noise of the crowd lessened, like the calm before a storm, Jan bit her lower lip. Without looking, she could sense A.D.'s tension beside her.

After the first three obstacles had been cleared, Jan strained to see how well her horse would handle the rails at the top of the hill. As Murty had predicted, Russian Eagle, an easy horse to steer, coped brilliantly and ran on among the leading group of eight towards the trickiest fence on the course, with a spread of nine feet from front to back on falling ground.

'Wow!' Annabel gasped. 'Did you see Eagle fly that?'

Jan grunted. Her teeth were clamped together. She couldn't speak if she'd wanted to. The big fence claimed three of Eagle's rivals.

Today's favourite had finished second in the Gold Cup at Cheltenham just over two weeks ago and was now pushing the three up front, who had quickened the pace on the far side of the track. Murty didn't panic; he was still travelling well within himself, ten lengths off the leaders, as the field thundered past the stands. Landing over the last fence in the straight, the second favourite hurtled his jockey into the ground. By now a quarter of the field were bystanders and the rumblings of the crowd had started to increase.

'I can't bear it – I can't see him.' Tears welled up in Annabel's eyes as she released Jan's forearm from a vice-like grip. 'I'm going to watch on TV.'

As the horses swung right and started back up the hill, Jan found her binoculars focused on one of the Order of Malta ambulances, which tracked the field along with the vet's car.

She tore her eyes away, pushing from her mind the thought that this was an omen. When she had refocused on Eagle, he was stretching out to clear the fence at the top of the hill. No one, she thought, could fail to admire the way he had taken it, touching down just behind the three leaders.

But the Gold Cup runner-up had started to use his normal tactic and suddenly cranked up the speed, hoping to outpace the slowcoaches.

Murty urged on Russian Eagle. The horse immediately stretched his neck; quickly passing the horse that was in front of him, he narrowed down the leader's margin to two lengths.

Rounding the final bend with just two fences left to jump, Jan watched her horse hang on like a terrier to the leaders' heels. Two from home they were neck and neck.

Coming to the last, Murty showed why he was the champion and with a display of dramatic bravado he asked Russian Eagle for a giant leap, which left his challenger a length down.

But the favourite wasn't beaten yet; his jockey lifted his stick for a forehand crack and punched piston-like fists through the air just above the horse's mane as he drove it back up to Russian Eagle's head.

Jan was totally rigid as she saw her horse's lead clawed back a few inches at a time. But Eagle's ears lay flat on his head as he was fighting for all he was worth; Murty didn't use his stick as he pushed his horse forward with every bone in his body. The crowd went wild as the two horses flew past the post together.

Jan would have collapsed had they not been packed on A.D.'s balcony like sardines in a tin.

She tried to speak, but nothing came.

Beside her, but as though he was a mile away, A.D. spoke. 'Jaysus; I think he did it!'

But Jan heard the doubt in his voice.

She stared anxiously at the horses on the track to try and gauge from the jockeys' reactions what they thought. Neither showed any sign of claiming victory.

Somehow, she managed to turn and saw Annabel pushing her way between A.D.'s dumbfounded guests towards her. There were tears flooding from her eyes and her face was ghostly with disappointment. She reached out a hand towards Jan and touched her shoulder. 'Oh, Jan, he was so, so brave!'

As she spoke, the course announcer's voice boomed around the stands.

'*Photograph for first place, number one and number sixteen.*'

Russian Eagle was number sixteen.

Annabel was shaking her head. 'He didn't hang on, did he?'

'Bel, he might have; I'm not sure and the jockeys don't know either – look at them!' Jan pointed down at the track, where the runners were trooping back in.

'But on the telly it was obvious.'

They went inside, where the final stages of the race were being replayed over the monitors. 'Bel, look at the angle,' Jan exclaimed. 'The camera's way behind the post. We still have a chance.'

Annabel was unconvinced. 'The commentator wasn't in any doubt.'

'Wasn't he? I didn't hear what he said.'

A.D. was behind them now. 'We'd better get down to the unsaddling enclosure,' he said, more soberly than before.

They didn't wait for the lift and ran down the stairs across to the parade to where the placed horses were already entering.

Murty on Eagle walked up to the second slot. Jan felt herself blanch, but the favourite was hanging back; its jockey was unwilling to commit himself to the winner's place.

Murty jumped down, expressionless, as Jan walked up to the horse's head. She patted Russian Eagle's neck. For a few moments it seemed as if the whole world was suspended in limbo, until the loudspeakers crackled into life.

'*Winner, number sixteen, Russian Eagle.*' For a moment, there was a deathly silence.

The massive crowd that had already gathered around the enclosure erupted into a huge roar that echoed off the back of the stands. Russian Eagle was taken completely by surprise. He jerked up his head and whipped round to take off, but Jan quickly grabbed the reins and hung on. 'It's OK, Eagle! It's OK! Good boy. You won!' she said to soothe him above the hullaba- loo. She handed the reins to Declan and he proudly led his horse into the winner's slot.

Jan felt as if she'd been holding her breath since the horses crossed the line and suddenly let out a gush of pent-up air. 'Jesus!' she hissed, shaking her head. 'I just can't believe he did it!'

Beside her, A.D. was speechless himself for a few minutes. But as it sank in, he turned and threw his arms around Jan in a massive bear hug.

'Jan, Jan, you genius! You did it! Right from the first time I saw you, choosing that horse, I thought – there's a woman who knows her own mind, and knows how to use it!' He laughed. 'I never dreamed you'd prove me right here in my homeland.'

He released Jan and she turned to Annabel, to see tears flowing down her face like a river. 'For God's sake, Bel, stop blubbing or you'll get me at it too,' Jan begged as she felt a prickle in her own eyes. 'Bloody hell,' she sniffed. 'We must look a right pair. Come on, use these,' Jan urged, offering her a wad of tissues she had stowed in her pocket, just in case.

'Jan I am so proud of you,' Bel sniffed.

'Shut up, you daft sod,' Jan teased. 'Let's go and give your hero a nice warm bath, then you can shower him with kisses. And, by the way, I do mean Eagle not Murty!'

16

'Hello, hello? Meg?'

'Mum! Where are you?'

'I'm in a great big hotel in Dublin – in Ireland.'

'Mum, we saw you, you were on the telly with Bel.'

'Did you watch it with Granny and Grandad?'

'Yes, and Matty. And Uncle Ben rang up. Mum, what's that splashing noise?'

'Sorry, I'm in the bath. It feels like my feet haven't touched the ground since Eagle won.'

'Was he nice, the man you had to talk to on the telly?'

'Yes, he was very nice. Everyone's been great, and Mr O'Hagan's having a big party for us at the hotel this evening.'

'A party? With dancing?'

'I don't know about dancing, but there'll be lovely food and everything.'

'Mum, when are you coming home?'

'Tomorrow, darling. Be good until then, won't you? I love you loads, you know that.'

'I love you too, Mum.'

Jan put the phone down and lay back among the bubbles in the big cast-iron tub. She was feeling a whole lot better than she had an hour earlier.

The immediate aftermath of Russian Eagle's victory at Fairyhouse had been utterly exhausting. In A.D.'s private suite, champagne corks had flown around like rockets on firework night. Even Dermot O'Hare had deigned to congratulate Jan with a kiss, although she was sure she could sense acrimony as he did.

After the presentation, the media interest and the sheer volume of good will from everyone she met had overwhelmed her. She was amazed by how much store the Irish punters put by a winning horse's trainer – much more so than its jockey, it had seemed to her. Murty himself was neither ebullient nor a stranger to major triumphs, but here, on his native soil, even he had been more exuberant than normal. Two hours after Russian Eagle had won the great race, Daragh had helped Jan and Annabel into the back of the Mercedes and taken them back to their hotel, with A.D.'s party invitation ringing in their ears.

When Jan felt more relaxed and almost back to normal, she climbed out of her bath and wrapped the big white bath sheet around her naked body and collapsed onto the giant bed, thinking back over the day's events and how, up until the showdown at Warwick only six weeks before, with a string of losing horses and facing the imminent defection of some of her owners, she had been seriously questioning herself about whether she would still be able to carry on in business by now.

There was a tap on her door. Annabel let herself in.

'Hi, Bel. How are you feeling?'

'Not quite so plastered as I did on the way back. I stood under the shower for twenty minutes and it seems to have helped.'

'You look all right,' Jan said, impressed by her friend's ability to look stunning wrapped in a bath sheet, with no make-up.

'Well, I don't feel it, but I expect I will improve later,' Annabel added, not wishing to dampen Jan's mood.

'You're going to have to get used to this, Bel.'

'Why? How many times do you think I'm going to win a race like this?'

Jan laughed. 'Don't ask me; I really didn't think we had a ghost of a chance today. I knew he would run his heart out, he always does, but the way he jumped the last – I don't think I'll forget that as long as I live.'

'I don't think there are many jockeys who could have pulled it off today. It really was a virtuoso performance.'

Jan nodded. 'It certainly took a lot of guts, if that's what you mean. I'm sure Murty was pretty pleased with it himself. I noticed during the video replays the twinkle in his eye, and he couldn't keep the smile off his face when he saw that jump at the last.'

'He's coming to the party tonight, you know.'

'Who else do you think will be there?' Jan mused.

'All the people who were in the box today, and a whole lot more of A.D.'s racing cronies, I suppose.'

'I wonder if the opera singer will show up?'

'She's such a nice woman, Siobhan, but surprisingly she's just not the least bit interested in racing, yet she and A.D. seem to get on amazingly well, despite the lack of kids.'

'There's more to him than meets the eye, I reckon,' Jan said thoughtfully.

Annabel nodded. 'You were lucky to meet him when you did, though.'

'I'll drink to that.'

🐎

A short time after Annabel had gone back to her room to get dressed, Jan's phone rang for the second time. She prepared herself for more congratulations and guessed she'd have to get used to handling it.

'Hi, Jan,' Tony Robertson said. 'That was fantastic. You must be ecstatic!'

'I am pretty ecstatic,' Jan said with a laugh. 'I am still struggling to believe it's happened.'

'You must be, especially after you assumed you wouldn't be winning any classy races for a few years – remember?'

'You have to go with the flow, though, don't you? I must confess I would never have dreamed of entering the horse; it was entirely A.D.'s idea. He had a fair idea what the opposition would be like, and he reckoned Eagle had a chance.'

'He must be very chuffed.'

'He is rather. He's organized a massive party here tonight – about sixty people, I reckon. God knows what it will be like at such short notice.'

'I wish I could be there with you, but I was wondering if I could take you out for our own little celebration dinner on Thursday – if you're back by then?'

'Of course I will be; we're all flying back tomorrow, though poor old Eagle's got to go via Luton.'

'Great! I'll see you Thursday.'

Jan put the phone down with a sigh and wished she felt as enthusiastic as Tony about the date.

🐎

A.D.'s victory party was held in one of the Shelbourne's private function rooms – a dinner for sixty people, a ceilidh band from Kilkenny, a dance floor and a discotheque.

The management were used to Mr O'Hagan's requests for lavish entertainment at short notice and knew what pleased him.

'Wow,' Annabel exclaimed, walking into a room decorated with beautiful flowers, specialist lighting and a mirrored ball on the ceiling. A 'U'-shaped table was laid with more flowers and candles of lavish dimensions.

'There must have been a wedding here over the weekend,' Jan remarked.

'You're such a cynic!' Annabel protested. 'It looks great and I think it's fantastically generous of A.D. to lay it on for us all.'

'All paid for by your joint horse.'

'Stop it, Jan! He's absolutely refused to let me pay any part of the hotel bill, by the way.'

'I'm only teasing, he's a great guy,' Jan sighed. 'Where is everyone, though?'

So far, the only other person they had seen was a waiter flitting in and out with more bottles of champagne.

'Drink?' Jan suggested.

Annabel shook her head. 'Any more champagne and I think I'll explode.'

'I suppose you're really glad you brought all those outfits now,' Jan remarked, looking at her friend's designer dress.

'Come on, Jan. I don't often get the chance to dress up these days.'

'True enough. Ah, look, here comes the band.'

The musicians set up, then started to play some discreet folk music as the other guests began to arrive. All of them came over and offered Jan their congratulations.

Eventually, when it looked as if all A.D.'s guests were assembled, the host arrived and placed himself at the head of the table, with Jan opposite him.

Everyone else was seated, at random it seemed, although, with a few apparent absentees, Jan was left with an empty space beside her. Unconcerned, A.D. ordered dinner to be served.

It was a magical spontaneous party, and entirely good-natured.

The band, swallowing Guinness as fast as they played, didn't let up for a moment and as the party went on some of the younger guests, including A.D.'s niece and nephew whom Jan had met the day before, stood up to demonstrate their skills at the Irish jig.

Jan was beginning to feel a bit overwhelmed again, but happily so. If anything was needed to bring home to her that she had arrived at a significant peak in her profession, this extravagant and exuberant function was pretty convincing. She looked over at A.D. and saw him beaming back at her – but not quite; she realized his smile was aimed at someone just beyond her right shoulder.

Relaxed, and mildly curious, she turned around. She saw a pair of lazy, chocolate brown eyes, wavy black hair, the familiar furrowed chin and slightly broken nose; and the thoughtful quirky smile on the well-remembered face.

'Eddie!' Jan shrieked, nearly falling off her chair, and a second later she was on her feet, throwing herself at him, hugging him for turning up from nowhere on the evening of her greatest success. 'What the hell are you doing here?'

'Pleased to see me, then?' he laughed, his arms wrapped around her, hugging her in return.

'You just don't know how much!' she said, and wondered if she could stop the tears flowing for the umpteenth time that day. As they released each other she stood back. 'God, you look so well – wherever you've been,' she added conspiratorially.

Eddie Sullivan, thirty years old, just over six feet tall, and well built, was in good shape after nearly a year in the Australian sun, riding, swimming or windsurfing most days of the week.

'Eddie,' A.D. boomed over the music, 'sit down. I kept a place for you next to our guest of honour.' He waved at the empty chair beside Jan.

Jan looked back at her host with a quizzical smile. 'A.D., what the hell have you been up to?'

'Just trying to think of the best possible present I could give my winning trainer,' the Irishman said with a shrug of his shoulders, before he turned to his neighbour.

Eddie turned the empty chair to face Jan and they both sat down.

'Jan, it's so great to see you! It was fantastic to watch Eagle win that race. Who would have believed, its just a year since I fell off the great lummox at Aintree . . .'

'You didn't fall off,' Jan interrupted indignantly.

'Well, after he and I parted company at the great track, who would have believed you'd be bringing him here to win a National?' Eddie shook his head. 'It's utterly incredible, only you could have done it.'

'Come on, Eddie. You know it's the horses that do the winning.'

'Just as you know it isn't only the horses. Anyway, Jan, I can't tell you how chuffed I am for you and Eagle, and Annabel, too, for that matter.'

'She's been a fantastic support, actually. So has A.D.' Jan

glanced at her backer, not wanting him to hear her praise him too much.

'Jan, you deserve it, you know you do. Now, tell me how it's all gone since I slept in that hay barn of yours last year?'

'Eddie, I don't want to be a dampener or anything, but after what went on last year, is it safe for you to be over here?'

'If you're asking has Dad paid back the half a million he owed to those Italians, the answer is definitely "No". But I don't suppose they'll catch up with me here for a bit. Not tonight, anyway,' he added with a laugh. 'Though I haven't been any-where near my beloved homeland since I left last year.'

'Oh good. I'd hate you to be whisked away before we've had a good chat and everything.'

'So, come on, tell me what has happened to bring you to this particular juncture?'

Eddie laughed and smiled as Jan told him all about the ups and downs that had occurred in her life since she'd been granted her professional licence, shortly after Eddie had disappeared.

She told him of the bitter hurt she'd felt at Angie Sharp befriending her, only to dupe her so completely, and about the scam the Sharps had been operating.

'But I don't see how it helped them,' Eddie interrupted, 'to have their good horses stopped.'

'It turns out they were running this massive tipping line, advertising in the papers and the Sunday tabloids. The punters had to phone a premium line and they were paying three quid a minute to listen to the tips. The Sharps had got quite a few jockeys and trainers in their pockets so they could manipulate results to suit their selections. They let their own horses win at the start of the season so they were able to build up a bit of form, encouraging the punters, and then they'd get them stopped. No doubt a bookmaker was involved somewhere along the line. It wasn't very subtle, but I guess it shifted the odds enough in their favour to keep the punters phoning; some of the papers today claim they were pulling in as much as a hundred thousand a week.'

'Good God! Some scam for a couple of old tinkers.'

'And their glamorous, totally bent daughter! I don't want to go on about that now, though. Thank God, with the help of A.D., we got out of it in the nick of time. But, Eddie, how on earth did you get here?'

'Well, that's all down to A.D.' Eddie glanced at their benefactor, chatting amiably on the other side of the table. 'Dad bumped into him at the races in Oz – I mean literally bumped into him, and A.D. recognized him. He's got a memory like an elephant, your backer. Anyway, Dad was pretty cagey about talking to him, but somehow A.D. knew about my connection with your yard and Russian Eagle, so in the end he persuaded Dad to ask me to get in touch with him when he was in Sydney for a couple of days. It was a bit risky for Dad to start letting on where we were, but I rang the number anyway. A.D. told me who he was and invited me up to his hotel.

'He told me his side of what you've just told me, about getting the licence and everything, and how he'd been impressed with Eagle's run at Aintree, having seen me and you buying the horse at Doncaster. He said he thought you'd be running the horse again soon, and if it ran well, he was going to try and buy it. And, if it had a chance, he'd run it in the Irish National. Actually, I thought it was all a load of bollocks and forgot about it, until he emailed me after Eagle had won at Warwick – then it was all on! So here I am.'

Jan shook her head in disbelief that these plots had been going on for months without her knowing; that A.D. had actually formed such a plan before he even owned the horse. 'You've got to hand it to him. He works hard to get what he wants.'

'And if you ask me, he does it with complete style. Now come on, Jan, we've done enough talking. The lights have gone down, the music's slow, and I reckon we could dance to this, don't you?'

Jan looked back at his big enquiring eyes. 'For God's sake, don't you start getting all soft with me, or I'll think you're after something.'

'Would I?'

On the small square of parquet flooring, several people were already dancing to the soft sounds that had taken over from the Irish jigs. Jan and Eddie found themselves a corner, where they didn't have to move too much and quietly laughed and talked some more. Occasionally their bodies touched – was it accidental? Jan wondered what it was that she was feeling.

'Do you know what?' she whispered. 'I'm sorry, but if I don't sit down soon I think I'm going to fall down.'

'That's fine,' Eddie said. 'Anyway, it looks like A.D's going to make a speech.'

Jan lay in the big bed in her room, wearing a long silk nightdress that Annabel had brought her for Christmas. Beneath the soft warmth of the Egyptian cotton duvet, she was glad of her friend's extravagance. It seemed right to go to bed in a hotel like this looking and feeling a little more special than usual.

It was two in the morning, twenty hours, she thought, since she had woken up to go and watch Declan give Russian Eagle his canter.

It felt like a month ago.

Today had given Jan the biggest buzz of her life, and had shown her the whole purpose and ambition of everyone involved in steeplechasing. To be feted by her peers and the general public who loved the sport, seemed to her as good as it could possibly get.

She smiled, remembering her parents' and Megan's excitement when they had spoken earlier in the evening, and Annabel's uncomplicated enthusiasm and delight at being a part of Russian Eagle's success. And Eddie, who had arrived completely out of the blue to witness her success.

She sighed contentedly. What a day!

As she finally gave in to her exhaustion and drifted into sleep, she wondered whether it could ever be as good again.

In the distance a gentle, persistent tapping on the door dragged her back from the brink of unconsciousness.

She blinked her eyes open in the darkness and listened again.

There was no doubt about it, someone was knocking on her door.

'It's half past two in the morning, for God's sake!' she whispered wearily.

Gingerly, she got out of bed and tiptoed to the door.

There it was again – three gentle taps.

'Hello,' she said huskily. 'Who's there?'

'Jan, it's me.'

Jan's shoulders heaved as she took a long, deep breath – a warm smile spread across her face.

She didn't answer. She grasped the china handle, slowly turned it, and eased open the door.

Outside, fully clothed, with his tie undone and his wavy hair dishevelled, stood Eddie Sullivan.

'Eddie,' Jan said quizzically, 'what are you doing? Are you lost?'

Eddie's enormous brown eyes looked back at her from under his dark brows. He shook his head and smiled. 'Not any more.' Tenderly he lifted her in his arms and gently carried her back into the room.